MW01134910

C. GOCKEL

ARCHANGEL DOWN

Copyright © 2015 C. Gockel

ISBN-13: 978-1530043675
ISBN-10: 1530043670

OTHER WORKS BY C.GOCKEL

THE ARCHANGEL PROJECT

Carl Sagan's Hunt for Intelligent Life in the Universe:
Part of Starbound, a multi-author anthology
Archangel Down
Noa's Ark
Heretic

THE I BRING THE FIRE SERIES

Wolves: I Bring the Fire Part I (free ebook)
Monsters: I Bring the Fire Part II
Chaos: I Bring the Fire Part III
In the Balance: I Bring the Fire Part 3.5
Fates: I Bring the Fire Part IV
The Slip: A Short Story (mostly) from Sleipnir's Point of Smell
Warriors: I Bring the Fire Part V
Ragnarok: I Bring the Fire Part VI
The Fire Bringers: An I Bring the Fire Short Story
Atomic: Part of Nightshade, a Multi-author Anthology
Magic After Midnight: Part of Once Upon a Curse a Mulit-author
Anthology

OTHER STORIES

Murphy's Star: A short story about "first" contact

Want to know about upcoming releases and
get sneak peeks and exclusive content?

Follow me on Tumblr: cgockel.tumblr.com
Facebook: www.facebook.com/CGockelWrites
Or email me: cgockel.publishing@gmail.com
Thank you again!

DEDICATION

To my dad, Jim Evans.
Thanks for getting me hooked on sci-fi, fantasy, and comic books.
I miss you.

CHAPTER 1

"We know you are a part of the Archangel Project."

Commander Noa Sato of the Galactic Fleet glared across the table. Two men wearing the dark green uniforms of planet Luddeccea's Local Guard glared back at her. Her arms were shackled behind her back to the cold metal chair she sat on. The room was chilly—she could smell the cold of it, along with the odors of various bodily fluids. Her back ached, her mouth was as dry as lizzar skin, and she thought the bright lights of the interrogation room might leave her permanently blind.

"I told you, I don't know what you're talking about," she spat.

"Then why are you here?"

"I'm on leave," she explained for the hundredth time. "I thought I'd spend my vacation visiting my brother on the planet where I grew up. Is that so difficult to understand?" Agitated, she spun her engagement and wedding rings around on her finger. Closing her eyes, she thought of her brother, Kenji, and inwardly begged his forgiveness. When they'd picked her up, she'd assumed this was all a misunderstanding. She hadn't meant to pull him into this.

"I've had enough!" said one of her inquisitors. A pair of sharp, pointed pliers emerged in his hand, and suddenly he was on Noa's side of the table. "Do you understand what I can do with these?"

Noa tried to keep from screaming ... and woke up in the

darkness, her whole body shaking, her breathing so fast and ragged her ribs hurt, cold air stinging her lungs. The darkness smelled like cold and various bodily fluids, an unhappy constant with the nightmare. She rubbed her eyes. But the rest had been just a dream. They hadn't used those pliers except to scare her during the interrogation. When she hadn't told them what they wanted to hear, they'd brought her to this camp.

She blinked. Was it unusually bright in the barracks? Stifling a groan, she sat up. Her vision immediately went black. She tried to access the reason why—and for the millionth time remembered her neural interface had been deactivated since she'd arrived here. Sucking in a sharp breath, she clutched her head, fingers drifting to the smooth, cool surface of the neural interface in her left temple. The guards were fond of parroting, "Freedom from information streams is the path to real wisdom," but it was torture, not freedom.

Noa's body swayed. Why was she dizzy? It couldn't be Luddeccea's gravity—the planet's gravity was the same as Earth's and standard starship grav. Was it malnutrition, or something more sinister? She bit her lip to stifle a bitter laugh. She was being slowly starved to death. How much more sinister could it get?

The spell finally passed, and she surveyed the barracks. All around her were rough wooden bunks four platforms tall. The beds were narrower than the single bunks on a starship, but each was shared by up to three women packed chest to back beneath thin blankets and without pillows. She could make out their faces—just barely—but it was definitely lighter in the barracks. Noa looked down at her bedmate, Ashley. Noa's skin was dark as straight Earth coffee. Ashley's was what Tim's people would call "peaches and cream." It made Ashley's delicate features easy to see, even

2

in low light. As she slept, clutching her crutch like a pillow, her face looked peaceful and her breathing was gentle. Not wanting to wake her, Noa gently folded her side of the blanket over Ashley's sleeping form. Slipping down the slats at the end of the bed, she padded to the window.

Peering through the dirty glass, she caught her breath. Sure enough, thick white flakes of snow drifted from the sky, sparkling in the camp's harsh spotlights. Their barracks was close to the barbed-wire fence that enclosed them, and she could just make out snow catching on the Luddeccean pines in the surrounding forest. Noa pressed a hand to the window. The snow on the dense foliage would throw off heat-seeking scanners, and the thick branches would throw off radar, but it wasn't bitterly cold—yet. If they were going to escape, now was the time. Her brow furrowed, and she touched her interface. She squinted at the clouds as though she could will herself to see through them. Somewhere above their heads, the satellite that was Time Gate 8 floated just outside the atmosphere above Luddeccea's equator. The gate allowed instantaneous travel to any other system that had a gate of its own. It also sent and received data. Time Gate 8 and the other satellites that orbited around Luddeccea's equator acted as relay stations for the vast data traffic of the ethernet. And, she thought more darkly, if her neural interface couldn't be activated, the satellites would serve as useful landmarks for navigation … if the snow let up.

Dropping her hand to her side, she balled it into a fist and bowed her head. As a pilot of the Galactic Republic Fleet she'd been given POW training. She was taught to stay put, to obey orders, and not to make foolish escape plans. She closed her eyes. But there was no war going on, and she wasn't the captive of some pirate clan. She was in a concentration camp on her home world, Luddeccea, which hadn't declared independence from the Republic. Opening

3

her eyes, she looked down at her wrist. A black 'H' and a number had been tattooed there, barely visible against her dark skin. She'd been captured, interrogated, and interned without a trial for being, in the guard's words, a "heretic." Not an admissible crime in the Republic. If the Fleet had known she was here, she'd have been rescued by now. Her hands formed fists at her sides. Kenji should have reported her missing. If he hadn't reported her missing, it had to mean he'd been interned, too … spinning on her heels, she went back to her bunk.

A few moments later, she was leaning over her bedmate, gently shaking her shoulder. "Ashley, Ashley, wake up, it's time to leave."

Ashley rolled over onto her back. Her eyes opened—visibly blue in the snow-brightness. She stared at Noa dumbly.

"Today is the day," Noa whispered. "It's snowing."

Ashley put a hand to her head and ran it through her sparse hair; they'd all been shaved when they arrived. A tattooed 'A' for augment stood out on her wrist like a black scar. Ashley's fingers went longingly to her neural interface just as Noa's had. About three centimeters in diameter, the interfaces were made of copper with titanium and polyfiber exteriors. At the center of each was a circular port that could be hardwired directly to external computer systems via cable, but it was more common to use the internal wireless transmitters. Around the central port, tiny drives, the width and breadth of fingernails, were arranged. When functioning, they could be used for app insertion. Normally, Noa thought neural interfaces looked like flowers—the tiny drives surrounding the central ports like petals. But like every prisoner in the camp, Ashley had a large, ugly, black polyfiber screw jammed into her interface port. The screw disrupted the flow of electrons between neurons and nanos and completely jammed their wireless transmitters.

4

It was a primitive but very effective way to keep inmates from accessing their neural interfaces and the wider universe with their minds.

"We have to get ready before the others get up," Noa whispered.

Ashley stared at her a beat too long, but then sat up and quietly handed Noa her crutch. Noa slid off the bed and down the ladder, crutch in hand, and waited for Ashley. When Ashley had first arrived at the camp, she had a cybernetic limb, her 'augment,' having lost her left leg to an accident as a teenager. The guards had ripped the leg off on Ashley's arrival—no anesthesia, of course. Noa scowled in the darkness, anger bubbling in her gut on Ashley's behalf. Noa's thumb went to the stumps of the fingers on her left hand—her ring finger and pinky had been removed for different reasons than Ashley's leg, but at least Noa's "surgery" had been quick.

Ashley stumbled over the side of the bed, and Noa helped her down the ladder. Instead of giving Ashley her noisy wooden crutch, Noa swung Ashley's arm over her shoulder. Together they went to the corner of the room. There was a waste bin there reeking of vomit. As they drew close, a few scrawny rats scrambled out over the edge. Ashley gasped, and Noa put a finger to her lip for silence as the filthy creatures darted into the shadows.

Holding back her bile, Noa gave Ashley her crutch, released her, and then rolled the waste bin to the side. Ashley immediately went to her good knee and lifted a small piece of floorboard. She pulled out a sack and carefully unwrapped it.

Inside were a few pieces of bread they'd painstakingly saved over the last two weeks. There were also a few tools in the bundle. Ashley was a cybernetics engineer. Noa wondered if it was her engineering ability, as much as her cybernetic leg, that had gotten her thrown in the camp. Noa's hand fluttered up to her interface; almost everyone but the most strident fundamentalist Luddecceans were augmented in some way or another in this day and age.

"It's all here," Ashley whispered, snapping Noa back to the present.

Noa's bunk mate had created the tools in the bundle from bits of glass, scavenged wire, and castaway cybernetic parts. Along with a precious pair of pliers to remove the bolt, there was also, miracles of miracles, a shattered com chip that Ashley had cemented together with nail polish she'd stolen from a guard. The size of a fingernail, the com chip glittered in the low light. Slipping the chip into a neural drive would give Ashley or Noa the ability to listen to the restricted frequencies the Luddecceans were using.

"Well done, Ashley," Noa whispered, patting the woman's shoulder. She couldn't help but notice that Ashley was trembling. Outside, she heard guards talking to one another, debating who would wake up which barracks. "Tie it up, and be ready," Noa said. "As soon as people start waking, we offer to take corpse patrol." No one wanted corpse patrol—it meant being last in the breakfast line—among other things.

Visibly shaking, Ashley replaced the board. Noa quickly rolled the waste bin back over it, and helped Ashley up.

Outside, she heard the guards laughing and their footsteps approaching. Any moment they'd come in.

Trembling beside her, Ashley said, "Noa, I can't go with you."

Noa looked at her sharply, uncertain of what she'd just heard. "What?"

Not meeting her eyes, clutching the tiny bundle to her stomach, Ashley said, "I'll slow you down."

"No," Noa lied. "You won't." Noa was taller by at least four

6

inches. Leaning down, she put her hands on Ashley's shoulders. There was a tear running down Ashley's cheek. Noa wiped it away without thinking. She felt her gut constrict. Ashley didn't look well; she was paler than even Tim had been—and he'd been blonde, blue-eyed, and genuine Aryan purist stock.

Ashley and Noa had bonded over their skin coloring when they first met. They were both throwbacks to an era people considered less enlightened, when humans had been many races instead of one. People like Noa and Ashley were reminders of that time; it made people nervous and, ironically, prejudiced. It had been a superficial reason to bond, and it could have backfired spectacularly when Noa had first voiced her escape ideas. But Noa had sensed bravery and mettle in Ashley and knew she wouldn't betray her. "I need you, Ashley," she whispered. She didn't want to carry out their escape plans alone.

Hunching her shoulders, Ashley looked at the floor.

Trying to ease her fears with a laugh, Noa said, "If you don't come, who will listen to all my crazy schemes and tell me they won't work? Who will tell me to shut up when I'm whining? Who will kick me when I snore?"

Ashley's eyes lifted.

Noa tilted her head and gave Ashley what Tim used to call her best "cornball grin." Although Noa had some acquaintance with corn, she wasn't sure what a cornball was—probably some Aryan-Europa purist isolationist thing Tim's people did—some sort of weird ball sport? Whatever it was, the grin had always worked on Tim and usually worked with her friend.

Instead, Ashley whimpered, "Don't make this worse! You don't need me, Noa. I showed you how to remove the bolt and turn your neural interface back on. You can move more quickly without me."

Noa squeezed her shoulder. "Ashley, Starmen do not leave Starmen behind."

"I'm not a Starman," Ashley protested, wiping her eyes.

"I can't leave you here," Noa whispered back. There was a part of her that wanted to, that was afraid of having to half-carry Ashley through the snow and wilderness. Starmen didn't give into fear.

Ashley closed her eyes. "Yes, you can, and you have to. You have to tell people about this place—if you tell them, they'll come for us and the nightmare will end."

"You could be dead before that happens," Noa whispered, the reek of the vomit in the bin creeping into her consciousness. People died here all the time—of illness, injuries, and starvation.

"I won't die," Ashley whispered.

Every muscle in Noa's body tensed. Ashley was too smart to believe that.

Putting her hand on Noa's arm, Ashley whispered, "And you have to go rescue your brother. From what you told me, he's in much worse danger than I am."

Noa swallowed. Most of her family had left Luddeccea—complaining that it was becoming more fundamentalist. But Noa's brother Kenji had left and then come back. Considering what Kenji was, that was especially crazy. Oh, nebulas, what would they do to Kenji? If they permanently deactivated his neural interface and deep neural implants—

The door to the barracks opened, and one of the guard women strode in. The guard was new and wore fresh Luddeccean Green—layers and layers of it. She looked so warm, Noa hugged herself instinctively. The guard had the amalgamation of East Asian-East Indian features that were most common: East Asian eyes, straight nose, full lips, tan skin, and black hair. She was very tall, and Noa noted enviously, well-fed. The woman bellowed, "Up, all of you!"

Around them, women cried and rose from their bunks.

Leaning to Ashley's ear, Noa whispered, "Do you want to wait until another day?" Her fingers twitched at her sides. The longer they stayed here, the weaker they became. But maybe Ashley's pallor was due to illness? Sometimes people here recovered from minor illnesses. Sometimes.

Ashley pushed the bundle at Noa's chest. Noa quickly tucked it in the waistband of the secondhand rags that served as pants. Her own clothes had been confiscated.

Ashley whispered, "If you don't go, I'll tell them you are planning to escape."

Rocking back on her feet, Noa's eyes went wide. The women in the barracks began stumbling into the line that went to the mess hall. Grabbing her crutch, Ashley hobbled quickly toward them. Noa chased her, feeling anger and dismay welling in her chest. "Ashley, wait … "

Ashley turned back. Wavering on her crutch, she hissed, "I'll scream, I swear it."

Noa stopped in her tracks.

"Why aren't you getting in line?" the guard bellowed at Ashley.

"I don't want to sleep with this woman anymore," Ashley said, shaking her crutch in Noa's direction. She curled up her lip and stammered, "Filthy African!"

Noa's jaw fell. It was the language of the European purists—a group to which Ashley didn't belong. She was like Noa—a random winner of a genetic lottery who looked like one of the old races. There were sharp chuckles from the women in line, maybe enjoying the irony of one perceived purist insulting another.

If the guard hadn't been new, she would have smelled the lie. Ashley and Noa had been friends since their arrival. But the guard was fooled. Huffing, she said, "Stupid Europa, get in line. And you—" She pointed at Noa.

Noa threw up her hands and moved to the line, but then her eyes slid to Ashley. The other woman was mouthing the words, "Go, Go, Go."

Noa's lip curled in despair and fury. Her eyes blurred—stupid, selfless, brave, Ashley. Noa was going to curse her name for years, she already knew it. Sucking in a sharp breath, she said to the guard, "I'm on corpse duty."

***

Noa watched the other women go to the mess, their shapes blurred by the snow and the dawn twilight. She could just make out Ashley hobbling on her crutch.

Noa looked heavenward. The snow-bearing clouds seemed to go on forever. There was no hope that she'd be able to navigate by Time Gate 8. She touched her interface, and her fingers slipped to the bolt blocking her data port. As soon as the bolt was removed and her neural interface was activated, she'd be able to find her way. She stroked the edges of the port, and her hand shook with hunger and weariness—or perhaps just yearning for connection. She'd be able to contact the Fleet, her family, everyone … she shook her head. Maybe not right away, not until she put some distance between herself and this place. Otherwise her signal might be targeted, and she'd be dust. But she'd be able to receive signals. Her heart clenched, thinking of her mother's voice. Her mother would have left a message as soon as Noa missed her weekly call. It had to be up there, suspended in the ether; Noa could receive it if she could just access the ethernet. The cold polyfiber of her interface burned her fingers, and Noa realized she'd been standing there, staring blankly at the clouds for much too long.

Exhaling and dropping her hand, she looked down the row of barracks. The snow was falling so thickly she couldn't see to the end. There was a large, open wagon two barracks away. The wagon looked like a thing out of the twenty-first century. It was made of rusty metal, with actual wheels. The source of locomotion, by contrast, looked prehistoric. The wagon was attached to a lizzar, a herbivorous animal native to Luddeccea that was lizard-like in appearance. It was as large as a cow. Instead of scales, fur, or feathers, it was covered by thick gray hide plates, as wide as a hand. It stood on four squat legs, had a short heavy tail, and a beak-like snout for ripping bark from trees. Noa had grown up in Luddeccean farm country surrounded by imported Earth livestock; lizzar made cows and even chickens look like geniuses. She watched as women from other barracks on corpse patrol threw bodies into the wagon. The smell of death didn't bother the lizzar a bit. It stood licking at the falling snowflakes. The smell of death didn't seem to bother the driver either. He sat unmoving at the front of the wagon, a barbed whip in his hand. Noa let out a breath in trepidation. There were no dead in her barracks. She had no corpse and no excuse to be near the vehicle. It was a sickening thing not to be relieved by the absence of death. What was she becoming?

Her skin heated despite the cold and her thumb found its way to the stumps of her fingers. Her fingers had been swollen when she first arrived; to steal her rings, the guards had cut off the last two digits. The memory of the pain didn't compare to the loss of those simple bands. After years as a widow, they were the only reminders of Timothy she kept on her person, and these people—animals—had stolen them. For a moment, she was so angry her vision went white as the snow. As her vision cleared, she spotted a barrel with a fire burning in it near the wagon. Two female guards were standing beside it warming their hands. Yelling for the driver's attention, the guards motioned for the man to get off the wagon. He perked up, hopped off, and followed them into a guard house. Noa's lip curled. For her husband's memory alone, she should take the barrel into one of the barracks, tip it over, and set this whole camp on fire.

Her feet started moving as though they had a will of their own. She pictured the flames rising up above the roof of the barracks, and it made welcome heat flare in her chest. And then she remembered Ashley's plea, "Tell people about this place," and swore. She heard her husband Tim's voice in her head, "Revenge isn't rational if it is suicidal, and it doesn't help anyone." She shook her head. Timothy was always so damned logical. "Damn you to Hell for being in my head all this time," she muttered. Her face crumpled, and she held back tears.

She drew to a stop and stood between the flaming barrel and the wagon. It was the first time she'd ever seen a corpse wagon unguarded and without a driver. In the guard house, she heard the guards and the driver; it sounded as though the guards were flirting with him. She almost snarled; how dare they laugh while they caused so much death and suffering? She imagined picking up the barrel, hurling it through the building's window, and their laughter ending. Her hands curled into fists. She'd never be able to lift it. She'd just burn herself. She looked at the wagon loaded with bodies, heard one of the female guards say, "We get so lonely sometimes," and bit her lip to keep from screaming. They deserved to die in flames. She heard the crunch of boots in snow, and looked frantically between the wagon and the flame.

***

"I should have set the whole damn place on fire," Noa projected the thought into her mental log as the wagon hit an exceptionally large pothole. She was shivering, colder than she'd ever been, and sick of it.

"Ehh … Lizzy, did you hear that?" the driver asked.

Her neural interface was dead, and she had spoken aloud instead. Quietly sucking in a breath, she said a prayer—silently this time—but her mind still reached for her neural interface, though it had been disabled for weeks.

"Must be going crazy," said the driver. Noa could barely hear him over the sound of Lizzy the lizzar's feet and the creak of the wagon wheels.

Noa's lips curled, even as her heart rate picked up in fear. She longed to get up and scream, "You despicable blob of blue-green algae! You have been to the camp. You are a monster to allow such horror." But then she'd have to kill him before he killed her, and he wouldn't show up to his destination on time. She needed to get out just before he reached his destination—whatever that was—and quietly escape without anyone being the wiser.

But she was so hungry … and so alone. She longed to open up her bundle, not just for the food, but to activate her neural interface and have the collective consciousness of humanity piped blissfully into her brain.

No, Noa, don't go down that road, she thought. You'll get out of this.

She bit her lip. She'd been in plenty of dire straits in the Galactic Fleet, but she'd never been in a situation this bad. Even the Asteroid War in System Six … she took a breath. At least, in that hell she'd had her crew mates.

Her one small relief now was that her fellows lay still and silent in the wagon. She had heard horror stories of barely-alive prisoners being thrown out with the dead.

She scrunched her eyes shut and took another breath, counting to ten as she did. Shutting her eyes was a mistake. Unable to see the meager light filtering through the blanket draped over her like a shroud, she focused on the feeling of the bodies around her. Where they should have been warm and soft, they were frozen and hard. She pictured their

13

cold, graying eyes. She opened her mouth, about to say, "Get a grip, Noa, Captain Kim escaped a hostage situation with this same ploy … " She caught herself just in time and restrained a sigh. After his cadaver-escaping-hostage experience, Kim had become a haunted man.

Her hand drifted to the bundle tucked in her waistband, drawn to the tools there. The rational part of her brain warned her that extracting the bolt was bound to be a noisy business … but the emotional part of her brain was screaming that if she went insane with loneliness, survival wouldn't be worth it. Her hands tightened around the bundle. She almost pulled it out, but then jerked her hand away. Closing her eyes, she tried to focus on happy thoughts, the kittens on her starship, her last lover—not Tim—she could never think of Timothy. He wasn't a happy thought. But, of course, telling herself not to think of her husband made her think of him, and made her thumb seek the stump of her ring finger. She could picture his dark blonde hair, slightly sunburnt cheeks, pale skin and ice-blue eyes. What would he say right now? "Don't think of me, woman, think of something happy." She bit back a smile and the hard edge of old grief. Think of something happy. She closed her eyes, and thought of her little brother Kenji …

***

The sunlight sliding through the window onto Kenji's bed seemed to have physical shape. It put his sleeping ten-year-old form in a natural spotlight. The spotlight effect was amplified by the midnight black walls of Kenji's room. Over the black paint he had put a map of the universe as it would appear from the core of Luddeccea. He longed to leave Luddeccea and explore the greater universe as much as she did, but for different reasons. Noa wanted excitement, adventure, and freedom. In Noa's mother's words, Kenji's fascination was much more "scientific." He'd agonized for months over how to make a cuboid-shaped room simulate a 360-degree spherical view. In the end, he'd made his bed the core and painted the constellations on the walls in a way that created an optical illusion of a sphere. Without an active neural interface, he'd tediously calculated the exact distortion he'd need to make the constellations appear realistic by entering formulas verbally into a computational device. Perhaps it hadn't been tedious; to Kenji, math was never tedious.

Kenji's eyelashes fluttered. Noa's fourteen-year-old self sat down beside him on the bed.

"Noa?" he whispered, rubbing the bandages over his data port.

Leaning forward, Noa took his other hand. His skin was tan, unlike hers, and instead of her fine tight coils, his hair hung in smooth black ringlets.

"I'm here, Kenny," she said. "How do you feel? Are you in pain?" Everyone received a neural interface in the soft spot at the left side of their skulls when they were just infants. The interfaces weren't activated until they were ten, when nanoparticles were injected into the central port. The nanos spread out over the surface of the brain in a net and could receive and send electrical pulses. Through the electrical pulses, sights, sounds, words, and even shadows of emotions could be received and sent. Secondary applications made arithmetic and memory tasks easier, too. Noa's "awakening" hadn't been a painful process; joining with the greater collective conscious had been, and still was, wonderful. As her neural interface had been gradually activated, she had been able to explore larger and larger parts of the universe with only her thoughts. But Kenji's "awakening" was different. Among other peculiarities, Kenji lacked the ability to read facial expressions. So doctors had sent some of the nanoparticles into deep structures of his brain to stimulate the regions that were at

15

work when humans saw a smile, a frown, or a flinch.

Kenji's eyelids ceased their fluttering, and his hazel eyes finally opened; in the bright sunlight they looked almost gold.

"No, I don't hurt," said Kenji, his voice and expression flat.

Noa smiled, not sure if the extra nanos had helped, but glad that he didn't hurt. A lot of the Satos' neighbors had disapproved of the family's decision to add the extra nanos, and she'd been worried about it herself. Her mom said it was the "Luddeccean influence" affecting Noa's reasoning. Her family was part of the fourth wave of settlers to Luddeccea, the "fourth families." They weren't part of the hard-core Luddeccean "first families" and "second families" that had migrated here to escape the coming Cyber Apocalypse and Alien Wars. It had been over four centuries since the first, primitive neural interfaces were designed and humans had begun exploring deep space. Neither of those conflicts had come to pass. Now, only the most fundamentalist Luddecceans didn't receive the neural interface—interfaces might be forbidden by Luddeccean gospel, but then, so was birth control. Most Luddecceans practiced birth control, and neural interfaces were even more popular than that. Still, many of the Satos' neighbors were against more drastic augmentation, like what had been done to Kenji. It would strip him of his "soul," they argued.

Noa had worried about that, and that it might hurt. But it didn't. Her smile broadened.

Kenji gasped. "You're happy."

Noa's eyes widened. He'd read her expression! "Yes." She hadn't sent that feeling to him through the net—his nanos were too new, and it would be a while before he was sending and receiving feelings or data.

Kenji's brow furrowed. "And you're surprised … " His eyes drifted down to her mouth. "And happy."

"Yes!" Noa cried, squeezing his hand. "Are you?"

"Yes," he whispered. And then he smiled. A little awkwardly, to be sure, but genuine. Kenji's smiles were always genuine.

"I feel … " he murmured. His hand tightened around hers. "Not alone."

***

The wagon jerked to a stop, and Noa's eyes bolted open. She heard shouts, and the roar of large engines, but not the distinctive whir of antigrav. She was at the destination; she'd fallen asleep and missed her proverbial stop.

Outside of the wagon someone shouted, "Detach that dumb lizzar and get that loaded up onto the dumper! Let's toss those corpses and bury them so we can get inside and get warm!"

Noa's heart stopped. So that was what they did with the dead. She heard the driver step down from the wagon, heard engines approaching, heard four loud squeals, and then the wagon was hoisted into the air. Noa lifted her blanket, crept over to the side, and peered down. She gulped. She was thirty feet above a deep pit in the dark, rich earth. She lifted her gaze. Beyond the pit was a field of low hillocks covered in snow. Her heart sank as she realized the hillocks were graves. "Focus on the positive, Noa," she reminded herself, and then realized there weren't many positives to focus on. "You're out of the camp … and being a first officer was boring you half to death. Stupid blue-green algae reports."

"Did you hear that?" someone said. "I swear this place is infested with spirits."

Her eyes went wide. Damn it, she'd spoken aloud. But then someone else said, "You're starting to hear things. These are augments, they don't have souls to be trapped in the afterlife. Human up!"

Noa's mouth fell at that. Shaking her head, she focused on the terrain around the graves. Through the falling snow she

17

made out low mountains and forest—the perfect hideout if she didn't freeze to death.

She heard engines to her right; she looked and saw enormous bulldozers. The platform the wagon was on started to incline and the frozen bodies started to slip. Scrambling forward, Noa grabbed the front edge of the wagon. She had to stay on top of the bodies or it would be all over. Clinging to the cold metal, part of her brain screamed that this was it, that the dirt from the bulldozers was going to be on top of her before she made it out of the pit. "Shut up, brain," she whispered. This time no one heard. The whirring of the engines and screeching of the dumper drowned her out. The wagon inclined more steeply and the back opened up. Her frozen companions started to slide into the open earth. Noa could hear shouts of surprise and alarm over the engine roars. Had they seen her? Tightening her grip, she waited for bullets … but none came … and the wagon stopped its incline. She looked down. The wagon was tilted at a seventy-degree angle, and there were still bodies at the bottom. She felt her fingers start to slip. Once she could have clung here like a xinbat for hours, but she was so weak. Her arms shook with cold and weariness. She heard more shouts, and then her fingers slipped from the front edge. Noa crashed onto the bodies below her, sending a few more toppling into the pit, but didn't slip in herself. She blinked, and found herself staring at a body of a woman whose mouth was frozen open in horror. Noa looked up fast, knowing that strange woman's face would be embedded in her consciousness forever. She shook her head and focused on the present and surviving. She couldn't see anyone outside the wagon, but she heard shouting. Above her head she heard the whir of antigrav.

There were more shouts, and the sound of engines turning off. One of the graveyard workers shouted, "The alien invasion is here! Quick, to your stations."

Noa's brow furrowed. What the solar core? She was
ranked high enough in the Galactic Fleet to be privy to
the intel the public didn't ordinarily hear: terrorist attacks
that were thwarted and not thwarted, plagues that didn't
respond to standard antivirals, antibiotics, or radiation
treatments; the latest in quantum drives, hidden jump
stations, and all intel on extraterrestrial life. There were no
aliens—well, not the kind that were sentient space-going
beings or that would be anytime soon. There was plenty of
blue-green algae, though. She frowned. She'd had to fill out
many a report on blue-green algae in her time in the fleet.
The Galactic Republic was so concerned with not disrupt-
ing the "natural habitat" of any potentially sentient being
that it went to great lengths to prove that even the bloody-
universal-blue-green algae they found all over the galaxy
didn't represent a hive mind. In all the cases Noa had
reviewed as first officer, it hadn't. She felt the muscles in her
neck tense and her skin heat in memory of the maze of bureaucracy she'd had to go through each time they came to
a semi-habitable world and she, as Acting First Officer, had
gotten the joy of compiling the reports from the scientists.
She should have stayed a pilot.

Shaking snow off her shoulders, she took a deep breath.
It didn't matter what the crazy Luddecceans believed about
aliens, what mattered was escape. She scrambled to the
edge of the wagon and peered over. Not a human in sight.
Hauling herself over the edge, she slid down to the dumper
platform, and jumped to the ground. Overhead she heard
cannon fire and more antigrav engines. Instead of an alien
vessel, she saw a single civilian flight vehicle—the kind that
could just get far enough out of atmosphere to traverse the
globe rapidly or rendezvous with Time Gate 8. It was being
rapidly pursued by one of the Luddeccean Guard's ships.

Noa didn't have time to wonder who it was. Ducking her head, she ran. She heard more cannon fire in the sky—so close the ground reverberated beneath her feet and her ears rang. But no one fired at her. She couldn't have planned a more brilliant decoy strategy. Threading her way between hillocks, she didn't stop until her heart felt like it would beat out of her chest and she was well into the trees. Her lungs burned and felt like they were filled with shards of glass. Her legs felt like they were made of rubber. Panting, she stooped and took out the bundle. She didn't reach for food first; she reached for the pliers.

Moments later, the bolt in her neural interface was discarded in the snow at her feet. With trembling fingers, she reached into the data port and found the damaged circuits. She snapped a few tiny levers back into place. And felt … nothing. She shook her head violently side to side, and her interface was reignited by the kinetic energy of the action. She felt the familiar buzz in her neurons, and she threw up her arms in joy. She had an urge to call her mother, the Fleet, anyone, but stifled it, remembering her signal might be detected. Instead, she set about searching the ethernet for proper escape music, or maybe what she needed was a direct link to the mind of a footballer on Mars sprinting in low gravity; that would lift her heart. She settled on a channel for Mars's premier stadium. Instead of a direct link to a footballer's brain, she heard an announcement: "The Republic has failed to heed the Luddeccean warnings of alien invasion. We will be alone in our struggle, but as Luddecceans we will prevail!" Noa blinked. Madness, obviously. She searched for a channel on Venus she liked for its dance music and got the same announcer, this time warning, "Disconnect your neural interfaces lest they be compromised by alien influence." Noa felt her heart tumble as she skittered through the stations. All were broadcasting the same announcer—all the off-world and planet-side channels had been compromised.

Swearing, and almost crying, she plucked the chip from the open bundle, put it into a spare slot, and immediately tuned into the Luddeccean secure channel—as she should have done immediately, she scolded herself. She heard a different man's voice, low and sonorous. "Team four has joined the pursuit, target will soon be down."

Belatedly, Noa realized the chase above her head was still going on.

Another voice crackled in her brain. "Should we give up the search for the lost prisoner?"

Noa held her breath.

"Negative, do not abort the search. Commander Noa Sato is considered a high security risk and extremely dangerous."

Noa's hackles rose. "Curse of bloody competency," she grumbled.

"We don't have her individual port reading," one of the voices said. "She must not have a locator."

Noa did have a locator—a Fleet supplied one. If there were any Fleet close by, they would have detected her. But, of course, the Galactic Fleet had devices that scrambled signals and even location. They didn't want shot-down personnel being trailed by terrorists. Unless they had a Fleet decoder—or until she tried to call for help—she would be as invisible as a phantom.

Another voice chimed in, "The screw jammed into her port should have a short-range locator. Try homing in on that."

Noa's eyes widened. She looked at the piece of polymer and metal at her feet. It was big enough to contain a locator chip. Picking it up, she hurled it through the air. And then, after stuffing some bread and snow in her mouth and letting it warm, she accessed some data her parents had made her download when she was just a girl. For an instant she worried that the ethernet bands used by her GPS would also have been hijacked—but a map seemingly etched in light appeared in the air before her—an illusion created by data as it interacted with her visual cortex. She saw her location as a single, red blinking light in a three-dimensional landscape. She concentrated—saved the data locally in case the GPS was hijacked, and then focused on finding the closest human habitation. There was a winter retreat town exactly twenty clicks away. She could make it … if she didn't freeze to death.

Curling her hands against her stomach for warmth, she set off through the pines. Just a few minutes later, Noa heard a howl so loud, it made every hair on the back of her neck stand on end. She heard a crack, snow fell all around her, and she ducked. A branch as thick as her leg landed not six steps away. The howling continued. Noa looked up. Where she stood there was only a breeze, but beyond the shelter of the pines' great trunks, the wind was whipping the tree tops like mad banners. She curled her hands more tightly against herself and kept going.

Over the Luddeccean channel, someone said, "Sato's data bolt has been found. Fan out!"

Another voice cracked, "We can't send a jump team from the cruisers. It's too windy."

"We've got men on the ground, divert them!" someone else said.

Nebulas. Scowling, Noa willed her legs to move faster— but they didn't. She cursed under her breath. She had to have more reserves than this.

In the sky above she heard the whir of antigrav engines, the scream of cannons, and then the roar of exploding cannon fire as it collided with a ship. Noa closed her eyes and said a brief prayer for the unknown person overhead.

A Luddeccean voice rang through her mind, over the secure channel. "The Archangel is down!" Stopping in her tracks, Noa spun in the direction of the explosions, memories of her interrogation flashing back to her at the word, "Archangel."

Someone on the channel gave coordinates for the crash site, and it seemed that every secure Luddeccean channel on the planet echoed the strange message. "I repeat: Archangel down, Archangel down!" The words exploded in her mind, and she felt a buzz in her head.

And then all voices went silent. Noa plugged the coordinates for the crash site into her neural interface's calculator app. Could there be any survivors? Could she reach them in time? The answer blinked back at her before she could even finish the thought: it would take hours to reach the craft on foot at her pathetic excuse for a jog. She couldn't help, or expect help, from any fallen angel.

CHAPTER TWO

He fell.

The ground rushed toward him, he swept past the limbs of towering Ponderosa pines to the ground of dead needles and rough stone, and he didn't feel pain. He was pain.

He opened his eyes and found himself flat on his back, bright lights burning his retinas, tubes in his mouth and nose. He heard the sound of rushing air, felt his lungs expand with a stab of agony, and then felt the air slowly seep back out. Dimly, he realized he was on a stretcher being pushed down a long, white hallway. Heat rushed down his cheeks.

"James," a familiar voice said.

His gaze followed the sound, and he found himself staring into his father's hazel eyes. They were red-rimmed with tears. His father never cried. "James! Stay with me," his father said. He pulled James's hand to his cheek. James blinked. His hand was pale next to his father's darker Eurasian skin. His mother was dark, too. His father and mother had struggled so hard to make sure that their blonde-haired, blue-eyed child wouldn't face any disadvantages. And he hadn't. James had had a wonderful life. A perfect life of mental stimulation, meaningful work, good friends, and adventure. He wanted to say so, but the mask over his face prevented him from speaking.

He heard shouting, and the sound of many footsteps, rubber on linoleum, a beeping long and slow, and someone saying, "Sir, you must step away."

"No," his father said. "No!"

His father's words echoed the feeling in James's heart. He couldn't swallow, but his body tried to. A gurgle rose up from the tubing, and the furious whir and beeping of machines became more furious still.

Blue-gloved hands wrapped around his father's shoulders, pulling him away, and James was moving through the long white hallway alone, the shouts becoming muted. He closed his eyes. He hadn't had a chance to say what he wanted to say—but the time capsule, his father would find it. Everything was in the time capsule … the world went dark behind his eyelids.

His eyes opened again. He was flat on his stomach instead of his back. Instead of pain he felt cold; it sizzled from his hands and the front of his legs and torso to his spine like an electric charge. He scrambled up, and for a moment he was suspended in a white blur. Trying to get his bearings, he spun in place. Was he in the hospital? But then why was it was cold? And there was no sound of beeping, footsteps, or the whine of antigrav stretchers—just a soft whisper.

His head ticked to the side, and the white blur came into focus. He found himself alone, outdoors—the ethernet strangely silent. He blinked. Beyond the snowflakes, there were trees. The whisper he heard was the sound of millions of snowflakes colliding with the pines, the ground, and his body.

Snow whispered.

He didn't think he'd ever noticed that before.

He blinked snowflakes from his lashes. The trees were Ponderosa Pines, which meant he was on Earth near the accident he'd just been dreaming of … no, remembering. He took a deep breath, and instead of the scent of pine, a different fragrance like mint and lavender flooded his senses—Luddeccean pine. He shook his head, blinked again, and saw that the trees he'd mistaken for Earth's Ponderosas had needles in gradients of red and purple, and silvery-gray bark. The morphology was almost identical to Ponderosas, hence his confusion. Similar gravity and climate on Earth and this planet had produced some of the most dramatic examples of convergent evolution in the galaxy.

How had he gotten here? He brushed snow from his chest and his hand encountered a strap. His eyes slipped down to a belt slung over his shoulder to his side ... a holster ... for the rifle on his back. Why did he have a rifle on his back?

He looked down at the outline his body had made in the snow. He must have fallen. Again. He shuddered, feeling a crawling sensation under his skin. Over the whisper of snow came the loud whine of antigrav engines above the treetops, ten kilometers away, south by southwest, and approaching at a rate that would put them here in 3.5 minutes.

He shook his head and clutched his temples as the recent past jolted to the forefront of his consciousness. He'd come to Luddeccea from Earth to visit with his parents at their vacation cottage—just as they had done every year since he was ten years old. The rifle was for hunting, as was the camouflage he was wearing. This year he'd come early. The recently elected Luddeccean government was very conservative. He'd heard things over the ethernet that made him suspect that the planet might have become inhospitable for outsiders. He had come to Luddeccea a week before his family, just to make sure things were safe.

He winced—the expression didn't go further than his eyes; his lips felt odd, stiff. The last thing he remembered was being in the shuttle he'd rented from the time gate ...

He'd had the proper authorizations; but, before he transmitted them, the Luddeccean Guard had begun firing. He blinked snow out of his eyes. His parents had said he was paranoid—things didn't get dangerous that quickly. James was a historian; his specialty was twentieth century Earth. Cuba had become dangerous in the 1950s very quickly … and apparently Luddeccea was undergoing such a dangerous revolution just as quickly. He couldn't remember ever being so unhappy to be right.

After the Guard had begun firing, he remembered a jolt as the shuttle's engines had been clipped. His body had been flung against his safety harness, and over the ethernet he'd heard, "Archangel down, Archangel down." Everything after that was a blank. But somehow he'd made his way here from the crash site …

He looked back at his footprints, rapidly filling with snow.

Archangel down. What could it mean? The ethernet was still silent—something must have become dislodged in his head in the crash. He shook his head in frustration and tried to access his own data banks. For a frightening moment he couldn't … but with another furious shake his neural interface kicked into gear. Although his specialty was twentieth century media, he had other historical data on hand. His neural interface picked up his last question and began to project images of archangels into his mind: illustrations from medieval manuscripts, paintings, and photo manipulations from the late 1900s and early 2000s, all of men with wings, often with weapons. At the same time the images flashed, nanos piped words. "Archangels: 'high angels,' mythical creatures, first imagined in 300 BC in the Judaic tradition: Gabriel, Michael, Raphael, Uriel, Raguel, Remiel, and Saraqael. Lucifer was also sometimes considered to have been an archangel before he fell from grace. Archangels were present in the religions of all the Abrahamic traditions: Judaism, Christianity, and Islam."

James exhaled a long breath. The Abrahamic traditions were popular on Luddeccea … had they been comparing him, a historian, to the devil? He was certain he could feel his synapses blinking in confusion at the lack of logic.

A shout on the ground drew him from his thoughts. James looked over his shoulder. The whine of antigrav was louder—as was the sound of wind above the trees. He still could not see anyone or even a ship; the snow was falling too densely. He stood, transfixed. The right thing to do would be to put his hands over his head, wait for an actual human, and explain the situation. If only they saw his authorization chip, they'd realize it was a mistake—he was a citizen of Earth, and purposely firing on him could be grounds for sanctions. Surely they'd merely deport him? On the other hand, if he ran, he would be a fugitive.

The approaching voices grew louder. He found himself backing away from his pursuers without conscious thought. He wanted to stop and think—but his body seemed to have a mind of its own.

… And then it occurred to him, in a bright moment of lucidity, that maybe his body had caught on to what his brain seemed determined to ignore. When he had told his parents the world might be unsafe for off-worlders, he thought maybe they'd have rocks thrown at their cottage windows—he didn't think he'd be shot out of the sky.

Could he reason with a government that broke the laws of the Republic under mythological pretexts?

Before his mind had even formulated an answer to that hypothetical, he found himself spinning in place. He started to run, calling on his data banks of the local terrain. A three-dimensional holo appeared to superimpose itself over the scene before him, an illusion his nanos were piping into his visual cortex. The perceived holo showed a map with a blinking light for him, the cottage a tiny block of light 234 kilometers away, and a refueling station twenty kilometers away demarked by a tiny glowing triangle. Could he catch a ride there? Or at least hide and find food and shelter before he died of exposure?

There was one other light. In his auditory apparatus the name "Commander Noa Sato" rang. He leaped over a large boulder, and, with the impact of landing, more memories hit him in a rush. Just before he'd been shot, he'd heard the Luddeccean authorities declare her "dangerous." An image of a woman in a crisp Fleet uniform came to his mind. Her eyes … Noa Sato's eyes, he was almost sure … were sliding to the side at someone out of the camera's line of vision. A wide smile was on her face. Her skin was so dark it made the drab gray of her uniform appear silver. Her cheeks were round and plump despite the sleek athleticism of her form. He knew, like he knew her name and face, that she was forty-two years old in the picture, though the Fleet's anti-aging regimen meant she looked closer to twenty-five. She looked vibrant, healthy, and very alive. In the cold, running for his life, the image impossibly made him want.

James felt the urge to frown, but his numb lips did not respond. He didn't know her … he couldn't remember anything about her other than that picture. She was in the opposite direction to his current course. He couldn't go to her. It was too risky. He stumbled, clutched his head, and stumbled again. His footsteps slowed, until he was standing, panting, staring at his feet, his breath curling in front of him.

He tried to move along his intended trajectory.

… And found he couldn't. The shouts rose behind the curtain of snow. Someone said, "It fell down here!"

It?

James looked in the direction he wanted to go, and then in the direction of Commander Sato. His feet moved toward the Commander … and at least he was moving away from the people calling him "it." At first he went slowly, but when he didn't stumble, he started to run faster. Every stride became longer, and faster, until the world was a blur. A fallen tree loomed before him, the crest of the felled trunk a meter and twenty-four centimeters high. He leapt over it before he'd had time to think—he had to have misjudged the height because he cleared it easily and landed lightly on his feet.

***

Noa wasn't running through the forest. She was shambling. Her limbs were cold, and it seemed that in every direction she could hear pursuers.

"Ashley," she muttered. "I am so angry with you… making me do this alone, making me leave you, making me so cold … for being right that you wouldn't have made it this far."

"Did you hear that?" someone shouted.

Noa didn't turn her head. Her Fleet-implanted locator app plotted the speaker as a glowing light a few meters behind her. She tried to run, but all that came to her limbs was a slightly faster shuffle.

She heard her own breath, raspy and loud. And she heard antigrav engines, the big kind, just clicks away. It was all strangely muted. By the snow? Or was she finally losing her mind? "I can't lose it now, I can't, I can't, I won't, I won't."

"I hear her," someone said.

Noa wanted to run, but sending that message to her limbs didn't work. It was like her body was a puppet that belonged to someone else. Without warning, the puppet master ripped her feet out from under her. Noa went sprawling forward, the front part of her body connecting with the cold ground. She heard men, too close behind, looked back, and only saw a large root jutting out of the snow. "Damn you for tripping me," she muttered, trying to drag herself to her feet. "Stupid root. I hope you die of rot. Or weevils. Or … " She groaned. It took too much energy to talk, and breathing sent daggers of ice into her lungs. She was on all fours, and somehow, she wasn't able to get up. So she crawled, hands burning with cold in the snow. She found the ability to speak again. "And damn you body. I hate you. Giving out on me at a time like this."

"Well, she still has energy enough to talk," someone said with a laugh. It wasn't a nice laugh.

The boot that connected with her side a few moments later shouldn't have taken her by surprise. Pain seared through her, but it was muted like sound in the snow. I'm sorry, body, she wanted to say, but couldn't. Sorry, I don't want to leave you yet. Don't give up on me.

Someone kicked her again. Lungs aching, she found herself staring up at white. Snow? Or had she fainted? She wasn't sure. But then her vision half-returned and she was looking at the dark arms of trees reaching for the sky. Someone said, "End of the line for you, throwback." She heard the click of a safety and found herself facing the barrel of a pistol. Beyond the pistol was a tan face, with Eurasian eyes, above a thick down coat in Luddeccean Green.

"Don't shoot her, Art," someone else said. "Command wants to interrogate her and to yank her port out. Fleet pulled a number on us."

"What the hell are you talking about, Joe?" said the guy holding the pistol.

Noa could actually hear the guy who must be Joe shrug, even though she couldn't see him. "Orders are orders."

The pistol pointed at Noa's nose slowly lowered.

Out of her line of sight, Noa heard a soft thud.

"What was that?" someone who wasn't Joe or Art said.

She willed her body to swivel in the snow, to knock the feet out from under her closest pursuer, and steal his pistol. Instead she just managed to scoot backward like an upside down snake. Did snakes move upside down? They were a recent addition to the Luddeccean fauna from Earth. A tiny, obviously useless, part of her brain tried to access the ethernet.

**

Over the sound of his breathing and his pounding feet, James heard someone say, "End of the line for you, throwback," and then the click of a safety.

He came to a skidding halt at the sound, and his vision pulsed, as though he were in a room where the lights were flickering.

"Don't shoot her, Art," said another voice. James blinked, and his vision normalized. He crept forward and peered around a tree. He saw what looked like a pile of rags on the ground, and four men in Luddeccean Green orbiting around it.

"Command wants to interrogate her again—and to yank her port out."

The words "interrogate" and "yank her port out," stood at the forefront of James's mind. The snow and storm disappeared as his neural interface crowded his mind with images of prisoners of war in WWII, and of victims of amateur port removals—their brains and nanos spilled out in back alleys.

He should run away from these savages. There were four of them, and only one of him.

He wanted to run. And couldn't.

He remembered a mountain climbing expedition to a sunken city along the San Andreas rift on Earth—he used to tell his students that he was a historian of the Indiana

Jones variety—after he explained who Indiana Jones was. On that particular trip, his companion's safety cord had slipped from the rock face. James had caught him and helped him to safety without a second thought ... and managed to pull his own shoulder out of its socket in the process.

Was he the type of person that simply couldn't turn away? But he wanted to turn away, and that person in the memory seemed like a completely different person.

James looked down at his feet half-buried in snow, immobile despite his wishes. He looked to the pile of rags that might be Noa Sato, and then to her pursuers. He couldn't run away—and he couldn't just haphazardly try to intervene—he'd be captured, too. How could he rescue her and keep his own skin? He needed a distraction ...

Gazing at the snow, he recalled another winter he'd spent here as a child. He'd thrown a snowball at his father's back, missed spectacularly, and hit a tree. His father had turned to the remains of the snowball before turning to James and lobbing a snowball back.

It wasn't much of a plan, but it was what he had. Kneeling down, James quickly made a snowball. He threw it at a tree thirty meters from his location, and hit it dead center.

"What was that?" said one of the men. Raising his rifle, the man looked toward the sound.

James made another snowball, and threw it at a tree a few meters from the first. His aim was unerring. He tilted his head; he'd been a terrible pitcher at cricket. Was fear improving his arm?

"What joker is throwing snowballs?" one of the other men said.

"Knock it off!" said another.

"Probably Jaurez. I'm going to check this out," said another, clicking the safety of his pistol and walking into the trees.

Swinging his rifle around without conscious thought, James found himself watching the man walk between the trees through the sights.

He'd never shot a human before. The realization hit James just as the man in the trees reached the remains of his snowballs on the silvery white tree trunks. James had a memory of watching some Fleet personnel boarding a shuttle back on Earth. It was right after a hostage standoff that had ended with the Fleet killing innocent civilians. James had shaken his head, turned to a professor colleague beside him, and said, "Violence is never the solution, not in this day and age."

Now his rifle was aimed at a man. Was he truly ready to shoot?

The man spun around, raising his firearm in James's direction. James pulled the trigger. The man's head jerked backward as the bullet hit and James felt … relief.

One of the men by the pile of rags screamed, "Pari!"

The same force that compelled him to find Commander Sato seemed to take hold of James. He moved from the tree he was hiding behind to another. A second man stepped into the trees. James's rifle was still raised, his eye still in the sights, and he pulled the trigger.

***

There was another soft thud, and then another rifle shot. Noa's body belatedly responded to her brain's order to move. Sitting up, she saw the first man crouched behind a tree. He had a heat-seeking screen up, and he was aiming it into a swirling blur beyond him. Noa managed to climb to her feet, and then wavered there like grass in the wind. Her pursuer wasn't paying attention to her. His face was on the screen, swinging it around, trying to find the source of the rifle shots … the snow was so thick that the heat screen was

34

a blur. He stopped, and over his shoulder, before Noa's eyes, a face emerged on the screen, very close, and very familiar.

Noa's body responded before her brain could even give it orders. She charged forward and delivered a blow to the side of the Luddeccean's head. It should have been enough to knock him over—but somehow wound up more like a tap.

"What the—" Joe let out a string of curse words. Before Noa knew what was happening, she was flat on her back in the snow again, the side of her jaw stinging, blood on her tongue, air whipping out of her lungs. There was the sound of a rifle shot, the crunch of snow, and the face she'd seen on the heat screen appeared above her. Bright blue eyes above high cheekbones, pale skin with a few freckles, all framed by dark blonde hair.

"Timothy," she whispered.

***

James stared down at the woman that might be Commander Noa Sato, the woman he had killed to defend—which seemed like it should be a milestone in his life—a marker, an event. But it wasn't. It felt as ordinary as breathing.

It was hard to reconcile the woman in the snow with the healthy, beautiful, laughing woman in his memory. This woman's cheeks were sunken, her hair was sparse, and her full lips were dry, split and bloody.

"Timothy," she whispered.

"No, my name is … James Sinclair." As the names spilled from his lips, they felt wrong. But they weren't. It was his name, a name with history. James was an ancient name, from Hebrew. It meant "he who grasps the heel" or "supplanter." Sinclair was Scottish, and it meant "bright and clear."

Why did it sound off? Because it was just a jumble of syllables that didn't sound like one who overthrew, and it didn't offer any clarity?

In the snow, the dark eyes of the woman rolled back as her head listed to the side. James took a step back. If this was Commander Sato, she didn't recognize him. Why was he drawn to her?

He heard the whisper of the snow falling on their bodies, and above the trees the sound of antigrav engines approaching. He remembered the expedition on the cliff face and catching the fallen man. Was it the instinct of a herd animal that compelled him to save her, or just a personality trait?

This woman was not part of his "herd," and logically, James knew she would be dead weight. Kneeling, he scooped her into his arms anyway. As he pulled her close, he smelled a raw stench of vomit, sweat, and unwashed clothing. He pulled her tighter, due to some instinct he could not name or fathom. Over those unappealing smells he felt something else—a rush of familiarity. Clutching her tighter still, he looked around. He saw four hover bikes in the trees. If he could start one, they could be at his parents' cottage in an hour or even less.

He carried the woman over to the bikes. They were oblong in shape with a padded seat that looked large enough for two, and a turbo engine at the back. Two antigrav engines, each about the diameter of a large serving platter and the height of his palm, jutted out from beneath it, the dull silver of the timefield bands that counteracted gravity gleaming in the low light. The timefield bands created a bubble in time—much like the ones created by the time gates that facilitated nearly instantaneous travel through space—but the fields generated by this craft were less precise and robust. The computations for the timefield were complex—the engine's location relative to the planet, solar system, galaxy, and universe had to be taken into account.

Warping time disrupted gravity's pull and created lift with a simple propeller mechanism, but these engines looked too large for a bike of this size—older tech, he suspected.

Sliding onto the seat, he slung the Commander awkwardly over his legs. The bike's controls looked antiquated. Besides the overly large engines and manual steering, there was a flat screen and actual dials. There didn't even appear to be a cable to connect to his data port. Dipping his chin, he focused on the dark screen and tried to pick up the bike's wireless signal—and got nothing.

He tried to access his data banks for information on the bike model, but drew a blank.

The Commander stirred. "Crazy, primitive, Luddeccean tech," she muttered, her voice barely audible.

James blinked down at her.

Her eyes were closed, but she continued to mumble. "Ignition controlled by retinal scan, scanner above the speedometer … remove the speedometer and hot-wire it. Just touch the yellow wire to the green port … Removing the speedometer will also remove the tracking device."

James heard shouting, and actual footsteps. He had only minutes before they would be in visual range. He ripped the main screen off at the front of the bike with one hand.

"Nebulas!" the Commander hissed. "You're strong for a figment of my imagination."

Too worried to ponder the statement, James almost dropped the screen.

"No!" She coughed. "Do the same to the other bikes, wire them up, activate them, and voice command them to go far away."

James held the broken bike component above her head. It seemed like a waste of time. He almost chucked the thing into the snow.

The Commander took a shaky breath. "Throw the one

you've got into the boot of one of the others when you do it."

The implications of that sank in. It was bound to be discovered that they'd stolen this bike. If they threw the tracking device into one of the other bikes, and the other bikes went to the wrong location, their pursuers could be diverted for hours. And he'd thought throwing a snowball at a tree for attention was clever.

"Do it!" the woman hissed.

His neural interface was blinking like the lights of a Christmas tree. He had less than two minutes. James swung Noa off his lap without paying attention to her landing. He left her cursing in the snow at the foot of the bike, and a part of him ached for it; but there was too little time for it to be helped. After ripping off the other speedometers, he quickly found the green port and yellow wire she was speaking of. He activated both bikes, gave them commands, and watched them zip off through the trees.

He heard the last bike engine rev. Spinning, he saw that the Commander had managed to get up, slide onto the seat, and activate the vehicle.

He looked back at the trail the other bikes had left in the snow. The search party on the ground was fifty-one seconds to visual range. She had his bike now, he'd slow her down and …

"Get on!" she ordered him.

James felt his mind stutter. She didn't seem to have the same ambivalence about rescuing him that he did rescuing her.

"What are you waiting for?" she asked.

Running forward, James jumped on, just barely fitting on the seat behind her.

"Hold on!" she commanded over the roar of the bike's engine and the search party. The bike rose before he had a chance to put on his safety belt, and he wrapped his arms around her waist. The bike was capable of soaring above the treetops—but the Commander kept it close to the ground, following the crater-like path the other bikes' antigrav engines had left in the snow … which was strange. She was the one who had told him to use the other bikes as a decoy. Before he had a chance to question, they were gliding over a large stream, not yet frozen over. The Commander immediately doubled back, but kept to the course of the stream. It wasn't in the precise direction he wanted to go, and he almost protested … and then realized the antigrav engines left no trace of their movement in the water. It was clever.

The Commander hit the accelerator and within minutes the sound of the antigrav engines in the sky was several dozen kilometers in the distance, and he could no longer hear the shouts of the ground party.

It should have been comforting. But without the threat of imminent death, James's brain started to replay how he came to be sitting behind a strange woman who was as thin as a scarecrow and reeking of disease. He tried to think back to when he had first rented the shuttle on Time Gate 8—wondering if somehow he'd managed to get the wrong authorization. But he couldn't remember being at the counter of the rental kiosk, or collecting the shuttle at the terminal. And then there was the time after the shuttle was shot that he couldn't remember, either.

James released a long breath. His arms tightened on the Commander's waist. She was a stranger, and just a shadow of the vision of her he had in his mind, but she felt real, familiar, and good. Between his knees he felt the Commander shiver. He could feel the edge of her ribs beneath the thin coat. He had an inexplicable desire to slip his hands up beneath her coat to feel her heartbeat.

The Commander shivered again, this time so violently he

was sure if his arms weren't around her she would fall off.

"Hope you can drive, figment of my imagination," the Commander said.

"My name is James," he said. And then, like a delayed reaction, he realized that she might be telling a joke. Why would she make light of the situation? He blinked, remembering when he caught his friend as he fell down the cliff. Afterward, James had said, "Next time you decide to plummet to your death, could you lose a few kilos?" He used to joke about death, too.

"My second wind just blew away," Noa said. "I think I'm going to … " She drew the bike to a stop. Water sloshed below them, spreading out in small waves.

"What?" said James.

She promptly slumped in his arms.

***

James stumbled through the snow, clutching Sato tightly to his chest. He kept his eyes closed—the snow was falling too thickly to see anything anyway. Instead he kept his mind focused on the glowing square in his mind's eye that was his parents' cottage. It was only ten meters away now.

He'd abandoned the bike about five kilometers ago when it had been almost out of fuel. He'd commanded the machine to continue along the river. Hopefully, when it was found, it would be sufficiently far away to throw off anyone who might discover it.

He shivered. He'd wrapped his coat around the Commander. At first, exertion had kept him warm, but then the very exertion that had kept him warm had caused the snow to melt into his clothes, and he was cold. He nearly tripped again. He was hungry, too, and there was a perplexing haze at the edges of his consciousness, as though all non-vital systems had been shut down. It was a relief in a way. He hadn't obsessed about his missing blocks of time or how he knew the Commander in exactly forty-five minutes and thirty-three seconds … Apparently, his brain thought a chronometer was a vital function. The observation almost brought a bitter smile to his lips—but they felt numb, and it didn't come.

The dot that was him and the square that was the cottage collided. James opened his eyes. He couldn't see the circle of pines that surrounded the remote retreat. The only thing he could see was the front stoop. A knee-high landscaping 'bot with a plow at the front was pushing snow away from the door. It flashed a red light at him, attempting a retinal scan. James dutifully met the red glow head on. The 'bot beeped in recognition, and before James even set his hand on the fingerprint recognition plate, the heavy wood door swung open. He stepped inside. It was warm—the 'bots had been expecting him. In the foyer, he paused. Everything was exactly as he remembered it. The floor was local limestone, the ceilings had exposed beams of Luddeccean pine. The walls were the same pine, but more finely sanded and stained a lighter color. He heard the whir of other housekeeping 'bots, and the distant hum of the furnace that heated water. James kicked off his boots and felt the familiar rush of warmth from the floors through his now-drenched socks. Familiar … and off. Something was missing.

His coat slid from the Commander's torso to the floor, bringing his attention to his mysterious burden. She had been absolutely silent since she'd passed out on the bike—he noticed with dismay that she was soaking wet, just as he was. Eyes still closed, she began to shiver. He didn't have time for his apprehension—as wrong as this place felt, it was still shelter.

He carried her to the bedroom. Dropping her on the bed, he put his hand on her forehead. Thirty-four degrees Celsius—she was mildly hypothermic. He flexed the fingers of his hand … he didn't remember having a temperature app. He didn't have time to ponder it. James quickly stripped her out of her wet clothes down to only her undergarments. For the first time he noticed that there were fresh scars on her left hand where her last finger and ring finger were missing. There were also two very small scars on her face—one beneath her eyebrow and one above. They didn't look like the aesthetic scarification that was popular a few years ago on Earth. There was another larger scar on her abdomen. Strange that she had not repaired the glaring imperfections. Besides those, she had visible bruising around her ribs and on her cheek. She was also visibly emaciated. She may have passed out from hunger as much as cold. For now, he couldn't help the hunger, but he could help with the cold.

Tucking her beneath the duvet, he stripped down himself and joined her. Removing her clothing had taken away some of the odors of filth that clung to her—but not all. For all the smell of death … there was something comforting about her presence. Maybe she'd only mistaken him for someone else earlier because she was exhausted from cold and hunger? Perhaps she'd wake up, they'd eat, and she'd remind him of how he knew her?

She shivered, and he put his hand over her heart. He could feel her rib cage too acutely, but the beat was steady.

Ten minutes later, the Commander's shivering ceased, and a quick check of her temple showed that her temperature had risen above hypothermic levels. His hand drifted down to her waist. He found that if he concentrated, he could hear her heartbeat over the sound of the wind outside, the furnace rumbling in the distance, and the house 'bots.

Settling into a semi-conscious haze with only the sound of her heart and his internal chronometer for company, he had an odd memory of being ten years old, in this very house, and curling up in this bed with a toy giraffe that played bedtime lullabies.

After four hours, six minutes, and thirty-seven seconds, the Commander shifted against him in a way that wasn't toy-like. Before James had a chance to come to full consciousness, she murmured drowsily. The tone of her voice was like a lover's, and his hand tightened on her hip, as though by reflex. Before he had time to fully process her murmur, or his reaction, she whispered, "Timothy ..."

The same body that had betrayed his logical mind and helped him find her, and was now gripping her hip in a way that was too familiar, betrayed him again. He responded without thinking.

CHAPTER THREE

Second Lieutenant Noa Sato leaned against the bar, staring at the empty dance floor. Crossing her arms, she frowned. It was her first night after finishing Officer Training School, and she'd wanted to dance. Unfortunately, her roommate wanted to catch up with her ex-boyfriend, and worse, the dance floor was empty. Noa stamped a high titanium heel in impatience. More friends would be here soon—but she wanted to let loose now.

"Excuse me, can I buy you a drink?"

Noa wasn't in the mood. She wasn't one for hook-ups—love sex though she might. What was the point in rolling in the sheets with a man who didn't feel the pressure to perform?

Without looking, she said, "No thanks."

"Oh, come on!" said the proposer, his voice indignant. "You have to realize what sort of internal anxieties I'm overcoming to talk to you!"

Expecting to hear some variation of "look at me, deigning to talk to someone who's an African throwback," Noa rolled her eyes. Turning to the speaker, she was prepared to give him a withering glare; instead, her eyes opened in shock. She expected to see tan skin, straight-to-wavy brown hair, and hazel-to-brown eyes. Instead the man before her was as pale as the moon, his eyes were bright blue, and his hair was dark blonde streaked with highlights that were nearly white.

The speaker lifted his hands and gestured at her. "I mean, look at you, you're … "

Noa's eyes narrowed. "I'm what?"

"Taller than me!" the man declared.

Noa's lips pursed, and one eyebrow shot up. In her seven-centi heels, that was definitely true. This particular pair of shoes had a collapsible heel by design. She could lower herself to his height and make him feel more comfortable—but she wouldn't.

He touched a hand to his chest. "I think you should consider that it takes a big man to love a taller woman."

Noa's jaw dropped.

The man's eyes went wide, and then his skin flushed red from the roots of his hair to the neck of his shirt. Putting a hand to his temple, he winced. "Nebulas, that came out wrong. Big heart, I mean, big heart!" He had lips so thin, Noa wondered how they could possibly sip from a glass, and a long, straight pointy nose—but those eyes, when they peeked at her—they were so wide they gave him an air of innocence, even if they were shockingly blue.

Noa found herself laughing. She held out her hand. "Second Lieutenant Noa Sato."

"Oh, I know!" said the man.

Noa's lips pursed.

Almost cautiously, the man said, "You did receive a commendation for your performance in hand-to-hand combat … " A mischievous smile tweaked at the corners of his thin lips. "I thought you were there when they gave you the ribbon in front of the rest of us."

Noa felt her cheeks get warm, but knew her skin would hide the evidence. "And what is your name?"

Taking her hand, he said, "Second Lieutenant Timothy Anderson."

A lot of men had wanted to shake Noa's hand since she

45

got that ribbon. Too many of them tried to crush the bones in her fingers to assert their masculinity. Pathetic in this day and age, really.

Timothy didn't try to break her hand, but neither was his handshake weak. It was just right. Noa found her whole body warming at the touch. She knew right then that she and Timothy would be lovers ... and that they would be together for a very, very, long time.

***

Noa was cold. She felt a chill deep in her bones, which was strange, because she was curled up with her back pressed to Timothy under a huge thick duvet, lying atop a mattress that was so soft and comfortable she thought that she may have to be antigravved out of it. She was so hungry that she could feel the sides of her stomach touching together—so hungry that she felt limp and dizzy from it. She heard the wind howl outside and actually smiled. Of course, because they got married yesterday, in Colorado of all places, in winter ... there had been a snowstorm. Noa loved snow.

Her eyelids fluttered briefly. She saw light wood-paneled walls, a rustic quilt on a chair ... the honeymoon suite. She sighed and closed her eyes.

She hadn't eaten at all during the wedding banquet. She'd been too busy greeting all their guests, too excited and too happy, that was why she was hungry. She shifted against Timothy and remembered with bemusement that they hadn't had sex the night after their wedding, either. Her mother had said they'd be too tired. And her mom had been right. She frowned. But she hadn't been too tired to dream ... terrible, frightening dreams. A concentration camp, and Timothy being dead, but then saving her and her saving Timothy.

She wiggled again, trying to get warm, and get closer to Tim. She felt fingers tighten on her hip. The cold ... the lack of marital consummation, these could be easily remedied. "Timothy," she whispered.

"I am not Timothy," said a masculine, strangely familiar voice, but not Tim.

With an undignified yelp, Noa rolled out of bed. Hitting the floor with jaw-rattling impact, she skittered like a crab on her hands until her back hit something solid. Literally, backed against the wall, she stared at the bed. It was a high mattress, box spring combo, very old fashioned, complete with a thick quilt, like the one on her honeymoon. A man was sitting there. He might have been Timothy's twin, a clone, or the type of animatronic that some people made so they didn't forget great-grandma, their partner, or their dead child.

After a beat too long, the not-Tim held up his hands as though in surrender. His jaw shifted from side to side oddly, and his brows drew together. "I am sorry," he said softly, as though she were a frightened ptery or bird. "I didn't mean to frighten you."

Noa felt bile rise in her throat. She had a moment of complete disorientation and wondered if she was still dreaming. She took a few shaky breaths, and nebulas, the cold still felt like it was clawing at her lungs even in the warm room.

"My name is James Sinclair," the stranger said. A part of her brain fumbled to draw up his name on the ethernet and found it still disconnected.

James's chin dipped to his chest and his eyes bored into hers. "Don't you know me?" There was an urgency in his voice that was disquieting.

Noa jerked her head in the negative. He pulled back and his eyes went to the ceiling, as though he was seeking some answer in the air. The picture of confusion—or dismay.

She gulped. His voice was too low and rich to be Timothy's. And he'd either bought an app to simulate the speech patterns of a wealthy Earther—probably European, maybe even British—or he was born into money. She didn't normally associate with either type of person. She looked down at herself … she was a skeleton … dressed in ratty underwear. She sniffed. And she stank. "It wasn't a dream," she muttered, her shoulders slumping. The escape, the concentration camp … her eyes fell on the scars on her lower abdomen, the thumb of her left hand touched the stumps of her ring finger and pinky … and Timothy was dead, and it hurt all over again.

"What dream?" the stranger said.

Noa blinked up at him. The likeness was extraordinary, and disturbing, but if she focused on him, she saw an artist's rendition of her late husband, not her Tim. James's hair color was the same—dark blonde, highlights of nearly platinum; he had the same skin tone, and blue eyes. But this man's lips were fuller, his nose not quite as long, his jaw more square, and his frame more muscular. He didn't have Tim's laugh lines, either. He had the sort of agelessness she associated with Earther plastic surgery and nano-repair. He looked to be late twenties, but could be anything from late twenties to early fifties. He was too perfect.

Her eyes narrowed. "Why was I … " She gestured to the bed. "With you?" And then she remembered the cold.

"You had—"

"Hypothermia," she said, dropping her eyes.

"A mild case," he said softly.

She shivered again with such force her spine hurt. In the periphery of her vision, she saw James sit up straighter—as though startled. She pulled her knees to her chest and curled into herself. James picked up the covering on the bed and walked over to her. Without preamble, he sat down beside her and draped the thick down quilt over them both, creating a welcome bubble of warmth, but she struggled not to scoot away. Scooting away would show fear—and she wasn't afraid—not really. She closed her eyes.

"Commander, the bed is warmer." His voice was a whisper, concerned.

"Here is fine," Noa said, even though the bed would be more comfortable. She didn't feel violated, but spooning with the doppelgänger of Tim was too much right now. She felt weak and disoriented, and she needed to get her bearings.

"Very well." After a pause, he said, "I'd hoped you'd recognize me."

She did, sort of. "Nope," she said, rubbing her temple.

"But I know you're Commander Noa Sato."

Noa dropped her hand. Her body tensed.

James didn't seem to notice. "I don't know how I know that."

Tension left her shoulders. In the grand scheme of things in her life that were wrong, that seemed the smallest to Noa. "I've been in the press a few times," she said. "You've probably seen me in holos or on the ethernet."

Leaning his head back, he gazed up at the ceiling. "Nothing makes sense. This is my parents' cottage—we were going to spend the holiday here together." He closed his eyes and massaged his lids. "I came here a week before them to verify that it was safe. I was shot out of the sky by the local forces. The last thing I remember hearing as my ship crashed was the Luddeccean authorities saying, 'Archangel down, Archangel down.'"

Noa blinked as her memories came back. "Say that again?" she said.

"Archangel down, Archangel down," James said, dropping his hand and blinking at the ceiling.

Noa's skin prickled. If she was remembering correctly, he

was saying that in the same voice with the same inflection as the Luddeccean who had first made the announcement … Which could have a lot of explanations. Voice chip for damaged vocal cords, natural ability to mimic …

Still not looking in her direction, a dazed expression in his eyes, he continued. "I knew that the locals were becoming more fanatic—what with the election of the new premier—but I had not realized the extent of the fanaticism." He shook his head. "I had all the right permits."

A glow bug lit in Noa's mind. "You are the one they shot out of the sky. You're the archangel."

James's head whipped to hers. "I am not an it."

Noa's lips pursed, uncertain where that had come from.

His jaw dropped and he looked away. "I don't know why they called me that, or why they shot me down."

Noa said softly, "Mistaken identity?"

James's face remained impassive.

The speed of the head turn just now, the way he'd ripped the screen off the hover … "You're augmented," Noa said.

Eyeing her and lifting a brow, he touched his data port. "Aren't we all?"

Noa sighed. "Yeah, it's ridiculous, but when were fundamentalists ever rational?" As soon as she said it, she felt off-kilter. Guilty. Earthers like him thought all Luddecceans were crazy. There were a lot of crazy fundamentalists on Luddeccea, but there were wonderful people, too. She'd been to Earth and met "extreme atheists;" she hadn't found them more moral or enlightened. She was ready to quip something defensive about all extremists, religious and irreligious being irrational, but James was touching the sides of his mouth with the fingers of both hands. The words died on her tongue at the odd gesture.

"I can't smile at your joke," he said, voice almost a whisper. "I can't frown, either."

Feeling a pinch of worry for the strange man, she leaned closer. His skin, where she could see it beneath his fingers, looked healthy—there was no sign of frostbite. She drew back, more pieces of the puzzle clicking together in her mind. "You have to be very augmented. They announced the coordinates of your crash over the channel. To reach me in time, you would have had to have run sixty-seven and a half kilometers per hour over mountainous terrain." The way he was patting his face … if he couldn't smile or frown, it meant he had augmentation there too, not just run-of-the-mill plastic surgery. But why?

James dropped his hands. "There was an accident, on Earth, before. I fell, the equivalent of many stories. I nearly died … " His head ticked to the side in a quick staccato movement. It reminded Noa of some of the compulsive tics Kenji used to have.

She sucked in a breath. An accident like he was describing would require facial augmentation, not just plastic surgery. If he was telling the truth, then maybe he'd received some damage to his augments during the crash? It would explain his inability to smile. But there was more to his story that didn't add up. "You had access to the secure Luddeccean channel if you heard their 'archangel down' message." And how had he known where she was? "Are you part of the Fleet?"

His jaw twitched, and he touched one side of his lip, and then looked down at his fingers. "I am not in the Fleet. I am a professor of history. I specialize in late 21st century. Most recently, I was in the process of reviewing discoveries I made along the San Andreas Rift."

Every hair on the back of her neck prickling, Noa interrupted him. "You killed three men."

For a heartbeat too long James was too still, his eyes on a place in the distance. When he spoke, his words came out as an uncertain stammer. "Yes … they kicked you, and were speculating on whether to kill you, talking about interrogating you and yanking out your port … and … I couldn't let it happen … I … I have hunted before, but never killed a human. I wasn't bothered by killing them, but I am bothered by the fact that I am not bothered, and I wonder if I should be … if that makes sense?"

Noa exhaled. Her hands flicked to her side—and she remembered being kicked—thanks to Fleet tech she was healing much faster than natural and it wasn't unbearably painful. "It does make sense," she said, and she did understand his ambivalence. She had pulled the trigger on more than a few unsavory individuals; it was harder than the holos made you believe. A man with no history of combat, nor apparently in a profession that would have given him training, killing three men? Her throat tightened. Of course, he'd just been shot out of the sky—probably because he was hyper-augmented. The situation was extreme—it could have pushed an ordinary man to extreme actions. And he hadn't hurt her, or ignored her, or dumped her off the snowmobile when she fainted. He had spooned with her scrawny, stinking self to save her from hypothermia.

"I feel … disconnected," James said. His face was turned away; his hand was on his data port.

"Because we're disconnected from the ethernet," Noa whispered.

His eyes narrowed and he shook his head, eyes roving around the room. "It's more than that. I feel off, Commander."

Noa's eyebrows rose. Something was off with James, but she didn't feel threatened. Instead she felt herself softening, seeing him for what he was—a civilian thrust into a war zone, a man who had overcome some physical and probably mental handicaps with augmentation. Her eyes grazed his perfect jaw line, the muscles and tendons in his shoulders that showed just above the comforter that covered them, and remembered the perfectly chiseled body below—his augmenters might have gone too far.

She sighed. "If you're not Fleet, you don't have to call me Commander."

Dropping his hand and turning to her, he said, "Very well, Ms. Sato." His jaw did that odd side to side shift, and he touched it in that self-conscious way.

He was too close for a stranger, and Noa fought the urge to pull away. "Just Noa is fine," she said, keeping her voice level. He turned away, and she felt herself relax. She reminded herself that he wasn't threatening, that he'd saved her, and there was no reason to be nervous or suspicious. Still, there was something else wrong with his story. "If you're not with the Fleet, how did you know my location?" She didn't remember her coordinates being broadcast, and her locator was Fleet secret tech.

"I saw your signal. I felt I had to find you." He gazed out the window.

Noa's brow furrowed. Her secure Fleet signal didn't rely on ethernet transmission at close ranges, but it was still secure and encrypted. Even if he'd tuned into the frequency, how would he have known it was her?

He shook his head—it was an odd movement—almost a shiver. "But I knew you were here. I hoped you could explain it."

Reaching up to clutch the edges of the duvet, she said, "I think the Luddecceans must have knocked out the satellite transmitter for this region—that's why the ethernet is down. Maybe the signals were scrambled as they were knocking down the satellite, and you accidentally tapped into the secure channel?" The Luddecceans and her own.

"A weak hypothesis," James said, perfectly sculpted profile

angled away from her. She felt herself relax, and realized if he had agreed with her, she might have been distrustful. His honesty made her instincts shout, "very strange" but not "danger." Or maybe she was just too hungry to feel danger. She sank against the wall, the sensation of her stomach curling in on itself overtaking her.

"Noa Sato … that is a Japanese name," James said, the lack of segue startling her.

"Yes," she ground out.

"My middle name is Hiro," said James, "after an uncle four generations back. My parents made me install a Japanese language chip so I could speak to Uncle Hiro and my grandmother Masako."

"Huh. I probably have that app," she said—or her mouth said automatically. She didn't feel as though her brain had taken any part in saying it. She felt as she had just before tumbling over the root in the forest, or slumping on the bike. She closed her eyes. None of it was a dream—not the concentration camp, Ashley or Kenji.

"Nihongo wakaru no? " said James, shifting beside her. "Honto?"

You understand Japanese? Her app translated. Really?

And she could understand his surprise … Japanese was no longer spoken, except by tiny enclaves of Japanese purists, and the app was rarely installed. To have two people in the same room with the app was rare, indeed. As she thought this, he rattled off in Japanese about how his great-great-something-or-other grandmother had left her purist family to be with his great-something-or-other British grandfather. It was a lot like Noa's family's story. Her parents had made her install the Japanese chip so she could talk to her 200-year-old purist Japanese great-great-great grandfather Jun Sato. And nebulas … like her, James didn't even look Japanese.

They could bond over that, but at the moment … bowing her head into her knees, Noa whined, "Get me food, James!"

He didn't move. "You'll be all right?"

Remembering his hunting rifle, Noa muttered, "What, do you have to go kill and skin it?"

"No, there is food in the kitchen."

"I'll be fine," Noa said, her stomach feeling like it was trying to devour itself. Remembering her first aid, and how it applied to starvation victims, she asked, "Do you have any soup? Something broth based?"

"I'll go check," he said, standing and giving Noa a view of the well-defined planes of his back and of his backside. She didn't even remember her brain telling her neck to lift her head. Scrunching her eyes shut, she groaned and banged her head against her duvet-covered knees.

James came back moments later with two sealed packets of soup in his hand. "Do you want me to warm the tomato or the chicken and rice—"

Seizing the chicken and rice packet from his hand, Noa ripped a corner open with her teeth and sucked out a mouthful of broth. James stared at her a moment and then did the same to the tomato soup. She raised her eyebrows at him.

Settling down beside her and draping the cover over himself, he said, "I'm hungry, too."

"Mmmmmmm…." Noa managed. The cheap cold broth from the packet was the most delicious thing she'd had in weeks. With each slurp she felt as if the cells in her body were rejoicing, the fuzziness at the edge of her consciousness was beginning to sharpen, and the nightmare of hunger and death of the camp starting to fade. Still sucking on the broth, she began to inspect her surroundings. The wall to her left had a huge window that was half-covered in snow. Outside it appeared to be close to evening—and the wind was howling madly. Inside … had James called this a cottage? The bedroom was nearly as large as the first floor of the house she'd grown up in. There was an unlit fireplace made of pale rough stones. She felt warmth beneath her bare feet—the floor was heated, which meant the fireplace was for decor more than function. There was a plush rug laid out over the wooden floor, and there wasn't a speck of dust anywhere. As she thought that, a tiny cylindrical cleaning 'bot a few hands wide and half as tall rolled out from under the bed. A light on top of it flashed in their direction and it turned away, obviously programmed to be as unobtrusive as possible. She lifted her eyes. On a dresser across the room another 'bot was hanging from the top of a mirror, wiping the glass clean. She frowned.

"You're definitely from Earth," she said.

"Yes," James answered, lifting an eyebrow.

Her frown deepened. Earthers. Luddecceans would hire actual people for help; even menial work was better than no work.

She shook her head. Tapping her data port, she said, "I was out for a whole four hours?"

"And six minutes and forty-seven seconds," said James. "Why were they chasing you?"

The lack of segue threw Noa for a second, but she shook it off. Highly augmented minds sometimes were … odd. "I was on leave to visit my brother. I was picked up on the street, interrogated, and incarcerated in what they called a re-education camp. I don't know why."

"They had you working, didn't they?" James said.

The hairs on the back of Noa's neck rose. "How did you know that?"

James looked at her sharply. "I didn't know, which is why I asked."

Noa scooted away from him just the same. He didn't seem to notice. Wiping his face, he said, "I'm just trying to understand what's going on. If I understand the big picture, maybe I'll understand why they shot me out of the sky, why I am missing huge chunks of my memory, and why I knew how to find you."

Noa felt the tension drain out of her shoulders. The words were clipped. He was frustrated, she decided, and confused, just like her. "Like I said, you're hyper-augmented … " She waved her hand around the room. "Rich and from Earth. Of course they don't like you. It's crazy, but you shouldn't waste your time trying to understand things that are crazy. Better to focus on how to blow the insanity wide open."

James shook his head. "How would they know any of that if I never sent them my authorizations?"

Noa drew back. How would they have known? One of her brows shot up. "You rented a shuttle on Time Gate 8, they beamed down your data."

Looking away, he was quiet for a long moment. "That doesn't feel right." His head did that compulsive tick thing. She heard one of the 'bots whir beneath the bed.

"The tattoo on your wrist, the forced labor … " he said quietly. "It sounds like other historical events. May I ask what they had you doing?"

Noa's body stiffened. "Things that should be done by a 'bot, even on Luddeccea."

James stared off into the distance again. She took a long suck on the soup. Soup, heated floors, a mattress, a quilt … Her left thumb went to the stumps of her ring and pinky fingers. She was safe, for now, and so many other people were not.

"The scars on your abdomen are old, but the injury on your hand has barely scabbed over—an accident during labor?" James said out of the blue.

Noa's whole body went still. She felt her heart rate increase, a prickle on her brow. "I … " Noa said. Her lips stayed parted. She remembered the guards holding her down, the ax, the pain—but more seeing them take away her rings, the rings Timothy gave her. "Can't talk about it," she said.

Without missing a beat, he said, "Who is Timothy?" And Noa felt like the atmosphere had become too thin.

She took a deep breath, smelled wood, floor polish, and James—he smelled impossibly good for a man who'd been on the run, and who now seemed set on mentally torturing her—and she smelled herself. "I reek," she said, because she couldn't say anything else.

James said nothing. Hopping to her feet, soup packet in a death grip, she looked around frantically, reminding herself he probably couldn't help his hyper-augmented brain. James hopped up immediately beside her. She was distantly aware of his fingers, just below her curled arm—as though he was preparing to catch her if she fell. Seeing a door slightly ajar, she said, "Bath?" She couldn't meet his eyes, but she saw him nod in the periphery of her vision. She set off toward the door without a backward glance.

***

James stood outside the bathroom, head bowed. For a moment he had a vision of Noa, lying at the bottom of the tub, her eyes wide open, her lips parted, and no air coming from her lungs. Stepping closer, he pressed his ear against the door. He felt static just beneath his skin. What was he doing? Why was he standing here obsessing?

Above the roar of the faucet, he heard the sound of Noa sloshing, and then he heard her sigh. He shook his head, irritated that the sound made him feel as though a burden had been lifted from his shoulders. He stepped back from the door and the edges of his vision went hazy. James felt himself waver on his feet. He was still hungry.

Backing away fast, he stumbled down the hall past the familiar pictures that felt unfamiliar and unreal. He stepped into the kitchen. There was something about the place that reminded him of the set of a play he'd once performed in during college. Going to the cupboard, he pulled more emergency rations out—sealed packets of soup, boxes of shelf-stable soy milk, crackers, and several jars of peanut butter. Going straight for the peanut butter, he grabbed a spoon from the correct drawer without a pause, opened the jar, and scooped a heaping helping into his mouth. Every taste bud in his mouth was jumping with joy. His eyebrows rose as he took another bite. He didn't remember loving peanut butter this much. Was it just hunger, or the fact that he'd nearly died … he smacked his lips and licked off all the salt. Or was it just that the peanut butter tasted real? He wanted to slow down and savor every gooey, oily, salty bite, but couldn't keep from shoveling spoonful after spoonful into his mouth. As his stomach started to fill, his mind returned to something else that felt very real: he and the Commander—Noa—were wanted by the local government.

The ethernet was still inaccessible, so they could not call in the Republic's authorities for help. Opening the soy milk container, he washed down a quarter of a jar of peanut butter. The Holocaust, the Gulags in the old Soviet Union, the Khmer Rouge, the rise of ISIL, and the North Korean slave state were all very interesting historical events—he had data on all of them stored in his banks. Now he was witnessing a similar regime first hand. What luck. He felt a bitter smile want to form, and then his neurons flared white hot. No, Noa had been the witness—they'd tortured her and forced her to work for them. He shouldn't have asked so many questions—her answers made him want to go back to the camp she escaped from and set it on fire. He felt heat flare beneath his skin; it was a worthless impulse. He had to keep them both out of the camps.

He plundered his databases. Cutting off communications to the outside was what fascist regimes did. But in successful, long running campaigns of population control, civilians were held in check by propaganda.

Soy milk and peanut butter still in hand, he strode to the living room. It was decorated in rustic chic. There were the wood-paneled walls, recessed lighting in the ceiling, a rug under a chest that passed for a coffee table, and a blue couch. Everything was as he remembered it, and yet it was still dream-like—something was missing.

Shaking off his unease, he went to the trunk and popped it open. He pulled out an ancient-looking device—a chunky flat box the width of both his hands and about three centimeters thick. It was an all-frequency receiver, tuned to the antenna on the roof. His parents kept it around for emergencies. He flipped open the device like a book. On one side was a screen, on the other was a series of buttons with worn letters and numbers on them. He pressed a button that had a barely discernible symbol, and the device—a "laptop," his father had called it—sprang to life. Or at least it lit up. It took a frustrating few seconds for a menu to appear. James touched the screen and a communications app opened. After a few more touches, the screen displayed a man with too-symmetrical Euro-Afro-Asian features in a neat Luddeccean Green high-necked suit. "Greetings, Luddecceans, this is Bob Wang in the Briefing Room. I have good news and bad news tonight. The good news is that the war with the aliens is going well. We have shut down the entire ethernet network above Luddeccea that was being used by the devil-invaders to spread misleading propaganda."

James's eyebrows rose. Aliens? Devil-invaders? That seemed about as far-fetched as archangels.

Dipping his chin, Bob looked directly into the camera. "The bad news is that a dangerous alien sympathizer has escaped from the secure detention center."

The word "sympathizer" rang in his mind. An image of Noa in her Fleet uniform burned through James's visual cortex. James fell back as though he'd been physically pushed into the cushions.

On the screen, Bob continued. "The escape was made with alien assistance."

James turned up the volume with a few keystrokes. Were they calling him an alien, or referring to some other assistance she'd received before he'd run into her?

"The authorities have secured the escape route, and it won't be used again; but the escapee is now at large in the Northwest Province. "

A holo of Noa sprang up beside Bob. In it, she appeared skeletal, with dark circles under her eyes, and had mangy, almost non-existent hair.

"This is Noa Sato," Bob Wang said. "Alien sympathizer. She is armed and considered extremely dangerous. If you see her, report her to authorities at once via the new landline network."

Bob waved a hand. "And now we'll take questions from civilians in our studio." The camera shifted to a man standing next to some bright studio lights. He was of average build and appearance, dressed in rough attire. "I'm Jorge Mendoza," the new man said. "I'm a farmer in the Southwest Province. How do we know an alien if we see one?"

Bob turned back to the main camera and Mr. Mendoza was no longer on the screen. "Well, Mr. Mendoza, that is the truly duplicitous nature of the alien scourge we are up against. It cannot be seen. The alien menaces that infiltrated our time gate and satellites are beings of pure energy, much like the djinn in the Final Book. They almost went undetected. They are capable of seizing and controlling augmented humans."

James had stopped breathing … and couldn't force his lungs to work. He hadn't run into Noa. He'd found her. Deliberately. Almost as though compelled… as though he'd had no choice.

Bob took a step closer to the camera. Hands raised to chest level, fingertips together, Bob said, "That is why it is important that you shut off your neural interfaces, lest the djinn hijack your free will, or make you a carrier and responsible for alien assimilation." Tilting his head, tone conversational, he added, "But not to worry. With your neural interfaces inactive, you are immune to alien influence. All the information you need can be obtained at your local authority and this station. Landlines will be available to all households soon."

Noa's voice cracked behind James. "What?" Twisting around on the couch, James saw her leaning in the door frame in a pair of flannel pajamas. He blinked. They were his father's flannel pajamas—his father had let them hang on the back of the bathroom door. There was a new packet of soup in her hand. Waving the soup, the Commander exclaimed, "That was a load of lizzar excrement!"

James stared at her. Not looking at him, she glared at the screen. In a voice several decibels too loud she said, "I'm on more alien subcommittees than I can count on two hands and I can tell you all the top-secret information we have on sentient galaxy traveling 'energy beings.'" Noa huffed, her nostrils flaring.

James blinked. "You can?"

Noa waved her hands. "Yes! Because there are none! None! Just a whole lot on non-sentient, stupid, heat guzzling, sunlight swilling, and H2O-choking blue-green algae-like organisms."

Her tirade was oddly comforting—except for the strange non sequitur about blue-green algae. Of course the Luddecceans were being crazy. There were no alien djinn-like creatures hell-bent on controlling humans through their neural interfaces … He knew this like he knew Noa's name … and when he thought about it, he realized it was so unlikely it was absurd. Humans themselves couldn't control other humans through their neural interfaces, or even lower life forms. He had a grainy memory of trying to control a cockroach through an interface in a seventh-grade science experiment. It had worked for a little while, but the cockroach had eventually regained control of its tiny brain and started resisting James's and his partner's input. Human brains were much more complex than cockroach neural networks. There were neural interface viruses that occasionally snuck by ethernet and implant scrubbers—but none had caused massive epidemics of remote control—just massive epidemics of headaches.

The screen flashed, catching his attention. James turned back to find an advertisement for non-ethernet dependent washing machines. A tiny row of text at the bottom of the screen advertised that a romantic comedy was playing next. He flipped the device back to the menu.

Noa walked over and sat down on the couch. "What were we just watching? Some sort of two-dimensional holo?"

"The frequency was in between the 54 and 216 MHZ range."

"Which is?" Noa said, bending her head to suck some soup from the packet.

"Television … TV," James said, referring to the devices that in the past had used those frequencies.

One of Noa's eyebrows shot up and her lips pursed.

"Speak in Basic, buddy."

James tried to formulate a succinct explanation, and settled on, "A two-dimensional holo." He adjusted the laptop on his knees. "How much did you hear?"

Noa sagged down at the opposite end of the sofa. "Enough to know that my guardian angel is apparently an alien, and I am an alien sympathizer."

James suddenly sensed that the laptop was about to fall off his thighs and moved his hands to stabilize it. He felt his nanos jump as he ran his hands over the cool plastic. The device was not unbalanced. "All the talk of demons, djinn, and devils ..."

Noa made a sound like, "Pfft." His eyes slid to her and she said, "Political and public types here are always putting their speeches into 'god' speak. They don't really believe it." She winced. "Well, maybe some of the political and public types do, and a large portion of the populace." Noa shrugged. "This isn't like Earth. It's a very religious place ... in some ways it's a good thing."

James found he could only stare at her.

Leaning back, Noa put a hand over her eyes. "Solar cores ... since before the Luddecceans founded the original colony on this planet, they have been railing against neural networks, and augmentation, and the search for non-human sentience since the Republic reestablished contact." This time her voice was softer. Tired. Parting the fingers of her hand, she peered at him and gave a tight smile. "Now they've managed to combine everything they hate in order to scare the populace and gain control." For a long moment she was quiet. "And you're caught in the middle ... I'm sorry."

James's brows rose.

"This is my home world." Noa sighed. "I sort of feel responsible for their craziness."

"Hmmm ..." was all he could manage. He suddenly knew what was missing from his memories of this cottage. He didn't remember the smells—the pungent scent of the wood floor and paneling, the natural fiber of the rug that was thrown in front of the couch, the cold ticklish fragrance of stone and ash in the fireplace. And the reason he knew that was missing was because with Noa so close he found himself inhaling the scent of soap, wet hair, and her. She was familiar, and good. It made him feel ... hope, anticipation ... and the urge to pull her onto his lap. The last realization made him draw back. She was visibly unwell. Her skin was stretched tight across her cheeks and had an unhealthy tinge to it; her body was skeletal, her hair unkempt. Aside from that, she wasn't his normal type: tastefully augmented, civilized, quiet, erudite ...

Noa's hand slipped from her face and dropped over the edge of the couch. Her eyelids slipped closed. From the rate of her breathing, James realized she was asleep. There was a raspy quality to it but it was steady and sure. He watched her for a few minutes, and then retrieved a blanket from the trunk. He draped it over her and her body relaxed. As she relaxed, he found he did, too. He turned the "television" back on and "surfed" the channels, the steady gentle rasp of Noa's breathing giving him the same peace he'd had when she'd been asleep in his arms.

And then the peace abruptly shattered.

CHAPTER FOUR

Noa's back was pressed against a wall. Timothy was leaning into her, his lips meeting hers. A bright light shone behind his head, and somewhere Kenji was screaming. In the twisted logic of dreams, Noa could see her brother, head bent, at the same interrogation table she'd been at, but this time they were using the pliers. She knew it was a dream—a nightmare—but she screamed, "Kenji!"

Her own voice woke her. She found herself staring at Tim. She screamed again, her legs bunching beneath her and pushing her backward. Tim reached toward her, lips parted, his eyes soft and worried. The expression was familiar, but his skin gave him away. It was nearly the same shade as Timothy's ... except that it didn't change. Timothy was so expressive that even his skin betrayed his feelings. He'd flush when he was worried or happy, turn completely scarlet when laughing, or when he was angry, or in the heat of passion. Her ribs ached with the force of her breathing, and she felt soft cushions behind her back. The not-Timothy had a boxy contraption on his legs. "I think you were dreaming ... about someone named Kenji?" he said quietly, carefully, in his highbrow Earther accent.

And it struck her—he, the not-Timothy, wasn't a dream. She sagged into the cushion, recent events coming back to her. "My brother," she said. "They've got him, too." She bit her lip. She had to save him. And then she remembered

Ashley and everyone else at the camp. She had to save them all.

From the "television" came the tinny sound of, "Update from the Briefing Room. The rebels in the Northwest Province have almost been neutralized."

Noa huffed softly. "Well, that's a load of lizzar droppings."

James's eyes slipped back to the screen. He put a hand beneath his chin and then self-consciously touched the edges of his lips. He'd said they were numb earlier … maybe they still were.

"It's difficult to say." He shifted in his seat. "It might be true, or may just be propaganda to dissuade others from going to the Northwest."

"It's propaganda," Noa said confidently. "The Northwest has been home to a lawless element since the third-wave settlers arrived. The mountains there are filled with caves. Even dropping a nuclear bomb on the region wouldn't take out the rebels." She frowned. "Although, I wouldn't call them rebels, so much as bandits."

Eyes on the screen but not really seeing it, she said, "We might go to the Northwest … there have to be some dissidents making their way there." Among them she might find someone skilled at hacking into data. She might be able to find where Kenji was held and alert the population about the camps via the landlines Bob Wang had mentioned.

"Do you think a landline could sync up with the population files somehow?" As she asked the question aloud, she tried to access the ethernet for information—and failed. She immediately sent a query to her own data files, but drew a blank.

"A landline could be used for data access," James said. "The original internet utilized landlines."

Noa blinked at him.

"The internet was the precursor to the ethernet," he said.

Noa gave him a smile. "I never realized how helpful it could be to have a history professor on hand." He turned toward her, brows still drawn together. He looked as though he was about to say something; but then, shaking his head, he turned away. Outside, the wind howled. She wondered if he was in shock.

Cocking her head toward the window, Noa hopefully mused aloud, "Of course, how would I get there? The bike's probably out of power."

"There is a hover in the garage," James said. "We could use that."

She didn't miss the word 'we.' It was the response she'd been fishing for, but still. "We? You'll come with me so easily?" she said with a bemused grin.

James was staring back at the screen. "I'd like to stay alive. I'm safer, the further I am from Luddeccean authorities."

Noa's blood went cold looking at his chiseled profile. She remembered what they'd done to Ashley. What would they do to someone as augmented as James? Give him a quick death—or slowly take him apart bit by bit? Before she realized what she was doing, she'd sat up and put a hand on his arm. "We won't let them get you," she said.

James's gaze dropped to her hand. Staring at her fingers, he said, "I sent the bike we were on to a settlement about 100 km from here. It should run out of fuel just before arriving in town. Hopefully, that will distract the authorities and keep them looking for us there."

Not sure if her proximity was making him uncomfortable or just her, Noa leaned back. Her eyebrows rose. "That's a nice bit of subterfuge, James."

He glanced at her. "I learn quickly."

She coughed involuntarily, not at his words.

His eyes dropped to her mouth. "We should probably pack and be prepared to leave."

Pounding her chest, Noa said, "Yes, you're right." She moved to throw her legs over the edge of the couch, but James dropped a hand on her knee. She looked down. Not on her knee—his hand was on a thick white duvet covering her knee. "Stay here and sleep," he said. "You don't sound well."

"I'm well enough," said Noa, but she felt tired. Exhausted, for no real reason. She'd slept, eaten. In irritation, she tried to move. But his hand was heavy. She scowled up at him. He leaned back slightly and his jaw moved side to side—as though he couldn't quite control it. One of his eyebrows rose, and he dipped his chin. "You don't know where anything is."

Noa took a breath, about to protest, but her lungs hurt and so did her injured side, and she was tired. She slumped back into the couch. He was right—she didn't know where anything was, she'd get in the way—getting some rest would be a better idea. She closed her eyes, and tried to relax, but consciousness was a buzz of static sizzling down her spine, refusing to let her drift off. As James walked away, her eyes slid to a dusty hologlobe in the corner, and to the cable he'd used to jack into the tel-ee-vision. After Tim died, she'd gotten in the habit of going to sleep with holos on.

She started rifling through the entertainment files in her neural apps. She'd watch Lightyears!— the sixty-three episode, true-life adventure, romance, drama of timefield pioneers Dr. Chandi Sood and pilot Raymond Bautista was practically a religion in the Fleet … it made even the toughest grunts get weepy.

Noa sat up, reached for the cable—and realized she couldn't access any of her entertainment files—she couldn't even listen to the story in her head. Her hands flew to her data port. Did she feel bent metal, stressed edges? She almost cried. The stupid screw they'd put in her! She fell back in the pillows, and felt the sting of tears in the corner of her eyes. They'd taken Lightyears! from her.

She put her hand over her eyes, and tried to breathe deeply. It was this sort of addiction to technology that her Luddeccean priests and teachers had always lectured against … She blinked at the dark ceiling. She tried to close her eyes, but she knew sleep wouldn't come.

***

Noa awoke on a sunny cloud. For a moment, the room was dim. She heard a tinny voice in the background say, "It is too late for that, my son."

Noa tugged at the cloud, and found herself on James's couch. The cloud was the duvet he'd gotten her. The "laptop" was open on the ottoman-coffee-table-trunk. Noa put a hand to her head and grimaced. Her hair felt like it had been sheared by a blind barber. Dropping her hand, she stretched. At least she had slept. After finishing his packing, James had found her sitting in front of the laptop desperately trying to find something to listen to that didn't feature augments possessed by aliens murdering their families. She'd needed background noise to sleep and James hadn't even watched Lightyears!, but he had these "move-ees" in his data banks. Apparently, he'd made his name as a history professor by finding an abandoned town littered with time capsules. Time capsules were sort of a misnomer. They weren't like the time bubbles created by time gates, but some low-tech things old Earthers used to do. They had put their favorite things in a box and buried it in the backyard. Noa had asked for something with space, adventure, and romance, and a lot of the capsules had the particular movies he'd selected in them—which was odd, because Noa hadn't been particularly impressed. The hero had some sort of hover car that would have sucked his head off in the jet engines. But James insisted the move-ees were very popular. He'd rattled on a bit to her about papers he'd written on "hero arcs."

Covering her mouth, she yawned. Last night she'd laughed when he'd gone off in lecture mode and had said, "Now you sound like a history professor," because he had, and maybe there was a part of her that still found that impossible. He'd reached her at speeds that would have been difficult for Fleet tech, and he'd killed her captors by himself—a lot for a history professor. When she'd made the joke, he'd turned to her and said, "Do I? I feel less and less like that person," and then gazed around the house as though he expected to see ghosts.

She shook herself. They both had ghosts. A normal person had to be even more rattled than she was by this situation. And she was rattled. It was worse than the Asteroid War in System Six. She rubbed her eyes again. The best way to handle things like Six was not to think about them … to focus on the immediate present.

She looked around the room. There were some clothes laid out for her, and no less than four jars of peanut butter on top of the trunk, all scraped clean. There were several boxes of opened soy milk that she didn't have to lift to know were drained, and empty soup packets. It was as though James had been the one who'd been in a work camp for weeks. He ate as much as several men his size.

Thinking about food, her stomach growled. Through the window she saw that snow still fell, but James was out shoveling. She could see the top of his blonde head among the drifts. She frowned and stood up. She'd been coddling herself long enough.

Pulling on the clothes laid out for her, she found her nose wrinkling up at the mess on the ottoman. By Fleet training, and an upbringing that had featured an explosion of rats among the native species, she did not like to leave a mess. After folding the duvet, she took James's trash to the kitchen, found the household incinerator-crusher beneath the sink, and dumped in the garbage. As she lifted her head and looked out the kitchen window, she was hit by a bolt of sunlight through the clouds. Her jaw tightened in the cheerful light. The snow was slowing; but, with James's earlier ruse, they probably had a few hours before company arrived. Just the same … she opened a soup packet and drained it swiftly, not even bothering to heat it up.

A few minutes later she strode into the living room just as James came in the front door. He was wearing a sweater rolled up at the sleeves. Covering his arms were tattoos. They looked like a twisting pattern of ivy and shimmered slightly in the sunlight that streamed in the door behind him.

She blinked. "Where did those come from?"

Following her gaze, he said, "We have to—" He stopped talking and drew his arms toward his face. "What are these?" he whispered.

Through the open door came the distant whir of engines. With a thought, Noa prompted her Fleet apps to identify the sound. It was a low altitude old-fashioned Luddeccean hover-carrier, the type that had been used in her youth to obliterate pirates that had terrorized southern sea lanes. She didn't remember one ever being used since then. They were huge and expensive. Her app placed it at twenty kilometers away—approaching at a speed of sixty kilometers an hour. It could go much faster—which meant they were using sensors … probably to search for them.

"I don't remember how I got these." James stared at the dark marks on his arms, the world around him forgotten.

"James? Are you in pain?"

James's head jerked up. Noa's hand was on his shoulders. She was looking him directly in the eye. He heard the ship outside, and he realized how he must look. He'd rushed in to rouse her, and now he was staring like an idiot at his arms … but he didn't remember how he got the tattoos. His eyes skimmed the house that he knew every inch of but felt like a set piece, and he blinked. Noa had folded the duvet and cleaned the ottoman. Those details seemed more memorable than the room itself.

"We have to leave, James."

The ship was getting closer. He met her eyes. They were no longer bloodshot. Her hands on his shoulders were firm.

"Yes," he said, rolling down his sleeves, as though covering the mystery and ignoring it could make it go away. "This way," he said, pulling away from her grip. She followed without a word. The lights flickered on as they entered the garage and he heard Noa breathe. "An LX 469." Voice a reverent-sounding whisper, she added, "Older model, but nice, very nice."

James had a hazy memory of saying nearly the same thing when his father got the vehicle. He'd been about fourteen, too young to drive on Earth, but in the 'wilds' of Luddeccea his father had let him. The craft was shaped like a teardrop. It was half as wide as James was tall, one and a half times as long. Even perched on its retractable wheels, it only came up to his mid-thigh. The top was glass reinforced with black steel supports at regular intervals, the front was rounded, the rear tapered to a single, large engine. The curve of antigrav engines peeked out from below. He tapped the button for the doors and there was a click— not a whoosh—and the sides lifted like wings. There wasn't a vacuum-tight seal; the LX was for near ground transport only, but it was small enough to slip through the trees.

He slipped into the seat and grabbed the wheel, and felt the now-familiar sense of wrong. Whenever he gripped the wheel before, he'd always felt a rush of nostalgia. Now … he only remembered the rush. He felt as though he was watching a holo of his life and not really living it. Sunlight spilled into the garage as the door lifted, and Noa slipped into the seat beside him. In the distance, he heard the approaching roar of the hover-carrier engines … that was real.

He hit the ignition. The antigrav engines whined, the craft lifted, and he retracted the wheels. They shot forward. In the periphery of his vision he saw Noa look back over her shoulder. "That carrier carries hundreds of troops, and smaller craft. Did they send it out just for us?"

James tilted his head. "There are a few other homes in this region."

"It's still crazy!" Noa protested. "The resources they're expending..."

James swung them around a large tree. "No one said they were logical."

Noa turned back around. "Why are you driving so slow?"

"I'm driving as fast as I can … " His jaw wanted to frown, and instead just shifted from side to side. He rolled his shoulders. "Don't you notice the trees?"

"You're following the manufacturer's guidelines, aren't you?"

James angled the craft around a tree and the centrifugal force pressed Noa into the door. He hoped it would make her be quiet so he could concentrate.

Being slammed into the door didn't deter her. "You are going too slow."

James didn't speed up. He just kept the craft angled toward the Northwest Province. He looked through the rear view cameras. The tree branches blocked the sky and the giant hover-carrier was completely invisible. Which meant their craft was invisible, too.

"Display topographical map," Noa growled, and a three-dimensional holo of the Luddeccean terrain appeared on the dash. The mountains appeared and the Xinshii Gorge. "We can't go this way," Noa said. "If we approach the gorge at this angle, it will be too wide and deep for us to cross."

She was right, and James adjusted their course. She looked over her shoulder and through the glass roof. "Can you go faster?"

"No," James said. The accelerator buttons were flush with the steering bar.

"You should let me drive," Noa said, her voice tight. "I'm a pilot." She tapped the dash meaningfully. The LX didn't have a cable outlet for neural interface control, but the steering bars were on a track that allowed it to be oriented in front of either passenger.

"I can't go any faster," he said. His eyes went to the rear view screen. There were still too many trees to see the hover-carrier. He could hear it—and it sounded louder—but he couldn't determine its exact location. The snow covered trees and ground, and the LX's own engines made it impossible to judge.

Noa rubbed her face. "I know this thing goes faster!"

"No, it doesn't! Especially not on this terrain—"

Over the sound of the craft's own engines, James heard more antigravs. Noa looked out the window and said, "There are antigrav bikes on either side of us. Go faster!"

"I'm barring it," James said, his fingers tightening uselessly on the steering bar and the acceleration control buttons.

"Give me the wheel!" Noa shouted.

James tried to plot the odds, the likelihood that his superior state of health and more likely faster reflexes would be an advantage over her experience.

"I am a pilot in the Galactic Fleet, James! Give me the goddamn wheel."

Before he could respond, she leaned across him, grabbed his hands, pulled back, and hurtled them upward. Luddeccean Green filled his vision. They were aimed at the belly of a hovering cruiser.

***

Gritting her teeth, Noa aimed the LX upward toward the Luddeccean craft hovering above the trees. It wasn't the carrier; rather a smaller, more maneuverable beast they'd sent out to drop charges and troops.

"What are you—" A nerve-searing crash from below cut James off.

Noa immediately pushed the bars, and the craft lunged down. She could feel the heat of plasma fire through the floor.

"That tree would have fallen right in front of us," James said. "How did you know?"

Eyes ahead, Noa gritted out, "It's what I would have done." The towering pine would have taken out a horizontal swerve—less need for a direct hit. She squeezed the accelerator. "Why isn't this thing going faster?" Noa hissed, angling the ship to the left so fast, James's shoulder slammed against the side door.

"I told you, it can't go faster," James said as Noa careened the vehicle toward a tree wider than their vessel. In the rear view screen she saw a bike directly behind them and her app went to work piecing together the make and model as Noa jerked the hover up sharply so they were rising nearly straight vertical. Gunfire erupted below, and Noa swung the ship to the side, colliding with a web of branches. They were buffeted by tree limbs, and the craft bumped like a wheeled vehicle on rocky ground.

In the calmest voice she could manage, Noa said, "James,

did you not disengage the turbo dampener when you got this thing?"

"That goes against the manufacturer's recommendations," James said. "It's technically my father's and—"

"They only make that recommendation so they can legally sell them to civilians," Noa said.

"I actually told my father that," James said, his voice sounding strangely far away.

"Next family gathering, bring it up again," Noa said, swerving hard just before they collided into the upper trunk of a tree, and then disengaging the antigrav. They free-fell for a few breathless nanoseconds as two bikes soared over their heads and past them. Restarting the antigrav, she banked hard right. Her hands were slick with sweat, and she felt at any moment the bars would slip from the three fingers of her left hand.

A tree exploded in a shower of needles, splinters, and flame to the left. Noa swung the craft hard as another tree exploded behind them. She heard another sound behind them—a whining noise that was louder than that of their antigrav engines.

"What is that?" James said, evidently hearing it, too.

"More bikes," Noa said, glancing in the rear view port. "They've got forward-mounted guns."

"We can't outrun them," James said.

"Nope," said Noa, jerking the craft hard left. Another tree exploded in what would have been their trajectory. A soft voice piped the make and model of the bikes into her mind. "The bikes are older tech," she said, reviewing the data. "They can only shoot forward—the cannons pack such a mean punch they need the forward momentum to negate the recoil. If you see one and you think I don't see it, please scream."

She saw James swivel in his seat. "I think I can do better," he said, bending into the back where the gear was. A moment later he reappeared with his hunting rifle.

Eyes still ahead, Noa said tightly, "Those guys are in armor. You're not going to hit the sweet spot between their face plates and chest armor at our speed."

"At least I will annoy them," James said.

And he had a point. "Annoy away," Noa gritted out, swinging them hard right. In her mind she was playing a map of their path. They were headed to the gorge. Lizzar balls.

James touched a button and a skylight rolled back. A moment later, James was standing half in and half out of the cab. In the periphery of her vision Noa saw a black blur fall from the sky and then a flare of flame. "They're dropping charges!" Noa shouted. " ... trying to keep us in a straight line."

A vehicle in the view screen was sliding into the path behind them. Noa waited for the moment it would be almost directly behind them to swerve. James's rifle cracked, and the moment never came. The driver went flying backward off his bike. Noa gaped, but she managed to raise their vehicle and hit the brakes in time for the riderless bike to careen below them and crash into a tree. She gunned the engine, heard two more cracks of James's rifle, one left, one right, and saw two more bikes go down.

"Nice shots, James," she whispered.

Slipping into the cab, he shook his head. "I can't believe I hit them. I'm not that good ... "

Noa blinked. "This is no time for self-doubt!" She almost told him to keep firing, but dark spheres falling from the sky made her breath catch. Each was about as wide as her arm was long, and they had flattened undersides with antigrav engines. Each had a seam around the center, like an equator. Cannons protruded from the equator, and Noa knew from experience they could fire in any direction. "Lizzar dung! Drones!"

James was up and out of the skylight before she could stop him. "Aim for the glass eyes!" She shouted. It wouldn't destroy the drone, but it would slow it down. She cursed. The eyes were only two centis and at this distance and speed ...

James's rifle cracked and a drone went spinning. He'd hit it ... Noa's jaw dropped.

His rifle cracked again and another drone slowed as it tried to reorient itself. The first drone was already back on their tail. James's rifle cracked as the cruiser above dropped more drones. She heard bullets whizzing overhead, and a charge exploding to their left. Noa did another hard turn, dropped nearly to the ground, and they flew beneath a tree in the process of toppling—trapping two drones at the same time. The sunlight overhead disappeared. Noa didn't have to look up ... she knew the main cruiser was up there. James's rifle cracked again and another drone spun out of their path only to reorient itself a moment later.

Noa took a deep breath. The gig was up. She thought of Kenji and of Ashley and the fact that she'd never be able to help them. They'd yank out her port ... and James, what they would do to him ... he had some crazy tech in him to be such an excellent shot.

Her jaw hardened. Filling her voice with every ounce of command she could muster, Noa shouted, "James, get down and close the hatch!"

James dropped into the vehicle and obeyed. "Safety harness," Noa said. He clicked it on, and God bless him for not arguing. Ahead she saw a clearing in the trees.

"Noa, no!" James said, "We can't fly over the Xinshii gorge—"

Noa swung the craft along the edge of the gorge—a drone

swept by them over the brink. The bottom of the gorge was 1,200 meters plus. Over the engines of the cruiser and the carrier she could hear the furious wail of the drone's anti-grav and propeller as it tried, impossibly, to adjust to the sudden disappearance of the ground.

And then the wail disappeared. She peeked into her rear view and saw the sky where the drone had been was now empty.

She heard James exhale. "I thought you were going to fly over the—"

Gripping the steering bars harder, Noa chanted, "Hail Mary, full of grace," not because she believed, but to give herself strength, to calm her heart that was beating so fast she felt her rib cage sting. Before she could lose her nerve, she swung the craft directly over the lip of the gorge, hit the brakes and cut the engine. For less than a heartbeat that seemed to last an eternity, they hovered without antigrav or engine.

And then they plunged.

***

James couldn't breathe, the water at the bottom of the Xinshii gorge was coming toward them too fast. The gorge was nearly as deep as Earth's Grand Canyon, and his neural interface began randomly calculating the strength and pro-cessing power needed for an antigrav engine to keep them aloft above a drop of 1,200 meters plus—more than the LX had, and Noa had cut the engines anyway.

Back pressed into the seat by the acceleration, James saw a light streak in the sky. A shooting star? An optical illu-sion? His malfunctioning brain and data port concocting a metaphor for his short life and flashing it through his visual cortex? He glanced down and all he saw was black water coming toward them faster and faster.

James had no words. But even if he had, they would

have been cut off by Noa's own utterance—a cry, a snarl, a scream of rage—it seemed to James to be all of those. Just before the craft hit the water, she pulled up on the rudder and engaged the antigrav engines, but it would never work—the engines would have to overcome the force of their fall and—

They hit the water with a resounding thwack before James could finish the thought. His vision splintered like shards of ice—another optical illusion? The last thing he would see before he died? The world went dark, and his head ricocheted against the seat. It took a moment to realize he was still alive, and that the impact had not been as much as he expected—the crack in his vision was an actual crack in the windshield, and water was oozing through the cracks in the skylight and the doors. Noa engaged the forward engine … he blinked … they were moving forward and up. A moment later they surged up out of the river, and instead of black he was surrounded by green … but not Luddeccean Green, the deeper green of the ivy that clung to the limestone walls of the gorge. The world that had been bright and sunny moments before was now bathed in shadow. James looked up, and saw the hulking shape of the hover-carrier just before Noa gunned the engine. An instant later, he was blinking in sunlight, and once again he thought he saw a shooting star.

"Damn it," Noa hissed. "We're carrying too much water."

That was when James felt the water around his ankles.

"Open the skylight, James!" Noa shouted.

He did what he was told—possibly because he was in shock. Noa hit the forward thrusters, gave more power to the antigrav engine, and angled them for some rocks jutting out of some rapids ahead at steep angles.

"Be careful," James said, "That will flip us—"

The craft hit the rocks, tipped over, and water poured out

through the skylight.

"—over," James said.

Noa spun the craft right side up and laughed. "Hold on, we're doing it again!" she shouted, taking them over some more rocks even as the sweeper ship dropped charges behind them.

"Close the skylight!" Noa commanded, and he did. Another charge went off in their wake, but the canyon curved sharply and Noa took the hover along the curve. Above them, the sweeper ship did not readjust as quickly. As they twisted around another corner, James looked over his shoulder. The sweeper ship was farther away, contained by its own inertia, but soon—

"As it picks up speed, it will overtake us and drop more charges," he said. He felt like his life had been very brief.

Leaning closer to the wheel, Noa said, "I know." She slid the craft around another bend in the canyon at full speed far closer to the walls than he ever would have.

"Tell me when you lose visual sight of them," Noa commanded.

James looked over his shoulder. "Now," he said, his body hitting the side door as Noa slid around another bend—his data banks registered that they were headed northwest. Maybe they'd be able to reach the rebels before the craft overhead blew them to smithereens.

Noa snarled. James turned around just in time to see the ship barreling straight toward a canyon wall.

***

Water was sloshing over Noa's feet. She heard the sound of drones and sweeper hovers fading into the distance. Northward, according to her locator app … she closed her eyes … and a little light flashed green in her mind. Smacking the steering wheel, she laughed in relief and amazement. James didn't make a peep. Worried, she turned toward him.

In the dim light, she couldn't see more than his silhouette. He was sitting very still, and very upright. Trying to get a rise out of him, she said, "Sometimes I amaze even myself." It was a reference to the ancient "move-ees" they'd watched the night before. If he was Fleet, she would have cracked a quip from Lightyears, but since he hadn't watched it, he wouldn't get the joke.

She got nothing from him, not even a, "That doesn't sound too hard." Which was, frankly, disappointing. Did she have to be the only one trying to laugh at barely-avoided death? She tried again. "I am the literal embodiment of ..." What was the character's name? "Han Solo. James, I think you should be impressed."

James's voice was curt when he responded. "They will turn back soon, resume looking, and find us."

Noa flashed him a grin that she doubted he'd be able to see in the darkness. "Not too soon. They'll figure we hadn't disengaged the turbo dampener, and have made it to the mountains. Got a flashlight in here? I don't have augmented eyeballs."

"I ... " James said. " ... do have augmented vision."

He said it like it was a new discovery to him, and Noa wondered how badly he'd been hurt when he'd been shot down.

"I also have a flashlight," James said, with more surety. "Just a moment."

A few seconds later, he pressed the flashlight into her hand. Turning it on, Noa lifted the door on her side and shone the light in directions the headlamps of the craft couldn't go. Behind them was a slim band of daylight, only a hand's width high above dark river water. Fortunately, the opening of the cave was much larger—just mostly below the river's surface.

"How did you know that the cave mouth would be large

enough for the craft?" James asked.

"It was just a hunch," said Noa.

"That's not reassuring," said James.

"We're alive, aren't we?" Noa said in what was supposed to be a calm rational voice, but came out angry and half-shouted.

James was quiet for a moment, but then he said, "Why haven't they found us?" He sounded irritated rather than relieved.

"You'd rather they did?"

"Of course not," he snapped. "But I want to understand."

There was an edge of something frantic in his tone. She remembered his words last night, "I'm just trying to understand ..." He wanted the world to make sense. So much of it didn't. Noa swung the light around to the front of the vehicle. They were parked in water, but up ahead was dryish rock. Suddenly feeling tired, she said, "Their sensors picked up the cave, but they've input the model of our vehicle into their computers. Our craft's manufacturer's description specifically says it is not meant to be an aquatic vehicle, and so this hiding place will be completely discounted without ever being reviewed by a human brain."

"How did you know this model was capable of submersion?" James asked.

Noa blinked and pointed the flashlight back at him. His sleeves were rolled up, and his tattoos were back. She wasn't sure if it was a trick of the light, but they didn't seem as dark this time. Remembering how he'd reacted to them before, she quickly brought her eyes back to his face. "When we hit the water last time, we survived."

"You didn't know we could survive the impact when you plunged us over a cliff?" James whispered, his eyes wide.

"Nope," said Noa, testing the water with a finger. She stared at the uneven waves around the digit and realized she was shaking from head to toe to fingertip. The cave was tropically warm due to the depth of the canyon, but the water was snow melt from the mountains.

"You risked our lives—"

"I risked a quick death versus a long painful death," Noa snapped, blowing her cool completely. She closed her eyes. Taking a deep breath, she opened them again. She met James's gaze. His expression was a blank mask.

"It was a Hail Mary move, James." She swallowed. Hadn't he heard her prayer? "I've seen what they've done to hyper-augments like you, and I know what they'd do to me."

His face didn't soften. Annoyed, Noa looked away. "I'd like to move us up to dry rock and let this boat drain while I disengage the turbo dampener," she said, as much to herself as to him. Gently pulsing the accelerator, she moved the craft forward. Sliding it up onto dry rock and turning it off, Noa said, "It is really lucky that we found this hidey-hole, I thought we were going to be stuck underwater, gulping at the air pockets as the ship slowly sank."

"Lovely imagery," said James dryly.

Stepping out of the vehicle, Noa shone the flashlight he'd given her down a long dark tunnel. "Maybe we'll discover a new species!" She tried to sound gleeful and carefree, to ease herself off of her adrenaline high, and to forget that she was still breathing too fast and trembling from it.

"What type of new species?" said James, sounding vaguely interested.

"A species like the one in the asteroid that tried to eat that spaceship in the move-ee last night," Noa said.

"A creature of that size and mass would have been detected by now," James said, climbing out of the craft.

Noa rolled her eyes in only semi-feigned exasperation. "I'm trying to lighten the mood here, James!"

James scowled at her. Noa's eyes dropped to his bare

arms. With each passing second, the tattoos seemed to be getting darker.

Shaking herself and leaning into the craft, she said, "Help me lift the seats up so I can access the turbo dampener ... do you have any tools?"

James didn't say anything, but he helped lift the seat and retrieve a toolbox from the boot. Handing him the flashlight as he deposited the tools beside her, she said, "Go behind me and hold this over my shoulder."

Rolling up her sleeves, Noa went about disengaging the dampening conduit. Since James wouldn't talk to her, she did it for herself. "Look at me, repairing the reverse power coupling!"

"You are joking," James said, now standing behind her.

Not the witty repertoire or joking camaraderie she would have gotten from her fellow veterans, but it was better than nothing. "Yep," said Noa. "I am Han Solo."

Silence.

"Work with me! I can't be the only one trying to crack jokes and raise spirits as we head on a course toward certain death."

"Why not raise our spirits by not sending us on a course to certain death?" James said, his voice testy.

She turned around. His face was unreadable. She felt her skin heat. "Too late for that. No matter where we go."

James was quiet. Noa put her hand over her mouth. The comment had been half barb and half justification for her risky actions, but she suddenly realized the truth of it. "They sent a hover-carrier after us." A ship that could carry auxiliary vehicles and hundreds of personnel. She wasn't finished with the turbo booster, but stood up, turned away from James, and took a breath that physically hurt—maybe just from the enormity of that sinking in. If the Luddeccean Guard wanted James and Noa so badly, even the mountains wouldn't keep them safe. They'd be too busy running to help stage resistance in any meaningful way. She closed her eyes, bowing her head. "There are thousands of people in the camps. How can we save them on the run?"

"Millions."

Noa spun to him. "What?"

Standing still as a statue, James said, "I'd estimate there are millions in the camps."

Noa gaped. "How do you estimate that?"

"When you were asleep, I watched the Briefing Room channel for a bit."

Noa's eyes narrowed at mention of the "news" station.

"There were some callers to the Briefing Room—"

"How did they call with the ethernet down?" Noa asked.

"Telephones."

When Noa blinked at him, he said, "They are devices that use the landlines they were talking about last night. Callers asked about missing family members and neighbors. According to Bob Wang, alien influence corrupted the data banks of many of the populace and they had been brainwashed into wandering from their homes and places of work—and the authorities were in the process of finding them and deprogramming them."

Noa's jaw fell. Her brain sort of blinked off with the sheer stupidity of it all. But when she finally spoke, the words came in a torrent. "That's crazy—massive viral attacks of that sort of magnitude don't happen when there is a biological interface. Even cockroaches can ward off thought control!"

James's jaw did that sideways movement; his eyebrows rose. "I did an experiment like that in seventh grade!"

Noa's shoulders fell and she looked at a puddle of still water on the cave floor. "I did too. But a lot of people on Luddeccea don't believe their kids should study neural nets." She'd only done that experiment because her parents had sent her and her siblings to a progressive fourth-wave school. She met James's eyes. "There are a lot of people here who don't believe in neural interfaces; and, even if they get one, they're ambivalent about them and only use them for emergencies. They arrange their kids' awakenings much later, they teach that the NI can be a direct ticket to the materialist culture of Old World sin, and that they are the antithesis of families."

She touched the stumps of her fingers. And in some ways they were right, she supposed. Getting her interface had only increased Noa's desire to get off world, to not become the happy housewife with six kids that Luddeccean culture encouraged. She pushed those thoughts aside. "So they're claiming there are millions of people who just wandered off due to alien mind control?"

Voice too level, James said, "In part. Other callers asked about workers in the New Valley." Noa lifted her gaze at the mention of Luddeccea's small but growing cybernetics hub. The planet might be anti-tech, but the solar system was loaded with the rare metals that made cybernetics hum. Luddeccea's New Valley was the perfect place to assemble the raw materials—cheap labor for the parts that had to be made by humans, with no need for an air dome, cosmic ray filters, or radioactive asteroid water. It was also where Ashley was from.

"The region is apparently a ghost town," James continued. "According to Bob Wang, the workers were relocated to secure locations."

Noa looked down at her tattoo. "They're secure, all right."

"It's all very reminiscent of the Third Reich," James said. "I'm sure many were exterminated … "

Her skin started to heat at his calm, and the hair at the back of her neck stood on end.

"... but not all," James continued. "The local government will need cheap and available labor while they transition Luddeccea's manufacturing to a system not reliant on augments."

He said it as though repeating a history lesson. She felt a prickle of sweat on her skin and it wasn't just from heat. Her hands balled into fists.

"Do you have any feelings on this matter, James?" She didn't try to hide the bitter edge to her voice.

"It makes me concerned about the possibility of being caught," he said.

For a few heart beats, Noa couldn't speak. "Don't you want to help?" she asked incredulously.

"I want us to stay alive," James ground out.

"Millions of people are dying. And you don't want to do anything about it?"

"No," he said levelly.

Noa rocked back on her feet. He wasn't a coward; he hadn't abandoned her—he'd taken care of her, very good care of her. But now he seemed remote, unfeeling. "You're inhuman," she whispered.

His chin dipped nearly to his chest. "According to the authorities," he hissed.

And then she felt a little disgusted—at herself for saying something so cruel, at the fundamentalists taking over her planet, but also at him for forsaking the other innocent people caught up in the same mess he was in.

Turning back to the hover with a growl of frustration, she began carefully scanning the wires and ports, looking for anything that might have been loosened when she disengaged the conduit. And she also began to think. The Fleet wouldn't let their own be arrested by locals without a court martial first. Which meant they didn't know Noa had been arrested in the first place ... and acts of genocide gave the

Fleet carte blanche authority to intervene. So they didn't know what was going on here, period. The Luddeccean authorities had managed to control the data packets that were being sent between Time Gate 8 and the wider galaxy by shutting down the ethernet, but that wouldn't be enough. She shook her head—how did they control the mouths of travelers? Were they restricting travel somehow? That would be difficult, and the Republic would be suspicious and would question it. Action would be slow in coming, bogged down by the Republic's near endless bureaucracy. She thumped her index finger on a wire and scowled. Still, she thought surely by now the Fleet would have an inkling …

She shook her head. Lifting herself out of the craft, she said, "I have to alert the Fleet." She felt a small wave of dizziness.

"The ethernet is down … How do you plan on doing it?"

Noa turned in his direction, tools shaking in her hands. Why wouldn't her hands stop shaking? "I'm not going to the Northwest Province to start."

"Where do you plan on going?"

Where indeed? She took a deep breath, felt a bite in her lungs and sweat forming on her palms. She did know where. "I'm heading to Luddeccea Prime. You can drop me off at the nearest magni-freight line."

She expected to hear "fine," maybe "if that's what you want," and at most, "you're crazy." James took another step closer to her. When he spoke, his voice was almost a shout. "You're going to do what?"

***

Noa met James's eyes. "You heard me."

He didn't want to believe what he'd heard. He didn't care about millions, but Noa … he shouldn't care, but he did. Dipping his chin, James said, "You're going to the capital,

90

the hub of the Luddeccean Guard, the location of the Central Authority of this world?"

"Yes," said Noa.

"No," said James, taking a step forward. She was so thin, her eye sockets sunken, her skin dry, and paler than he remembered. She was in no shape to go anywhere, much less to Luddeccea Prime. Noa didn't back up, didn't even wobble on her feet. She lifted her chin higher, as though she was challenging him.

He paused mid-step. Was he challenging her? A vision of swinging her over his shoulder, throwing her into the LX, and taking her to the Northwest Province flickered through his mind. And then he remembered finding her in the snow … She'd escaped a concentration camp; she would escape him. Or hate him. His vision went black for a moment. That was not acceptable. He took another step forward.

This time Noa did react. "Are you going to try to stop me?" Noa said, throwing up her hands. The pliers flew one way, and the pulse reader flew another, landing in water with a plop. And then Noa did back away, holding her hands in front of her. They were visibly shaking and she was looking at them with alarm … as though they weren't her own. He could empathize.

Straightening and dropping her hands, she turned to the water. "I still need that," she whispered, her voice slightly breathless.

He was barely listening. James felt like snarling—and couldn't, just as he couldn't smile or frown. She was going to get herself killed if she went to Prime. It shouldn't be his business, but it was; and it made anger and frustration burn in his mind like a white hot solar flare. "I'll get the pulse reader," he ground out. He had to get away from her, just for a moment.

James walked past Noa before she could protest. He kicked off his shoes, and then peeled off his slacks and his sweater. Noa's jaw fell. The tattoos that had been on his arm ran down his torso and his legs too—and they were very dark now. As he bent to put down his sweater, he paused, lifted his arms much as she did moments before, and then looked down at his body. His back was to her, so she couldn't read his expression—but from the way he practically leapt into the water, she got the impression that he was trying to run away from what he'd seen.

Noa watched his head disappear. She put a hand through her not-quite-existent hair—she was still shaking. And breathing hard. She felt a gust of wind could knock her over. She trembled again, this time with foreboding. What was wrong with her body? When James had stalked toward her, she hadn't been afraid, just aggravated. But when the tools had slipped through her hands … that had been scary. She wasn't clumsy. She didn't run out of breath. She didn't shake like a leaf.

Her jaw hardened. She'd been in a concentration camp for weeks, that was what was wrong with her. And others were still there. She growled in frustration, and her eyes dropped to the water where James was. It was very calm … she felt a stab of worry and checked her chronometer app. It had been two minutes and thirty-three seconds since he'd plunged in. She walked to the edge of the water. "James?" she shouted. "James?" The surface of the water remained eerily calm.

Grabbing the flashlight, knowing it had to be waterproof, she kicked off her shoes and dove in, the cold water hitting her like a physical blow. For a moment she saw an underwater world straight from a fairytale. But then the light flickered and the frigid blackness wrapped around her. She could see nothing, not even the surface.

CHAPTER FIVE

It felt as though every centimeter of his skin was tightening and constricting to ward off the frigid waters in the cave. And he swore he felt all his cells cry for oxygen, and then sigh, as they gave up and realized none was forthcoming. His muscles stiffened—from the cold, or the lack of air, he wasn't certain. It was unpleasant. But even if he didn't have the lost tool as a goal, he would not have wanted to return to the surface. The world beneath the water was quiet, undemanding, and fascinating. Soaring through the water over a forest of pastel-colored stalagmites on the cave floor, he caught sight of small fish-like creatures with enormous eyes. The same soft hues as the stalagmites, they darted among the columns. He dove farther, searching among the column roots for the gauge, and was struck by a memory: a smaller version of himself asking his mother, "Why do the colors leave when it gets dark?" His mother had told him about the limitations and advantages of rod and cone cells in the retina—and how in darkness, the cones, the color receptors, could not receive enough light to be effective. Rods, by contrast, could be activated by as few as six photons. The shimmering colors of the underwater world defied that memory. A product of his augmentation? The only thing that told him it was dark was that the periphery of his vision was nearly black, as though looking through binoculars. He had no memory of when his vision was augmented. It was very strange. And wonderful just the same.

Catching a glint of something at the bottom of the watery cave, he dove deeper still. The blackness on the edges of his vision expanded, the pressure in his ears and chest increased, and his world shrank. He had to keep his eyes glued to the glimmer, or he would veer off course. It took a few minutes, but he did reach the fallen gauge. He wrapped his hand around the hand grip and brought it to his eyes. The tool was blurry, and it seemed to shimmer, and he was filled with a wave of panic. Something was wrong again, he could feel it, yet he wasn't sure what it was. He blinked in the depths, and called up every memory he had of being in a pool, a lake, or an ocean … and realized he hadn't exhaled … he hadn't even felt the need to. The water above him suddenly seemed solid, the cold completely frigid, and he was certain his muscles were going rigid. With a terrified kick, he propelled himself upward. As he got closer to the surface, he heard splashing, and Noa's voice, muted by the water.

He erupted through the surface and sucked in a long breath—to reassure himself that he still could.

"James!" Noa screamed.

Treading water, he turned toward her and lifted the gauge. "I found it," he said, because it was easier than saying, "I don't seem to need oxygen."

Splashing in the shallows, Noa said, "You were underwater for eight minutes." She ran a hand over her head. "How are you even—you don't have gills—I'd be able to see them."

He blinked at her, and an image of the implants along the front of the neck some divers and special ops agents sported flitted through his mind. Kicking to the shore, James searched his data banks. "Even without augmentation, humans are capable of staying beneath water for over ten minutes. It just requires training." It required years of training, packing air just before the dive, and staying motionless underwater. He didn't share that, though. Ducking his head, he climbed out of the water and shook himself off. The warm air on his skin felt wonderful, his muscles loosened, and he took another deep breath.

Noa didn't say anything for two long minutes. And then she looked down at the flashlight in her hand, now unlit. "I tried to dive after you, but your flashlight broke. Who doesn't have a waterproof flashlight?"

James blinked at her. She was soaked through and shivering. "I'll finish the repairs," he said, because he could. Disengaging the dampener wasn't a skill he had, but checking the charge in the ports was basic. He needed to not think about her fragile body in the cold water, trying to save him when he apparently didn't need saving.

He shook water out of his hair and then glanced down. Before his eyes, patterns were reappearing on his arms and torso. They were leaf-like shapes that were split by tiny veins of paler skin. He ran his hands over them. They had a slight texture, like scales. He tried to remember when he'd received them, and his memory was like a gray wall. He felt colder than he did in the water, though the air was warm. He remembered the Briefing Room, and Bob Wang describing aliens taking over the bodies of augments … he blinked his eyes. An alien of pure energy stuck in an augment would still have to breathe, and a being of pure energy wouldn't have … scales.

"James, what's wrong?" Noa said.

"I … " he stared at the leaf-like patterns becoming noticeably darker. "I can't remember where these came from."

Noa shifted on her feet. "Do they hurt?" she asked. Hadn't she asked that earlier?

"They … " He felt his skin warming, and the edge of hunger that had begun to bite beneath the surface started to fade. "No."

Noa took an audible breath. "We need to get out of here, James, both of us."

James thought of the sweeper ship, the drones that would invariably be coming back. He wanted to tear at his skin with his fingernails, even if the rising patterns felt good. "You're right," he said. Turning quickly, he strode to the craft and went to work. As he did, he heard the pteranodon-like birds of the planet call outside the cave, and near his feet water lapped against the shore. But Noa was silent. Which at first was a relief. And then it was a worry. The woman seemed to like to talk. But maybe she was reconsidering her plan?

"All done," he said unnecessarily. Lowering the seats back into place, he climbed to his feet.

He found Noa staring at him, arms wrapped around herself. "You can drop me off at the northeast junction," she said.

She had obviously not reconsidered. James's jaw shifted. He couldn't force her to do something, but perhaps he could reason with her? "Going to Luddeccea Prime is dangerous … "

She glared at him. "That isn't a good reason not to do something that needs to be done."

James felt heavy, like his neurons were misfiring. "You'll die." He blinked at his own words, amazed that was the first thing that came to his mind, not his death, although he was worried about that, too. He gulped.

Noa's mouth fell open, but instead of arguing, she just panted.

James pressed on. "You're breathing hard … you're half-starved … "

Her face softened.

"It's too risky," James said, shaking his head.

"It's the riskiest course of action," Noa admitted.

James's body sagged with relief. He tried unsuccessfully to smile.

"But it has the highest reward," said Noa. "We get to Time Gate 8, we call the Fleet, they'll have a cruiser there in minutes. They have ships on standby at other gates just for this sort of thing. We could be completely safe within days, not hunted like rats for potentially months."

James tried to run estimates of their chance for success … and could not. There were too many unknown variables. And yet, what she said about highest rewards—that was rational. Although saying a lottery had higher rewards than conscientiously saving for fifty years was also rational. He felt a shiver spread like a wave through his body. He imagined her, in a bright white interrogation room, body spilled out over a steel table, her neural interface yanked from her head, her eyes open and empty, and felt his skin prickle at the intensity of the vision. He took a step toward her, fists tightening.

Unmoving, eyes on his hands, Noa whispered, "You have to let me go, James."

James stopped. Letting her go would be the rational thing to do … it was her decision, he didn't have to go along with it. He opened his mouth, wanting to say he'd take her to the magni-freight line. "I will go with you to Luddeccea Prime," he said, the words surprising him with their smoothness. He looked down. He felt like he did when he'd wanted to run away from her the night before. What was wrong with him? He stared at a black puddle on the cave floor. It gave him no answers … just his reflection framed by inky darkness. His reflection faded, and his imagination conjured up Noa in an interrogation room, her port ripped out … to let that happen would be … failure.

"You will?"

His reflection on the surface of the obsidian-like puddle

returned, and he lifted his eyes. Noa was smiling wildly, her teeth white against her dark lips. That smile filled his eyes, and his neurons and nanos sang with a sensation of victory. His jaw shifted. Despite the stupidity of what he'd just offered, he wanted to echo the smile with one of his own. He stepped closer to her, as though pulled by a string, and then stopped short. His fists balled at his sides. He wanted more than just that smile—and the realization filled him with frustration that was more than sexual. She was in a profession he didn't particularly admire, she was too loud, and he was beginning to doubt her sanity.

Noa's smile disappeared. Her lips parted slightly. He blinked and in the same instant, Noa stepped away. Her wet clothes made her gauntness more apparent. He remembered the image of the smiling woman in his memory. Maybe he was attracted to an idealized Noa that used to be?

Rubbing her arms, Noa stumbled, and it hit him with the force of a blow. "I have spare clothes for you to wear," he said hastily. She was obviously cold, and ill, and he should have offered them before. She didn't argue, just said, "We have to hurry," so softly it was as though she were reminding herself.

After digging out spare clothes for her, he went to grab fresh clothing of his own. Hearing the craft rev a few minutes later, he turned to see that she'd already dressed and hopped into the craft before he'd had time to put on his sweater. He blinked. He had countless memories of waiting for women to get ready, and even making jokes about their lack of expediency. Feeling slightly abashed, he balled his sweater into his fist, and hopped into the craft—not even complaining that Noa was at the wheel.

A few minutes later, they were zipping through the canyon—not over the main river, but along minor tributaries.

"They are probably stopping all vehicles entering the capital," James said. Part of him hoped that, if he pointed out all the dangers, she'd turn back.

"Yep," said Noa. "I have a plan."

The craft darted through a patch of sunlight and James looked down at his arm. His "tattoos" were darkening; where the sunlight flooded in the window of the hover, they were darkest of all. They felt good, and that felt wrong. He studied the veins on the markings. Holding his hand above his arm, he watched as the markings started to fade in the shadow of his hand. Maybe this was an augmentation that had happened after he fell? He felt a cold bolt of panic. He didn't remember waking up after the doctors wheeled him down the hallway. But no, he'd told his parents he was coming to Luddeccea. That had happened after the accident on Earth … hadn't it?

"Why are you still not wearing your sweater?"

Noa's question drew James from his confusing thoughts, and it was, surprisingly, a relief to escape.

"Who doesn't wear a shirt in the middle of winter?" she continued. "It's just …" She gestured at the air between her and himself.

"Is this some breach in etiquette?" James asked. He had memories of people in the Luddeccean countryside not wearing shirts, or much else, in the summer.

"Well, it isn't exactly high-class," Noa said. She leaned forward and scowled, eyes straight ahead.

James raised an eyebrow at the look of ire. "Is my naked chest bothering you?" Seeing the tattoos bothered him, but they weren't obscene.

"I … no … of course not!" Noa stammered.

The transparency of the lie lit a little spark in his mind, a wicked, twisted little spark. She did say she wanted him to help her lighten the mood. "Maybe you are not so much

Han Solo as the etiquette and protocol droid?" His lips didn't turn up at the jibe, though they wanted to.

Noa hunched at the wheel. Her nostrils flared. Her lips turned down. And then up. "Okay, that is actually kind of funny."

And he felt that same sensation of victory he'd felt earlier when she'd smiled.

"So, here's my plan," Noa said, her smile getting broader. "It's kind of crazy—"

"We are heading into the capital, the fortress of our enemies, the figurative belly of the beast—how much crazier can it get?" And he had strange tattoos, augmented vision, didn't need oxygen, was too good a shot, and he was too fast—but he couldn't bring himself to say all of that.

"You're really getting the hang of this!" Noa laughed.

It took a few moments for James to process that his completely honest question had been interpreted as a joke. Seeing her happy made him happy and that was irritating. "Onward to the Death Star," he said dryly, apparently unable to help himself.

Noa laughed aloud, and it felt like a victory and a defeat of all that was logical in the universe.

***

The Universe was packed. The floor of the Earth night club throbbed with a pounding beat. Normally, these were things Noa enjoyed. But right now they were getting on her nerves. She peered around the corner of the booth she'd commandeered and looked for Tim. He'd gone off to get drinks. They were supposed to meet friends here.

Catching her unspoken question over their shared ethernet connection, Tim spoke into her mind. "I got our drinks, making my way back to the table now."

Noa squinted, trying to see him. The room was pulsing with blue strobe lights, and bodies were writhing on the dance floor, a step below where the booths were located.

Timothy's thought came, "Ugh, I just spilled half my beer."

Noa's lips pursed. Over the ethernet she said, "I know what's bugging me. This place is just too damn crowded." On Earth they were close to people all the time. Humans were inescapable; even in "wilderness areas," humanity was only a shout away. There were no wilds on Earth. On Luddeccea she was always looking for a crowd; here she wanted space.

"I'm not going to argue. More packed than a starship," Tim muttered. She thought she saw him holding two beers atop his head, and sent the image to him with a thought.

"Yep, that's me," Tim replied, his thoughts a soothing balm in the noise and the crowd. Probably to make her laugh, he spun in place in time with the beat, beers still on his head. She smiled, but over the ethernet chided, "Don't spill my drink."

The music stopped suddenly, and the dancers slowed. The flashing strobe light dimmed, and Noa lost sight of Tim. A single man's voice singing a haunting melody floated through the room:

"We sent our probes out into the dark,
Hoping ours was not an uncommon part,
But the probes came back, and we found out
We are alone in the black, alone in the black ... "

Noa glanced up at the speakers. It was a song she'd heard for the first time a few days ago. Humanity's inability to find another sentient space-going race was a frequent theme in art on Earth—it was as though timefield bands and having ten settled systems linked a heartbeat away by time gates wasn't something to celebrate. Earthlings' romanticized first contact. It might have been Noa's Luddeccean upbringing, but the prospect of eventual alien contact stirred mixed emotions in her. She wanted to be there the day they met another sentient space-going race—but another part of her realized *such a race was equally likely to be friend or foe.*

Music throbbed again through the speakers, and the singer's voice became a wail:

"Dance! Dance! Dance all night!

We have to make our own light!"

… and then his words were overcome by the sounds of an electronic sitar and drums. The strobe light flashed again.

Noa turned in her seat, and caught sight of a man staring at her. Facial tattoos had been in fashion last time she'd been to Earth, now scarification was the thing; you could tell who was an Earther by the raised scars that swirled around their eyes. In another month the scars would be gone, replaced by something else. Noa shook her head, "So much wasted energy," she thought.

Over the ethernet, Tim quipped, "Keeps the surgi-centers in business." Noa laughed. The man who'd been staring at her started to point in her direction—maybe because Noa's scars were natural and not fashionable, maybe because she was a throwback. The man nudged his date—and she scowled at Noa. Rolling her eyes, Noa scanned the crowd. She saw Tim again, just a few paces away, eyes on the drinks he now carried in front of him. In the blue strobe light his pale skin shone like the moon. His blonde hair had been bleached by the sun during training in the Sahara, and it glowed.

Noa smiled at him.

Catching her eyes, Tim smiled back. "Hey, gorgeous," he whispered in Noa's mind. He was only two steps away when a man stepped in front of him and shoved him hard. The drinks spilled, and the man's voice boomed above the sound of the music. "Throwback Purist! What are you doing here?"

Noa was up in an instant, but a crowd of people were already dragging the man away. Tim was glaring and running a hand through his hair when she reached him. A man who'd helped drag the boorish man away blinked between the two of them. "Oh, you're together. Sorry about that."

Noa sighed. As if being visibly of one race was only ac-ceptable if you were with someone who was not—or you were with a throwback of a different race. That proved you thought "correctly." She huffed. Incidents like this one were too common on Earth. On Luddeccea she'd faced racism too; but, in the small farming community where her parents lived, everyone knew her, and she was always accepted there.

"I can't wait to get back into space," Tim grumbled over the ethernet, putting a hand on her hip.

She knew what he meant. In the Fleet, racism was prac-tically non-existent. The joke was that the Fleet treated every-one like throwbacks.

She turned to him, a warm feeling in her stomach. She was about to say, "Let's get out of here," when he began to fade before her eyes. Noa's stomach fell, and she realized she was in a dream ... dreaming of Tim. "No wait! Timothy!" she said, just wanting to have him for a moment longer, but he just kept fading, the bar scene disappearing with him, until all that was left was darkness.

***

Noa blinked. And found darkness, and for a moment thought she was still dreaming. "Timothy!" she called. And then she felt the prickle of hay beneath her back, and the side to side sway of the magni-freight car. She almost cried. It had been years since she'd had a dream where Timothy vanished before her eyes like that. Why of all times was she having one now?

She heard hay crunch, and a dim light flickered on. James's face was suddenly suspended above her, his body too close—and his face too similar to Timothy's own. That was why she had the dream.

"Noa, are you alright?" he asked, with his too perfect, too Earther intonation.

For a moment, she could only stare at him. His eyes were wide, his brow drawn—he looked worried. She averted her gaze to the hem of the blanket. Sometimes, when she looked at him, she felt she was looking at an impostor, not a real human being.

The car swayed, and Noa looked up at the ceiling as though searching for something she'd lost there. "Stupid hay, it is too prickly," she said, to say something, anything, that wasn't about the dream she just had.

James took an audible breath, and then, mimicking Noa's voice perfectly, said, "This freight car is the perfect way to get to Luddeccea Prime." No grin tugged at the corners of his lips. Tim would have cracked up halfway through that joke. James wasn't Timothy, but he wasn't an impostor, he was himself.

"Shut up," said Noa, but she smiled, trying to let him know she was grateful that he had changed the subject. He was picking up on the witty banter thing, at last.

James narrowed his eyes. His jaw moved from side to side as though he was trying to grin. "I don't think you mean that."

"Yes, I do." Noa glowered, but it was feigned. In the freight transport container behind them some cows lowed.

"If more than five minutes pass without conversation, you talk. Or prompt me to talk," James parried.

Raising an eyebrow, Noa put a hand to her chest as though she were affronted. "Are you calling me a chatter-box?"

James looked up at the ceiling as though searching for something hidden in the eaves, just as she had a moment ago.

"Never mind, I'm going back to sleep," Noa said, rolling onto her side. James flicked off the light.

Beneath them, the track the freight container was elevated on must have hit a rise, because the container rocked. They'd dumped the hovercraft in the forest a few days ago. They couldn't refuel it—their faces were all over "television"—so they'd hopped on this freight transport. The hay was prickly, but soft. This container and the half dozen behind and in front of it were hitched together, and hovered on a magnetized track. It was less energy-intensive than antigrav. The rocking usually put Noa to sleep.

Noa shifted beneath the blanket she shared with James. It smelled like him. No man should smell as good as James did, especially not after a few days without a bath. Scowling, she closed her eyes. As much as he gave her nightmares, she was attracted to him on some base level; she caught herself observing him too closely, and she felt herself flushing when he was close. That attraction ran smack into a wall in her heart or her head or both. He looked too much like Timothy and had the same sort of constantly curious mind Tim had. But Timothy wouldn't have thought twice about going to Prime; Timothy, even more than Noa, would always do the right thing. She closed her eyes. She was beginning to like James, but she wasn't sure she respected him. It was annoying that he had to be so good-looking.

Sleep didn't come, even with the gentle rocking of the car, although she was warm and not hungry.

She sighed. "You have to admit, hopping a ride in this freight car was a pretty good non-crazy idea."

"Four minutes and thirty-five seconds," James said dryly.

Putting a hand to the side, Noa found her canteen. "Admit it," she said and took a swig. James was silent. Returning the canteen to its spot, she plucked up the flashlight—recovered from its dip in the water—and shone it at James.

He scrunched his eyes in the spotlight, and held up a hand. She knew him much better after a few long boring days in a freight car. His father was a cybernetics expert, his mother was a biomechanical engineer—occupations that made perfect sense for the parents of a hyper-augment. She knew he didn't have a grip over all of his augmented bits; he was not sure how fast he could run or how strong he was, and the mysterious origins of his tattoos bothered him—but whenever a beam of sunlight streamed into the car, he invariably wound up sunning himself in it, shirt open, the tattoos turning black on his pale skin. He didn't need to shave, though he had a touch of stubble and didn't look like he'd had his facial hair follicles surgically depleted. Also, she'd never met anyone who ate as much as he did. She'd thought he'd overdone it when she saw how much food he'd packed, but now they were nearly out.

She realized that she was still shining the light on him, and he was blinking furiously.

She dropped the light guiltily—and then realized the spotlight had been like a wall between them. Flustered by how close he was, she looked away.

Taking a long breath, James said, "It's probably more comfortable than a cave in the Northwest Province ..." his voice trailed off.

"But?" said Noa, shoving him back with her shoulder and instantly regretting it.

"I can't help thinking about the Nazis loading the Jews into cattle cars."

Noa rolled her eyes. He was obsessed with this.

James continued. "We've done the work for the Luddeccean Guard, loading ourselves onto our century's version of a cattle car."

The transport jostled as it hit a bump in the track ... as though emphasizing James's point. Noa groaned. "Not with the Nazi's again, James!" She put a hand over her eyes. "And nothing about ISIL, or North Korea, or the gulags of the

USSA—"

"USSR," James said. "The Union of Soviet Socialist Republics."

"Whatever!" said Noa. "They're dead and gone!"

"The impulse for genocide and reigns of terror isn't gone, it's alive and well here."

Groaning, Noa dropped her head to her knees and banged it several times. He'd filled her in on all of those despotic regimes, and she had to admit, he had a point; but she didn't want to think about it. They'd be in the thick of it soon enough. She'd already been in the thick of it on her own.

Not catching the not-so-subtle body language, or not caring, James slipped into professor mode. "Usually, this sort of fascist, self-destructive upheaval comes about because of corruption within, or from intolerable stress from without."

Hoping he would get to the point and change the subject, Noa groaned again. Loudly.

James kept going. "I don't know of any external pressures on Luddeccea right now."

And that rankled. Against her better judgment, she found herself drawn into his useless philosophical meanderings. Again. "Of course you don't know about the external pressures … you are an external pressure."

James blinked. "What? Me?"

Noa waved the flashlight. "The original settlers to this place didn't want to be part of the Republic. You guys just showed up—"

"You"—he pointed at her chest—"are a member of the Galactic Fleet of the Republic, you are 'you guys.'"

Aiming the flashlight in his eyes, Noa ignored his commentary. "The Republic showed up, offered to build the time gate to allow Fleet and traders through. Luddeccea said no—but then the third-wave plague broke out, a vote was held, the yes votes just barely prevailed, and this planet joined up. Now that there are no longer huge epidemics, and the place has been basically tamed, off-worlders are moving in, building enormous houses, not hiring locals, driving up real estate prices and making it hard for young people to buy farm land … " She gestured at him absently. "And looking so pretty with all your augmentations and leading easily impressionable youth astray."

"Looking so pretty?" said James, an eyebrow shooting up.

"But that's not the same as having two superpowers wage war on your turf like what happened in North Korea," said Noa. She thought it was a pretty good recovery, even if it slightly negated her point.

James exhaled. "You are right, it is not as extreme as the influence wars on old Earth. The local regime … it is corrupt, though, too."

Noa tilted her head. "It's static more than corrupt. The same families have held sway in Luddeccea since the founding of the first colony … but you can still have a very nice life here if you want to start a farm and make babies."

"Isn't 'static' the same thing as stagnant … and isn't that corrupt?" James said.

Noa shook her head. "Maybe a little. But it isn't like the way you described Earth's Middle East in the early 2000s. You don't have to bribe officials. Business permits are slow, but you can get them." She tapped her foot and frowned. Her baby sister had complained it was harder to do if you were female, too. Noa thought she'd been exaggerating— her sister had tried to start a composting plant when she was fourteen, based on a science fair project she'd done. That had been a little ambitious for a fourteen-year-old, in Noa's opinion, and Noa could see where the authorities might not trust a kid to follow safety protocols. Noa rubbed the back of her neck. But she'd also understood why her sister had been hurt and angry when a twenty-year-old boy from one of the old families had taken her idea and had gotten a permit for it right away. That incident was shortly after Noa went to the Fleet, and shortly before her sister had graduated and moved to Earth for schooling. One by one, her other siblings had followed, and then her parents. Kenji had gone off world for a while, too—but then had come home.

James tilted his head. "If ambitious men cannot get ahead by legal means, they will do so by criminal means … I remember reading the new Premier isn't from a First Wave family; he's just very good at promoting their agenda."

Noa stared at her feet, her thoughts catching on the words "ambitious" and "criminal." "I've been called ambitious and criminal, and I'm not a fanatic."

James lifted an eyebrow. "Really?"

"How do you think I knew how to hotwire a grav bike? I borrowed one from a neighborhood Guard patrol when I was a teenager."

James blinked. "Why would you need to hotwire a vehicle you were borrowing?"

Noa looked up at the roof. "I didn't ask to borrow it first." She tilted her head. "Although it wasn't technically a crime, since the charges were dropped when I told them I was going to join the Fleet as soon as I graduated. The judge's last words to me were, 'good luck and good riddance.'" She tapped her chin. "So maybe I wasn't really a criminal since I was never charged. Although I did hop transports like this too, I just never got caught. If you don't get caught, is it really a crime?"

"That seems like something a criminal mind might ask."

Noa grinned at the wry humor. "But I'm not a criminal. I joined the Fleet and flew straight, figuratively, if not literally."

"And if you had stayed here?" James asked.

Noa rolled her eyes. "Not worth thinking about. There would be nowhere for me to go, especially as a woman. The Republic may grant women rights, but culturally, on this planet … " She shook her head. The law was only the first step in such things. "My family wasn't like that … and they all left." She touched the scars on her abdomen self-consciously. "My mom always said the Luddecceans are slightly cult-like, and cults need to make babies. When babies need to be made, women can't be out making a living."

After a long moment, James said, "Which leads to a third reason why such fanaticism might be taking hold … maybe they really believe what they say?"

Noa shook her head, bored with the mental exercise that took them nowhere. "Why does it matter why it is happening? At this point, it only matters that it is happening. Our job is to alert the Fleet. They can come here and straighten it out."

Taking a deep breath, James closed his eyes and rubbed his jaw. "If I understand why this is happening … " He looked away. "There are so many things I do not understand. Things that should bother you too … like how I found you, and how I knew your name."

"Those things really do not concern me more than staying alive and not dying," Noa said.

"They should concern you more," James said softly.

There was a quiet that stretched too long. Taking his hand on impulse, Noa batted her eyelashes at him. "Is this the point where you tell me you're an alien, James?"

His gaze met hers, and his fingers tightened. "No." She had a moment where she thought he might kiss her. She felt herself flush, realizing a part of her wanted that … but Noa told herself it was too much emotion, too fast, brought on by too extreme circumstances—that she had too much to do. The transport jostled and Noa felt it all the way to her bones. She was also just so tired. Leaning back against the wall, she pointedly looked straight ahead. James didn't let go of her hand.

So quietly that he was hard to hear above the rattle of the connections between cars, and the lowing of the cows, James said, "Something is wrong with my neural interface and my brain, Noa."

Noa thought of her nightmares, and her flashbacks, and nudged him again. "We've both got broken brains."

Flexing his fingers in hers, he whispered, "You say the most unreassuring things."

Noa stared down at their entwined hands, dark on light. It brought back so many memories, and she couldn't bring herself to tear away. Instead she said, "James … will you put on a move-ee?" They'd been watching a lot of move-ees and tee-vee programs to pass the time when they weren't eating or training. Noa had assigned herself a calisthenics routine to try and recover her strength. She should do that right now … she liked working out, the meditative quality of it … although lately it was exhausting in a way she wasn't used to. Before her muscles ached, she felt inexplicably drained.

James took his hand away as he pulled out the laptop. She put hers in her lap and out of reach. As music started to play, she had a moment of apprehension. "What is this?"

"Schindler's List," James replied.

"Is this about ISIS or North Korea?"

"No."

"Is it happy?" Noa asked.

That was met with silence.

Curling her legs up, Noa banged her head against her knees. "James, I just escaped a 're-education camp.' Have mercy!"

James stopped the playback. "Would you like to continue the series we started before? You seemed to find that amusing."

Noa laughed, thinking of the space exploration "sitcom" he'd shown her before. "Yeah, that ship was hilarious. They would have flip-flopped through space." She'd laughed until she'd cried watching the opening credits.

"So—"

She waved a hand. "Something new."

James used a finger to navigate through tiny icons on the archaic screen. A show came on, obviously set on old Earth. It was some sort of detective show, with some sort of psychopath type as the lead. He had nearly augment-like abilities of recall. It was entertaining enough, but confusing: little text boxes popped on the screen occasionally. "What are those?" Noa asked.

"At that point in history, instead of thought-to-thought communication, humans used to send text messages on phones—the little black rectangles you occasionally see them speaking into—that were connected by satellite. Those squares of text superimposed on the frame reflect what he'd see on his phone."

Noa cocked her head. "Sort of like a prototype of thought-to-thought ethernet?"

"That is when they say it began," James said.

And Noa could see that. Sure, texting was to thought-to-thought communication like paper and ink was to painting on cave walls, but it was a start. If she could have it now … what she wouldn't give to be in contact with Kenji, her other siblings, parents, or her friends in Luddeccea Prime … Still, just to be contrary, or maybe just to talk, she tsked. "Poor, poor, primitive savages."

"Yes, they were practically chimpanzees," James replied. And bless him for joking. Noa grinned, but her smile almost immediately began to fade. "I think I remember reading about 'texting' actually … the text messages facilitated some of the early democracy movements, right?"

"Yes," said James, gaze still on the screen.

"The people of Luddeccea don't even have access to that," Noa said, her heart sinking.

"No," said James. He turned to her, his face blue in the laptop's glare, his features as always too perfect. "Do you still want to continue to Prime?"

Noa's jaw hardened. She thought of the camp and Ashley. She thought of her brother—he had been in Luddeccea Prime when she arrived planet-side—was he now in a camp? Had they hurt him? In Prime they had to have some sort of computerized record-keeping. The same person who'd helped them access one of the shuttles to Time Gate 8 might be able to find Kenji.

"I need to go there even more than before," she whispered.

She was dimly aware of James's Adam's apple bobbing. At last he said, "We will go there, then."

She closed her eyes at the word "we." She was ridiculously grateful not to be alone in this, and she wanted to drape herself over him, but also to pull away. She sat perfectly still, instead, and let herself be distracted by the antics of a consulting detective.

CHAPTER SIX

From the top of the freight car, James watched the suburbs of Luddeccea Prime roll slowly by. Luddeccea Prime was closer to the equator, and the homes were built with heat reduction in mind. They were low-slung adobe creations with deep awnings. Lights burned inside the buildings, and shone through wide floor-to-ceiling windows open to the evening breezes. There was nothing to suggest that there was anything amiss on Luddeccea. But sometimes, marching down the quiet streets, James spotted men in uniform stopping pedestrians and ground transports.

He had wondered many times, back when he was safe on Earth, what he would do if he were to find himself in one of the genocidal events he'd studied. He'd always fancied that he would choose to resist. But he didn't feel like resisting now; he didn't feel any sort of moral compulsion to help these people. He felt as though he was watching a bad play, and all he wanted to do was leave the theater.

He gazed down at the ground rolling past them. It would be easy enough to jump from the roof. The train was traveling at only thirty kilometers per hour, and it had stopped occasionally for other trains, cars, and once a wheeled busload of children. He could easily disappear into the darkness of the early evening. He could catch the next freight train going in the opposite direction. It would be the logical, sane thing to do. He wanted to do it, he really did.

But he couldn't make himself leave Noa; she was the only thing in this nightmarish drama that felt real. He sighed. And he couldn't make himself bind and gag her and drag her to some place safe, he thought ruefully.

A pinprick of light falling in the sky caught his eye.

"Another meteorite?" Noa whispered, so close he almost started. "That's strange," she continued in a hushed voice. "If there was going to be a meteor shower during my visit, Kenji would have told me. He would have wanted to go to the countryside away from all the light pollution to watch."

James shook his head. He had no idea if a meteor shower was expected. But they'd seen dozens of falling stars over the past few nights when they'd dared to peek out of the freight car, even some during the day.

Noa sighed, and then said, "Ready?" James turned to her. Like him, she was on hands and knees, and like him, she wore a pack on her back with the remains of their scant supplies. The white of her teeth flashed briefly in the gloom, and then the smile was gone. She was less than a meter from him, and that felt far away. He'd become accustomed to physical contact, or the promise of it, at all times. Not that there had been anything untoward … which was strange. His former self, the person he'd been before he woke up in the snow, had been confident. Overly confident, maybe. He had a faded memory of being called "a presumptuous ass."

"No, I'm not ready," he said, predicting the straightforward observation would make her laugh. He was rewarded with another grin, but it disappeared too quickly. She took a long breath. Was it his imagination, or did her arms tremble slightly?

"Let's go," she said, turning her focus to the back of the train. "Let the revolution begin."

James sighed; but his sigh did not provoke even a chuckle

from Noa. His only hope at this point was that this first part of the mission would fail, that she'd reconsider, and that they could hop off this train while they still had time and head for the Northwest Province.

Traveling on hands and knees, they reached the third to last car. In the caboose, there were four train operators who had fed the cows and occasionally checked the cars for stowaways. The cows were still alive, but they hadn't done a very good job with the latter, obviously.

Noa and James's goal was to subdue the operators, steal their uniforms and their identification, and then hop off the moving train and make their way to the city proper by hover—hired or stolen—before the freight cars arrived at their destination. In the city, they'd find a programmer who could hack their retinal scans into the Luddeccean time gate mechanic crew's database. Noa was sure they could find a retired Fleet officer to do it; James was less sure. But he also didn't have a better idea; or rather, the idea he did have, running to the Northwest Province, had gotten him nowhere.

Reaching the end of the car, Noa slipped down. James followed. The animals in the car beyond began to low. Noa went to the door between the freight cars. It had a simple latch mechanism, a vertical handle that only had to be lifted. Noa gripped it and gritted her teeth, and then gasped and dropped her hand. "What? Today they lock it?" she snapped.

James blinked, remembering how easily they'd slipped into the car of cows, hay bales, and wooden crates a day ago. "Perhaps because we've been stopping more frequently?" he suggested, taking the handle and gently lifting. It was definitely locked … maybe she'd back down?

"We'll have to confront them in the caboose," Noa said with a frustrated-sounding huff. "Not as ideal as our original plan."

Much more dangerous than their original plan is what she meant. James jiggled the handle. "I think it has a little give," he said, not sure if he was lying or hoping.

Noa held up her hands. "Don't—"

James yanked it up sharply. There was a loud crack, and the whole mechanism disengaged from the door.

"—break it," Noa finished.

"Maybe it was rusty?" James said, turning it over in his hands. He didn't see any rust; yet, he had broken it as easily as a toy. He tossed the lock aside. It made him think of his tattoos, night vision, and ability to stay underwater without breathing. He felt a stab of inner panic.

"Actually, this might work … " Noa said, snapping James from his thoughts. She reached into the hole in the door and winked. "Yep." There was a click. She swung the door open and disappeared within. James looked longingly at the ground rushing past. He knew that he could jump and survive with only a few scratches. His skin prickled with annoyance. But he wouldn't do that, no matter how much he wanted to, despite the fact that he thought it was the better idea. He couldn't leave Noa. He followed her into the car.

He immediately hit a wall of the worst smell he'd ever encountered. Putting his arm over his face, he gasped, "Methane."

"You can't smell methane, James," Noa said, her voice barely audible over the sudden lowing of beasts.

James dropped his arm. He was sure he smelled methane, along with animal smells, hay, the faint odor of rot, dampness, and a hint of Root, a popular native stimulant that was very addictive and illegal on both Luddeccea and Earth.

"Although, there's probably plenty of methane in here,"

Noa said, looking around. "What you smell is cow. And what posh cows they are. These bovines are destined for the dinner plates of the high chancellors. Look at them, each with its own stall and feed bin, not packed like—"

James put a finger to his lips. Noa raised an eyebrow in his direction and fell silent. James tilted his head to the far door. Over the lowing of the cows and the rattle of the car on the tracks he heard someone say, "Something is getting them excited."

Noa loped to the door with surprising stealth. The cows still lowed and stamped their hooves in her wake. They stamped more vigorously when James passed down the center aisle between them. His passage was not as quiet as Noa's. He took his place beside her at the hinge side of the door, just as Noa had made him practice.

He heard the click of the lock. The door swung open and two men stepped in, both brandishing stunners.

James shut the door—gently. Outside a remaining agent said, "Hey, Bart—what 'cha doin'—you know I forgot my keys." Noa stepped forward, wrapped one arm around the first man's neck, and in one smooth motion she lifted the man's own stunner and stunned his companion with it before either could call out. As soon as the stunned man went down, James dragged him into a stall that held bales of hay instead of a cow. The man Noa was trying to choke struggled, and Noa stunned him as well. Lowering him to the ground, Noa nodded for James to pull him away. As James did so, she went swiftly to the door, opened it, and took shelter behind it.

A man stumbled in. "Oh, thanks, Bart—"

Noa hit him with the stunner an instant later.

"Well done," James said, stifling a sigh … against grim odds, it looked as though her plan might succeed, and they would not be going to the Northwest Province. Noa was still thin, but her training and surety of movement had compensated for any lingering frailty.

Without acknowledging the compliment, Noa looked at the downed men and exhaled audibly. "Wasn't hard, they're just civilians." She sat down on her heels and felt one man's pulse. "They'll all be fine. Nothing worse than a headache." Noa closed her eyes briefly. "Thank you, random factors of the universe."

James didn't comment. That was one of her goals, that civilians not be hurt. They were, in her words, "just caught up in events beyond their control." Which was their own situation as well. James hadn't argued with her assessment, even if the logical part of him said they'd be less likely to be identified if the train personnel were dead.

Opening her eyes, she whispered, "There's one more. I didn't hear anyone while we were above. Did you?"

James shook his head. Noa went to the door, pushed it barely ajar, and cautiously peered out the crack.

And then James heard a piece of hay break behind him and a soft exhalation, and he knew without turning that there was a man behind him, approximately 1.8542 meters tall. He could smell Root on the man's breath. He heard the soft brush of skin on hard plastic and knew the man had a stunner. Spinning counterclockwise, James kicked up and out with a leg and hit the man squarely in the chin. There was a sound he didn't recognize, a sort of snap, as the man flew backward over the hay bales he must have been hiding behind. Spittle flew from the man's mouth, and James caught a heady whiff of the drug.

Noa gasped, ran over, and dropped beside the man. She was silent for one minute and forty-five seconds.

"What's wrong?" James asked.

Noa looked up at him. For thirty-three seconds, she did not respond. And then she said in a hushed voice, "You broke his neck."

Gazing down at the man, James noticed the impossible angle of his head for the first time. "I acted on instinct."

"That was a mighty good instinctive roundhouse kick," Noa said, and James could hear the tension in her jaw.

James didn't answer. He had a hazy memory from his life on Earth; he'd been behind the controls of a hover, with a woman sitting next to him. She'd been a colleague and a lover, though he couldn't remember feeling anything for her. She had said to him, "You drive very responsibly." He had replied, "If I hit someone and they died or were injured, I'd never forgive myself." He hadn't been lying; but now, staring down at the man whose life he had ended, he felt nothing.

"James … " Noa said.

James turned his gaze to her.

"Really good instincts, for a history teacher," Noa said. "What are you hiding from me?"

James took a step back. For the first time, he felt something … terror, and the potential for failure of something he could not name. "Noa … I don't know."

Noa's shoulders fell. For another ten seconds, she was silent. And then she shook her head. "Let's tie these guys up, take their uniforms and identification, and get out of here."

James took a deep breath. The charge in his body dissipated; but, instead of relief, he felt grief. He stared down at the dead man. He remembered a time on Earth when he'd watched a stranger's funeral procession from afar, and mourned in a vague existential way. James had that sensation now, but not for the dead man. He mourned for himself, the man he once had been.

***

From the back of the hover cab, Noa handed the driver the identification she'd stolen from the two train operators who looked the most like James and herself.

In the dim light of the cab, the driver looked down at the identification documents. They were primitive things, little booklets with a picture and relevant bio-data. The most high-tech thing about them was a two-dimensional holographic image of the Luddeccean emblem: a dove with a green branch in its mouth. She supposed that societies became paper bound when they had no ethernet.

The driver rifled through the booklets, taking his time. He glanced up at her and James, and back down again.

Her left thumb went to her rings—and found them gone. Her jaw tightened, and her eyes flitted to James. Like her, he was wearing the train uniform, complete with a brimmed cap pulled low to hide his blue eyes. Like her, his face was caked with dust from the gravel bed along the track. It made his pale skin darker, and her dark skin lighter. She'd added darker dirt to her jaw to give her the appearance of stubble. None of the train operators had been female.

She caught the driver's eye in the rear view mirror. He looked suspicious—as well he should be. Two train hands would never pay for a cab from the suburbs to the capital proper—they would have taken a hover bus. The man met her gaze in the mirror. "Port of Call?" he said.

Forcing her voice down an octave, hoping it didn't sound too contrived, Noa said, "Yes."

He stared at her a moment. Turning his head, he spit out the window. Noa's heart beat so fast that her ribs hurt. She was dimly aware of James slipping the damn protein bar into his pocket and his hand going to the latch of the door.

The driver grunted. "I want to be paid up front."

Noa's body relaxed, and then stiffened again when he said, "Seventy credits, no less."

It was highway robbery. The driver spat again. Noa

ground her teeth, but she slipped out the credits and handed them to the man.

Without a word he set the cab into gear. He didn't look
frightened, as presumably he would be if he recognized
Noa or James from the "tee-vee" broadcasts. Her eyes
narrowed at the back of the man's neck. Or maybe he just
knew the Luddeccean alien-devil spiel was lizzar excrement?

Sitting back in her seat, her eyes went to James. His hand
was still on the handle of the door, his chin was dipped,
and his eyes were drilling into the back of the driver's head.

Seventeen minutes later, they stepped out of the hover
cab into the hot, humid air of Prime's Port of Call district.
As the hover lifted and soared away, Noa surveyed the
surroundings. Port of Call was between the train yards, the
Tri-center's spaceport, and the sea port. It looked almost
exactly as she remembered it. Squat pastel-colored stucco
buildings lined the narrow two-lane street. None of the
buildings were taller than four stories; all had deep-sloped
overhangs, to block the tropical sun and prying eyes from
windows that were most often open to the breeze. Almost
to a one, they had gleaming spiral windmills on the roof
that by day drew energy from the wind and sun, and by
night still derived power from the ocean breezes. Only a
few had hover parking on their rooftops. In the city, such
amenities were taxed to the teeth to prevent sky congestion.

The sky itself looked different. Since they'd left the train,
cloud cover had moved in. She felt a gentle drop of rain on
her cheek. From where she stood, she could see the silhouette of the Ark, the vessel the first Luddecceans had arrived
in, rising up in the direction of the Tri-Center. Built like the
space shuttles of the twentieth century, but far more massive, the Ark looked like a mid-rise apartment building or
warehouse, not a spaceship. A planet-wide monument and

122

museum, it was lit from within and appeared reassuringly normal. However, there would usually have been a steady stream of ships leaving the spaceport behind the Ark. Today the area above the spaceport that usually looked like a column of descending and ascending elevators was strangely dark. Port of Call smelled like salty air and hover exhaust, but the normal smell of sun-baked garbage was absent. Dropping her eyes, Noa exclaimed under her breath, "Where are the rats? There should be rats."

"No, there shouldn't be," James said, sounding professorial. "They're an invasive species. They've destroyed huge swathes of the local ecosystems, spread disease, and … "

"And they're disgusting," Noa said. She blanched and stuck out her tongue. "Creepy, naked tails. I know some people say they make great pets, but get your hand bitten once, or find them gnawing on human corpses … " She sucked in a breath. Rat bodies writhed like so many snakes in her memories of the abandoned asteroid mines around Six … she shivered. "I convinced the captain of the last ship I was on, to keep a bunch of kittens because of the rat problem." And because kittens were cute.

"I was going to say—"

Noa waved a hand. "That's not the point. In this part of town they should be practically coming out here and saying hello." Cheeky little beasts.

James dipped his chin. Voice hushed he said, "Just about every totalitarian regime gains power by solving some problems."

Noa shoved her hands into her pockets, although the night was warm. "I never thought not seeing rats would make me uneasy," she muttered. She looked down the street. She didn't see the usual prostitutes, and there were fewer land cars than usual. There were plenty of people … yet fewer than normal.

Beside her, James said, "The meteor shower continues."

Noa raised her face to the cloudy sky and saw pinpricks of light shooting through the clouds, exploding before they collided with the earth—but still, far too low.

Movement not sixty meters away caught her eye. Wiping a few raindrops from her face, she saw men in Local Guard uniform inspecting the papers of some nervous-looking civilians. Ignoring the natural fireworks display, Noa grabbed James's arm, guided him down a nearby alley, and then down another. She hadn't let the hover pilot drop them off too close to their destination. In the event he reported them, she didn't want their path to be too obvious.

She turned left and walked under some clothes clipped to a line being rapidly pulled in by an inhabitant in the flats above. Her head jerked up at the plain white men's shirts and women's slips. They looked like things she had sewn at the camp. It was startling to see them out of the context of Taser-wielding guards and the drone of sewing machines. It was also strange to see them line-dried. She shook her head. Even simple devices had become ethernet dependent over the last few hundred years. She shouldn't be too surprised that newer laundry machines no longer functioned.

Resuming her path, her eyebrows lifted as James ripped open another protein bar. "You're unusually quiet," he said, before practically inhaling the thing.

"I'm focusing," Noa said, which was the truth … but not the complete truth. They had murdered a train worker. By the smell of the Root on his breath, he'd been in the cow car desperately sneaking a chew. An addict, obviously, but he hadn't deserved to die. There had been one civilian death in her revolution already. Her eyes slipped to James. She was certain he hadn't meant to kill the man, but she thought of him ripping the lock from the cattle car's metal door, and the way he'd peered down his perfect nose at it and suggested he'd been able to do it because it was rusted. He didn't know his own capabilities … which made him dangerous, like a child with a loaded weapon. She closed her eyes. She'd have to deal with it later. They had perhaps an hour before the team in the train car would be discovered.

At last, she reached the place she had in mind. She guided James down a dark stairwell to a nondescript black door. She knocked a few times, keeping her chin down and her cap pulled low so the security camera didn't get a clear view of her face.

For a too-long moment, nothing happened. "Does this place have a name?" James whispered.

"Hell's Crater," Noa muttered, keeping her chin dipped and her voice gruff.

"And I thought we were just going to hell in the figurative sense," James muttered. Noa smirked, glanced up at him, and realized all of the dust had washed off his face in the rain—and probably off her face as well. Just as she realized that, the door swung open.

Adjusting her shoulders, trying to appear broader, Noa stepped in with James. She was briefly blinded by lights as bright as the Luddeccean interrogation room. As her eyes adjusted, Noa saw a burly guard she fortunately didn't recognize. He was standing behind a podium with a thick open book, partially blocking a short hallway that led to some more stairs. Noa thought she made out mug shots on one side of the book's pages and a list on the other. Her stomach sank. But she took the pack she was carrying off her back and put it in some lockers just before the podium. She motioned for James to do the same. In her pack were the stunners, and James's pack contained his rifle, carefully disassembled. They'd be nearly defenseless, but it couldn't be helped.

"Sorry, guys," the guard barked. "I gotta see your IDs."

Noa swallowed. This was not normally the sort of place where IDs were checked … and even if the dirt of their disguises hadn't been washed away by the drizzle outside, they never would have passed muster in the bright light of the hallway. Her eyes flitted to James. His chin was dipped low, eyes on the security guard, and she could feel his readiness to fight.

Noa took a deep breath and made a leap of faith. Reaching into her pocket, she pulled out the billfold-like ID and handed it to the guard. Turning to James, she jerked her head in the guard's direction. Thankfully, taking the hint, he handed his ID over. The guard looked at the pictures in his hand, looked at them, and down at the pictures again. He looked over at the book, and ran his fingers over the names.

"These IDs check out," he said, head bent over the podium. Not lifting his eyes, he said, "The pictures look old." He handed the IDs back, still not looking at them. "You might want to have them updated." He coughed into his hand. "We get some slack for being a Fleet establishment, but sometimes, the Local Guard checks in here."

Noa nodded, and said, "We understand. Thank you." She wasn't sure if the guard recognized her—but she was sure he knew the IDs were fake.

Turning to James, she said, "Come on," and led him down the hallway to the dark descending stairwell beyond. She noticed that the hologlobe that usually played a Fleet recruitment recording in the hall was gone, as was the two-dimensional old time recruitment poster that used to hang on the ceiling above the stairs. A chill descended on her, even though the hallway was as hot and humid as it had been outside.

Beside her, James whispered, "He lied … he lied for us. I can't believe it. Although … there is a wonderful

126

little-known account of a mixed-race man living in Nazi Germany, titled Destined to Witness. He was saved by purposeful acts of disambiguation by—"

"James," Noa hissed as a man appeared at the foot of the steps, a wave of sound from the room following as he did. "Shhh ..."

"Ah, right," James said, stepping to the side to let the man pass.

Noa could hear music thumping as they approached the bottom of the steps and the heavy metal door that separated the stairwell from the club. The humid smell of the hallway was replaced by a hint of Root and tobacco. James bumped Noa's shoulder with his. "Have I ever entered a more wretched hive of scum and villainy?"

Noa snapped, "These are mostly former Fleet personnel!" There were a lot of veterans on Luddeccea. The planet may have been ambivalent about joining the Republic, but Luddecceans were over-represented in the military, and especially over-represented in the ranks of grunts. If you were a Luddeccean from a lesser family aspiring to more than baby-making, Fleet was the way to go. Luddecceans made great spacers; they were farm kids used to hard work and doing without. And Luddeccea's only recent conquest of native bacteria, fungi, and viral infections meant that Luddecceans were more likely to accept the risk of death that went along with space exploration and keeping order in the asteroid belts. Many Luddeccean veterans settled on other worlds when they left the Fleet, but some came back … and when they did, they came here. She felt protective of them. They were her people, more than other spacers or Luddeccean civilians. She glared up at James.

His eyes narrowed, and his jaw twitched. "I was trying to lighten the mood." One of his eyebrows lifted. "I was under the impression you liked that sort of thing."

Noa squeezed her eyes shut, remembering the movie he'd mangled the line from. She'd missed the joke in his deadpan delivery. Timothy would have been blushing from hairline to neck, and biting a smile to keep from laughing aloud. He wasn't Tim. She released a breath. Not meeting his eyes, she nudged him with her shoulder. "Yeah, thanks. It was funny."

"Please, contain your mirth," he said dryly.

The wryness of his tone made her smirk. Putting her hand on the door latch, she said, "Now let's try and find someone I recognize, who can play programmer for us." She swallowed. "Without us being recognized."

Turning his head to her sharply, James said, "You said no one from Fleet would be likely to turn us in."

Wincing, Noa looked up at the ceiling. "Well, almost no one." Without waiting for a response, Noa opened the door and stepped into the room beyond.

***

Hell's Crater was almost exactly as Noa remembered it. Smokey and badly lit, it smelled like too many bodies and spilled drinks. But when her eyes grazed the crowd, she saw that things were different. It wasn't as full as usual. The hologlobe at the bar's end wasn't playing live sports; it was playing an old holodrama instead. And when she peered into cubbies and nooks, her eyes actually went wide with shock. Some of the patrons were linked to each other via cables. Hell's Crater wasn't stuffy, but it also wasn't the sort of establishment where this sort of thing usually went on.

Normally, direct neural interface communication was achieved by ethernet; but, with the ethernet down, cables or "hard links" could substitute. Noa felt a near-constant desire to link, but she didn't feel compelled to hard link. There was more risk involved in linking with hardware; it was easier to catch a bug of the biological or electronic variety. Also, the ethernet relay stations for thought trans-missions had built-in gates to help keep errant thoughts and emotions from slipping through. With a hard link, the nearly subconscious observation that your data partner had nice biceps would be transmitted straight to his brain. And the way human brains worked, that observation was likely to be followed with thoughts even more explicit. Sex was so often a result of a hard link that "hard linking" was a meta-phor for sex. Noa had some Fleet apps installed to provide filtering for her own thought transmissions; however, the apps couldn't shield her from a stranger's musings.

Realizing she probably looked like a kid who'd just found porn playing on her grandmother's hologlobe, she smoothed her expression. Squinting in the gloom, looking for someone she recognized, she saw a few hard linkers were smiling a little too broadly, eyes rolled back in their heads. A hard linked woman in one of the booths began to visibly moan, her mouth agape and eyes glazed. Her part-ner grunted, his hand beneath the table, his arm moving furiously. Noa had seen more explicit antics on some of her shore leaves, but nothing like it at Hell's Crater. She shook her head—so why now? The security guard's words came back to her. "We get some slack for being a Fleet establish-ment." She sighed. They were here because they didn't have anywhere else to go. She looked around the bar to see how the other patrons reacted. Some of them were laughing and pointing; others were shaking their heads. She noticed a man at a table directly across from the couple; he took credits from a man and then handed him a hard link. Noa's eyebrows shot up. Apparently this was where people came to buy hardware; that would explain the festivities. Her eyes narrowed as she inspected the seller. He was wearing a glowing necklace. The necklace lit Eurasian features that were more perfect than James's. He'd definitely had work done ... also not typical of this place. Fleet people were more likely than Luddecceans to have plastic surgery for major scars—but "pretty" wasn't an ideal. Just before she turned away from the man, he caught her gaze. His eyes widened a fraction, and he lifted his glass in her direction and leered. Noa's stomach churned.

Beside her, James whispered, "You know him?"

Noa stepped toward an empty booth in the corner. "No, but he makes my creep detector buzz."

"Is that an app?" James whispered in her ear.

Noa had no idea if he was joking, which made it funnier. Covering what had to be a goofy grin with a cough, she slid into the booth and tried to observe everyone discreetly. James had just taken a seat across from her when the door flew open. The guy they'd passed on the way up the stairs lunged in, eyes wide, shouting something into the din. Noa couldn't hear the words, but she could read his lips: "Patrol!"

The holo went silent, but the noise in the room increased. There were a few cries, a few shouts, and around them people started yanking cables from their ports. James lurched to his feet, and Noa did, too. Other patrons were already ahead of them, running to the back door, but before Noa had slid out of the booth, the door in the back burst open and men in Luddeccean Green blocked their exit.

Noa's eyes darted across the room, looking for a place to hide. There had been a time when alcohol was prohibited on Luddeccea. Maybe there was a hideaway behind the bar?

"Noa," James hissed. Her eyes snapped to him—he was staring at someone not two steps from the table.

CHAPTER SEVEN

James's muscles tensed. He heard shouting and saw people dropping hard links to the ground as they pressed in a mob toward the exits. A part of his mind noted the anomaly of it—hard linking wasn't illegal in the Republic. It was necessary for psychotherapy or neural interface repair. It was, however, typically found to be in poor taste in public places. He remembered half-seriously suggesting to a girlfriend that they hard link in the backroom during a particularly tedious event. She'd suggested he go hard link himself.

At the same time his mind processed these thoughts, his eyes remained fixed on the "creep." The man shuffled toward the table—fortunately, effectively blocking the Guard's view of Noa and James. Hands in the pockets of a long trench coat, the stranger looked James up and down without ever meeting his eyes, and then he looked at Noa and smiled.

Her eyes narrowed at the man. "Do I know you?"

James heard footsteps on the stairs, and shouts of, "This is an ID check, stay calm!" James's eyes darted around the room, looking for an escape, but he heard the Guard at both exits. For a brief moment his vision went black. They'd run through a blizzard, fallen into a gorge, crashed into a canyon wall, hidden in a magni-freight car … this couldn't be their end … not in a bar. But of course it could be; it was magical thinking to suppose otherwise.

There were whispers and screams, and someone cried,

"Dear God, dear God."

More magical thinking. But what was the alternative? He told himself they would get out of this. His vision returned, and he was once more staring at the stranger, but he couldn't move. He was frozen in place, his mind scrambling for a viable course of action and finding none.

Chuckling despite the chaos, the stranger slid into the booth across from James, blocking Noa's escape. Pulling his hand from his pocket, the stranger put a stiff plastic necklace on the table. "Put this on, Noa."

James looked to her, surprised the man knew her name. Realizing the man's frame wasn't blocking the view to others in the room, James leaned as far as he could in his seat, turned his head to Noa, and put a hand to the side of his face visible to the crowd.

Noa didn't move. "Who are you?" she demanded.

The man's smile widened, but he didn't show teeth. "It will hide you from the patrol." The smile lasted too long without changing, and was too symmetrical.

Sliding toward him in her seat, Noa said, "Get out of my way … "

The man frowned. The necklace he wore went dark. Halting, Noa gaped. James did, too. Where an instant before there had been a handsome if artificial-looking face, what appeared now was the face of a man who was pudgy and overweight. He had a thin unkempt beard, above which his cheeks and forehead glistened with sweat. His nose was long, pointed and European, but his eyes were narrow and red-rimmed. He lacked a distinct chin.

"I'm only trying to help you, Noa," he said, his lower lip quivering.

"Dan Chow," said Noa. James's eyes slid to her. She recognized "Dan" obviously, but didn't look overjoyed to see him. Her eyes darted to the necklace. Dipping her chin toward James, she said, "If you're going to help me, you've got to help my friend."

"We don't have time for games," Dan said. Around the table the crowd was being pushed backward. James heard shouts from the patrol, "Take out your IDs!"

"Lizzar dung. You've been playing a game since we came in," Noa hissed back.

Dan's eyes slipped to the crowd and back to Noa. He looked down his too-long nose at James and sniffed. "Fine, Noa. Keep your toys." James felt heat flash beneath his skin, but instead of sweating, he shivered.

"My friend," Noa said, and the heat cooled.

The man's lips quirked up in a small smile. He snorted. "Really?" Pulling out another necklace, he slid it across the table to James. Leaning back, Dan said, "And he looks like a throwback, too ..." James raised an eyebrow. He remembered, in his past, getting into shouting matches with people who used that slur. Now ... he told himself that it was just their circumstances forcing him to keep a level head. But the slur felt wrong, like his name, an incorrect label, a jumble of syllables.

Taking the necklace proffered to her, Noa slid it on her neck—and she vanished. In her place was a woman with paler skin, straight black hair that cut off just above her shoulders, eyes that were narrower and lips that weren't as full. She still wore the clothing they'd stolen from the train operators—it looked out of place. Her face looked perfectly made up with makeup that was sophisticated, but not too heavy. The tiny scars above and below her eye were gone.

It was a look he normally would like, but now it set him on edge. Noa was the only thing that felt real to him. The hologram—he was sure that was what it was—took away his one tether to reality. He gave his head a tiny shake. He had to get over it. Picking up his own necklace, he inspected it briefly. It looked and felt like a slender band of light-weight plastic. Slipping it on, his mind whirred. To work, holographic projections required smoke at the very least. In the hologlobes, rapidly oscillating beads reflected cyan, magenta, and yellow depending on the holographic data received. The necklace had no such medium to operate in.

As the latch at the back of James's necklace clicked, Dan said, "Now you're both more attractive." Dan's necklace was on again, his face once again artificially handsome.

Noa—or the hologram she wore—rolled her eyes, and James found himself doing the same.

"Hide your hands," Dan commanded.

Glancing down, James saw Noa's hands were still dark and his were still light. They both slipped their hands beneath the table as Dan pushed some ID billfolds out on the tabletop.

At that moment, a Luddeccean patrolman sidled up to the table. "IDs please!"

Dan nodded at the ID billfolds. "Right there, Sir."

Beneath the table, Noa's hand went to James's arm, and he could feel her tension in her fingers.

The guard picked up the billfolds. As he flipped through them, James had the distinct impression that time was slowing. He cast furtive glances around the Guardman, noting there were no less than fifteen other members of the Guard in the room. All armed with stunners, and more lethally, laser pistols.

The Guard's eyes went to James and then to Noa, and back again. James's muscles coiled, ready to fight. Noa's fingers tightened even more. Tipping his helmet, the Guard gave a wink to James and a smile to Noa. Nodding to Dan, the guard put the IDs back on the table. "Thank you for your cooperation," he said, and strode away.

Dan chuckled. "I wonder if I should feel jealous or proud

that he found you two ladies interesting."

Noa made a barely audible gagging noise.

At the table where the two lovers had been hardwired together, James heard a woman's voice, "Please, no!" and a Luddeccean Guard saying, "You are under arrest!" Noa went completely quiet and still. There were more sounds of protests, and scuffling, as other patrons were shoved up against the bars and tabletops.

James's eyes slid to Noa's and her holographic disguise met his gaze.

"Easy ladies," Dan whispered. "Haven't I just proved that you have nothing to worry about?"

Despite his assurances, Dan didn't speak again until the Luddeccean Guard had cleared out of the room, taking a substantial number of patrons with them. And then he said, "Fancy meeting you here, Noa."

Noa's holographic illusion fixed Dan with a glare. "What's your game, Dan?"

Dan cocked his head, and one side of his lip curled. "I go by Ghost now. Aren't you going to thank me?"

"You didn't do it out of the goodness of your heart … " Noa tilted her head. "... Dan."

Dan frowned and leaned across the table. "I could just as equally ask what your game is, Noa. You need something, too. You were off in one of their re-education camps—"

Noa recoiled as though she'd been struck.

Dan gave her a thin smile. "Didn't think I'd know about that, did you?"

Noa's jaw hardened. "You knew about that, but didn't help?"

Dan's lower lip trembled. And James smelled something familiar. He'd smelled it when Noa had darted off his bed and in the cattle car just before he clipped the man in the chin. Noa had been afraid. Had the man in the cattle car been afraid? Was Dan afraid? James's eyes dropped from the man's artificially generated face to Dan's hands. They had a barely perceptible tremor.

"You were too afraid to help," James said flatly.

Noa snorted. "Good call."

James couldn't meet her eyes. He'd almost been too afraid to, too. Dan's eyes flicked to James, and then went back to Noa. "I was too smart to get involved."

"You've always been too smart, haven't you, Dan?" Noa snapped.

"Ever seen tech like this?" Dan said, stroking his neck.

Noa's holo's eyes narrowed to slits.

Dan leered. "Oh, your precious Fleet would love these, wouldn't they? Are you sorry that you didn't recommend me for a promotion now?"

Huffing, Noa shook her head. "I had nothing to do with that."

"You could have put in a good word for me," Dan snapped.

She snapped right back, "Get to the point. Why are you helping us? Just to gloat? To show off your shiny new tech?"

Dan sniffed. "Maybe." He tilted his head. "Although I am curious as to how you escaped the camp." He leaned closer to Noa. "That would seem to be a feat that would require divine assistance."

James almost jerked back at the word "divine," and felt all his nanos and neurons fire at once. The Luddeccean Guard had broadcast the falling of an "Archangel." Had Dan heard the broadcast? Had he somehow pieced together James's "identity"? What would it mean if he had?

Without missing a beat, Noa said, "What are you getting at, Dan?" James didn't think he'd be able to speak as smoothly.

Dan's brow furrowed and a light went on in his neural

136

port. "The Archangel Project. I know you were involved."

All the neurons and nanos in James's skull lit again, and the charge spread to every inch of his skin. Dan knew ... he had to know James was the supposed Archangel. And then another neuron flickered brightly in his mind. Noa had never said she was involved in the Archangel Project.

Noa's jaw dropped. Her eyes flitted to James. Did she look guilty, or just confused?

"Dan," she said, meeting the man's gaze. "I'm not part of the Archangel Project." She sighed. Bowing her head, she leaned on her elbows, her shoulders slumping. "But you're not the first person to ask me about it. The Luddeccean Guard asked me about it when ... " Noa shifted in her seat. "I'd never even heard of the project," Noa finished, "Not until they asked."

A light flashed near Dan's neural port. "But how did you escape?"

With one finger, Noa traced an engraving of some initials carved into the table top. "It's not a pretty story." Rubbing her upper arms, she said, "I don't want to talk about it."

Dan leaned back, tapped his neural port, and the light went out. "I believe you." His forehead furrowed.

"What do you know about the Archangel Project?" Noa asked, leaning toward Dan.

Dan snorted. His eyes flicked to James, and for the first time James felt as though he was being looked at instead of looked through. Looking away, Dan blinked rapidly and waved a hand. "That the time of angels has come. Or aliens, or devils, or djinn. Who knows?"

"You're too smart to believe any of that, Dan," said Noa.

Narrowing his eyes at Noa, Dan frowned. "It's Ghost." And then he looked away and wiped a hand down his face. "Surveying my options ... " He muttered in a voice so low it was almost inaudible. "Hoped you had something special

137

… "

"What do you mean?" Noa asked.

Dan glared at her. James's eyes fell on the ignored IDs on the table. On a whim, he plucked them up and flipped through them briefly. He saw Noa's holographic image in one, another woman who looked startlingly similar to Noa's ulterior appearance in the second – he supposed that was what he looked like. The third had a picture of Dan's holographic avatar. James read the name "Hung See." And suddenly James knew why Dan had approached them. Sliding the IDs to Noa, James said, "He's on the run, too. That's why he's hiding his identity from the Guard, and he's looking for help."

Dan sat up very straight. He glared at James. Noa, by contrast, smiled. "Last I heard, the new Luddeccean Premier had hired you on; in your words, they 'recognized your talent.' Why would one of their own be hiding?"

Dan looked away. "I'm not one of them, obviously. They barely appreciated me. I built their non-ethernet dependent systems—a closed system that could never be infected by external influence. I gave them the computing power of a time gate at a scale that is … " His eyes closed and a look of bliss passed over his features. " … At a scale that is impossibly small."

"And they turned on you," Noa said. Her avatar's jaw appeared to harden. "Because the mind that could build that sort of computing power—"

"Luddites," Dan hissed.

"By definition, actually," said James, remembering the origins of the Luddeccean name.

Dan scowled at him. Noa's lips flattened, not like she was angry, but like she was trying to conceal a smile.

James's own lips wanted to pull up—but didn't. He touched the side of his mouth self-consciously.

Leaning toward Dan, Noa practically crooned, "You need help, Dan. Which is why you helped us."

Dan sat perfectly still. He didn't blink, or swallow, but his necklace flickered, and for a moment, James could see the red eyes and sweaty face of the real man. A passing barman, a bowl of peanuts and boiled soybeans in either hand, stopped and gaped.

Noa said quickly, "We'd like to see a menu, we're hungry." The man put the two bowls of snacks on the table, nodded, and left quickly.

James's eyes fell heavily on the peanuts. He could see their oil glistening in the low light. Before he'd even thought about it, he'd scooped up the contents of the bowl and shoveled them into his mouth.

"How lady-like," said Dan as James bolted down the peanuts. James shrugged. The taste of the peanut oil and salt on his tongue made his taste buds sing.

"Your makeup is running, Dan," Noa said.

Dan blinked, and Noa tapped her necklace meaningfully. Dan's eyes went wide. He tapped his necklace and the hologram flickered back to life. Gaze shifting around the room, he picked up the fake IDs from the table and said, "We need to get out of here. Follow me if you want my help."

Without looking back, Dan slipped out of the booth and walked toward the back door.

Palming the soybeans, James looked at Noa—or the hologram that concealed her face. "He let us keep the hologram projectors," he said.

Noa looked past him and her brow furrowed. Following her gaze, James saw the bartender pointing in their direction and whispering to a patron sitting alone at the bar. James's mind whirled through his recent memories. He was certain he hadn't seen that patron before.

"Because he knows we have to follow him," Noa said.

The patron at the bar got up and walked with quick steps to the front door.

Noa's eyes got wide. Slipping from the booth, she whispered, "And we have to hurry!"

***

Barging through Hell's Crater's backdoor, Noa plunged into the alley beyond. From the main street she heard a shout. "Patrol, this way."

"I see Dan," James said, grabbing her arm and pulling her in the opposite direction. Noa blinked. There were no streetlights, and she was unable to see anything. She let herself be drawn in that direction, trusting James's augmented vision.

She heard pounding footsteps behind them. She plugged the sound of the steps into a Fleet app. Her gut twisted. "There's ten of them." She remembered the stunners and laser pistols they'd carried, and their threats to rip her port out—she wasn't sure which would be better.

James yanked her sideways into another alley at a four-way intersection. It had stopped raining; they passed under several rows of clothing hung out to dry. The pavement was still slick though, and everything smelled damp. The alley was partially blocked with dumpsters, and they bent low to hide behind the dumpsters' bulks.

"I saw him go this way," James said. "He took off his disguise."

"Because the light they emit is a beacon in these dark alleys," Noa gasped, ripping her necklace off and jamming it into her pocket.

James did likewise. "Nice to have you back," he murmured. Someone shouted, and the group that had been following them split in opposite directions.

"Five still after us," she said. "Keep moving." James nodded, and set off at a quick trot. Behind them Noa heard the

Guards knocking on doors and banging their rifle butts on dumpsters. A shot made her jump, and both of them quickened their pace. They ran under another row of clothing, and past a hover on cinder blocks, and found themselves at a main thoroughfare. Late night shoppers and some men who looked as though they had just finished work at the boat yards were walking down the street. Over the sound of her loud, raspy breathing, Noa heard the sound of a hover bus taking off.

James stopped and peered left around a corner. "Patrolmen, three more of them. But Dan went right, I saw him—see him!"

Behind them there was another shot into a dumpster. "We have to make a break for it." Noa said, gritting her teeth. Her lungs burned and her ears rang with the sound of bullets impacting on metal.

"Right," whispered James. Grabbing her arm again, he said, "Now, before I lose sight of him!" He gave a yank, and they bolted to the right. She heard the patrolmen on the street shout, "There they are!" Noa urged her legs to go faster ... she was a very fast runner. Was. Past tense. But James pulled her along. "Down this alley," he said, yanking her left.

They tore down another alleyway with laundry above. Noa's eyes widened. It was one of the alleys they'd passed through earlier.

James yanked her right, and left, and Noa saw the main thoroughfare where the cab had first put them down. She heard troops shouting ahead and behind. Noa's breath was ragged in her ears. Her skin was clammy with the ambient humidity.

James stopped. "I saw him go this way ... but we should have caught up to him ... he wasn't moving that fast."

Tearing her arm away, Noa looked for something that she

could use as a weapon, a broken bottle, an old two-by-four, anything. "No garbage, nothing I can use to bash someone's head in," Noa hissed. "I'm really not liking the new regime, even if there are no rats."

"This wasn't sticking out last time we were here … " James said.

Noa looked over her shoulder. James was staring at a brick protruding from a wall where the outer layer of stucco was peeling away. Before she could tell him to stop worrying about it, he pushed it into the wall. It moved with a scrape … and a portion of the wall flickered … or rather, did the inverse of flickering. It went darker, reappeared, and went dark again. The unflickering wall was barely wider than Noa's shoulders, and no higher than her chest.

"Another hologram," James whispered, just audible over the sound of footsteps closing in on the intersections at either end of the alleyway. He took a step back and put a hand to his chin as though pondering a deep and weighty question.

If the situation hadn't been so dire, Noa might have laughed. "Just the time for your inner professor to pop out," she muttered.

"What?" said James, blinking at her.

Without a word, she spun him sideways. "Down!" she whispered, pushing him through the unflickering space. A heartbeat later she followed. She felt rather than saw stone walls scrape against her back as she passed through the narrow space. And then her side hit something firm even as the walls fell away in front and behind her. Stumbling, she found herself gasping for breath, side pressed to James's chest, staring back the way she came. "Shhhhh …." James said, and she realized he meant her breathing. She took one last deep gasp and tried to relax her demanding lungs. Looking back the way she came, she found herself staring through the hole in the wall they'd just come through. On this side, it looked like a flickering curtain of light ... if it was flickering on the outside too ....

Before she could finish the thought, the curtain of light abruptly stabilized just as Luddeccean troops converged right in front of the space. For a moment she thought they'd seen James and her disappear. She bit her lip, afraid to hope and afraid to move, lest the sound of their steps give them away. A man she identified as the Captain by his uniform said, "Did you see them?"

Outside, a sergeant said, "No, sir," and gulped audibly.

Noa's body sagged in relief, and James, perhaps thinking she was about to faint, wrapped his arms around her. She almost pulled away, out of habit or pride or both, and then realized she was shaking, and her legs were weak. What was wrong with her?

The Captain looked back and forth down the alleyway. "You must have mistaken the direction they took." From his hip, he pulled a device slightly larger than the "cell" phones that the characters in the old tee-vee programs used. Putting it to his face, the officer pressed a button. The device buzzed, and he spoke into it. "Patrols, I want you at the corners of ... " He walked away before Noa could hear the rest.

The patrol split in opposite directions, and their footsteps faded down the alleyway.

Closing her eyes, Noa took a breath so long and deep she could feel it stinging in her lungs.

James whispered in her ear, "I think it's safe to move."

Noa didn't want to move. The way her legs were trembling, she was afraid she really might faint. She wanted to catch her breath, and stay safely supported in James's arms. Instead she pulled away. Finding the necklace in her pocket, she clicked the edges together—it lit a scant few centis of dark, and then abruptly shut off. It hadn't been enough to see past a lizzar's nose, and Noa didn't even bother to ask for James's. Instead, peering into the blackness, she asked, "Can you see?" There was a wall behind James, that much she was sure of. Maybe it was some sort of hallway?

James didn't answer. When she glanced back, she found him staring down at her. In the dim light he looked like he was glowering. "You're not well."

"I'm—" She almost said "fine." But then a cough wracked through her. She barely muffled it with her hand. " … recovering."

James's hands balled into fists at his side and he did not move until Noa caught her breath again. Then, squinting into the dark, he said, "I see a door."

"Let's go," Noa said—though it came out more a gasp. "Lead the way."

Instead of walking ahead of her, he put a hand on the small of her back and guided her down the hall. With only the faint light of the hologram behind them, it was soon pitch black. The world was only her breathing, their footsteps, the smell of old mortar, her sweat, and James. As usual, he smelled good. It made her a tiny bit jealous. James took slow steps, either because he was afraid to tire her out, or because he couldn't see well. She almost wished she'd had her vision augmented—and then her mind conjured up Ashley and her missing limb. Would her captors in the camp have removed her eyeballs, if she had had nano-augmented night vision? The thought made her shiver, and James pressed his hand on her back more firmly.

"I'm fine," she muttered proactively.

She heard James exhale, felt his breath close to her ear, and shivered again. "And my eyes are not rolling," he said in his deadpan tone.

A laugh that sounded too much like a cough cracked out

144

of her, and tears prickled the corners of her eyes. "I will be fine," she said. She pressed a hand to his side reassuringly—reassuring to him, to her, she wasn't sure. And then she caught herself, realizing how inappropriate the gesture was. She pulled away, but not before she felt the warmth of his skin through his shirt, and the tautness of the muscles of his abdomen.

James said nothing and Noa's mind wandered in the dark and near silence. "It was lucky you saw that brick ..." They had passed through so many alleys that all looked nearly identical.

"Stop here," James said, not dropping his hand.

As Noa obeyed, a thought occurred to her. "Do you have some sort of holographic memory app running at all times?"

The hand on her back stiffened. For a too long moment there was silence, and then James said, "I didn't have a holographic memory before the accident ... but ... I ... believe I do ... now."

Noa felt a flash of concern. "James, you have to turn that off." Noa had a holographic memory app like all Fleet personnel. But standard procedure was to dump the contents. Keeping so much data on hand tended to bog down normal processing of the nano and neural variety.

She felt a brush of his breath against her temple. "I ... don't think I can."

The stutter in his voice ... he was just as broken as she was. Noa's hand slipped to where his upper arm would be—and found it. She gave him a pat ... the same sort of pat she'd give to a fellow pilot, she told herself. "We'll find someone who can make you better, James. As soon as we get out of here, I promise."

"Thank you," he whispered, and she felt his breath on her forehead, and realized their bodies were facing one another,

145

with scant centis between them. Unaccountably flustered, Noa spun around and threw out her arms. "Which way is that door?" In the same breath, she found a knob. She gave it a twist. It didn't budge. She rolled back on her feet. "Figured that he'd lock it … "

James murmured, "I'd thought … hoped … he'd left the brick out on purpose for us to find and escape our pursuers."

Putting a hand on her hips, Noa scowled in the dark. "Pfft. Nope, that was an accident, I'm sure."

She heard James exhale softly. "How far do you trust this Dan?"

"Not further than I can see," Noa said, running a hand over the seam between the door and the wall. "He is a malignant narcissist. He imagines he is a genius, and he is; but not that much of a genius."

"If he invented the necklace holograms, his genius is exceptional. The light of the holograms had nothing to reflect off of. Presumably he was manipulating individual photons … but such utilization of quantum mechanics outside of a closed environment isn't possible."

"Not yet," Noa countered. "But it's been speculated about for years." That much had been reported in the press, that she could speak about. It was also one of the Fleet Intel's projects.

"Speculated about, maybe," James said. "But I haven't heard of any working prototypes."

"Neither have I," Noa muttered, her shoulders falling. Not even in the classified briefings she'd attended. She shook her head. "But Ghost—Dan—isn't that smart." She stamped her foot and looked at the door—or tried to in the pitch blackness. "More of a problem is that he is a coward."

"Should we seek help from someone else?" James asked. "You don't like him or trust him—which makes me not like or trust him."

"I don't, you're right." Noa wrapped her arms around herself, hit by a sudden new certainty. "But it has to be Dan. He knows we're here. If we don't let him join us, he will try to turn us in for amnesty." The thumb of her left hand went to the stumps of her missing fingers. She took a shaky breath. "I hope we can convince him it's in his best interests to be on our side."

She felt James's hand drop on her shoulder. Voice too even, he said, "If he doesn't help us, I'll kill him."

Noa froze at his words. She believed that he would kill Ghost. So would she. Maybe. If forced. It sounded as though James had no qualms about it. She remembered him confessing that he hadn't felt bad for killing her attackers in the forest. She shook her head. She wouldn't have had qualms about killing them either; and, if his voice was too even—well, his apps were wonky.

Her heart sped up. But then how did he imitate voices so well? Her breath caught; but then she shook her head again, remembering his stutter when he apologized for killing the train operator. The expression of emotion and the imitation of voices were two different things …

"Get back," James said, and she noticed his voice had become gruffer.

Noa backed away, and James threw himself against the door. There was a thud, and then another, and then the low moan of bending steel. There was another loud thud, a bang, and the sharp sound of metal crashing against metal. The door that had been in front of her fell and she was bathed in putrid green light. She threw up her hands against the glare. As her eyes adjusted, she saw a landing and a stairwell beyond the fallen door. Striding forward onto the landing, she motioned for James.

She almost shouted Dan's name, but gritted her teeth

instead. Dan wasn't the only person who'd been passed over for promotions. Starship Captains required tact and a certain amount of verbal restraint. In every evaluation she'd had since Tim died, she'd come up short on both counts. Before Tim died, she had someone she could vent to, always just a thought away. Afterward … well, it was a lot harder to smile at the politician you thought was a mother-eating rodent from the asteroid colonies in Six, when there was no one you could be secretly honest with. What had one officer said over beers? "In the event of a first contact scenario, Commander Sato would be the last person I'd want on a bridge. She'd tell the green sons-of-bitches exactly what she thought of them."

Her nostrils flared and she balled her hands into fists. It wasn't that she couldn't be diplomatic. It was just that she hated it, so much that she wasn't sure even a starship captaincy was worth the trouble.

But if they didn't have Dan on their side, he could be dangerous. She bit the inside of her cheek. She thought of Ashley and Kenji. More than rank was at stake. "Ghost—think of him as Ghost," she muttered softly to herself. "Feed his vanity."

James must have heard because he gave a low huff.

"It will be hard, but worth it," Noa promised James and herself. "Even if it makes my skin crawl." Ghost was skilled enough to get them authorized to travel up to Time Gate 8. And … she paused at the top of the stairs. He'd known that she'd been sent to a camp; that meant, he'd know where Kenji was, too. Her heart hammered in her chest. "Ghost, we'll help you," she called out as sweetly as she could manage.

From the bottom of the stairs, Ghost's voice rang out, "You made it … I'm sorry. I had to run, you understand. But you made it, that's good." His voice was plaintive, like

148

a frightened child. In a child, Noa could have forgiven his simpering. She bit back the snarl that came to her lips. Instead of saying, "No thanks to you," Noa said, "Yes, isn't it wonderful? Now we can work together." She smiled down at him from the landing.

Ghost stood at the bottom of the stairs, no longer wearing the holographic necklace. He was holding a laser rifle, but wasn't aiming it. He sniffed. "I don't need your help, you know."

Noa's fingernails dug into her palm. James, her silent shadow, strode forward suddenly, the metal wire of the landing groaning beneath his feet, the expression on his face as impassive as a statue. Noa caught his arm and he stopped. At the bottom of the stairwell Ghost shuffled backward and raised the rifle shakily. Her eyes widened in alarm. James was scaring Ghost—and that was not good. She mouthed the word "wait," and then said, "Of course you don't need our help, Ghost."

Ghost huffed. "I'm just investigating my options ... there are others who could use my services. Others with more money and faster ships."

Noa's brow creased, but she licked her lips and said, "Can we come down and talk about your services?"

Ghost was quiet for a long moment. But then he cleared his throat and lowered the rifle. Puffing out his chest, he sniffed again. "You can come down."

James looked at her sharply. Slipping his hand up to her elbow, chin dipped, eyes on hers, lips so close she could feel his breath, he whispered in Japanese, "Is it safe?"

"Yes," she replied in the same dead language.

"I'll go first," he whispered.

He was being protective. Touching and out of place. Noa shook her head. In Japanese she said, "No, you'll frighten him."

Downstairs, she heard Ghost clear his throat again.

James didn't drop her elbow. She wanted to tell him that Ghost was too much of a coward for direct confrontation. But Ghost was probably listening, and he was smart enough to feed their words through an interpreter app at some point. The less they insulted him, the better.

Without waiting for James to drop her elbow, Noa spun out of his grip and went down the stairs. By the bottom of the steps, she felt her legs giving out again. She found herself grasping the handrail too tightly, wishing James still had her elbow, and carefully watching where she put her feet.

At the bottom of the steps, she lifted her head—and stifled a scream. Behind Ghost was a floor-to -ceiling pile of limbs and semi-dismembered corpses, piled like logs bathed in the vile green light. She backed into James, and would have fallen over if he hadn't caught her. She was in the wagon again, the frozen elbows and knees of dead bodies jamming into her back and side.

"They're just sex 'bots," Ghost said.

She blinked, and saw that the mannequin-like faces of what she'd taken to be bodies were too perfect in death to be from humans. More obvious were the wires jutting out of amputated limbs and torsos.

Noa's diplomacy left her. "Still creepy as Hell, Dan!"

Ghost—Dan—rolled on his feet. He actually looked slightly ashamed. "Yes, but I need the parts, and people keep throwing them away. They're illegal now, you know."

Noa shivered unaccountably. Sex 'bots were expensive. She knew only one person who could afford to have one. The penalty for having one must be immense if people were throwing them away. She didn't approve of sex 'bots, but she found her eyes roaming the pile for the face of the one she knew, and was a little surprised she felt relief when she didn't see it.

"This way," said Ghost, leading them through a door Noa hadn't noticed. They followed him down a long hallway of poured concrete and exposed pipes. Her brow furrowed, remembering Dan's—Ghost's—psyche profile. He was all about showing status. If he was living in a place like this, he was in more trouble than he let on.

Ghost took them to a dark room that was too warm. It was cluttered with loose electronic equipment in disarray, and what appeared to be furniture covered by sheets. There was a floor-to-ceiling geothermal energy converter at one end of the room. There were also food pouches next to a wave oven and an industrial faucet with a bathtub-sized sink. Noa's eyebrows rose. There was a surprisingly clean, large towel folded neatly beside the sink—as though he was using it for a bath. Ghost was definitely in more trouble than he was letting on. She swallowed. Ghost could disguise his face, and had fake IDs, if he was in trouble. Her eyes slid to James. He'd walked past her and was standing with his back to the geothermal converter, arms crossed, eyes on Ghost.

She heard the screech of chair legs on the floor, and turned to see Ghost clearing a space in the center of the room, pushing some furniture covered with a sheet. The sheet abruptly slid off, revealing a sex 'bot in a ball gown sitting on an elaborately carved high-backed chair. Half of her head was cracked open.

Noa's eyes went wide. Ghost, catching her expression, said, "She didn't get me. And I needed her processor for something."

Noa closed her eyes briefly, unsure if Ghost was telling a joke. She reminded herself that no matter how life-like the 'bots were, they weren't alive, and didn't care if they lived or died. It still made her feel sick. She opened her eyes and found James's eyes on hers, his expression unreadable.

Ghost pulled a cloth away from another piece of furniture, thankfully, only revealing another high-backed chair. He sat down, and motioned for Noa to take a seat on a rickety-looking folding chair nearby. He didn't gesture to James at all.

Noa's lips pursed at the slights to her and to James, but held her tongue.

As she sat down, Ghost leaned forward in his seat and smacked his hands together. "Now, to discuss my fees."

James beat her to the rejoinder. "How can you tell us a fee if you don't know the service?"

Ghost jerked his head back, and his eyes narrowed at James. Noa's eyebrow rose, and she remembered Ghost's 'divine intervention' comment at the table. Ghost had to have been following the secure channel communications. Did he know James was the figurative Archangel? Ghost was too smart to believe in aliens, but he might have heard of James killing four men during their escape. That could be why he was afraid.

Eyes coming back to Noa, Ghost said, "I know what you need."

Crossing her legs, Noa leaned back in her chair. "Really?"

Looking heavenward, he gave a leering grin. "You need someone to shut off the defense grid so you can slip your ship out of orbit."

Noa's mouth fell open. What Ghost was proposing was next to impossible. The defense grid's passcodes would be a lot more secure than a mechanic's personnel files. His proposal was also so far out of left field that it left her speechless. Her eyes met James's. He'd been leaning against the geothermal converter, but now he'd taken a step forward. His head was cocked, and one eyebrow was up in an expression that she recognized by now. It clearly said,

"What is this crazy person thinking?"

Ghost bounced in his seat, drawing Noa's eyes back to him.

"Where do you plan to go? Which of the in-system colonies? There is Atlantia and Libertas ..." Ghost asked. His eyes narrowed and he raised a finger. "Oh, I know. Libertas is the most self-sufficient colony this side of the time gate. You'll hole up there. The local food, water, and oxygen should last another few decades." He nodded and smiled, as though pleased with himself. His eyes slid to the side. "With enough money, we could buy out Libertas's natives." His head bobbled, his smile remained frozen on his face, and his eyes slid back to Noa.

Noa blinked. Leaning forward, she said, "I have a better plan. One easier than turning off the defense grid. I'm going to bring the armada here. I just need someone who can get James and me to Time Gate 8, we'll send off a message and—"

Ghost started to giggle.

"What?" Noa said.

Wiping his eyes, Ghost said, "You're joking."

Noa's eyes slid to James, and both of them looked at Ghost.

Ceasing his manic giggles, Ghost's gaze flitted between them. "You really don't know?"

"Know what?" asked Noa.

"Silly woman," Ghost said. "There are no more flights to Time Gate 8. There are no flights out of atmosphere, period." His head bobbed, and he looked away. "Well, except for the contingent of the local armada surrounding the station in a Mexican standoff. They periodically refuel and do supply runs."

Noa's mind reeled. Without Time Gate 8, it would take a Fleet ship nearly ten years to reach Luddeccea at light speed from Time Gate 7 … if they left right away. Her brow constricted. And they wouldn't leave right away—a mission of that scope would take months of planning. She shook her head. There had to be a way to reclaim Time Gate 8. "Have terrorists taken over the gate?" Noa asked.

Ghost blinked at Noa. And then he said, "Aliens have control of Time Gate 8." His eyes went to James, and she had an uneasy feeling in her gut.

Noa tilted her head and said sharply, "That's Luddeccean lunacy. None of the Fleet intel has any indication of space-going sentient races—energy beings or not. You're too smart to believe that, Ghost."

Ghost shifted in his seat and dropped his eyes. "I didn't believe it at first, Noa. But the evidence, it's indisputable—the energy beings, they've taken over the station." He met her gaze, and his eyes were pleading. "I have access to Luddeccean intel. The station's personnel, the travelers, hardly any of them escaped during the takeover. If it hadn't been for a Luddeccean agent who planted a plasma detonator on the station long enough to temporarily damage the gate's self defense mechanisms, no one would have escaped at all. As it was, well, Time Gate 8's portal functionality was permanently disabled along with it. The gate's defenses were temporarily shut down—just long enough for some vessels to escape the station."

Noa's jaw went slack. All the words he said had registered, and yet they weren't fitting together in her head.

She was vaguely aware of James asking, "When did this happen?" Ghost gave a reply, and James said, "Be more specific. I need to know when … to the hour, and minute, and second."

Noa was dumbstruck. The station was under control of an alien force shooting ships from the sky? How could something like that happen without the Fleet having some inkling beforehand? It was too big, too much. There would have been signs. She had been privy to every suspected first contact, and all had come to nothing.

"That is impossible," she dimly heard James say. "The station could not have been under alien control at that time—"

"The meteor showers," Noa exclaimed, lifting her head. She hadn't realized she'd dropped her face into her hands. "They aren't natural, are they?"

Ghost turned to her with a sidelong glance at James. "No. Of course not. That is the station knocking ships out of the sky." He looked at a point on the floor just before her feet. "And the self-defense grid knocking down people trying to escape Luddeccea and head to Libertas, or other in-system colonies."

"The self-defense forces are knocking down people trying to get off world?" James asked.

Ghost cleared his throat. "And anyone trying to re-enter. All off-planet trade has been suspended. You didn't know?"

James mutely shook his head.

Noa dragged her hands down her face, her body feeling heavier and colder by the minute. "We have to let the Fleet know what is going on. We have to bring them here."

Ghost sighed. "Even at light speed, without a functional jump gate it will take ten years for the Fleet to get here from Time Gate 7."

"There's another," Noa said.

"Another what?" James asked.

Ghost's eyes went wide. "They have one? In this system? Why haven't they used it?"

Noa massaged her temples. "It went offline a few weeks ago."

"What went offline?" James asked.

"There's another time gate," Ghost said. His security

clearance hadn't been high enough to know its exact location, but he must have heard rumors that they existed.

"Another time gate?" said James.

Noa let out a breath. "Military only." It wasn't something civilians were generally privy to—or even all Fleet personnel. The Fleet had hidden gates in every inhabited system that was part of the Republic … and in some systems that technically weren't part of the Republic, or even inhabited.

Ghost shook his head, very fast, causing the loose skin near his chin to jiggle. "We can't use it, Noa. What if it was taken over by the same aliens who—"

"There are no aliens!" Noa said. "The weapon systems on Time Gate 8 are malfunctioning, or there are terrorists, or it's all a ruse that the Luddeccean government is using as an excuse to seize control."

"Noa … " James said, his voice a whisper.

"Then how do you explain—" Ghost said.

Noa closed her eyes. "Even if this Time Gate 8 is … " She waved a hand. "Possessed, the military time gate is a possibility. It is at the edge of the Kanakah Cloud. It was struck by a large asteroid according to its video feeds."

"They could have been faked," James said, his voice hushed.

"It wasn't faked," Noa said. "We have confirmation from more than one source. A repair mission was in the planning stages."

"If it's not functional—" Ghost sputtered.

"You can fix it, Ghost!" Noa exclaimed. "And escaping this system would be better than holing up on Libertas until their food runs out." She leaned closer. "And you know it will. The colony may be self-sufficient, but it won't be sufficient to feed all the miners in the asteroid belts in this system."

Ghost's mouth snapped shut. She saw his Adam's apple

bob. And then he nodded and his voice became confident. "Yes, of course I could fix it, if it is at all fixable." His beady eyes narrowed. "I still want to be paid."

James interjected, "Do we even have a ship?" and Noa resisted the urge to wince.

Ghost looked at James and then back at Noa.

"I've got a ship," she said.

"You do?" said James.

Ghost sniffed and sat back in his chair. "I can tell this is going to cost you," he said.

"I have a ship in mind," said Noa.

"In mind?" said Ghost.

"One that we will have to steal," James said, rolling his eyes.

Noa's lips pursed. She really shouldn't be surprised that he'd put that together … still …

Ghost looked at James sharply. One of Ghost's eyebrows rose, and then he looked back to Noa. "Is that true?"

"Steal is a harsh word," said Noa. "We'd actually be appropriating a ship and utilizing it for its intended mission … keeping the people of Luddeccea safe."

Ghost squinted at her and frowned. James's eyes widened. She knew that look. He understood what she was getting at, and moreover …

Rolling up his sleeves, exposing tattoo-stained skin, he stepped toward her. "No, no, no … "

"It's the best option," Noa countered.

James raised an arm in the direction they just came. "When you do something … " His hand made a fist. " … ridiculous, and you somehow manage to not die, do you think to yourself, 'I made a mistake, how can I possibly get myself killed next time?'"

Noa sniffed. Typical professor, using too many words when one or two would do. Death wish, she wanted to say, the words you're looking for are death wish.

James took another step closer. "You can barely—"

Noa thought of barely making it down the steps, of struggling to keep up with him. She waited for James to say any of that, but his eyes shot to Ghost, and back to Noa, and his jaw snapped shut, his blue eyes boring into hers. She exhaled in relief. He didn't want to reveal how weak she was.

"Noa ..." He tilted his head. "You can't do this."

A moment ago, she'd thought he understood her. Something inside her shattered, but she straightened her spine. "I have to do this ... I have to try."

Clearing his throat, Ghost looked hesitantly between James and Noa. "Have to do what?"

Noa's jaw tightened. Telling Ghost her plan would mean that if he was captured by the authorities, there would be no way to pull it off. On the other hand ... malignant narcissist though he might be, Ghost was a genius, and he had built the Luddecceans' new main computer. If anyone could shut off the defense grid and help her pull off what she wanted to do now, it would have to be Ghost. He'd need to start preparing as soon as possible.

Before she'd made up her mind how much to reveal, James gave it away. "She plans to steal the Ark."

Ghost choked on his own spit.

CHAPTER EIGHT

"The Ark," Ghost sputtered, "No ... no ... no ... that is just as illogical as ... " He waved at James with a finger. " ... suggests."

Ghost didn't use James's name, or even say "your friend." It sent ripples of static beneath James's skin. He suspected James was ... something else. He felt a cold settling in the pit of his stomach. The time table for his escape from Time Gate 8 was wrong. He'd left a full day after the explosion that had briefly incapacitated Gate 8's defenses, and the shuttle he'd been in was not the type that could hover in orbit for extended periods.

"His name is James Sinclair," Noa snapped. "Professor Sinclair if you must."

James looked up and found her glaring at Ghost, arms crossed. The sharp angles of the gesture highlighted how emaciated she was. He couldn't let her die ...

Ghost snorted. "Professor?"

James blinked at him. "I'm a history professor." The words felt hollow, wrong, abstract, and a jumble.

"Really?" said Ghost.

"Ask him about his time capsules," Noa said, her voice dry.

Ghost leaned forward in his seat. "Time capsules?"

James lifted his chin. He had a speech for that. "Time capsules were popular on old Earth. I discovered a town along the San Andreas rift that had been— "

"Stop!" said Noa. She spun to Ghost. "We don't have time to talk about time capsules." She waved a hand. "Or hero arcs from the mov-ees within the time capsules."

James's mouth fell open and then snapped shut. It was true, the speech he had in his mind lasted for nearly fifty-five minutes. Every word was memorized, but none felt real. The passion behind them was gone—stolen by the need to stay alive, maybe?

Massaging her temple, Noa groaned. "Focus, D—Ghost. The Ark is perfect." She sat up straighter in her chair, and as her body unwound, it made her look frailer instead of stronger. She was still painfully thin.

"It has near light speed capabilities," Noa continued, her form becoming animated, her face glowing in her excitement and giving her an illusion of health. "Its hull is robust enough to withstand deep space travel and time surfing once we get to the Kanakah Gate. It is kept stocked with decades' worth of S-rations, it can lift out of orbit without any planet-side assistance; and, even if its offensive weapons are worth their weight in meezle guano, the aft cannon was designed to crack large asteroids and should be enough to temporarily disable any ships from the armada in our path."

James took a step back, closer to the soothing warmth of the geothermal generator. He wondered if anyone could be as logically unreasonable as Noa; she almost had him convinced. He had rolled up his sleeves, almost unconsciously, and now he ran his fingers over the dark stains. Was she being unreasonable? If the Fleet couldn't come by Time Gate 8, it would take them ten years to get to Luddeccea from the nearest other portal, Time Gate 7 … if they didn't get the military gate open, that was. Ten years was a long time to survive on the run planet side, but was taking the Ark to a hidden gate really a viable option?

Even as a non-native of Luddeccea, James knew about the Ark. It was the vessel that had brought the first colonists to Luddeccea. It was over 300 years old, but it was kept in working order by Republic law. In the event of an emergency, it could, theoretically, be used to help evacuate civilians. It would be more than adequate for a ride to the edge of the Kanakah Cloud. Even if they couldn't make the military gate operational, the Ark was stocked with enough provisions to get them to Time Gate 7. But …

Ghost thumped his chest as though trying to clear something from his lungs. "No, no, no. Stealing the Ark would be ludicrous!" He shook his head. "You're wasting my time."

Standing, Noa stepped toward the small man. "Ghost, it's our best hope … and think about it. No one would expect anyone to steal the Ark."

James had been to the museum that housed the Ark as a child. It was located in a courtyard between the museum and the spaceport spokes of the Tri-Center building. While waiting for their flight, his family had passed the time exploring the Ark's cramped living quarters and the museum's exhibits. At one point James had even peered down the long hallway that led past the massive security that kept tourists and travelers out of the Central Authority wing. No one uninvited went there; it was where all local civilian and military operations were coordinated.

James took a step away from the geothermal unit's heat. "Because there is no more heavily guarded location on the planet than the Tri-Center."

Noa put her hands behind her back. She opened her mouth … and no sound came out. She took a deep breath. "Technically, it's only close to the most secure location on the planet."

James crossed his arms.

Tilting her head, Noa said, "However, the Ark's not in the secure wing."

Clearing his throat, Ghost said, "Commander, the spaceport is swarming with troops right now. They don't want anyone leaving."

"Are there any more troops than usual in the museum wing?" Noa asked.

A strange look came to Ghost's eyes. "No."

Noa rolled her hands, as though urging Ghost to say more. "And if there is any sort of disturbance in the area, where is the Central Authority most likely to concentrate their forces?"

Ghost's eyes went wide. "The spaceport and Central Authority."

"Exactly," said Noa.

Ghost rubbed his chin. "Huh."

"There are guards at the museum," James protested.

Noa's eyes narrowed. "You've been to it?"

"My father took me there when I was a little boy," James said, the memory hazy and dull in his mind. "I remember one of those guards talking to me—"

Noa sighed. "If he was any spacer officer worth his salt, he wouldn't be chatting with little kids while he was on duty."

"But—" James started to protest.

Noa's voice was soft. "Unless they were hired on more as tour guides." She looked away. "They are practically civilians."

"This might just work," Ghost murmured.

Noa nodded. "The men posted around the Ark are for the most part semi-retired members of the Luddeccea Local Guard. If I'm right, it's the least guarded deep space vessel on the whole planet." Her eyes slid to Ghost.

The little man was nodding, his beady eyes wide. "Yes,

yes, you're right." His pupils seemed to lose focus for a moment, and then began moving rapidly back and forth. Ghost was mentally accessing some data, obviously. James met Noa's eyes. Her chin was lowered, as though daring him to say something. He didn't look away, but he didn't know what to say, either. Her plan could get them killed— but so would staying on Luddeccea. His mind tumbled over all the odds and obstacles. He searched his data banks for a Prime street map—and miraculously found one. He began plotting distances in his mind, eyes still on Noa's.

Ghost giggled, interrupting their stare down and James's thoughts. "During a local emergency the museum guards' primary job is to help evacuate civilians." Ghost smiled. "They most likely won't even be there if we manage to trip an alarm."

James's head jerked, another obstacle coming to his mind. "The Ark is over 300 years old. It doesn't operate by even local ethernet ... Who will fly it?"

Putting a hand over her chest, Noa said, "Me, of course. I've flown the Andromeda; it's the same model as the Ark."

James searched his data banks. The Andromeda was the same class of ship. He tilted his head. They'd still need to get into the museum complex. Which seemed doubtful ...

Ghost frowned. "How did you get to fly the Andromeda?"

Waving a hand, Noa smiled. "Admiral Sung took me aboard when it was docked off Venus."

"Sung," Ghost muttered. His eyes narrowed at Noa. James found himself stepping toward Ghost, his hands curling into fists. Ghost's eyes darted to James, and he flinched and looked away. "She blocked my promotion," he said in a tremulous voice.

James realized he was on a trajectory toward the little man without even thinking on it. He stopped mid-stride.

"I had nothing to do with it," Noa said. "You know that."

Ghost shook his head and sniffed. "The Ark's a big ship. You would need a crew."

James wondered if flying 300-year-old ships was one of his undiscovered abilities. He blinked … and couldn't even draw up schematics for the bridge.

Noa cocked her head. "Give me access to the population records. I'll find members of the Fleet who are desperate to get off this rock."

"That will cost you," Ghost said, straightening in his seat. "I do have other options, other people who need to get off this planet, who can pay me much better."

Noa leaned forward. "What good is money going to do you in this system? Libertas is going to be hopping with food riots within months as asteroid miners flood in. That planet is so poor their Local Guard is made up of bare-ly-trained, part-time volunteers. They won't be able to protect you, Ghost."

James's gaze flicked between the two Fleet officers. Steal-ing the Ark would be riskier in the short run, but in the long run it could have the highest reward. He wasn't sure whether or not he wanted Noa to succeed in this bargain with Ghost.

"I don't want to wind up on Earth a beggar!" Ghost snapped. "All of my savings are here." Looking down his nose at Noa, he said, "Which reminds me, I want to be paid in Galactic Credits, not Luddeccean currency."

"How much do you want?" Noa said.

Ghost swallowed. Instead of answering, he said, "Also, you need to get the funds within three days."

James blinked. "Why?"

Ghost's eyes slid between Noa and James. "Because the Luddecceans have begun outfitting patrols with instanta-neous DNA identification kits. They aren't tied to the ethernet, so all offenders' DNA has to be downloaded to the kits on a regular basis." Looking at the floor, he muttered, "Time consuming and wasteful … clunky bits of machinery … but blasted things would be beyond my control to hack into between uploads." Shaking his head, he looked up at Noa. "They already have you and me on file, no doubt, and the attention we drew at Hell's Crater will have them scanning the booth. They'll know we were there … " His eyes slid to James and narrowed. "And they may have their eyes out for you, too."

James's brows rose. If the Guard weren't aware it was Noa and him at the bar, they would be soon, and then they'd be on alert for them here, not in the Northwest Province. Even Ghost's holographic disguises—

"Even your holographic disguises aren't going to work then, Ghost," Noa said. "So let's not waste time. Give us access to your files so I can retrieve Fleet members' names and addresses."

James's apps started working again. There was a side entrance to the museum complex labeled as a pedestrian path—

"I'm not giving you access to my files until you pay me," Ghost said.

Jaw hard, Noa asked, "How much do you want?"

"50,000 credits," Ghost replied.

The apps in James's brain stopped working. His head whipped to Ghost. The man was playing with them.

"15,000 now," Noa said. "10,000 when we reach Sol System."

"20,000 now," said Ghost. "20,000 when we reach Sol."

"15,000 now," said Noa. "15,000 when we reach Sol. That's my final offer."

Ghost shifted in his seat.

Stepping closer to him, Noa said, "It's the best offer you're going to get. 50,000 credits isn't going to go far when Libertas erupts in food riots."

Shoulders tight, Ghost drew his arms across his chest. "If we survive stealing the Ark."

Noa waved a hand. "We'll be fine once we reach light speed."

It was nearly impossible to track ships at near light speed. They would move faster than they could be traced. And there was the issue of time distortion, too. Time would move much faster on the Ark than it would on Luddeccea, causing all sorts of logistical problems for pursuit. James rolled his eyes. Once again, Noa was being truthful, but was omitting important details … like how they were going to get 15,000 credits in under three days.

CHAPTER NINE

In the darkness of Prime's sewers, Noa stumbled, and instantly felt James's hand on her arm. Water dripped in the distance. Her locator app said 400 meters to the left, but with the echo in Luddeccea in the cement channels, it was hard to tell. She brushed away James's hand, more out of habit than conviction. She was shaking, exhausted, and strung out. She wasn't sure if it was because she'd pushed herself too far physically so soon after leaving the camp—or if she was just overwhelmed by all she had to do.

"One foot at a time, Noa," she muttered. "It could be worse."

Ghost hadn't given them new disguises, but he had at least given her and James data chips with maps of the sewer system. The tropical city received heavy amounts of rain during the late winter months. Right now there was only a tiny trickle down the center of the tunnel, but in a few more weeks the place would be flooded. In spring, summer, fall, and early winter, Prime was bone dry. The first and second wave settlers had built an elaborate tunnel and cistern system to handle the alternating flooding and drought. Noa and James had traveled four blocks unhindered by Luddeccea's Guard, but Ghost had warned that the Guard kept watch over sensitive areas—beneath the spaceport, government buildings, and official residences—and had even begun sporadic patrols beneath Port of Call. For that reason they were using James's augmented vision, and the occasional street lights filtering through manholes, to find their way.

She listened for sounds of human footsteps, but she didn't hear even the skitter of rats. James, a dark shadowy shape beside her, whispered, "I suppose you have a plan for acquiring 15,000 credits," and the break in the near silence was such a relief she almost laughed. She'd expected he'd ask that a lot sooner. Instead, he'd just followed her. A cough from her own lungs surprised her before she could answer.

"Does it involve storming the Tri-Center's secure wing?" he asked. In the dimness it was hard to see, but she had the impression that his jaw was shifting in an attempt to smile, and he'd lifted an eyebrow.

Thumping her chest, she summoned a smirk. "What if it did?" She had to stay cocky, optimistic, brave …

James drew to a stop. She could just barely make out his features in the dark. "Don't joke." A hover rumbled softly overhead, and the sound echoed through a drain.

She wanted to return with a witty rejoinder. A joke was always appropriate when you were going to steal the Ark, which even she could admit was almost a suicide mission. Her stomach was tying in knots, but the thought of thousands—maybe millions of people if James was right—tortured and dying kept her going. If she didn't laugh at times like these, she would go mad with the weight of it all. Instead of laughing, she coughed, and the force of it was like nails hitting her lungs.

"Noa," James said. "I need to know what your plan is. If I don't know what the plan is, I can't calculate the odds of its success."

Noa suddenly didn't feel like joking. Her blood went cold. "Calculate the odds of success?" Her jaw dropped, and her face twisted in disgust. "Some things are worth more than any odds."

"I don't want to throw our lives away," James snapped.

"It's not throwing your life away if it's the right thing to do," Noa said, feeling a burn in her lungs; she didn't know whether it was from the coughing, or the heat of anger.

James's head cocked. "Yes, it is."

His voice was too even, and maybe it was the dim light of the sewers but he looked completely emotionless. Alarm bells went off in her mind. She thought of the man he'd killed on the train, of the way he'd dispassionately said he'd kill Ghost, and of the way Ghost kept subtly alluding to James not being human. It would explain his dispassion, his apathy ...

She felt herself tremble with rage, not weariness. No, James wasn't an alien. He was worse. He was a spoiled Earthling who let himself be protected by a Fleet disproportionately made up of Luddecceans and people from the newer worlds—people whose lives weren't so sheltered that they forgot that some things were worth dying for.

"If that's what you believe, then go!" Noa hissed. "These tunnels can take you right out of Prime!"

James didn't move, but his fists balled at his sides.

And Noa had had enough—of his looking for every flaw, for his cowardice, laziness, apathy, or whatever the solar cores it was that would let him turn away from the suffering of millions.

Flinging up her arm, pointing to the nearest exit from the city, Noa hissed, "Go!"

***

"Go!"

The word hit James like a physical blow. His mind went still, and his vision flickered. And then his neurons roared to life, and it was like an alarm had gone off in his mind and body and every nano and cell was screaming, "Fail-

169

ure!"

He wavered on his feet. Noa stood before him, staring up at him, brows drawn, lips curled. All he could see was her, whether because of a fluke of his augmented vision that tunneled in the dark, or because … because …

"Get moving!" Noa said.

He couldn't leave her. He'd never been able to leave her, and now he could only stand helplessly trying to formulate a way to make this better. He didn't think millions were worth dying for. But it occurred to him that he would die for her—not precisely happily, or bravely—he just couldn't help himself. But he didn't think that would reassure her.

Noa's head whipped around into the gloom, and she took a step back.

Before James could say a word, she threw up a hand and motioned for silence. And then he heard it, a soft thumping too light to be human. It was followed by a light cheeping.

"Rats?" he whispered.

Shaking her head in the negative, Noa padded off in the direction of the sound. James followed. Ten steps later, the source of the noise became apparent. In a beam of streetlight fractured by a manhole cover, a small, serpentine creature swayed back and forth like a cobra. As they drew closer, he saw it was less like a serpent, and more like an Earth ermine. It had large eyes and tufted ears, with dirty gray fur that might be white if it were clean. It had ten limbs, and was currently standing on the back four, its other tiny paws curled to its belly.

His mind searched his data banks and he found a match for the creature. His nanos piped: "Werfle, name derived from English 'Weasel' — extremely rare, venomous, native to Luddeccea, master escape artists. Omnivorous, but favors meat. Population has grown since rats have become an invasive species on Luddeccea. Sometimes semi-domesticated. Experimental data on cognitive ability not available as Luddeccea has outlawed animal experimentation."

James had never seen a werfle before. He was struck by how high its forehead was, and how the large eyes met his almost appraisingly.

Noa sat on her heels, and the creature dropped to all ten legs. When it hopped cautiously toward her, it used only its front and hind-most limb pairs, the middle three pairs curled up to its stomach. He thought he'd heard werfles could carry their prey with their middle limbs for many kilometers.

Noa took off the outer jacket of the train uniform and held it before her like a hammock. James's eyes widened, realizing what she intended. "They're venomous!" he said.

Noa snorted as the creature hopped into the outstretched fabric. "Did you notice he's wearing a collar? His venom has already been milked."

James blinked. Sure enough, the werfle wore a thin red collar around its neck.

"Someone's pet," Noa murmured, looking down at the tiny form rolling onto its back in her arms. "But he's in bad shape."

On its back, the creature opened its mouth wide and made a high-pitched cry. James noted that he could see its ribs through its sparse, dirty fur.

Noa murmured, "I know you're hungry, little one." She sighed. "You lost your family, didn't you? And there aren't any more rats in the sewers." She wrapped the creature in her jacket so only its head was exposed, pulled it to her stomach, and ran a long dark finger down its exposed chin.

Without looking at James, she stood up. "What are you still doing here? You think stealing the Ark is 'illogical,' and are afraid of stealing 15,000 credits from the Central Authority."

The darkness in James's vision returned … He lifted his eyes from the softly sighing werfle to Noa. He almost asked if she intended to keep the animal, and then stopped himself. He felt as though gears were clicking into place in his mind. Of course she'd keep it. She surmised it had lost its family. It was starving. It was her.

It was a needless burden that she shouldn't take on. He could confront her and they could fight about it, and she could demand once again that he go. And he wouldn't be able to.

Meeting her eyes, he sighed. "I don't believe that stealing the Ark is completely illogical." He looked up at the dark cement ceiling above their heads. "I think it is near suicidal … but since learning that the time gate has been disabled, I realize staying here would be suicidal, too." He felt a flair of static and irritation beneath his skin. "I can't think of a better ship to buy or steal."

Noa looked up at him for the first time since she picked up the animal. Her finger ceased rubbing its chin.

"I will help you steal the Ark," James said.

Noa's jaw tightened. "I don't need your help."

In her arms, the werfle made another soft cry of hunger. Noa soothed it with her finger.

James blinked down at it, and searched his data banks. Although they preferred meat, werfle "chow" was often made with soy. Searching his pocket, he pulled out one of the remaining soybeans from Hell's Crater. He offered one to the tiny beast. It sniffed his finger cautiously, but then took the proffered bean. "You need all the help you can get," James said.

Noa's shoulders fell. She watched the creature noisily chew the soy bean. After two minutes and thirty seconds she said, "Fine, let's go."

It was two more blocks before James dared to speak to

Noa again. "Please tell me acquiring the 15,000 credits doesn't involve raiding Central Authority … not that I am not committed to stealing the Ark, but maybe we could come up with a better way to get the money?"

Noa snorted. "Do you really think the Central Authority would have 15,000 Galactic Credits lying around?"

James blinked in the darkness. Of course they wouldn't. It wasn't a bank. Far in the distance he heard water dripping. He remembered the intense feeling of failure that had radiated through his very being just minutes ago. "It was all hypothetical," he murmured.

"I'd do it if I had to," Noa said. "But I was planning on borrowing the money from a friend."

James cocked his head toward her. Noa gave him what she'd informed him back in the freight car was her "patented cornball grin." He'd had to explain that cornball was not a sport. In her arms, the werfle purred. Rolling his eyes, James looked away.

"I think I'll name him Fluffy," Noa said.

Irritation flickered under his skin again in a buzz of static. "He isn't fluffy, his fur is short. That name doesn't even make sense."

"They are fluffy when they're kits," Noa said. "We named our werfles Fluffy back on our farm."

"You named more than one werfle Fluffy? How is that even practical? They wouldn't know which one you were calling."

"Not at the same time!" Noa whispered. "After the first died, we named the second werfle Fluffy. That way we didn't slip up and call werfle number two Fluffy, when his name was actually Rex, or Spot or something. Calling him by a dead werfle's name would have been rude and weird."

"But technically, you were calling him by the dead werfle's name," James protested, feeling the static again.

"Fluffy was the dead werfle's name even if it was also werfle number two's name."

Noa huffed. "Fine, if you don't like Fluffy, choose another name."

James looked down at the creature. After eating the soybeans, it had rolled over on its back. Snuggled against Noa's stomach as she rubbed its chin, its lips seemed to stretch in a smile. Irritation flared beneath his skin like static. "I wouldn't even think you'd like werfles. They look like rats."

Noa's eyes went wide and she gasped. "They look nothing like rats. Their noses aren't long and pointy, their eyes aren't small and beady, they're clean—well, when they have access to clean water, they're clean. Their tails aren't naked, and they don't eat people." She lifted the creature to her nose. "They eat rats. They're cute, they're friendly, and they're intelligent—smartest creature on Luddeccea—at least as smart as ravens as far as anyone can tell."

James swore the creature's smile actually grew wider as it touched its nose to Noa's. The static beneath James's skin turned to heat. "Fine, call it Carl Sagan if it's so smart."

"Carl Sagan?" said Noa.

"Twentieth-century scientist," James muttered, looking away from the whiskered snout of the werfle. "He theorized that there was intelligent life in the universe, just that it hadn't visited us."

"Carl Sagan," said Noa. He could hear the smile in her voice, and the world lightened. "I like it."

The creature purred. Noa beamed up at James, and he wanted to smile back despite himself.

They approached an intersection in the sewers. Looking above, Noa said, "We're almost there." She frowned, and he saw some emotion flicker across her face. Worry, maybe?

"This person you're going to ask for a loan, do you think they'll turn us in?" James asked.

Noa shot him a glare.

"I have to ask," he said.

Noa looked away. "No, it's not that." Her shoulders fell. "I'm actually more concerned about whether Ghost will be able to shut off the defense grid. If he can't, this is all for nothing." Her brow furrowed. "I know he built the new main computer, so he'd know the weaknesses; but he'll have to exploit the weaknesses through a landline … which is slower, if you explained it to me correctly. And he isn't as smart as he thinks he is."

James's head tilted. She'd said something similar before. "He created the holographic necklaces."

Noa snorted. "They are tricks of the light."

"I think you underestimate their sophistication," James said.

Noa's jaw became set. She lifted her chin. "No, I don't underestimate it. I've known real geniuses, my little brother …" Her voice trailed off and her jaw softened. "Ghost … he doesn't have the tenacity to put his mind to work. In the Fleet, as soon as he had a disagreement with someone, or he thought someone didn't kiss his behind enough, he'd say he was being underutilized and ask to be transferred. There is a lot of hard work behind genius and invention. Only to a real genius, like my brother, it's not work, it's compulsion. Kenji, he can seem dismissive sometimes, but it's just that he's wrapped up in his own brain, and he sometimes forgets other people exist … but he's actually humble, and if you ask him to explain something in a way mere mortals can understand, he will. He's excited to share his passions with everyone."

James didn't know what to say. He never did when she spoke of her brother. Talking about Kenji always made Noa quieter. It made her fidget with the stumps of her fingers, and her eyes drift away.

"Kenji discovered that fifteen percent of Time Gate 8's power expenditure was unnecessary," Noa whispered softly. Her thumb grazed the place where her fingers used to be. "The thing has been hanging in the sky for a hundred years, and some of its auto maintenance features have built themselves up to be so big—they actually built in unintentional redundancies. He was working on fixing that … " She took a breath. "He'd been stationed planet-side … " Her brow furrowed. "He wouldn't have been on the station when the explosions happened." He heard her swallow and saw her lips turn down. "I don't think."

She drew to a halt beneath a manhole, a ladder beneath it on the wall. Tucking the bundle that was Carl Sagan into her shirt, she said, "We're here."

"I can go first," James suggested, but she was already scaling the ladder.

CHAPTER TEN

As James crept after Noa in the darkness of a small side street, he heard footsteps, the murmur of voices, and shouts from patrols. Closer to him, he heard Noa's breathing. It was too loud and too fast. Still, she didn't hesitate as she guided him around a corner. They were in a neighborhood a few kilometers beyond Port of Call. The buildings were still stucco, but they were surrounded by high- wrought iron fences covered with red-leaved ivy and bright white and yellow flowers. Most had at least one hover parked on the rooftop between solar cell wind turbines.

Noa reached a gate in a fence that looked no different from the rest. "There should be a buzzer … " Noa muttered, gently probing among the flowering vines as Carl Sagan peeked out the neck of her shirt. A moment later, James heard the sound of a doorbell ringing in the home beyond. And then there was silence … for two minutes and forty-five seconds.

"This person—"

"Eliza."

"How well do you know her?" James whispered.

"We're practically family," Noa whispered. "Great, great, great, great aunt thrice removed."

The answer didn't fill James with confidence. Fifty meters down the street there came the shout of a patrol.

"Could she have been arrested?" James asked as another precious thirty seconds went by. He scanned the small street for a manhole and saw none.

"She was one of the original settlers," Noa whispered back. "They couldn't have possibly arrested her."

"One of the first settlers?" James protested. "But that would make her—"

"Really, really old," Noa finished.

"And a fanatic!" James whispered back.

"Ahhhh … " Noa winced. "No … sometimes we wished she were. She has some eccentricities … "

"What kind of eccentricities?" James said.

Noa turned to him, her mouth opened, but before any sound came out a beam of light at the intersection caught James's eye. Arm looping around Noa's waist, he pressed her and himself into the ivy. Her dark eyes widened and met his.

"We can climb the fence," James whispered.

Noa shook her head. "No, there are alarms. Would draw even more attention."

At the intersection, someone called out, "I think I see someone! You there, show yourselves."

"Nebulas," Noa hissed.

"Fight or flight?" James said, hand tightening on her waist. Noa closed her eyes. A flashlight beam caressed the curve of her back just peeking out from the flowers and leaves. James ducked his head into the space of her shoulder and neck and breathed deep, his arm tightened around her.

Noa didn't answer.

"You there," the man called again. "I see you." James could see the flashlight beam bouncing. He counted no fewer than six pairs of footsteps. He remembered the laser pistols of the Guard in the bar. At that thought, a red spotter beam grazed the ivy above Noa's head and began to drop. James took a deep breath. He wanted to explode from his skin. He felt trapped in a nightmare, knowing what would happen and helpless to do anything about it. The tracer dropped to a centi from her head … and then there was a creak of metal and darkness came too quickly for James's vision to adapt.

"Quick, inside," a raspy voice whispered.

James blinked. The gate had opened between them and the approaching patrol, and a stooped figure was standing there, wobbling on a cane. He blinked again, and two exceptionally bright blue eyes came into focus. The eyes were situated in a face more wrinkled and worn than any he had ever seen.

"Halt!" cried the patrol officer. James heard the troops break into a run.

Before he could gather his wits, Noa pulled him through the gate into the garden between the ivy- covered fence and a lavender stucco home. The gate slammed behind them. From the house came the thunderous sound of a piano playing the opening to Carlos Chen's Time Gate Ten Overture. Behind him, he heard the woman cry in a warbling voice, "Fluffy! Fluffy! Where are you!"

James blinked. He felt Noa lean against him, the barest soft touch of her breast against his upper arm, and the faintest brush of her breath against his ear. His body went warm, his vision lightened, and gravity seemed to dissipate. What was the reason for this sudden intimacy? It struck him that he didn't care.

"Fluffy is a popular name for pets in our family, " Noa whispered and then pulled away from him.

The lightness in the vision dissipated. His skin prickled, and he would have frowned at her if he could have. The Guard was so close and she was joking?

Noa grabbed his hand and pulled him toward the house. A patrol man outside the gate shouted, "Hands above your head!" The Guard was only a few meters away now.

The old woman cried, "Oh, Officers, thank goodness you're here! Have you seen my cat?"

James glanced down at his feet, trying to walk as silently as he could. He saw a pathway of sparkling recycled glass beads beneath his feet. His and Noa's feet crunched slightly as they walked—no, stalked—but thankfully, the piano music covered the noise. On either side of them were walls of pink and lavender flowers as high as his head. They were headed toward the steps of a back stoop encrusted with a blue mosaic set into white stone. A door atop the stoop was open to a kitchen from which the piano music poured, and warm yellow light glowed. Just before they reached the steps, a voice, young and male, whispered from the wall of flowers to their left. "This way, quickly. Eliza says they'll ask to come inside next, and she doesn't want us to be found."

Noa dragged James in the direction of the voice down a path so narrow James wouldn't have seen it if they hadn't been right beside it. The path curved around to the side of the house. He quickly found himself staring over Noa's shoulder into the darkness of a door, just slightly ajar. He was completely unable to see inside, although the tops of the flowers were well-lit by the kitchen light. Apparently, his augmented vision had trouble adjusting to sudden differences in brightness.

"Ma'am?" said another officer, less than five meters behind him just beyond the fence laden with ivy and head-high flowers.

"She's a brown and black tortoise shell," the old woman continued.

"I thought I saw someone hiding in the vines, Sir," said the man who'd spotted them.

"Ohhh!" squealed the old woman. "That was her, that was her!"

"Are you sure, Ma'am?" said someone else just before James and Noa stooped to enter the darkened door. James's vision slowly adjusted, and he found himself in what might have been a gardener's shed, except it was set into the main building of the house. In front of him was a wall of old-fashioned pruning equipment, shovels and spades of every sort, rakes, gloves, aprons, and little houses he estimated were for the pteranodon-like creatures that flew in Luddeccea's skies.

He heard the door click behind them, and the male voice said, "I'll show you the way."

James turned toward the man and his eyes went wide. Striding through the shed toward the wall of gardening supplies was a young man with Mediterranean features too symmetrical to be natural. He appeared to be wearing only a pink apron. The man strode by them … and … he was only wearing a pink apron.

Apparently unconcerned with his nudity, the man went to the wall and lifted a spade. The wall opened with a click. Turning to James and Noa, he beckoned with a hand and whispered, "This way, Noa."

"I can barely see, Sixty," Noa said.

"Oh, it is dark," the man who was apparently "Sixty" answered. "But Eliza told me not to turn on the light until you were inside the safe room." The man stood ramrod straight by the door without a word after that statement.

"Maybe if you gave me your hand, Sixty?" Noa suggested.

"Of course," said Sixty, lifting an arm James could not help but notice was well-muscled.

James's vision darkened. Guiding Noa past Sixty, he said, "I can see fine," even if at that moment he couldn't.

Standing oddly still, Sixty didn't put down his hand as James led Noa into the narrow half meter-by-three meter space beyond. It was completely devoid of furniture, and there were handles set into the white-painted walls at regular intervals. James drew up short, the compact space making his neurons and nanos pulse in alarm.

"What is it?" Noa whispered.

"It's—"

The door to the garden tool room shut, a light flicked on, and white flashed behind James's eyes as they struggled to adjust. Noa's hand dropped from his and he felt her spin around.

"Sound and light proof!" exclaimed Sixty.

James turned around, rapidly blinking his eyes. As his eyes recovered, he found Sixty standing not ten centis from Noa's nose. The man was smiling brightly. Clutching the coat that contained Carl Sagan, now completely hidden in the folds of fabric, Noa stumbled back against James's chest with a yelp. James put a hand on her shoulder, and he heard her swallow.

"I was going to say cramped," James finished. He saw no sign of another exit.

"Please tell me you're wearing more than an apron, Sixty," Noa whined in a way quite unlike her.

"You know a lie would go against my programming," Sixty said. "And I was cooking—I have a new cooking app. Of course I would be wearing an apron." He looked up at James and held out his hand. "You haven't introduced me to your companion."

James stared down at the hand, an inkling beginning to form at the back of his mind.

Noa sighed. "James, this is Sixty—"

"6T9," the man corrected. "The number, the letter, and the number again." He smiled and winked.

James stared at the hand. The inkling in his mind became a 99.99% certainty.

"6T9," Noa said. "This is James."

"Hello, James," said 6T9, hand still outstretched. Looking to Noa, he said, "Noa, are you and James in a mutually exclusive sexual relationship?"

James's hand on Noa's shoulder tightened. He almost said "Yes," estimating it would end the line of questioning.

"Why are you asking?" Noa said.

Hand still outstretched, 6T9 said, "Because James is a fine specimen of the masculine gender. Sometimes Eliza likes it when I and—"

"Not interested." The words spilled from James's mouth in the same unconscious way he'd pulled the trigger in the forest, or kicked the man on the train.

Finally dropping his hand, 6T9 shrugged. "I have to ask. It's part of my programming. Please do not take offense."

"You are a ... " James could not bring himself to finish.

Noa sighed and rubbed her temples.

6T9 smiled. "A sex 'bot. A very high-end one." He winked again.

James echoed Noa's sigh. Most 'bots were designed with a function in mind, and being human- formed was rarely the most ideal for that function—whether it was cleaning a home, sailing through the clouds of gas giants, or doing archaeological digs. It took a lot of processing power to move like a human, smile like a human, and sound like a human when speaking. When you created a 'bot that could do all those things, you didn't leave a lot of room for processors that could do other things. Like thinking. Sex 'bots were designed for their primary function, and that involved looking like a human. James had heard that they were very good at their primary function, but he hadn't indulged. It was considered extremely gauche. However, it wasn't just that. He remembered being really drunk and telling a friend, "Even when I'm this pissed, as soon as they open their mouths, I feel let down and annoyed." He must have had some need to connect on an intellectual level ... His head jerked at the unconscious past tense. Not must have had. He was the same person, no matter how different that person sometimes felt. He looked at the vacant expression on the 'bot's face and felt a mild revulsion sparked by more than just his preference for women. Some things he still had in common with that other him.

6T9 lifted his head, as though hearing a far-off sound. "I am supposed to turn on the monitors to the rest of the house now." He turned around, exposing his back side.

"Couldn't you put on some clothes?" Noa groaned.

Grabbing a handle on the far wall, 6T9 looked over his shoulder. "You know I can wear clothes, Noa. And I am wearing an article of clothing." The 'bot's head tilted. "Was that a rhetorical question?"

"It was a request," James supplied, intensely irritated by the 'bot after only a few minutes.

"Oh," said 6T9, opening a cupboard and pulling out a hologlobe that had a tail of cords trailing from its underside into the wall. It was hardwired—of course, if the signal was transmitted wirelessly, it could be picked up with signal augmenters.

"I don't have any other clothes down here," 6T9 said. He turned around so only the front of his pink apron was showing and Noa muttered, "Thank you," and wiped her eyes.

"Whatever for?" said 6T9, the hologlobe flickering to life in his hand. Neither Noa nor James bothered to answer. They both turned their attention to the globe. In it, James saw the old woman he'd briefly seen before, apparently in her kitchen. With her were two Luddeccean Guard members. The woman's voice filled the room. "Would you boys like some fish stew?" James shifted agitatedly on his feet and looked up at the ceiling feeling as though it might fall on his head. She was suggesting they stay?

"Ma'am, we can't have any when we are on duty," said a man who appeared to have a lot of ribbons on his chest.

"But it smells delicious," said the other.

6T9 smiled. "It is delicious. I have a fantastic cooking app."

"Well, I'll do anything to help the fellows who find my cat," said the old woman.

"Why is she encouraging them to stay?" James asked.

"Where are the others?" asked Noa.

"Probably looking about the house," said 6T9.

The globe flickered again, and James was staring at what appeared to be a sitting room. One trooper was staring at a chess set. It was set up on a coffee table next to an enormous blue couch draped with a knitted afghan. Pieces were arranged on the board as though it had been halted mid-game.

"Ma'am, is there someone else in the house?" one of the troopers asked.

"Oh, no," Eliza's voice replied from out of the globe's glow. A moment later, she wobbled into view. "I was playing with a friend on Earth over the ethernet."

6T9 made a sound that sounded like a sigh. "I'm not a good enough player to offer her sufficient stimulation."

"Shame about those aliens, I may never finish my game," Eliza said breezily.

"Ma'am," one of the Patrolmen said, "I hope you've turned off your neural net."

"Turned it off?" said the old woman. "Son, I am one of the original settlers. I never fooled with any of that new-fangled gadgetry! I chat with my Earth friends via holo chat." She harrumphed, and the trooper actually tipped his helmet.

"Sorry, ma'am, just had to say so."

"There were more troopers," James said.

The globe flickered, and James was looking at two troopers in what looked to be a laundry room. "That's just to your left," said 6T9 cheerfully.

Before James could take a breath, the globe flickered again, and the gardening room came into view. There were two troopers in the room, stunners upraised. "And that," said 6T9, "is the room to your right."

"Shhhh … " said Noa.

In the globe, one of the troopers approached the wall of equipment and reached toward the wall.

"Oh," said 6T9, "perhaps they know we are here." James glanced up at the 'bot. His face was completely serene.

James's eyes dropped back to the globe just in time to see the trooper's fingers passing within inches of the spade. James found one of his hands balling into a fist, the other on Noa's back.

Instead of picking up the spade, the trooper picked up one of the pteranodon houses. Stunner upraised in his opposite hand, he turned to his companion and said, "This is really well done."

His companion shook his head and swung his flashlight beam around the room. "Don't take granny's ptery house."

"I wasn't going to," the first protested.

"Come on," said his companion. "There are still rooms to check upstairs."

The globe flickered once more, and James saw four troopers in the kitchen around a table eating bowls of soup. "This is really good!" said one.

"Undisciplined." Noa shook her head. "Eliza is still an old fox."

"Oh, yes, she is," said 6T9. "I call her my silver fox."

"Please don't tell me any more," Noa said, throwing up a hand.

"That comment wasn't gratuitous at all," said 6T9.

"But you wander off on gratuitous tangents all the time," Noa said. "And I'm trying to nip it in the bud."

6T9 tilted his head. "I like to nip—"

"Shut up," said Noa.

6T9's mouth snapped shut, and James found himself unexpectedly feeling pity for the 'bot. In the twenty-first century, humankind had hoped for so much from robots, androids, and AI—and feared so much, too. But that was before Moore's Law ran smack into Moore's Wall—significant improvements in computer processing power hadn't been made in centuries. Instead, humankind had plugged into perhaps the most sophisticated processor in the universe with nanos and neural nets … their own minds. Augmented with nano storage, and apps for memorization tasks and computations, humans could do all the feats they'd imagined AIs would do. 'Bots, on the other hand, seemed like simple humans.

A few breathless minutes later, in the hologlobe the Luddeccean patrolmen said goodbye to Eliza.

Her head bobbled, and she grinned and waved as they left—the perfect granny. As soon as she shut the door behind them, her demeanor changed completely. Her eyes went to slits. She looked directly up at one of the cameras and shook her cane.

"That is the sign for us to go up," 6T9 said. Putting the hologlobe back in the cabinet, 6T9 jumped up, grabbed another handle set into the ceiling, and pulled. A chunk of the ceiling opened up and 6T9 pulled down a ladder. He was about to start up it when Noa said, "I'll go first. I don't need the view of your moon and saber."

Lifting his chin, 6T9 smiled. "I know those metaphors. They have sexual overtones."

From above came a cackle. "I quite like the view of your

moon and saber, 6T9!"

6T9 pointed up. "Eliza quite likes my—"

"Shut up," Noa grumbled, sliding by him, arms protectively around the still completely-hidden Carl Sagan.

6T9's mouth snapped shut.

From above, Eliza said, "Noa, are you insulting the love of my life?"

Noa snorted.

6T9's face went blank. He turned to James, and for just a moment James thought he saw a flicker of something—concern maybe?

But then 6T9 smiled at James. "Would you like a view of my moon and saber?"

"No," said James.

"After you then," said 6T9, holding up a hand, a pleasant smile on his face and all trace of concern gone.

For a moment, James froze. 'Bots of all sorts could "feel" concern for matters within their primary function—James's dig 'bots "fretted" often enough about the proper force to use when clearing dust from artifacts—although "voiced concerns" was perhaps a better description than "fretted." But what about the last statement could concern a sex 'bot, James couldn't imagine. Shaking his head, he hastily climbed up the ladder.

***

Noa ducked her head and crawled out of a narrow doorway into Eliza's kitchen. She blinked back over her shoulder. The doorway was cleverly disguised as a kitchen cabinet. Scrambling to her feet, wobbling only a little in exhaustion, she smiled at Eliza, a snappy comment on 6T9's nudity on her tongue. The comment died as she looked at Eliza for the first time in proper lighting. It had been only a few years since she'd last visited Eliza—but the woman seemed to have aged decades in that time. She was shorter, more

stooped. Her hair, once steel gray, was now completely white, thin and wispy, and didn't completely conceal
her scalp—although Noa noted that the fine wisps were
strategically collected with a colorful rose bloom pin right
above the spot her data port would be. Her face seemed to
have collapsed in on itself in wrinkles. Inwardly, Noa's heart
sank, but with some effort she was able to keep the smile
on her face. Carl Sagan poked his nose out of the cocoon of
her jacket. She stroked her fingers between his ears.

"So you've got a young man at last," Eliza cackled, leaning
on her cane. "About time."

Noa scowled as the werfle ran up behind her shoulder.
"I do not have a young man," she hissed in irritation. Eliza
had never remarried, and the implication that Noa was better off with a significant other was downright hypocritical.

"Really?" said Eliza, her voice wheezy, high, and chiding,
an impish smile on her thin lips.

Before Noa could retort, James poked his head out and
nodded politely up at Eliza.

The old woman's eyes went wide, the chiding smile vanished. "He looks like—"

Tim. It wasn't just Noa who saw the resemblance, and
Noa wasn't sure how that made her feel. She shook her
head, to say, no, we're not a couple, or no, don't talk about
Tim, please.

"Like who?" James asked, climbing to his feet and dusting
himself off.

"Like he's hungry!" Eliza said brightly, in true Luddeccean grandmotherly fashion. Noa nodded her head at Eliza
in acknowledgment of the small mercy.

Thumping her cane, Eliza commanded, "6T9, get these
people"—Carl Sagan chirped from Noa's shoulder—"and
their werfle some soup!"

Poking his head out of the cabinet door, 6T9 stared up at

Carl Sagan. "That's not a rat?"

Noa barely heard Eliza's response. On shaky legs, she sank gratefully into a chair. Following her, Eliza said, "And while he's doing that, I expect you to tell me all about how you came to be on the Luddeccean Most Wanted list." Her voice lowered and her eyes narrowed sharply. "And then you can tell me why you need my help." There was accusation in that voice, and oddly it made Noa smile with relief. As much as Eliza's body had aged, her mind was still sharp.

***

At Eliza's table, Noa sat with a half-eaten bowl of soup before her. 6T9's cooking app was very good, but Noa couldn't finish. Carl Sagan was lapping from a bowl of broth in the corner. Next to her, James was on his third bowl of the stuff. 6T9 had left the room to prepare rooms for James and Noa to sleep in.

Eliza was sitting in front of her, nervously playing with some beads around her neck. Her eyes were still bright and sharp—Noa's relief at that was tempered by the fact that the more of her story she told, the deeper Eliza's frown lines became.

"So," Noa said, "I think at this point the best option is to bring in outside assistance."

"The fastest any deep space vessel can reach the next time gate is 9.633 years," Eliza said. She exhaled shakily.

Noa leaned back in her seat. She wasn't sure how many details of the hidden time gate to reveal—she trusted Eliza, but good intentions weren't enough to hide the truth if someone were to pry loose your neural net. And Eliza still had her neural net in place, that was for certain. Although Noa couldn't see the port, the old woman's observations were too precise to be anything but net enhancement. One of Eliza's eyebrows rose. "And frankly my dear, I don't think I'll live that long."

Before Noa's brain and net had a chance to process that reply, 6T9 walked into the kitchen and interjected, "The doctor said you're perfectly healthy. The cancer you had was completely eradicated by the immunotherapy and the plaques in your heart and brain were removed by nanos."

"It isn't my health I'm worried about, dear," Eliza said.

6T9 came over to the table; it put his derriere closer than was comfortable to Noa's nose. He'd thankfully put on a pair of boxer briefs beneath his apron—hot pink boxer briefs—but it was still disquieting. She found herself leaning away from him. Where he sat between Eliza and Noa, one of James's eyebrows rose.

"If not your health, then what, darling?" 6T9 said, leaning over the table, putting a hand on Eliza's shoulder. His expression was such a facsimile of human concern that Noa nearly shivered. She didn't mind 'bots that looked like 'bots, but the ones that looked human and talked like humans made her uneasy. It was, as her military psyche training taught her, too easy to bond with a human-like 'bot—a faulty glitch in the emotional centers of the human brain. For that reason, military 'bots never looked human, so no commander ever felt guilty sending a drone on a self-destruct mission.

Eliza was silent. Noa's eyebrows rose. 6T9 hadn't heard her conversations, and Eliza hadn't told 6T9 that possessing a 'bot was illegal ... If she had, 6T9 might have wiped his memory and turned himself in. Eliza was risking her life for a 'bot ... Noa rubbed her temples. If she didn't need Eliza's money, she might call her on it. Out of the corner of her eye, she caught James's gaze on her, inscrutable, emotionless, and probably judgmental. She got the feeling he didn't approve of 6T9. She wished she could reach him through the ethernet to reassure him that she didn't approve of 6T9 either.

"You contributed to the premier's campaign fund," said 6T9, snapping Noa back to the present.

"What?" said Noa, eyes going wide in alarm. Apparently, Eliza had been discussing some politics with her 'bot. James sat up straighter in his chair.

Waving a hand at Noa and James, Eliza said, "Don't worry, I never supported his policies."

"Then why did you fund him?" James said.

"Because he was going to win," Eliza snapped.

"You said contributing to his campaign fund would protect you against vicious gossip and wagging tongues," said 6T9. "That's what you're afraid of, right?" He shook his head and tsked. "You shouldn't be. Gossip won't kill."

Noa sighed. Gossip was all the danger 6T9 could conceive of, she supposed. It was probably beyond his processing power to understand that they were in the midst of a genocide.

Turning to 6T9, voice soft, Eliza said, "My money won't protect me anymore, dear."

6T9's head tilted to the side. "Why not?"

Eliza gave a wry smile. "Because I don't think there will be any more elections."

"But that is part of the charter, elections every six years," 6T9 protested.

"They will change it," said Eliza.

Next to her, James sighed and put down his spoon. "If history is any indication they'll find a way."

Noa took a deep breath. "Yep."

Eyes glued to Eliza, 6T9 said, "I do not understand."

"Don't worry about it, darling," said Eliza.

6T9's expression softened immediately. "Okay." He smiled a smile of utter peace and contentment—because an end to worry was simple as an order when you were a 'bot.

Stroking her beads, Eliza said, "Why don't you go upstairs, prepare some towels and clothes for Noa and James, too. You gave them separate rooms, right?"

6T9 nodded, and Eliza smiled brightly. "I'll join you shortly."

6T9's smile dropped. Dipping his chin, he raised an eyebrow and then winked at Eliza, giving a look that Noa supposed would be "smoldering" ... if you didn't know it came from a 'bot. She glanced between James's light features, and 6T9's more conventional tan skin and brown eyes. Both of them were two of the most beautiful examples of masculinity she'd been around in a while. And she wasn't attracted to either of them, for very different reasons. She smiled bitterly to herself. It was unfair, but sadly convenient.

"I will be expecting you," 6T9 said in a low voice.

Putting a hand to her chest, Eliza giggled like a schoolgirl. "Yes, sir."

Noa rolled her eyes as 6T9 prowled out of the room. As soon as he was out of sight, Noa turned back to Eliza. "You see why this is so important, then."

Looking at the table, Eliza fidgeted with her place mat. "Yes ... but I must consider my options. 9.633 years ... "

"There is a faster way," said Noa.

Eliza's eyes narrowed. "You said you need money to help finance a mission ... I know you have no ship, so you must be stealing one, and I don't know how you can get by the grid ... "

"I have a plan. But the less you know the better."

"So you say," said Eliza, looking away. "To get past the blockade you'd need either a very big ship or a very small one, but a very small one wouldn't last in deep space ... a big ship ... " she rocked in her chair.

Eliza's eyes slipped to James. He was dipping a roll in a plate of rinseed oil. It struck Noa that he looked too big for the tiny table, and just the simple act of dipping the bread seemed a feat of difficult maneuvering for his large frame.

"Are you privy to the whole plan?"

James put the bread down. "Yes."

Noa prepared herself for Eliza to pry him for details, but instead she said, "What do you think of it?"

"That it is near suicidal," James replied.

"And yet you are going along with it," Eliza said. Her voice had become softer as the night had worn on. Her eyes were drooping. "May I ask why?"

One of James's eyebrows rose as they did when he was telling a joke. "I'm still asking myself that."

"You are a wry one," Eliza chuckled. "And what is your answer?"

James was quiet for a long time. Noa found herself shifting in her seat.

"I am a hyper-augment … " His head ticked, and straw-blonde hair fell into his eyes. He pushed it back. "I don't have a lot of options, and … " He looked at Noa, and then away and shrugged.

Eliza stared at a spot on the table between her and Noa. "This is a big decision for me."

Noa's jaw got hard. "So many lives are at stake, Eliza." Kenji's life was at stake. Her thumb went to the stumps of her fingers.

"Including my life," the old woman said.

Noa sat back in her seat. "You're a founder of the colony … surely if you just got rid of 6T9 … "

Eliza's nostrils flared.

Noa felt her skin heat in anger. "He is a 'bot."

"But I'm not," Eliza said.

"Of course not," Noa said, not sure where this was going.

Eliza's eyes became pained. "You think he is just a sex toy, but he's not. He's my hands, my arms, my legs." Her hand shook. "My body is falling apart, no one can fix that at this point; but my mind is still alive thanks to nanos and apps. Without 6T9, they'll find some way to put me in a home. They don't allow nano flushes or apps anymore." Her eyes dropped. "I'll become a vegetable." For a moment it looked like Eliza might burst into tears.

Noa released a breath. "Eliza … " She reached toward the old woman.

"And if I'm going to die," Eliza said, "I want to be having as much sex as I can with the most beautiful man I can for as long I can."

Noa's hand fell.

Eliza's thin eyebrows waggled, and she giggled, her bony shoulders rising. "He really is excellent," she whispered. "It took me centuries to get lovin' like I've got now."

From the doorway came 6T9's voice. "Did you call me, Eliza?"

Eliza turned to him. "No, I … " Her brow creased even more. "Actually, I think I could use your help getting up the stairs."

6T9 strode into the kitchen, thankfully wearing pajama bottoms. "You know I live to sweep you off your feet."

"Eliza … " Noa said.

Eliza waved her hand. "You know where the spare rooms are … I'll give you my answer in the morning. I need to sleep on it."

Kneeling beside her, 6T9 said, "I hope you won't sleep too much."

Eliza waggled her eyebrows again and let him help her into his arms. "Oh, you … " she giggled as 6T9 gently stood, nuzzling her neck as he carried her from the room.

Noa put her elbows on the table and stared at her bowl of half-eaten soup. She dropped her head in her hands.

"That sounded like a 'probably not'?" James said.

Noa felt sick to her stomach. She was asking Eliza to give

up more than a toy. She was asking her to give up her freedom, her independence … and her very life.

"What do we do now?"

Head still in her hands, Noa sighed. "Sleep, I guess."

"I meant if she says no?"

Noa rubbed her eyes. "I have no idea."

***

When Noa woke from a nightmare at 25:43 Luddeccean Time, even though James was dozing, he knew it. Since he'd awakened in the snow, he had been unable to truly sleep. His body was still, his eyes were closed, his breathing was slowed, his temperature was lower than normal, and memories were tripping through his mind in a semi-dreamlike way. At the same time his mind almost dreamed, there was, off in the corners of his neural net, a running inventory of what was still going on around him—minus vision, of course. At 01:00, Noa went downstairs and he heard her start to pace back and forth. That brought him out of his semi-conscious state. With his augmented hearing, even from the second floor he could hear her sigh.

It was comfortably warm in the room. He hadn't even bothered with a sheet. The bed was as large as the one in his parents' cottage, and as comfortable. But it was the first time he'd slept without Noa since he arrived in Luddeccea. When she wasn't with him, there was a part of him looking for her. He supposed that was because she had been the one constant since he arrived.

Sitting up, he shook off the last vestiges of his doze—an image of Ghost's face flickering from a perfect hologram—and swung his legs over the edge of the bed. Just before he stood up, he caught sight of the skin of his arms. He swallowed … and part of him registered that was a very peculiar reaction to unease. Was he trying to devour his disquiet? It didn't work; the strange markings on his skin had him still on edge. Earlier when he'd taken a shower, the strange tattoos had risen in stark black relief on his skin. They hadn't disappeared like they normally did; they'd only faded. He exhaled sharply. They always made him nervous, but they were too regular to be some nano-inspired tumor. He closed his eyes. He could do nothing about them right now. If he abandoned Noa and made a run for the Northwest or Northeast Province, it was doubtful he could find anyone with the experience and equipment to explain all the aspects of his hyper-augmentation to him. If they succeeded with Noa's plan, on Earth he'd reunite with his parents. They could help him recover the memories locked away in his mind. James drew his hand across the slightly raised flesh of the designs. When they were faint, they looked less like a leaf pattern and more like … feathers. The thought made him bolt up from the bed. He pulled on the long-sleeved train operator uniform shirt before he left the room to hide the tattoos—from either himself or Noa, he didn't know which.

Minutes later, he found Noa in the room with the chess board. She was standing by a bookshelf, staring at a small glowing hologlobe. In it, many people, all facing the camera, were smiling back at her. As he padded forward, Noa jumped. Spinning in his direction, her body dropped to a semi-crouch before she caught herself and stood up straight. Carl Sagan poked his bewhiskered nose out from between some books.

Wrapping her arms around herself, Noa asked, "Did I wake you?"

James shook his head. "I wasn't really sleeping." Which was the truth, if not the full extent of it. He walked toward the holo, and his head tilted. He saw Noa in the holo, near the front. She looked to be about twelve. An older man had his arm draped protectively over her shoulder, and the younger Noa had her own arm wrapped around a boy slightly shorter than her. Noa's mouth was split in a wide grin, and she had her chin resting on the boy's shoulder. The boy wasn't smiling, but he had one of Noa's hands in his. No one in the holo shared Noa's unique coloring, but … "They are your family," he said. He could see Noa's small, delicate, rounded nose on a man's face, her wide lips on another woman, her brows on another, her high cheekbones on someone else. The boy whose shoulder her chin rested on looked like Noa, but he was tan instead of dark brown, his eyes were so light they were almost gold, and he had wavy hair instead of her tight curls.

Pointing to the boy, Noa said, "That is my brother, Kenji." Her thumb caressed the place her missing fingers would have been. She bowed her head, touched the globe, and it went dark. She touched another globe, and it flickered to life, casting her profile in sharp relief. Like him, she'd taken a shower. She also must have cut her hair. It was now tight against her head and paradoxically looked thicker than before. The angle of the light emphasized the indentations of the scars on her cheek and forehead, but also her high cheekbones, her full lips, her wide eyes, and the overall smoothness of her dark skin—the way the bluish light caressed it, it looked almost like velvet.

"The older woman at the center, that is Eliza," Noa said, pointing at the new holo. James followed her finger. In the holo, there was a man and a woman who both appeared to be about sixty, if they weren't augmented. Around them stood eight younger men and women. There was something restrained in their expressions. They weren't smiling as brightly as the people in the other holo.

"That is her late husband and children. It must have been taken about twenty years after the colony was founded." Her brow furrowed. "Eliza had twelve kids … the original settlers favored big families."

James stared at the globe. Sometimes a cold or flu swept across Earth. He'd even caught one that had kept him flat on his back for a week while the nanos cleaned him up, but he'd never known anyone who'd died in an epidemic. "There are eight in this holo … "

"Yes," Noa said. "Four more died in another epidemic. Her husband died, too. I think it must have been shortly after this holo was made—he was maybe forty-seven?"

"Forty-seven … but they look so much older than that in this holo."

Noa shrugged. "Life was hard then." She shook her head. "It was some sort of virus. Caused a disease like meningitis. He wouldn't take a nano-treatment. Eliza and the children that survived did." Noa's brow furrowed. "I think that is when she started to reject the Luddeccean philosophy. She bought a lot of land after the virus wiped out half of the first, second, and third wave settlers. Sold it and used it to send her kids to Sol System for school. Three didn't come back. The other—her last daughter—died a few years back."

James drew closer to Noa. "Why didn't Eliza leave?"

Noa sighed. "Probably because her descendants wouldn't approve of 6T9."

"You don't seem to approve, either." As he said the words, he thought he felt a gust of cold air sweep the room.

Gazing at the holo, Noa sighed, the light of the globe shining in her eyes. "I don't normally approve of sex 'bots, or animatronics, no. People become addicted to them, forget that they're not human, give love and affection to machines that don't care one way or another, and that are expensive and energy hogs to boot."

"6T9 seems to care about Eliza … " His voice trailed off. He wasn't sure why he was playing devil's advocate. And where was the cold air coming from? He looked over his shoulder at an air vent—but it wasn't on.

Noa frowned. "It's his programming to mimic emotions. It's his programming to care about her feelings and her well being. But it isn't real … 'bots don't care about anything, not really, not their owners or even themselves. He'd wipe his memory and shut himself down if he realized he was endangering her."

James thought of contemplating leaving Noa to her fate in the forest. "You make 'bots sound better than humans."

Noa raised her eyes to his. "No, they're not—they're just programmed that way. To be afraid, to want to live, to want to avoid pain, and to do the right thing anyway, that is far more than any 'bot can do or be."

James felt as though gravity had lessened and the chill in the room had dissipated.

Noa looked down. "People who think they love 'bots … well, real love is compromise and sacrifice and not always easy, but it makes you better because you have to be a better person. And having a person who loves you back … they're doing more than following a script." She looked away quickly. His eyes slipped down her body. She wore a pair of light coral silk pajamas. Designed for life near the equator, the top had no sleeves. The color contrasted sharply with her dark skin and it might have looked enticing on the Noa in his memory, but it made the hard angles of her emaciated body stand out even more. She wrapped her arms around herself again. James wanted to put an arm around her, but didn't.

Noa sighed, walked over to the couch, and flopped down. "But in Eliza's case … I don't know." Leaning her head against the back of the sofa, she put a hand on her forehead.

James sat down beside her. Leaning back as she was, he retrieved some data on sex 'bots from his data archives.

In the twenty-first century, there were some people who thought that sex 'bots would replace fellow humans as the sexual partners of choice. The thinking went that their appearance could be perfect and their personalities could be "perfect" as well. But with nano technology and improvements in surgery, almost anyone with enough money who wanted could have the appearance they desired, at least until they reached an advanced age like Eliza's, when systems broke down too fast for even technology to keep up. The "perfect" personality varied with the individual, and 'bots were limited in that regard, as Noa put it, to "scripts." The end of the human race hadn't happened with humans becoming so seduced by 'bots that they forgot to reproduce.

"Everyone deserves the chance to be loved," Noa said, snapping him from his reverie. "Here on Luddeccea, it's hard for older women. Love and sex are for marriage and children. It's not uncommon for men past one hundred to marry girls in their twenties, or women with frozen eggs in their sixties who can still carry a baby to term." Her brow furrowed. "When Eliza's first husband died, she was too old, and didn't have frozen eggs. She worked so hard to put her remaining kids through school away from this system, and her business was here and she was alone … I think … " She shrugged. "There are extenuating circumstances, I suppose."

Leaning back, James rolled his head toward her. Noa had curled into a ball at the corner of the couch. She closed her eyes. "I'm so hungry," she said softly. "Do you have any of those soybeans you filched from the bar on you?"

"I gave those to Carl Sagan," James said.

"Damn," Noa said.

James remembered the soup she hadn't finished earlier—she'd said she was full. So he'd finished it for her. Still, there was plenty to eat in the kitchen … He tripped over a memory of himself as a young man staying at his grandparent's condo in London. As his grandparents had retired, his grandfather had said, "Help yourself to anything if you're hungry."

He looked down at the pajamas Eliza had provided for him. "Noa," he said. "Do you think Eliza would really mind if you helped yourself to some food?"

Noa was silent. James looked up and found her eyes wide, her lips parted. With his augmented vision he just barely made out the black H on her wrist. "No," she said. "No, she wouldn't mind." She didn't move from her seat. She looked distressed—and she was silent, which proved it. His mind was a maze of unanswered questions and locked doors, but his unknown couldn't be worse than her known.

"Let me go make you something," James said. He had fuzzy memories of cooking elaborate meals—he didn't think he could recreate them. But following instructions on the back of a soup packet seemed possible. And he wouldn't mind a snack himself.

Noa's mouth dropped open again. Shaking her head, she looked away. "Sure, yes, thanks, that would be great."

James left her there and padded into the kitchen. He found the small remainder of the admittedly excellent soup tucked in the refrigeration unit, still in a pot. Putting the pot on the gas stove, he struggled to turn it on—the electric spark would not light. And then he noticed a box of old-fashioned matches sitting off to the side. His eyebrows lifted. He looked at the stove and shook his head. The electronic spark must have been disabled with the ethernet shut down. He struck a match, turned on the gas, and watched the flame leap to life. Shaking out the match, he almost sighed. Welcome to 1984 … and then, at memory of that particular year, and the novel by Orwell of the same name, he almost smiled wryly. But of course the smile didn't come.

Self-consciously touching the corner of his lips, he found a large spoon and begin to stir the pot as the soup slowly heated. Some of the soup splattered on his arm and he rolled up his sleeves. As the soup warmed, he began to notice the markings on the arm exposed to the steam becoming more prominent. Dropping the spoon, he pulled his hand away. He heard a shuffling noise, and turned to see Carl Sagan standing on his hind legs sniffing at the air, staring at James. He hastily rolled down his sleeves again.

***

Noa caressed the tiny hologlobe she'd found on the end table next to the couch. It fit easily in her palm and her fingers left streaks in the dusty surface. Light flickered from within the globe. James re-entered the room, bowls of soup in hand, and Carl Sagan followed in his wake. Perhaps enchanted by the fragrance of the soup, the werfle's bewhiskered nose twitched as he sniffed.

"That looks to be old," James said as the picture in the hologlobe emerged like a scene rising out of fog. It was one of the old globes that only had one holo in them, too. You could tell by the way the colors were muted. "What is it?" James asked.

Noa shook her head and put it on the coffee table in front of the couch, her mouth watering at the smell of soup.

As she took her first slurp, the sound in the globe crackled. "I met Jun at a transport station in Nigeria." The 'smoke' in the globe solidified and a man and woman appeared. The man looked East Asian; the woman was African in appearance with skin as dark as Noa's. She wore a Japanese yukata, but the bright yellow, blue, and geometric-patterned garment appeared to be cut from traditional Nigerian cloth. They both had sparkling augments in their temples smaller than modern ones, without all the external

203

drives for app insertion.

Noa smiled. "That's my great-great-great grandmother and grandfather! Eliza never knew them." Her head tilted. "I wonder why Eliza has this?"

Noa traced the phantom figure of the man in the holo with a finger. He was visibly ethnically Japanese, with a slightly hooked nose, almond-shaped eyes, slender chin and slight frame. "Both our families were purist groups."

The hologlobe came to life, and the image of Noa's grandmother within it shook her head. "Purist groups, they're like religious sects, they always urge women to have a lot of babies. Controlling women's fertility is how they maintain their existence. But ever since I was a little girl, I knew that wasn't what I wanted. I didn't want to be in any of the careers that were slightly acceptable to girls—nursing and teaching—I wanted to build rocket ships!"

Noa's smile faded. She could see why Eliza might have this. Purist groups, religious sects … her own home planet. It was true, she supposed. If Noa's own parents hadn't been outsiders here, that would have been her life. As it was, she'd still felt the pressure to conform to that lifestyle. Nice girls didn't "borrow" antigrav bikes, hop onto freight cars, or spend years mastering martial arts. Nice girls were demure, modest and let the men in their lives take the risks while they tended the home fires. Maybe her risk-taking personality as a kid was just a counterbalance to that pressure? To prove to herself that she could be brave and fierce? And maybe the reason why she'd wanted to be a pilot, and then later, part of command, was because it was the furthest from the status in Luddeccean society she could imagine being? She put her spoon down. Maybe, if she hadn't been from Luddeccea, she would have been happy with some other career; maybe she could have been perfectly content as an engineer, or one of the Fleet's analysts.

But the risk-taking had altered her brain chemistry, wired her for risks ... she had hated being First Officer.

The voices in the holo changed to static. Picking it up and surveying the bottom, James said, "A penny for your thoughts?"

Noa blinked up at him.

Catching her gaze, he added, "It's a very old expression. It means ... "

"I know what it means," Noa said with a wave of her hand. Her brow furrowed. "Not that I know what a penny is ... " Her eyes slid to the side.

"It was a unit of currency that ... " James's voice drifted off. "Actually, I'm not interested in reciting the history of the penny. I'm wondering what you're thinking and if it will somehow get me into trouble."

Noa laughed and swallowed another spoonful of soup. "I was actually just thinking about every damn report I've had to do on blue-green algae."

James said in a cautious voice, "Sounds harmless enough." His eyes slid to hers. "It is harmless, isn't it?"

"I can't begin to tell you how harmless it is, except for the kind that excreted hydrochloric acid."

James's eyebrows shot up. Noa waved a hand. "No, it was great, actually. The discovery of that algae was the only time anything interesting happened. The Republic's Committee on the Search for Sentient Space-going Races is so obsessed with the search for sentient life that even blue-green algae has to go through fourteen different tests for sentience on the off chance that it could be a hive-mind organism."

James's brows constricted. "It could be ... "

Swallowing a spoonful of soup, Noa groaned. "But it's not! It hasn't been. I've cataloged over 100 species since I became First Officer aboard the Sugihara."

"I thought you were a pilot, not a scientist?"

Noa dropped her spoon. "No, but I'm good at whipping up reports—" She raised her fingers to make air quotes. "—in plain Basic." Dropping her hands, she said, "I hate it. And then getting the sign-offs from the Fleet and the inter-Republic agencies … it's such a pain in the ass, and it has to go to someone who is meticulous, organized, and charming." She harrumphed.

As she finished her soup, she spouted off about all the stupid, redundant things she had to do to obtain authorization for a Fleet ship even to enter the atmosphere of a planet with blue-green algae swimming in its H2O. Talking was better than nightmares. It was better than thinking about contingency plans if Eliza didn't come through. But by the time she was almost, but not-quite-done with her rant, she leaned back and realized aloud, "I'm boring even myself!" She looked over at James. "You're cursing the fact that this is all going down in your holographic memory, aren't you?"

He raised an eyebrow. "Not out loud."

She laughed softly and closed her eyes, and leaned her head back, just for a moment.

When she opened her eyes, it was still dark, but she heard the pterys outside announcing the imminent rise of the sun within the hour. There was a light streaming from the hallway, beyond the living room, backlighting 6T9's half-clothed form and Eliza's bent frame. Eliza had one hand on the 'bot; the other was wrapped around a cane.

"I've made up my mind," Eliza said. "I won't lend you the money."

Noa sat up with a start. During the night her feet had somehow managed to find their way onto James's lap. She might have flushed with embarrassment, but Eliza's words had chilled her to the bone. James was sitting up in his seat, leaning forward, wide-eyed.

"But I will pay you to book two flights of passage."

"What?" said Noa, wondering if she had wandered into another bad dream.

"One for me," Eliza said nervously. "One for 6T9."

"Oh, where are we going?" said 6T9, looking back and forth between the humans, a slight smile on his lips.

"That's impossible," Noa protested, swinging her legs off the couch and standing up.

James stood up beside her. "Eliza," James said, "Noa hasn't told me her plans for procuring the ship we need—but I know they will be very dangerous. You do not have the physical strength."

Noa remembered nearly falling down the stairs last night at Ghost's place, and struggling to climb up the ladder from the safe room. Maybe she didn't have the physical strength, either.

"6T9 will be my strength," Eliza said, patting his arm. "He will carry me if necessary."

"I am programmed to sweep her off her feet, literally and figuratively," 6T9 said with a proud smile.

"6T9 will be an energy hog," Noa said. That was the other reason AIs and 'bots never took hold. They consumed massive amounts of power.

"I'll keep him in sleep mode when he's not needed!" Eliza said.

Noa took a deep breath. "Eliza, if you get hurt, you'll endanger the whole mission, everyone on it, and everyone on Luddeccea."

Eliza looked down, and her knuckles went white.

"If we pull this off, we'll get help here in a few months," Noa whispered. If they could get past the gauntlet of the Local Guard above Luddeccea Prime, if they could coax the Ark to light speed, and if they could reach the Kanakah Cloud and activate the Fleet's time gate …

Eliza looked up suddenly. "I'm going," she whispered. "I gave my life for this colony, and my children's and husband's lives for their philosophy." Her wrinkled face crumpled further. "I'm being selfish now … " She took a deep breath and stood taller. She nodded. "If I'm badly hurt while trying to take the ship, you can leave me behind."

"And me, too," said 6T9. He pulled Eliza's hand to his stomach and gazed down at her. "I won't leave you."

Eliza beamed up at him. "I know. That's why I won't leave you behind, either."

Noa resisted the urge to growl. Eliza was anthropomorphizing him, and it would cost the team power and trouble with nothing in return. 6T9 wasn't the brightest 'bot on the assembly line. He'd be useless aboard the ship.

Eliza's eyes flashed toward her. "I can offer you more than just my money. You can use my hover, and my time, and I'll do anything you ask … but I'm leaving this place, and 6T9 is coming with me." She drew herself up to her full height—diminished though it was. "Take it or leave it."

CHAPTER ELEVEN

James's feet splashed in the thankfully shallow runoff water in the circular tunnel of the Luddeccea Prime's main sewer line. On his back he carried a pack stuffed with credits. Noa had wanted Eliza to drive them closer to Ghost's abode; unfortunately, Eliza was too shaky to pilot the hover. She'd been relying on an "ethernet chauffeur" for years. So now they were hiking again, this time without Carl Sagan.

"She's crazy," Noa grumbled beside him. Her breathing was slightly labored, although their pace wasn't particularly fast. "You saw how she thinks of 6T9 as a person!"

James tilted his head. "Eliza is the only person on the planet who has any experience in the Ark."

"She won't make it to the Ark! She's too frail. She'll be injured and shot … " Noa waved a hand.

"If she makes it, she may be useful, but if she is shot, you can leave her behind," James said. Noa might have experience flying the same model ship as the Ark, but every ship had its idiosyncrasies—even James knew that.

Drawing up short and spinning toward him, Noa said, "How can you say that?"

James came to a halt and tried to work out what had offended her.

"She's like an aunt to me!" Noa said. "A crazy aunt, but an aunt just the same! How can you suggest I just leave her?"

James stared at her. "Because that is her wish?"

Noa frowned. "How can you be so unfeeling?" she hissed.

James tilted his head. He didn't have any feelings toward Eliza, either positive or negative; but, if Noa was injured, he knew he couldn't leave her behind. It wasn't rational, and he had no explanation for it. "I have feelings," he said. Noa drew back. She took a breath, and then turned away. "If we didn't have so little time … I would have convinced her not to come."

Breathing heavily, she continued on the path back to Ghost's lair. "As it is—" They reached a wide fork in the tunnel. The faint echo of voices sounded from the left. James grabbed her arm and drew her against the wall. Noa's eyes met his. She didn't speak or ask questions, but she inclined her chin to a branch off the main line just across from them. It was much smaller, just wide enough to crawl through, and it was at shoulder height. James nodded; the voices were getting closer, and they had to hide. They moved to the other side of the tunnel. Noa reached up and gritted her teeth. James had a memory of helping a girlfriend up onto a horse. Looping his hands, he nudged her with his shoulders. Dropping her eyes, she caught his meaning immediately. She slipped a boot between his fingers, gave a bounce at the same time he gave a lift, and she disappeared down the shaft a few moments later. James followed, the sound of the Guard sloshing in shallow water echoing in his ears.

***

Heart beating in her throat, Noa sat with her back to the wall in the thankfully drier secondary sewer shaft. She held her breath, afraid even that could give them away. She felt James's legs brush hers and could just make out the sound of his breathing. Light from the Guard's flashlights reflected from the water in the sewers, and for a moment she could almost make out his features across from her. A few minutes ago she'd felt so angry at him for his lack of compassion that she thought she might self-combust. That feeling was gone now, and all she felt was relief that he was here and she wasn't alone.

From the tunnel, she heard the sound of retreating footsteps and a patrolman say, "This tunnel is clear." The patrol had just missed them. They must not have seen the small tributary they were hiding in. The patrol didn't have a map of the sewers stored in their neural nets like James and Noa did.

Noa closed her eyes and waited for the sound of their voices and footsteps to fade. Lifting her head, she mouthed the word, "safe?" knowing that James would be able to read her lips even in the nearly pitch blackness of the narrow shaft.

"Yes," he whispered.

James scooted to the comparatively brighter main tunnel and then lowered himself down. Noa followed. Her arms shook as she lowered herself, but James caught her and she landed gently. Feeling a bit guilty for the way she'd snapped at him earlier, Noa whispered, "We make a good team."

He didn't reply. "Thanks for the lift earlier." She sighed and started down the tunnel. "I don't know who will be more a danger to the team—Eliza or me." She ground her teeth. What they were planning to do—well, they had no plan, and little hope.

"Leg-up," James whispered.

"What?" Noa said.

"In equestrian circles, we call that lift a 'leg-up.'"

"You were in equestrian circles?" Noa asked.

"I just remembered, I used to play polo."

Noa stopped in a slanting beam of sunlight coming through a grate above their heads. She had to throw a hand over her mouth to keep from laughing aloud at the completely random statement. Biting said hand to stifle the chortle, she looked up at James. He raised an eyebrow and whispered, "I am glad you find that amusing."

"Rich much?" she asked, resuming her path down the tunnel. Horses—polo—enormous off-world country "cottage"?

James looked heavenward.

"Should I have told Ghost we could have given him double his money on arrival at Sol Station?" Noa chided in a hushed voice.

James stopped short. His jaw twitched—as it did when she expected a smile or a frown. "No … I … since the accident, I am not sure … "

Noa's smile dropped. "The augments … your family … " Enhanced sight, his appearance, his strength—James's augments were state of the art. "They spent it all on you."

James looked at the ground. "I think maybe … "

Noa put her hand on his arm. "Hey, at least you're here."

James looked up at her. Raising both brows, he looked pointedly down at the puddled water beneath their feet and then up at her. "Joy," he said.

And Noa had to bite back her laughter again. As they continued down the tunnel, her eyes slid to James. She could just barely see him in the dim tunnel. He carried the backpack swung over one shoulder. She trusted him implicitly with the burden. He could have left her behind long ago—but he hadn't. And he wasn't Fleet, or Luddeccean, but of all the off-worlder civilians to be stuck with, well, she could have done much worse. And he had that dry wit of his. She smiled to herself.

"What?" James whispered.

They had too many serious moments ahead of them. She wasn't about to let the ball of levity drop in this moment of calm. Alluding to a silly tee-vee show from the United States in the 1970s, Noa whispered, "The six-million credit man."

James didn't smile, of course. But she knew he found it funny, when, in a perfect imitation of the strange sound effects of the show, he said, "Sprrrrroooooooyoooyoooinnn-ngggg."

***

"He's not answering," Noa whispered. She was hanging on a rusty ladder about a meter from James's head, rapping on an equally metal hatch. The ladder continued up to a man-hole. Sunlight was streaming over Noa, turning her skin to dark orange. Occasionally someone would walk overhead and Noa would press herself to the wall.

"Maybe I can break the lock?" James said, remembering the train.

"Yeah, I think you'll have to," Noa said, giving a tug to the door handle. Dust fell into James's eyes and mouth. He coughed and blinked upward.

Noa was staring at a piece of metal in her hands. The narrow hatch was slightly ajar in front of her. "Okay, that was really rusty," she whispered.

Because it had made her smile before, James made the same sound effect from the 1970s television show. Biting her lip, she gave him a dirty look. "Don't make me laugh—" A shadow passed above her and she pressed her slender frame against the wall. The shadow didn't slow. Noa pulled away from the wall with a sigh that James could barely hear, but could see. And then he saw her mouth drop open and heard her gasp.

"What is it?" James said, his body already dropping into a crouch, preparing to jump up to the ladder.

Dropping her head to face him, Noa put a finger to her lips, and then without explanation, she slid forward through the hatch; it slipped closed behind her with a soft clang.

Above the manhole someone stopped and James jumped back. "A rat down there?" someone said.

"Damn things hitchhike on spaceships all the time," said someone else.

"Not anymore," said another voice. "And good riddance." There was a sound of retreating footsteps. Jumping, James caught the lowest rung of the ladder with ease, and pulled himself up from a dead hang. He reached the hatch, and saw that not just the lock had come off, but a portion of the ancient brick surrounding the door. He didn't reflect on it, just opened the ancient door marked with the seal of a defunct electrical utility. Where there should have been the darkness of Ghost's hideout there was blinding light— and no Noa. Pressing himself to his stomach, he slithered through the narrow space, using his elbows to propel himself forward. He heard the door clang behind him as his head popped out of the narrow access shaft. He gasped. Instead of the unkempt room he remembered, there was brightness, and where the geothermal heater had been was a chrome column four meters wide, burnished so brightly he could see his own reflection and Noa's as she stood to the side of the entrance shaft, craning her neck upward.

"What's going on?" he said, pulling himself out of the shaft.

"I don't know," she whispered. The light was so bright, so natural, that for a moment James was transported to a memory of a church of the New Era with white walls and sunlight streaming through the roof. He lifted his eyes, and saw the ceiling that had been barely above his head before was now vaulted several stories high. Neat metal ducts protruded from the column at regular angles above their heads. He looked down. Below them was wire flooring, and below that he could see machinery that was eerily silent. Turning slowly in place, he saw a podium with gauges set into it, and a keyboard, much like the one on his laptops. He heard Noa's footsteps. Spinning, he found her lifting a hand toward the chrome cylinder. Her hand passed right through. "It's a hologram of the Ark's engine room," she said, her voice hushed. She inclined her head to the chrome column. "That must be a holo of a fission reactor ... but I can't figure out what it's projected on."

"Another one of Ghost's creations," James said, reaching out to touch the keyboard. The illusion was so real he saw the shadow of his hand on the keys. When his fingers passed through the holographic keyboard, he almost sighed in dismay.

From around the giant column came Ghost's mutter, "Oh, no, that doesn't sound good at all."

Noa's eyes met his, her lips parted but she didn't even whisper.

Ghost's voice echoed again. "But then how to fix it? Hmmm ... "

Holding out her hands, Noa slowly walked around the chrome column. James quickly fell into step behind her.

They found Ghost with his back to them, staring down at another console, muttering, "That sounds better, but still not good—"

"That's because nothing good ever came out of a holodeck," Noa said, referring to a television show they had watched. She gave a wink to James. He wanted to frown at her. The "holodeck" they were in was ingenious, breathtaking, and deserved some respect.

Ghost spun around, eyes wide, nostrils flared. "I'm impressed your education was sophisticated enough to make that reference, Sato."

Noa shrugged and smiled. "Already preparing to go with us?" Her eyes narrowed. "Maybe you don't have as many options as you said you did?"

The hologram dissipated, and for a moment James could see nothing. His eyes adjusted, and he found himself in the familiar darkness of Ghost's basement. Where the shiny chrome nuclear core had been, there was now the geothermal generator. All of the furniture in the room had been pushed to the side.

Ghost's eyes narrowed. "The Ark is the only boat of all my potential escape craft that I don't know like the back of my hand. I was merely educating myself on the peculiarities of its engineering before you returned with my credits."

Lowering her chin, Noa glared at Ghost for all of thirty seconds. He sniffled and wiped the side of his nose.

Jaw tight, she indicated the floor with a tilt of her chin. "James, let's give him the credits."

James dropped the backpack with the credits on the floor.

"The deposit's all there," Noa said.

Ghost looked down at the floor, and then up at Noa. He didn't ask questions about how they acquired the money, or even pick up the backpack, but James thought he saw a light by the side of his head flash in the direction of the credit-laden bag.

"You'll give us access to the population data?" Noa asked.

Lifting his gaze, Ghost said, "Yes." He tapped his head. "It's all in here … "

Noa leaned back, and her lip curled slightly. "I'm not interested in some dirty hard link."

Ghost sniffed. "I wasn't going to suggest it. I was only thinking of the best way to get the most up-to-date data from the Luddeccean main computer to—"

James's neurons fired like fireworks on Unification Day. "Up-to-date data from the main computer—but that would require the ethernet if you're not hard linking into it."

Noa's eyes went wide. "Ghost, if you're using some other sort of remote signal, their amplifiers could catch it."

216

"It's not like that." He smirked, and his eyes shone. "There is no signal to pick up."

Noa's jaw dropped. "You have some sort of landline—"

Ghost beamed. "No."

James's mind spun, thinking of the holograms that had to be the result of applications of quantum theory, and came up with another conceivable application. "Does it rely on quantum entanglement?" Theoretically, entangled particles could be in the same state in two different places at once, and such states could be measured and used to communicate between one place and anywhere else in the universe.

Noa huffed. "It's not quantum magic."

Ghost's smile dropped. His lip quivered. "No," he said, leveling his gaze at James.

"Then how—" James began.

"I use it all the time and they still haven't found me." Ghost said, beginning to pace. "But how to get the data to you and allow you to sort through it?" His eyes widened. "Oh, the Ark's antiquated interfaces have given me an idea!"

James was blinded by a bright flash of light, but then the light dimmed, and he found Noa and himself facing a semi-transparent wall. Between them were two consoles like the one James and Noa had just seen, complete with keyboards. In front of each, the wall blinked with illuminated text: Please input search parameters.

"You couldn't have made it voice-activated?" Noa said, looking down at the keypad.

"If you don't mind, I'd like to study the engineering systems of the Ark without interruption," Ghost snapped back.

Noa glared at him but went to the keypad. She pressed down on a key and said, "My finger is hitting empty air."

Waving his hand, Ghost said, "It still registers your input."

Noa slowly plunked out a query and the semi-transparent wall of light began scrolling with names. Noa's eyes went wide. "This works. James, why don't you commit all the sewer, electrical, and service tunnels here in Prime to memory, and streets and alleys, too?"

"Will do," James said. His own mental map was not that complete. He bent to his console, but his eyes went through the wall, now filled with names. Ghost was staring at engineering schematics, similarly projected in the air before him.

Catching his gaze, Ghost said, "I don't just want to upload the schematics to my memory app—I want to commit them to my neurons—and really understand them." He sighed. "I have a feeling it will be a bumpy ride."

James suspected Ghost was right. He nodded at the inventor. Noa might not like or trust him, but James was beginning to respect his intellect. The man flushed slightly, and then his eyes went back to the schematics.

Bending over his console, James typed the request for sewer lines into the air pad, and began committing the results to memory. Beside him, he heard Noa gasp.

Ghost spun around, and James turned to her sharply.

Noa put a hand to her mouth. Eyes wide, she said, "Kenji."

James looked at the light screen. The young man from the holograph was there. He looked considerably older now—older even than Noa. He hadn't taken age suppressors, obviously.

From the other side of the light screen, Ghost sneered. "They gave him my job."

James's eyes slid to the other data besides Kenji's picture. There was his title, "Lead Analyst, Computing Systems," and a home address.

"They didn't arrest him?" Noa said.

"Arrest him?" Ghost said. "He works for them." Inclining his head toward Noa, he said, "He probably turned you in."

Noa's hands fell to her side. "He's my brother!"

Ghost shrugged.

"He didn't turn me in!" Noa said, her voice rising.

Ghost's chin dipped.

"Where's the evidence? Show me the evidence!" Noa demanded, stepping through the wall of light.

Ghost shuffled backward and held up his hands. "I don't ... "

"You don't have any!" Noa retorted. "You were always jealous of him! You're not half the genius he is, and you've always been jealous!"

Eyes wide, Ghost took a step back. "I just ... "

Noa took a step forward. "You just—"

James caught her shoulder just as her body was bisected by light. "Noa," he whispered, "We still need Ghost's help."

He felt her body rise and fall as she took a deep breath. She closed her eyes and stepped back, not meeting Ghost's eyes.

Ghost harrumphed. "Your brother is a lunatic."

James glared at him. Lip trembling, Ghost turned away. James looked back to Noa. She wouldn't meet his eyes.

CHAPTER TWELVE

Noa walked along the promenade of Time Gate 1, hovering in Earth's orbit. The promenade went the circumference of the gate, and was as wide as an eight-hover roadway. A skylight over her head let her see the entirety of the gate. Time Gate 1 was shaped like a ring; her feet were in the direction of its outer rim, her head its inner. The outer rim had twelve "jewels" set into it. From where she stood they looked tiny, but each was as large as a mid-rise building. Each had engines and defensive arrays—although the defensive arrays had never been used in Sol System's gate. These "jewels" were studded with docked ships. She heard a hum and instinctively looked up. The skylights in the inner rim were bisected by giant timefield bands. The bands were glowing now. They looked like liquid lightning, and then the lightning turned to rainbow colors and spread out in an enormous sphere within Time Gate 1's center. It was a breathtaking sight, one that Noa hardly believed could be created by humans. The rainbow sphere disintegrated and the hum died. Where a moment before she had seen the opposite side of the time gate, now there were two large freighters and a number of smaller passenger vehicles. The memory of the bubble bursting stayed etched in her mind. She sent it to Timothy without even blinking her eyes. "Always beautiful," Tim replied from where he was stationed aboard the Sun-Sin, the fighter-carrier that was their home, currently docked for maintenance at moon base.

"I forgot what gate Kenji's at," Noa said over the ether, dropping her gaze and searching the ethernet for departure information. "How did I not put that in my memo-app?"

"A-03," Tim reminded her over the frequency. And then his thoughts gently nudged her. "Shouldn't the Senior Lieutenant of a fighter squadron remember the destination of her mission without having to rely on a memo app?" Noa rolled her eyes and let him feel it. She'd just been promoted to the leader of her squadron aboard the fighter carrier Sun-Sin. Tim was an engineer for the enormous carrier, a position out of her line of command, allowing their relationship to be completely above board. Although she had aspirations for a Captaincy; that rank would complicate things, and for now their situation was perfect. "Don't you have a toilet line leaking near the engine to repair, Lieutenant?" she teased right back.

"Ha, ha … but yes, I have to report to duty in three minutes and fifty-six seconds. I better sign-off. Enjoy your leave with your brother, and don't get into any trouble—I know that's hard for you."

"You stay out of trouble," Noa responded, mostly to keep him on the line.

"Yeah, I'll be sure to put up the out-of-order signs." Because she knew Tim, she could "hear" the dry humor in his "voice" and feel his annoyance with the task in her bones. "Love you," he said, and then their connection shut down. Noa stopped on the promenade. For the first time, she saw the crowds swirling around her … and for the first time, she felt alone even though she could see Kenji now, sitting at his gate, eyes glued to an e-reader. He wore funny little old-fashioned glasses. Lately, he didn't want anyone "messing with his eyes." In her mind she felt the tickle of messages piling up, and a restaurant she passed on the concourse sent a little ping to her personal line, trying to get her attention and remind her that they had the best won-ton mein off-planet. Ignoring all of it, she strode over to Kenji. Although she made no effort to hide her approach, he didn't look up until she leaned over and said, "Hey, Little Brother!" He visibly jumped in his seat.

Grinning, Noa teased him. "If you were connected to the ethernet, you could have set your app to let you know when I approached."

Dropping his gaze back to his e-reader, Kenji said, "Or you could have just said hello before you were standing right over me." Adjusting the fragile-looking lenses in front of his eyes, he muttered, "Technology kills human decency."

Noa sat down beside him. "Giving you warning wouldn't be any fun."

To her relief, instead of becoming defensive, Kenji gave a sort of clumsy half-smile. "Sisters."

Smiling at him, Noa said, "Brothers."

Kenji's long fingers drifted down the side of his e-reader. "Go on," Kenji said. "Tell me what an idiot I'm being, leaving the firm and going back to Luddeccea."

Noa bit the inside of her lip. "Sounds like everyone else already has." And she agreed with them. He'd wound up disappointed with his job at the university. Politics at the academic level were the most bitter because the stakes were so low, her father always said. But then Kenji's love of numbers and abstract mathematical theorems had gotten him a position in a prestigious firm that specialized in extraterrestrial arbitrage. He could have advanced as high as he wanted if he just worked for it. On Luddeccea, as a member of the Fourth Family settler class, he'd hit a glass ceiling.

Apparently mistaking her answer for approval, Kenji glanced over at her. "I'm glad someone understands."

Noa felt her gut constrict. She was naturally honest, but she also loved her brother, She didn't want their last meeting before he headed home to end in a fight.

Looking away, he shook his head. "I've just had enough of

this place." A cleaning 'bot whirred by, and he drew back as though from a bad smell. "I thought technology would make us better, but it just takes away our dignity."

Noa couldn't restrain herself. "You'd rather be cleaning floors than playing with mathematical theorems?"

Kenji pushed the delicate lenses up his nose. "Maybe the person who was good at floor cleaning would rather be doing it."

"Or maybe they'd rather just enjoy their dole," said Noa, "and writing bad poetry, or whatever they do for self-fulfillment."

Kenji frowned. "We clutter our minds with so much data, we've lost the ability to think critically about what we actually know; and we've lost a connection with our spiritual selves in an avalanche of electronic stimuli … the dole isn't worth that."

Noa groaned. That was language straight from Luddeccean philosophy.

Kenji's shoulders sank. He looked away. "Noa … I know you don't believe in things like that but … being here, being constantly inundated with everything … it makes me feel lonely." His shoulders rose and fell. "I know it's supposed to make us feel connected, but it doesn't make me feel that way; it just makes me feel like another cog."

Pushing up his glasses again, he said, "Working on Luddeccea, I'll be doing meaningful work on our time gate, improving its systems. It's so old … "

Noa tilted her head. All the time gates were old and needed repairs directed by a human mind. The gates were programmed to repair themselves, but over the years some of the repairs no longer made sense. She looked around. The commercial sections of the time gates were always kept sleek and clean; but station staff complained that the living quarters sections had "roads to nowhere," hallways built for 'bot *access that were no longer used, and huge rooms of computer servers that hummed with power—but whose exact functions were no longer known. She couldn't deny that it was work that needed to be done. And unlike extraterrestrial arbitrage, people would actually see the benefit of it. Nebulas, if Lud-deccea's gate broke down and there was a famine ...*

She put her hand on Kenji's. "You're right, it is important work. And I'm proud of you for following your heart."

Kenji lifted his chin.

"And you have experience with the local culture, unlike most programmers who won't get on too well with the Lud-deccean First Families," Noa added, her lip curling a little in disgust.

For a moment Kenji's smile faded.

Squeezing his hand, Noa said, "I'm proud of you, Little Brother." He smiled back. Swooping in for a hug, Noa said, "And I love you."

Over a loudspeaker, an announcer called boarding for his flight.

"That's me," Kenji said, pulling away from her embrace.

Noa blinked. He had tears in his eyes. He stood up hurried-ly, and Noa stood with him. Grabbing her hand, Kenji said, "I think you're the only person who understands me." Looking down at her hand, he said, "I love you too, Noa."

And then before she could reply, he pulled his hand away, and she was staring at the back of his head as he headed for the boarding tunnel.

***

Noa crossed her arms and bowed her head in Ghost's dreary basement. Kenji loved her—he would never hurt her—and as much as he respected some aspects of Lud-deccean philosophy, he had to know it was out of control. Somehow they'd tricked him into serving them, and as for her being missing ... well, maybe they'd made up a horrible story about her dying, or told him that the vid message she'd sent from the ancient Luddeccean vid booth was from off-system, or a computer simulation … or … there were hundreds of things they could have told him. And maybe he went along with it because he believed them, or because he was afraid.

"Noa?" said James.

Noa jumped at his voice—she smiled wanly in his direction without really seeing him. Her mind was focused on the memory of Kenji at Time Gate 1, hazy with the distortion of time, saying he loved her.

Her memory might be dim, but one thing was crystal clear. She still had to save her brother.

***

"This screen is too small," Noa complained, sitting beside James on Eliza's living room couch. His laptop was balanced on his knees. The hard line connected between his port and the machine kept getting in the way of his fingers, making his skin buzz with irritation. They were in the safe room. 6T9 was seated nearby, in the process of rebooting. The hologlobe showed that Luddeccean guardsmen were still upstairs in Eliza's kitchen drinking milk and eating cookies.

Noa had been quiet the whole trip back. Granted, when they'd crept out of the sewer near Eliza's house and slipped into the boot of Eliza's hover in broad daylight, silence had been a necessity. And then after Eliza nearly plowed said hover into the side of her home and a Luddeccean Guardsman had helped the old woman navigate into her rooftop garage, silence had been even more necessary. They'd just had enough time to exit the boot and run down to the safe room before the whole patrol had showed up at Eliza's door, making sure she was okay. Of course Eliza had felt compelled to offer the Guard milk and cookies.

"Can you enlarge this small section?" Noa said, pointing to a portion of the screen displaying the electrical network.

They were reviewing the electrical lines and sewer system of the city. Noa wanted to plan a "distraction" to draw the patrols away while they stole the Ark. They could have done this on Ghost's light screens, but Noa didn't trust Ghost, and insisted they keep their plans secret from him until the last possible moment.

Reaching forward, James got his hand caught in the cord, and the plug popped out of the socket. The screen went dark. He felt his neurons go black in frustration. James's eyes slid down to the cord. "Noa," he said, holding up the end of the wire. "There is a faster and easier way to do this."

Noa leaned back in her seat. She looked away.

"I know you are still troubled about your brother. You don't have to worry about hiding it," James said. He'd had the odd errant thought about Noa—what if one slipped? He felt something within him alight with certainty. He could hide thoughts, couldn't he? He was sure he could, but how did he know he could? His head ticked.

"You're right." Beside him, Noa cast a furtive gaze in his direction. Rubbing her temples, she said, "It would be faster and I need it in my data banks as well."

For once James was glad his face showed little emotion. It occurred to him that he was curious about what errant thoughts Noa might have about him, and he was glad that curiosity couldn't show in his expression.

"Give it here," Noa said.

James handed her the cable. Looking at it, Noa sighed, and then plugged it into her port. Her dark eyes briefly met his. No words passed over the link, but an emotion coalesced in the depths of Noa's limbic system, a surge of neural activity that James's mind had no difficulty in interpreting. There was something about looking at him that

226

repelled her.

***

Noa hadn't hard linked with anyone since Timothy and looking at his doppelgänger was strange, and disquieting, and she wanted to pull away. The feeling rose in her before all her apps were up, and it raced at the speed of electrons to James's mind. She expected to feel something from him, shock at least—the emotion was not flattering, and sometimes she got the feeling James was at least superficially attracted to her. She was still too scrawny, but she was experienced enough to realize that for some people opportunity and proximity were three-quarters of attraction. They'd had a lot of proximity in the past few days, and he'd been more physically demonstrative than he needed to be. Before she could even say, "I'm sorry," aloud or with her thoughts, he said in her mind, "Let's review the plans, then."

Maybe he hadn't felt it? Perhaps the shielding had been adequate after all? He turned his head so he was facing away and touched the air. The engineering plans seemingly flickered to life in front of their noses, but actually it was just an illusion transmitted directly to their visual cortexes. If 6T9 were to awaken, he wouldn't see what they were pointing at.

She had too much to do right now. Worrying over hurting James's feelings was not what she needed. In Ghost's basement she'd memorized all the Fleet personnel that were planet side. She wasn't sure whom to approach first … if they believed in the "alien" invasion, if they believed she was a sympathizer, even a member of the Fleet might betray her. Hell, they'd be more likely to betray her. If they believed she was a danger to the planet, they'd turn her in, not for a reward, but out of duty. And then there was still the matter of how she would save Kenji.

First things first. Her jaw hardened, and she set her

memo-apps to work. She began saving the schematics for the sewer lines and electrical grid to her mind, as well as a recent map of the city. She'd just completed those tasks when 6T9, apparently done rebooting, piped up, "Oh, fun! Do you have a three-way link?"

"We're done," said James, too quickly.

He pulled the hard link from his own neural port without warning. Noa leaned back slightly. He had felt her repulsion, she knew it, that was why he was pulling out of the link so quickly. But she hadn't felt his recognition of her emotion—or anything personal at all, which meant he had better shielding than her. Which was very strange. Fleet mental shielding was designed to resist torture. That he had something that might even be better …

"Oh, how sad," said 6T9. "Eliza would have found it so titillating."

"Yep, we're done," said Noa. She looked at the hologlobe. "And the Guards upstairs are done, too. Let's go up." The small safe room suddenly felt cramped.

6T9 pulled down the ladder and they made their way into the kitchen. Eliza was there sipping a cup of tea, reading a strange grayish pamphlet thing that was nearly as wide as the table. The front had Noa's picture on it and was captioned in big, black letters, "Alien sympathizer still at large."

Before Noa could ask any questions about their visit, James said, "Is that a newspaper?"

Eliza blinked up at him. "Why yes, it is. It's how they keep us in line."

6T9 went over to Eliza, but before he reached her, Eliza flipped the paper over so he couldn't see Noa's picture. Instead there was a picture of a happily-smiling family with black polybolts in their data ports and a headline that read, "Permanent Data Port Deactivation Gives Luddecceans

Peace of Mind," and beneath that in smaller letters, "Luddeccean Premier makes it free—council discussing making it mandatory." Noa's stomach did an uncomfortable flip-flop. She hadn't seen any civilians with their ports jammed, but that day was coming.

Paying no attention to the newspaper, 6T9 went directly to Eliza and looked into her eyes, as though trying to see evidence of a concussion. "Eliza, are you having a moment of confusion? The stated purpose of the Prime Tribune is to keep the populace informed."

"I remember that is what they say," said Eliza. "Don't worry."

"Oh," said 6T9. He kissed her head and straightened with a smile. "I won't worry, if you say so." With that, he began clearing the plates away from the table. Eliza sighed.

James went and read over her shoulder. "I extracted a newspaper from the 2000s from a garbage heap on Earth. Is this published daily?"

"Yes," said Eliza.

"How interesting … they are reprising this technology," James said, sounding not unlike the professor he claimed to be.

Clenching her fists, Noa checked herself. Was. He was a professor. "So they're taking us back to the 2000s level of technology," Noa muttered, partly to stamp those suspicious thoughts out of her mind. "Great."

James looked up at her. "More like the 1950s level of technology."

Noa felt a cold coil of dread in her gut … not that an extra fifty years of backwardness should matter so much. Keeping her fear out of her voice, she quipped, "Even better. Anything in it that might be useful?"

"They know you're in the city," said Eliza, eyes scanning the pages. "They're imposing a curfew at sundown."

"Well, at least we know they know," said Noa, walking over to the table. She said, "Anything else?"

"The daughter of one of the first colonists just died," said Eliza. "Do you remember her, Noa? She came to your elementary school and told you all what it was like to be a little girl at the time of the first colonization."

Noa looked over Eliza's shoulder. In slightly smudged ink there was a picture of a woman who looked even more ancient than Eliza. "Up until a few years ago," Eliza said, "Grace Lao took nano treatments like me. But lately she's been returning to her Christian faith and the Luddeccean philosophy … she decided she didn't believe in the treatments anymore, they were vanity and against the will of God. She died from a faulty heart valve … could have been replaced so easily, even at her age." She snorted. "Even at my age." Eliza's eyes narrowed. "Not able to reproduce and no longer of any use."

From where he was scraping dishes, 6T9 piped up, "She still could have practiced!" Eliza tittered at that, but Noa's eyes were riveted to the page. Beneath Grace's obituary, were more … and she said, "I recognize one of the names." She closed her eyes. Her hand went to her stomach.

"Who?" said Eliza.

"Manuel," said Noa. "Oliver Manuel."

"He was only eighteen months old … " said Eliza.

"I knew his parents," Noa rubbed her eyes and began pulling their address up in her mind. The location gave her a start; it was worth risking Eliza's driving for. "Eliza, get ready to fly your hover. We'll go offer our condolences to his parents."

Eliza looked at her watch. "Noa, there will be a curfew tonight; we won't make it back in time."

Noa looked down at the picture of Oliver Manuel. "They'll help us," she whispered. "And if they don't help us, no one will."

And no one else lived as close to her little brother.

***

James was flat on his stomach in the boot of Eliza's hover. Noa was beside him, and 6T9 on the far side of her. The back seat was pushed down so they could stretch. Eliza was driving, Carl Sagan hopping on and off her lap. If Eliza was stopped, they could pull the seat back up quickly and curl into fetal position and in Noa's words, "Pray they don't search the vehicle."

"This thing itches," Noa said, scratching at the base of a pink wig Eliza had loaned her. Eliza had also loaned both of them her makeup. The tan liquids and powders made James look darker and Noa look lighter, and both of them look pasty and unnatural, but they were going to need to get out of the hover at the Manuels' residence, and were bound to be seen.

"How are you not itching?" Noa demanded, turning her head in his direction.

James touched the blue wig he wore self-consciously. "It's no different than wearing a hat."

"It is a lot different than wearing a hat," Noa protested. "It feels like I'm wearing a hot, tight helmet filled with fleas!"

"We could be doing much more exciting things with our bodies in this tight confined space than tear at your wigs," 6T9 said, without any apparent segue.

Rolling onto her stomach, and in the process, closer to James, Noa shouted at Eliza, "He just touched my ass! Did you not turn off his flirt app?"

"I may have forgotten," said Eliza. "I like him flirty, and the pink wig may be confusing him. His processor is old."

Noa slid even closer to James, the full length of her side pressing against his. He was less repellent than a sex 'bot. He wasn't precisely relieved.

"6T9," snapped Noa. "It's me, not Eliza, keep your hands off."

"Oh, it is you, Noa," James heard 6T9 say. "I'm finding the strange locale, the wig, and the makeup confusing."

"How can you get me confused with Eliza when she's right there, in the front seat?" Noa said.

6T9's skull started making a beeping sound.

"Don't overload his circuits, Noa!" Eliza snapped, turning her head in their direction.

"Keep your eyes on the sky!" James and Noa screamed in unison.

"Turn your eyes on me anytime you want, my darling," said 6T9.

Eliza blew him kisses, and the frantic beeping from 6T9's skull stopped.

"Oh, Lord, if we succeed, we'll have this day in, day out," Noa said, slapping a hand over her face. The hover stopped abruptly and Noa, James, and 6T9 nearly flew into the front seats.

"That hover came out of nowhere," Eliza said.

Noa sighed. When the craft resumed its journey, she nudged James with an elbow. "You've been unusually quiet."

He tried to think of a witty reply, and couldn't.

"Aren't you going to tell me how ridiculous my plan is?" Noa asked him.

"I have already stated my objections to your so-called plan," James said. Noa intended to show up at the Manuels' door without giving them any prior notice. James believed it would be better to approach them incrementally—send Eliza over, have her gently probe and see if they were dissatisfied enough with the administration to leave. Noa had agreed with him, but then said they didn't have time, and that had been the end of it.

"You never listen to my objections," James commented.

"I listen, I take them into account. I just never agree," said Noa.

James stared up at the roof of the craft. What was he doing here? His vision darkened. He'd failed. Failed at what? His head ticked rapidly three times to the side.

"Hey," Noa whispered. "You okay?"

The compulsive movement ceased. James lay mute for a moment. The proper response was, I'm wanted by fundamentalist Luddeccean lunatics, stuffed in the boot of a hover with another Luddeccean lunatic and a sex 'bot being driven by someone who isn't fit to park it in a garage. Of course I am not okay. He felt as though his consciousness was condensing again. It was so cold in the hover. Did Eliza really need the air at full blast? But all he said was, "I'm hungry." As he said the words, he realized they were true, and his vision was getting fuzzy at the edges again.

Noa's brow furrowed. "You just ate … "

He shook his head in annoyance. "I was there, I remember."

"We're here!" 6T9 shouted.

The hover started wavering wildly, and Noa and James slid across the floor toward 6T9. "Just let me land this thing!" Eliza shouted.

Noa put her head under her arms in a crash position. The craft lurched sideways, and James rapidly assumed the same pose. 6T9 crooned, "Darling, you drive like you're in the Mars Rally 6000."

The Mars Rally 6000 was a demolition rally. James blinked beneath his arms. "Well, he isn't wrong."

Noa huffed in what sounded like a laugh, but then the hover hit ground, bounced, and bounced again and all James could hear was Noa's and his teeth rattling, 6T9's head bouncing, and a frantic-sounding squeak from Carl Sagan. James thought the worst was over when Eliza cut the engines, but then the hover settled down before the risers could engage. Metal screeched against metal. James felt as though his eardrums and the auditory regions of his brain were burning with agitation.

He barely had time to catch his breath or for his frantic nanos and neurons to cool before Noa said, "Let's go," and slipped over to open the side hatch. Mercifully warm air from outdoors flooded the hover.

James considered just lying on the floor with his head down.

"James, are you alright?" 6T9 said, scooting closer. "If you were injured during the landing, I give excellent back massages." James hastily scrambled to his knees and crawled out of the side hatch after Noa, Carl Sagan hot on his heels. Noa was already at the door to the Manuels' residence, hand on a brass knocker. The building was a two-story white stucco townhome with red tiles. It and its identical neighbors had covered balconies on both levels to shield the windows from the equatorial sun. Beneath the sheltered stoop, the light at the corner of the porch was already on; its blue-white glow made Noa's pink wig appear almost lavender. James reached her just as she let the knocker fall. She stood facing straight ahead, back straight, eyes on the door's peephole. James looked around, surveying the surroundings. The Manuels' home was on a cul-de-sac, set off of a narrow street. All the townhomes on the cul-de-sac and street had narrow front lawns with palm-like trees near the street, and neat sidewalks paved with recycled glass of various colors. Each had a short driveway in the front; Eliza had managed to land her hover squarely at the center of the Manuels'.

James tilted his head, listening—the sun was close to setting and the nocturnal pterys were starting to sing their songs. A rustling in the ferns close to the house made him turn sharply—just in time to see a white cat dart across the street. At Noa's feet, Carl Sagan stood up on his back four legs and hissed at it. Other than himself and Noa, he saw no humans outside, but he did see a few children's toys left on the lawns. There were none in front of the Manuels' house, he noted. Noa had promised that the Manuels would help them. Their son had been born with a faulty heart that had had to be replaced regularly with artificial devices as the boy grew. Noa was certain the Luddeccean philosophy had managed to kill the boy.

"Can you hear if anyone's home, James?" Noa muttered. She scratched at the base of her pink wig, and then adjusted the dark glasses she wore.

James turned his attention to the door and tried to focus. The ptery's cries seemed to increase in volume, the cat that he knew was four meters away sounded as though it was just a few steps behind him, and the sound of Eliza being helped out of the hover by 6T9 was deafening. His head jerked to the side, and those extraneous sounds faded. Behind the door he heard the very faint sound of breathing.

"Someone is home," he said.

Noa looked around. Turning back to the door, she took off her glasses, spit on her fingers, and rubbed a long stripe across her cheek.

Behind the door, James heard a gasp. And then a soft voice. "It's Lieutenant Commander—Commander Noa Sato. Go quickly!"

He heard feet racing from the door inside the house. And then he heard the sound of marching boots. In the cul-de-sac he couldn't see anyone, but he estimated they couldn't be more than 400 meters away. There were no gaps between the houses; the ferns were too small.

"Patrol on the way," Noa said, evidently hearing it, too.

The door swung inward just as the words were out of

her mouth. A man stood there. He was of indeterminable ethnicity: brown skin, dark brown hair, light brown eyes and medium build, which was to say, normal. What wasn't normal was the flare of his nostrils, and the sweat on his brow in the cool night air. Carl Sagan darted between his feet and into the house. The man didn't appear to notice. He stared at Noa open-mouthed, and then his eyes swept to James, 6T9, and Eliza.

"Lieutenant Manuel—" Noa began softly.

The man waved them inside, whispering, "It's almost curfew."

Noa and James immediately entered, and Eliza and 6T9 followed. Just before they crossed the threshold, 6T9 swept the old woman into his arms and cooed, "Milady."

"Hurry, darling!" said Eliza, for once not giggling at his flirtations. Thankfully, 6T9 didn't argue—but the Lieutenant looked at him in alarm. A moment later, he shook his head and darted outside the house, slamming the door behind him. Outside, James heard the troopers turn into the cul-de-sac.

CHAPTER THIRTEEN

"Manuel?" said Noa as the door slammed behind her. She shivered, and not just because the Manuels seemed to have set the air conditioning too high. James grabbed her arm and pulled her back. From outside the house she heard the sound of breaking glass, and the slightest band of blue-white light peeking through the curtains disappeared. She heard loud footsteps over the sound of her heart, and almost immediately heard a Guardsman say, "You there, what are you doing? It's past curfew!"

Inside, a woman's voice whispered, "Grandmother, are you injured?"

"I'm fine," Eliza whispered back.

Beyond the door, Noa heard Manuel say, "My porch light was blinking ... broke the damn thing trying to replace it."

The Guard's voice went from accusing to solicitous. "Do you need help?"

"Yeah, that would be great."

A second later, yellow light broke between the cracks in the curtain. The Guard said, "There you go. Just to follow procedure, may I see your identification?"

"Of course," said Manuel.

"This way, all of you," the woman whispered. Noa turned and saw a slender woman with long straight hair who must be Dr. Hisha Manuel. She was leading 6T9 to what looked like a small cluttered kitchen.

As he entered the kitchen just behind Noa, James muttered dryly, "I hope that they don't invite the Guard in for milk and cookies." Noa gave him a sidelong smile, but he was looking away from her.

"That would be crazy," the woman whispered.

"Crazy like a fox," said Eliza.

6T9 growled. "My silver fox."

Hisha dropped her hand from the 'bot's arm. "You're not her grandson?" Hisha asked in a cautious voice.

Gently setting Eliza down by a chair, 6T9 said cheerfully, "No, I am her personal cybernetic consort."

The hand that hadn't been on 6T9's arm fluttered to Hisha's chest. She looked between Noa, James, 6T9, and Eliza, swallowing audibly. The woman sidled to the sink. "My husband will be back in just a moment, Commander." Looking away from Noa, she washed her hands in the sink—concentrating on the hand that had touched 6T9 … which … sadly, Noa sort of understood. Touching a walking, talking, sex toy was a little disquieting, although she knew intellectually sex 'bots were programmed to practice scrupulous hygiene. Her eyes flitted to the 'bot. He didn't seem to have noticed the slight. Despite herself, Noa still felt for him. Which was why 'bots were so dangerous. Worrying about 'bots distracted people from worrying about their fellow humans.

The front door slammed, and Noa breathed out a sigh of relief when she heard only Manuel's footsteps hurriedly coming down the hall. Standing straighter, Noa stepped forward. "I'm sorry about your loss," she said, before anything else. Manuel raised his chin. When Tim had died, Noa had felt empty … afloat. Manuel looked angry, and something else; she couldn't put her finger on it.

The engineer hadn't changed much in the past few years. His hair had gone gray at the temples. It was longer, too. She noted it flopped over the spot where his neural interface was. He was sporting about three days' worth of stubble; but he was still in decent shape, as was his wife, who was a doctor. She could be useful. And they would be motivated to help her ... if Noa had correctly surmised the reason for their son's death.

"You have a plan, Commander?" Manuel said.

"I have a plan to summon the Fleet," Noa replied.

Smiling tightly, he said, "Commander, I hoped that you were coming to say they were on their way ... that maybe by some miracle they were already on the edge of our system's space."

"No," said Noa. "We have to go get them."

Manuel's eyes slipped to 6T9 and back to Noa. "Who is 'we'?"

Noa didn't flinch. "So far, only the people you see in this room —"

" —and the 'bot," added Eliza hastily.

6T9 looked at Eliza. "Why are we summoning the Fleet?"

"6T9," said Eliza. "Please shut down for now."

"Yes, ma'am," the 'bot said. He abruptly went silent; he'd been producing a barely audible hum, Noa realized. His eyes went dark.

Manuel looked at Noa, his forehead written with lines of concern. And then he took Hisha's hand. They looked at each other; and, before Noa could say another word, Manuel said, "We're in."

"We'll do anything," Hisha said. There was desperation in her voice, not anger. To Noa it seemed too fast, too easy, and that didn't feel right. But, if Manuel was going to turn them in, he would have done so already. Wouldn't he? Noa's eyes sought James's, but he was looking at the ceiling. Her hands clenched at her sides. She wanted the Manuels' help too much, but for the wrong reasons. Kenji was so close ... the map of the city flashed in her visual cortex ... if she could only get a chance to see him ...

James said, "There's someone upstairs," and Noa snapped from her reverie.

"A cat!" said Hisha.

Noa's shoulders relaxed, but then James said, "You are lying." He stepped quickly to Noa's side, but kept his eyes on the Manuels. She felt a warmth rising in her chest that she hadn't felt since she'd returned to her home planet—trust—the kind of trust that only happened between comrades-at-arms.

Dipping her chin, Noa demanded, "What are you hiding?" An elaborate ruse to find out what her end game was?

It was Manuel's turn to hold up his hands. She saw his Adam's apple bob. "My son."

Eliza gasped, and Noa rolled back on her feet. James tilted his head. "But the obituary ... "

"False," said Manuel.

"But the body ... " Noa said.

Hisha spoke. "It was an animatronic—a 'bot someone had commissioned when their child died. I knew about it. They're illegal now so I begged it off them and then faked a death certificate. Some of my patients had their augmented children taken away, or they just vanished. Oliver would have been next."

Manuel took a step toward Noa. "Do you understand now, why we'll do anything?" A baby's cry from upstairs mournfully punctuated the question. Noa's heart sank.

***

James paced through the house, listening for sounds outside, and occasionally peeked through the blinds. Since their arrival, he hadn't seen nor heard more than a cat. He also listened as Noa related her plans to Manuel. Afterward, he heard Manuel say, "Dan Chow ... don't trust him; but you're right, he needs to leave. Since he built the system that controls the ground defenses, he's probably the best bet to shut them down. Still, you have the Local Guard to deal with. You need weapons … "

"I was hoping you could help with that," said Noa.

"And," continued Manuel, "you need more than an electrical transformer station explosion to keep the Luddeccean Guard at bay while you steal the Ark." A transformer explosion was an idea James and Noa had floated as an idea to distract the Guard.

James padded back to the kitchen and found Noa sitting at the table with the engineer and Eliza. Eliza had fallen asleep in her seat. She was leaning against 6T9. The 'bot was standing beside her, hand on her slumped shoulder. 6T9 was in an energy-conserving "sleep mode." Although he was upright, his eyes were dull and dry instead of shiny and wet. James hadn't realized how much that contributed to a life-like appearance. 6T9 was also mercifully silent.

Noa inhaled sharply. Leaning on her elbows, she said, "I know, but I don't have a better idea."

"I do," Manuel responded.

Noa sat back in her seat. "What do you have in mind?"

From the front room James heard the sound of Hisha's footsteps on the stairs.

"Protests," said Manuel. "Some of us have been planning them even before Time Gate 8 was destroyed. I can organize a 'spontaneous' show of civil disobedience within days." He waved a hand. "And we have access to weapons and explosives for those of us who will be aboard the Ark."

"We need more engineers for the Ark," Noa said. "A ship that size will need a crew. I've got a list of Fleet personnel in my data banks, but I don't know whom to trust."

Manuel nodded quickly. "I can find you a crew."

At that moment, Hisha walked into the room with a child clutched in her arms. He appeared to be sleeping, his head pressed to her shoulder.

"He's beautiful," Noa said, although the child's thick, fleshy face was distorted by its own weight, and one of his sagging arms was visibly cybernetic as well—plastic and steel that the Manuels hadn't bothered to cover with synth-skin. His 'beauty' was subjective, James decided. He had a hazy memory of saying such things himself in the past. But he also remembered confiding in a friend that he didn't want children because they were a "burden," "expensive," and "drooling pools of disease."

Manuel slid out a chair, and Hisha's body sagged into it, giving credence to James's observation about children being a burden. The woman twisted her body, and James could see a dark wet stain of drool on her shoulder, giving credence to that observation as well. Manuel cleared his throat. "And my wife, she doesn't have combat experience, but she would be useful aboard the Ark … "

Noa was silent.

"I'm not afraid," Hisha said quickly, her eyes getting wide. "I …would do anything … For my child, I would even kill."

Noa looked back and forth between the couple. Her lips flattened.

"You just … you have to let us bring him," said Manuel. "You can't make it to the Ark without our help. You don't know which members of the veteran's community have fallen for the Luddeccean philosophy, you don't know whom you can trust. I do. And you know you can trust me—" He looked at his wife, rubbed his chin, and looked back to Noa. "You can trust us."

Noa's chair screeched against the floor as she scooted backward. "No. Manuel, I can't take the three of you … " Her eyes fell on the sleeping child and up to Hisha. Her lips thinned, and she turned back to the Lieutenant. "Manuel, I'll take you, yes … " She looked back at Hisha. "But Hisha, you and Oliver have to stay here; you don't want to bring your child into this."

"I have to get him off the planet," said Hisha, clutching the child tighter, the pitch of her voice noticeably higher. "His heart will have to be replaced in a few months! It won't be big enough for him for very long—he's growing so fast."

Voice tremulous, Manuel added, "I know, best case scenario you can get to the gate in the cloud in two Luddeccean months, but who knows how long it could take for the Fleet to plan a campaign after that? It will get caught up in bureaucracy."

Noa's voice was soft as she replied. "You know that, when we commandeer the Ark it's going to be bloody. If something happens to your son during the firefight, you won't be able to focus on anything else." Rubbing her temple, she sighed audibly. "A child will disrupt everyone's focus."

"I'll sedate him," Hisha said.

"That isn't what I mean," said Noa.

James's brow rose, not sure what she did mean.

"Hisha," Noa implored, "Please stay here, for your child's sake."

"We won't have anything to remain here for, if Oliver dies," Hisha said. "And he will die if he stays here. We know that … we will stick with the mission … even if … " She swallowed.

Noa put her hand down too heavily on the table. She released a long breath. "I don't like it," Noa ground out, leaning back in her chair.

James looked between the couple and Noa, weighing their arguments. Stepping closer to Noa, he said, "We don't have time to find another engineer … and finding a doctor was pure luck."

Noa looked up at him sharply.

"Each time we contact someone, Noa, we put ourselves

at risk for being turned in. We are better off accepting their help and the risk to their child." He waved his hand at Oliver, still asleep on his mother's shoulder.

Noa crossed her arms. "The risk to bring the child on the ship—and then, once he's aboard—"

James shrugged. "If your objection is based on the risk to the child, there is no argument. He may die trying to escape; he will die if he stays here."

He heard Hisha gulp at his words, and Manuel shifted in his chair.

"I'm not just worried about the risk to the child," Noa snapped. "I'm worried that the child may endanger the entire crew."

James looked at the baby. His small cybernetic hand clenched in his sleep.

"Please," said Hisha. "We'll work hard. We won't let ourselves be distracted."

"Of course you'll be distracted!" Noa said.

Oliver stirred in his sleep, and Hisha shushed him. Eliza sank lower against 6T9's thigh. A whirring noise came from the 'bot's chest for a few moments and then went silent.

Noa sighed. She cradled her elbow with one hand, and massaged her temple with the other. For three heavy minutes the only sound was Hisha patting Oliver's back.

"He can come," Noa said at last.

"You won't regret it," Hisha said.

Noa's jaw tightened. "I do already."

With his hyper-augmented hearing, James picked up a thud above, and then another. Dropping his hand to Noa's shoulder, he exclaimed, "Someone is on the roof!"

Manuel cleared his throat. "Those are members of the opposition movement. I summoned them when you first arrived with the change in light bulb."

Noa looked at him sharply. "Military?"

Smiling tightly, Manuel said, "Not even close. Kids. None over twenty-five. It would be better if you hid in another room."

"You don't trust them?" said James, feeling alarm flare in his mind.

Standing from the table, Manuel said, "I trust them to cause unrest. I don't trust them to hold their tongues if they are arrested." He looked at Noa. "The less they know about you—"

"—the better," Noa said, standing. She looked at Manuel. "They traveled across the roofs?"

Manuel shrugged. "It's the easiest, safest way. Even the sewers are being patrolled now."

"Huh," said Noa, her eyes narrowing slightly. "How far does the rooftop highway go?"

"About a quarter mile," said Manuel.

Noa didn't reply, but the barest hint of a smile crossed her lips. James felt his neurons alight with alarm.

Noa snapped toward 6T9. "Wake up, 'bot, we're moving out." James could no longer see her face, but he could hear that same ghost of a smile in her voice.

***

"James, can you hear them?" Noa whispered.

They were so close that he could feel her breath against his cheek. Both of them were sitting next to the door to the bedroom they were hiding in, listening to the "opposition meeting" going on below. He could hear every chair squeak, every elbow on the table, and next to him he could hear Noa's breathing, faint and raspy. Across the room, on a bed, he could hear Eliza snoring softly, with 6T9 sitting beside her in hibernation mode.

"Yes," he said. "I can hear them very well."

Noa took a long breath. Again James heard a slight rasp. She'd started breathing heavily when they came up the stairs.

"Hard link with me, James," Noa said. "I want to hear, too."

For a moment, James sat motionless. The memory of her revulsion still stung. Below them the opposition members greeted each other. He heard hands clasping, and what he was fairly certain was backs being thumped.

"I'm sorry about last time," she said, averting her gaze. "You ... reminded me of someone. It's ... strange. I'll keep a better handle on it this time."

James wanted to ask who, and then he realized he probably knew. The mysterious Timothy. He remembered her darting up and away from him when they'd been huddled in his parents' cottage after he'd asked her who Timothy was. He nodded at her and retrieved the hard link, nestled next to his laptop in a small bag.

A moment later, opposite ends of the port were in each of their data drives. For a fleeting instant, Noa was unguarded. For less than a second, James could sense something, which was withdrawn and concealed quickly; then, Noa's filtering app must have kicked in, because he could feel nothing at all. It was disquieting, and also disappointing, he couldn't say why.

Downstairs, he heard the tone of the conversation shift, and quickly began relaying the words, exactly as he heard them ... and suddenly found himself in the kitchen surrounded by medium height, slightly tan, faceless people. He blinked. The kitchen was blurry and out of focus.

Noa appeared among the faces. She was wearing her fleet uniform.

"Fleet-issued avatar for these sorts of mental conferences," the vision of Noa said, her avatar gesturing to the mental imagery. She looked exactly as she did in his earliest memory of her. He felt the familiar thrum of want, and

246

was glad he could hide it from her. She was so close in the mental and physical worlds.

Not party to his thoughts—or desires, literally or figuratively—Noa continued, "I'm trying to imagine exactly what's going on."

James looked around the blurry kitchen and filled in the details for her. The faceless opposition members he couldn't picture—they hadn't had a chance to see them—but he knew their gender by their voices, and their weight by the sound of their footsteps and the way the chairs sounded as they slid across the floor. So he filled in those sparse details, too. An instant later, the mental image of the kitchen was exactly as he remembered it, and the tan placeholder people had more human appearance.

Noa's avatar shook her head. "Of course, you've got that holographic memory app running, you would remember everything." Her avatar walked through one of the opposition leaders and bent down to look at the table. "I can't believe you remembered the wood grain, though." Straightening, her avatar looked around. "This is amazing." She backed away from the table, where the constructs of the opposition leaders were drinking and complimenting the food.

"Don't you have an avatar?" Noa's avatar asked him.

"Several," he said, activating his avatar app.

Noa blinked—or, her avatar did.

James let his avatar look down at itself. His mental persona was wearing what he'd wear to a lecture hall— high-necked long silver jacket with patched elbows, black trousers, and polished shoes.

Noa laughed, or her avatar did, and she was exactly the image of the healthy vibrant woman from James's memory. "Patches on your elbows? Of course … I forgot. You're a history professor! For a moment there … " She looked around the mental space. "Well, I've only seen this sort of detail in internal 'scapes created for military ops, or in history class."

James shrugged. Since the opposition leaders were still talking about things that didn't seem terribly important, he changed the scene to the interior of 10 Downing Street, residence of the Prime Minister of England. He gave it the décor that it sported during Margaret Thatcher's administration.

"Amazing," Noa's avatar said again, taking in the antiquated furnishings. She let an emotion sift through. Emotions from another person over a hard link were like seeing an image through fog. Not as powerful as an emotion that belonged to yourself, but somehow more rewarding than hard data. He felt his real lips in the physical world want to curl up. She was feeling wonder. Although he couldn't smile, his avatar could and did. Noa's avatar beamed back at him. "And it's nice to see you smile."

In the physical realm, he touched the side of his face. "It is nice to be able to smile." She walked over to the desk and peered down at it. "No wood grain."

James tilted his head. "Nothing before the fall is as clear."

Noa's avatar looked up at him, brow furrowed. "The fall …"

James changed the scene, and Noa shrieked as she found herself falling down past the Ponderosa pines. She jumped at the 'impact,' and he switched the scene to a generic white room.

"It was a miracle you didn't die," she whispered. "With the organ damage you would have received … they had to augment you."

A miracle? To James, something felt off with that assessment, and he felt a chill race along the neurons beneath his skin. Down below, he heard Manuel explaining, "So I said that I used the signal for a reason ... " and he changed the scene back to the kitchen. Noa's avatar turned and gazed on the generic avatars of the opposition with laser-like focus. Manuel told the opposition that they needed to stage protests before rapid DNA testing was the norm—which James thought was a weak premise for a hasty gathering of forces—but the opposition ate it up. When it was over, and the opposition forces were leaving, Noa made him replay the conversations that occurred while they had been distracted. As Manuel and Hisha were saying their goodbyes, Noa's avatar whispered in his mind, "We'd better unlink. I get the feeling that Manuel and Hisha would be scandalized if they found us hard linking in their house." She winked and smiled. Considering her revulsion, James didn't find it funny. Maybe due to his lack of reaction to the joke, or her own distaste for him, Noa yanked out her link too quickly for comfort. Just before their link was severed, James sensed her concealing something again. Winding the cord around his hand, he wondered, was it just revulsion she was hiding, or something else?

Standing quickly, Noa took a deep breath and slipped out the door. Tucking the cord away, James followed. As soon as he stepped into the hallway, he felt the world shrinking and growing dark at the edges. He heard Noa ask, "A hidden stairwell?"

At her words, his world came into focus again. Manuel was standing at the end of the hallway by a floor-to-ceiling block of shelves loaded with toys, physical books, and replicas of starships. It was situated at a forty-five degree angle, like a door ajar.

Manuel shook his head. "No, not really. This house is so small, I tried to utilize every bit of space efficiently." He pulled on one side of the shelf, and the unit opened fully to the steep stairwell beyond. "It wouldn't be a good place to hide. All the townhomes are built to the same plan, and any patrol searching places would know there's a hidden space behind the shelves, if that's what you're wondering."

"Nah," said Noa. "I was just admiring your handiwork." She peered into the space beyond, and played with the door herself, opening and closing it. "Nice workmanship. No squeaky hinges for you."

Manuel snorted. "I am an engineer."

Noa tapped his shoulder with a fist. "You think this is small after living on a starship?"

Face visibly flushing, Manuel mumbled, "Yeah, yeah, I know."

Her brow furrowed, and she said, "You said that any patrol would know that this space was here—but you have piles of rope, a rope ladder, and climbing equipment?" James's world began to get dark again. He heard Manuel reply, "That is part of our fire safety evacuation kit. We're responsible parents, Commander." James could no longer see the equipment; the hallway became progressively darker and more blurry, tunneling into a narrower and narrower frame. He remembered a snippet of innocuous conversation a few minutes before. When Hisha had asked the visitors if they were hungry, one had said, "I'm so hungry, I feel like my stomach is eating itself." Like a chain reaction, that memory sparked others from before the fall. He'd made similar statements on occasion and had felt that sensation before. The room felt suddenly very cold, although the temperature had not dropped. Suddenly he found it was a struggle to stand upright.

"Are you alright?" Manuel said, his concerned face blurry on the periphery of James's vision.

"I'm starving," he said. But he felt the hunger in his mind, not his body, and he knew that was very wrong.

***

Noa opened her eyes to darkness, in the too-chill house. She was lying on the floor in the spare bedroom, a blanket thrown over her. Tomorrow, she'd meet her crew. In 48 hours' time, they'd be in space, bound for the Kanakah Cloud and the hidden time gate. The most important thing she could do right now, before all that excitement, was sleep. She sat up anyway.

Her eyes slid toward James. He was lying on his back, his eyes closed. Illuminated by a single beam of a fluorescent street lamp slanting through a crack in the blinds, his skin appeared blue. Maybe it was that bluish cast, the fact that his lips were fuller than Timothy's, the slightly aquiline curve of his nose, or the delicate wing-like shape of his eyebrows, but he looked more Japanese than Caucasian—even with his square jaw. His eyelids didn't flutter as Noa gazed down at him.

She took a deep breath—and felt as though she'd barely breathed at all. Jitters, maybe? Or apprehension? As a fighter pilot, she'd participated in clearing the asteroid belt of System Six. The fire power of the carrier that played base to the fighter squadrons hadn't been at all useful in the tight conditions of Six's belt. Worse, the asteroid minerals dampened drone sensors; so, human pilots had to go in. When a squadron went in for a sweep between the densely packed asteroids and the pirates, it was pretty much guaranteed that only two-thirds would come back out.

In those sorts of conditions, pilots began developing rituals before each mission. Noa would kiss Timothy on the cheek three times before she left. She would perform the sign of the cross although she was only Christian by heritage. Then she would slip her wedding rings in a tiny carbon fiber envelope that she tucked into the left pocket of the under layer she wore under her g-suit. Once, after thirty-six missions, after she'd slipped her rings into that pocket, Timothy had kissed her an extra time. She'd taken her rings out, put them back on her fingers, and went through the ritual all over again. The protection such rituals gave might have only been mental—but that didn't make them any less important. She fiddled with the stumps of her fingers.

As important as ritual was the people on your team. She took a breath and bit her lip. During the System Six campaign, she'd piloted a six-person bomber. Like everyone, she was expected to fly thirty-two missions. But during mission seven, she'd sustained a third-degree burn that melted her skin and locked her elbow. While she'd recovered, her first crew continued to fly. They'd been shot down during the first mission without her. Her next crew was fresher than Noa. When she'd finished her thirty-two missions, they still had seven more to do. They begged her to stay on because she was their "lucky credit." She'd been so afraid … but she stayed on as their pilot. Tim had been furious.

Her eyes slid to James. He'd been part of her crew for a while now. Mentally, she'd begun to depend on him being there. She took another deep breath that felt shallow and sounded weak. She'd been depending on him physically as well. She remembered every time he'd literally pulled her out of a jam. She was afraid … but she had to do this alone.

Carefully pushing aside her blanket, she grabbed the small bag she was using as a pillow, and padded to the doorway and out into the hall. She was wearing the clothing she'd worn when she'd arrived at the Manuels' house, so there was no need to change. She slipped to the bookshelf door, opened it silently, and crept into the claustrophobic closet-like room beyond. Opening her backpack, she pulled out a flashlight she'd brought along, flipped it on to the lowest setting, and found the rope ladder and coil of rope.

Hoisting it over her shoulder, she began to climb the stairs. At the top she found herself winded and silently cursing the camp. She'd once been so fit. Gritting her teeth, she undid the lock. Turning off her flashlight, she opened the door, slipped out onto the roof, and waited for her vision to adjust. The night was warmer than the townhome and she found herself almost sighing with pleasure. Luddeccea's satellites may not have been connecting the ethernet to the planet's denizens, but their glowing forms did give light to the rooftops. She gazed upward. She thought she could make out Time Gate 8 …

Light to the east caught her eye, and she saw what looked like a meteorite falling to earth. Noa's jaw hardened. A ship that had tried to leave? A Guard vessel shot down by Time Gate 8's defenses? Gritting her teeth, she focused on the mission at hand. In her mind, she pulled up her map to Kenji's house and let it flicker behind her eyes—it was in a building across from this very townhome complex. There were four streets she'd have to cross between there and here, but she could make it. She carefully began making her way across the roof. It had a slight grade to let the winter rains drain off, and between each unit in the complex there was a short wall as high as her hip. The Manuels had toys still strewn across their roof and a hammock. Treading lightly, she climbed over the first wall. The Manuels' neighbors had small potted trees in giant planters, and a vegetable garden in neat boxes. She skirted between the plants, hopped over the next wall, and loped toward the next, her breathing getting ragged and fast too quickly. She was approaching the next wall between townhomes when a familiar voice whispered behind her, "What are you doing?"

The voice might have been familiar, but she was on a mission and her instincts were hardwired. She spun, and would have delivered a kick to James's lower legs—a kick

253

that she could have followed with a rapid-fire kick to his chin as he fell—if James hadn't jumped half a meter in the air and missed the first pass. By that time Noa's brain was catching up with her feet, although if the quick parlay hadn't completely winded her, her brain might not have caught up before the second kick.

Nearly falling over, she panted, "Sorry."

Landing lightly despite his size, James said again, "What are you doing?" His face was as expressive as it was during sleep—which was to say, not very. Remembering his avatar's smile was like remembering a surreal but happy dream.

"It doesn't concern you. Don't worry about it," Noa said.

James's gaze shifted in what was exactly the direction of Kenji's house as the ptery flew. "You're going to Kenji's home, aren't you?" he said.

Straightening, Noa silently cursed the fact that he'd seen her little brother's location when they were at Ghost's.

"It doesn't concern you," she said again.

James took a step closer. "Of course it concerns me. You could be caught." His head did that ticky thing. "And then I'd have to find a way to get you out."

Noa actually laughed; fortunately, almost silently. The camaraderie she sensed between them was real. "Yeah, I'd do the same for you," she said. "But you don't have to come with me."

"Of course I do," he muttered. His hands clenched at his sides. "I have to. I don't know why … I wish I did. Then I could kill that part of me, and probably live a lot longer." He said it in that deadpan voice of his, and Noa had to fight to keep from laughing out loud.

"You're funny," she said, turning back to hop over the wall.

"I wasn't joking," he retorted.

Which made Noa giggle softly despite herself. "I can hear your eyes rolling," she said as she slipped along the next rooftop. She felt her spirits lifting. These things were easier when you had someone to crack jokes with.

"My eyes do not make a sound when—" Breathing heavily as she loped along, she flashed a grin at him. He did roll his eyes. "Everything is a joke to you." He couldn't smile in the physical world, but his eyes were much more expressive. Maybe making up for the things his mouth couldn't do? The exaggerated eye rolls and brow lifts were funnier on his too-perfect features. Some esthetic augments wouldn't be so expressive for fear of wrinkles—not that there weren't cures for such things—but the barest hint of a wrinkle that came with a frown, a scowl, or a smile was considered a blemish. His candid expressions showed a lack of vanity that was refreshing.

Panting, she came to the next wall between roofs.

"Noa," James said, not appearing even slightly winded, "I am not well versed in tactics ... but I have watched a lot of twenty-first century crime dramas."

Noa contained a snort at that, but only barely.

"Even if Kenji would never turn you in ... won't the authorities have people waiting for you at Kenji's house?"

"Of course they will," said Noa. "We'll have to figure out a way to sneak in when we get closer."

They reached the corner of the next wall, and she gestured with her head in the direction of his building. "He lives on the third floor of the mid-rise you can't see, but is just beyond the fern trees." She paused to catch her breath.

James was silent. When she looked up at him, he said softly, "Noa, you are not well."

Quickly returning to a lope, Noa waved a hand. "I know. Still recovering from the camp." She panted. "You'd think, being so much lighter, it would make it easier." Without her volition, her feet slowed to a walk.

"No, you're not recovering. You're getting worse," James said, putting a hand on her arm.

Noa jerked her arm away and broke into a lope again. A moment later, they reached the end of the block of townhomes. She attached the top of the ladder to a rooftop behind some enormous fern trees. She half-slid, half-climbed to the bottom, and then peered down the street. "I don't hear any patrols," she said.

"Nor do I," said James.

Noa looked back at the ladder. "Might as well leave it … can probably walk through the rest of the complex." She inclined her head toward a wall of fern trees that demarcated the edge of the townhome development. Perhaps twice as tall as the townhomes, they obstructed the view of her brother's buildings.

"Let's continue on the ground," she said, heading in the direction of the trees. The street had lamps, but it was an older section of the neighborhood, and there were plenty of trees and ferns to hide among … and truthfully, she didn't want to scale another roof right now; she was tired. She needed to conserve her strength. She bit the inside of her lip. Was she sick, as James had said? So many women had gotten sick in the camp. Of course, she had to have been exposed to something. She shook her head. Illness had a mental component. She would will herself through this; she could have her breakdown later, on the Ark, once they got past the blockade. Ducking her chin, she broke into a lope again, but she was grateful that she needed to stop and check to see if the coast was clear between clumps of vegetation and shadow.

A few minutes later, they reached the fern trees. The trees were part of a narrow stretch of "urban forest." Civic planners had put a path down the center of it. Skirting the path,

Noa led James toward Kenji's building.

After long minutes of silence, James said softly, "Who will fly the Ark if you are caught?"

"I don't know." Noa panted, and her gut constricted. "Maybe Ghost could share the engineering designs of the ship, and one of the Fleet personnel could fly it?"

"Do you think a pilot could be prepared in less than forty-eight hours?" James asked.

"Maybe," said Noa, panting heavily.

James continued, his breathing regular, his lope easy, "I'm not a tactical expert … but it seems once the protests take place, it will be difficult to stage them again. At least some of the leaders will be captured."

Noa only grunted. She tasted bile on her tongue.

James was mercifully silent for a few more minutes, but then he asked in a light voice, "Is it standard military procedure to rescue a single individual at the possible expense of the mission?"

"If that person is of strategic importance, yes. Starmen don't leave Starmen behind." Noa said it to herself, to James, and to the universe at large. She could barely hear her own words over the sound of her panting.

"But he is working for the other side," said James.

"They've deceived him," Noa hissed. "You don't understand how vulnerable he is!"

She drew to a stop, her locator app telling her they were in the correct place. She went to the edge of the trees. Kenji's building was across a field of open parkland the size of one city block. She didn't need an app to know the distance. The city was built on a plan. A block was 500 meters. Between her location and Kenji's building, there was a playground, a dog walk area, plenty of trees and shrubs, and a "nature walk" that cut a circuitous route through the field. He'd chosen the home so he could be close to nature even in the city; he hated crowds. Now, for Noa, it meant plenty of places to hide.

Her eyes scanned the building and she picked out his unit. Noa's breath caught in her throat. "I see him!" she said. She didn't think she'd ever really believe in God, but she did at that moment. She felt so much relief swell in her chest that it was almost physically painful. A part of her hadn't believed Ghost when he'd said Kenji was still free—she thought it was false data to lead her astray. To lead her here to be captured …

"I see him, too," James said.

Noa scanned the park. She didn't see any Guards on the trails. She looked to the roof of the building, and didn't see any snipers, but James was right. They would be waiting for her inside. So she had to keep her time within the building limited. She scanned the balconies. Maybe she could climb up on the outside; she still had her coil of rope. She remembered James jumping half a meter in the air. If they could just reach the second level, between the rope and his augments, they could make it. She took a deep breath and felt fear turn her limbs to cold lead. Maybe James could make it … Her hands and limbs were shaking, not with fear, but with exhaustion. She gritted her teeth. She'd made a career of taking action despite her fear. She crept closer to the edge of the field. They'd thought they'd catch her—but she'd steal him out from beneath their noses.

She took another step forward.

"Noa," James whispered.

She took another step.

"Noa," James whispered again.

She opened her mouth, about to tell him her plans, when he hit her from the side and behind, knocking her flat to the ground behind a small cluster of ferns just before the forest edge.

She lay in the damp earth, without protest, certain he'd knocked her down for good reason. Her heart beat in her ears, she could see nothing and hear nothing. His weight made her ribs and her lungs ache.

"What are you doing?" James whispered, his voice urgent. "You almost walked into the spotlights!"

Noa peered out over the dark field. "What spotlights?"

"You don't see them?" James whispered, shifting his weight and allowing her to breathe a little more.

"No, I don't, get off me!" Noa said, trying to pull herself out from beneath his hovering body to the edge of the cluster of ferns to get a better look. James knocked her flat again.

"What are you doing?" Noa snapped.

He didn't answer, but she felt his hand at her temple—or his fist, rather—and heard the click of a hard link being inserted, and suddenly the scene before her transformed. Spotlights were sweeping through every inch of the park. They were mounted on the roof of Kenji's building. Noa's eyes widened. In the physical world she saw only darkness, but superimposed over the shadows were men in camouflage wearing elaborate eye gear—a lot like night vision goggles from the old military museum. A team of four was moving in James's and Noa's direction. They stopped and dropped below a low embankment about 400 meters away. She made out the shapes of rifles on their backs. Noa's shock raced across the hard link before she could stop it.

James's voice came in her mind. "You did not see?"

Noa trembled with rage and helplessness. She projected the dark park she did see. She looked up at the spotlights, and mentally cursed in every language and dialect she knew. James was still on top of her, but his avatar appeared just in front of her. "Well, that language was colorful," he said. She felt nothing when he said it, no flash of amusement, nothing, but his avatar did raise a brow.

Noa let her avatar stand beside his.

"What is your plan?" he said.

Scanning the balconies with James's eyes, Noa saw Guards there as well. Her dismay slipped across the hard link before she realized she still hadn't battened down the apps that hid her emotions. "I'll figure something out," her avatar said. She hadn't thought it would be easy.

James's avatar turned to hers. She didn't feel any emotion over the link; but his avatar's brows were drawn, and his lips were turned down. It was strange how alien a frown looked on his usually stoic face. Noa's avatar looked away quickly and back to the scene before her and the spotlights she hadn't seen. "It's light just outside of the visual spectrum," she mused through her avatar.

In the periphery of her vision she could see his avatar blinking. "Ah ... you're right," James murmured. "Ultraviolet. I didn't know I could do that."

"How well can you see my brother?" Noa's avatar asked. "Do you have telescopic vision as well?"

The perspective changed so quickly, it was like watching the zoom on a hologlobe. Suddenly, she was sitting down on Kenji's balcony looking up at him through the glass doors. To her immense relief, Kenji didn't look harmed, or even nervous. He held a cup of tea; his hand wasn't even shaking. His clothing was neat and pressed, he'd gained a little weight, in a good way, and his hair didn't show the telltale signs of fidgeting it always revealed when he was nervous. "He looks good, at least," she breathed.

"He looks very well," James said.

Noa's heart pounded in her chest. "They didn't incarcerate him because they wanted to use him as bait," she said into his mind.

"But they thought you were incarcerated—why would

they need to do that if you were already locked up?"

"They must have just released him."

"Then why doesn't he look half-starved like you do?" James's avatar said, and she was shocked by the anger in his voice.

Noa couldn't answer. In the physical world, she struggled to get up, to crawl closer, but James grabbed her, and like the devil on the shoulder in a Luddeccean holo he said, "He never went to the camps, Noa."

Noa frowned. As though that meant anything. Her mind spun ... "Because he's brilliant ... they'd still find a use for him. Especially since they don't rely on the ethernet, they'd find his mind indispensable. They probably threatened him ... said they'd hurt me if he didn't cooperate. I've got to get him out of there, I can't let them use him!"

"He doesn't look like someone who is worried about his sister dying," James said, as Kenji took a neat sip of tea. Before she could retort, James said, "He seems quite safe. By trying to save him you'd be putting his life at risk, wouldn't you? The men we saw in the field were armed." He didn't look at her when he said it. His voice was light, almost curious, as though it weren't a question of life or death but a mental exercise. "Noa?"

"Of course I have to save him!" she shouted over the mental link, though she remained silent where they hid behind the shrubs. "He'd do anything for me—anything for this planet and his people!"

James's avatar tilted his head. She felt nothing from him, but his avatar looked doubtful. "If he would do anything for his people ... would he want you to risk your life and the mission to save him?"

"He ... he ... " Noa's avatar crumbled to the floor of her brother's apartment. Behind the ferns, in the physical world, her head fell to the damp earth. She locked down all her emotions before they rose in a deluge.

***

Kenji had his arm through Noa's. He guided her through the penthouse apartment on Luddeccea, threading them past the party guests. It wasn't his apartment; that was below in the same building. This one belonged to someone from the First Families. Noa noted that the furnishings were simple and tasteful, the carpeting below her feet was as soft as her bunk, and there was a prayer room off to one side. A crucifix was prominently displayed on the wall, flower vases and three books directly below it. Noa knew without looking that the book directly below the crucifix was a Bible, to the left would be the Torah, and the right would be a Koran. The owner of the apartment was Christian, obviously, but all of Luddec-ceans gave respect to the Three Books. The room was empty. It would be in bad taste to step inside a prayer room during a party ... which begged the question of why put the prayer room in a central location in the home, and leave the double doors wide open—but First Families always made sure the prayer room was in a prominent location.

Her brother patted her arm, snapping her attention back to him. Kenji was smiling, just a quirk of the lips, but on Kenji that was a sign that he was ecstatic. They reached the floor-to-ceiling windows that were the western wall of the abode, and he said, "You won't see a view like this on Earth."

The penthouse overlooked a park in the heart of Prime, the main city on their home world. The sky was crystalline blue, and there wasn't a rim of smog that followed the horizon. Noa's eyes roved over the tops of the strand of fern trees that marked an urban nature trail. She thought she could make out a complex of homes between their branches, but with the angle it was difficult to tell. Beyond the homes she saw a few buildings and then ...

"The ocean," said Kenji, "without a large stain of sewage

just offshore."

"You're right, it's nothing like Earth," Noa said ... or a shell of Noa said. She had a strange sensation as though she was here, and not here. She was half a being. Her hand instinctively went to the scars on her abdomen, still in the process of healing. At the last moment, she jerked her hand away, and nervously fidgeted with her rings instead.

Kenji didn't seem to notice. Still beaming, he said, "You should move back here. Exciting things are happening." Part of her wanted to say yes. To go back to the starship where she and Tim were stationed ... had been stationed ... felt like a return to prison. It was the walls—the gray industrial metal walls of the whole damn ship, even the room they shared. The small three-meter-by-three meter space that was their home hadn't been so bleak with Tim to tease her, to smile at her, or even to shout or scream. Even their fights had been life, their life, and now it was broken. She could fill her half-life with crystal blue skies and verdant green, find a new life here in the place where she had once lived.

Her thumb twisted the rings around her finger. The grief counselor had said not to make any decisions before the end of one Terran year. Noa closed her eyes.

She heard a change in the conversation among the guests as at least twenty divergent conversations merged into one soft murmur.

"My friend is here!" Kenji said. "Come, I'll introduce you to him."

Before she could protest, Kenji spun her around. A man whom Noa didn't recognize strode through the front door. His uniform and the ribbons on his chest marked him as a Captain in the Luddeccean Guard.

"Yon is amazing," Kenji said. "He worked his way up the ranks, and he's not even a First."

That he had made it to Captain in the Guard without

263

being a First Family member spoke volumes about his competence. But Noa couldn't help notice that he didn't smile as they approached. "Captain Yon, this is my sister Noa, I told you about her," Kenji said. "She is scheduled to re-enlist in the Fleet in a few months. You should talk her out of it. She was a hero during the Belt Battles of System 6. She's a pilot and would be a great addition to the Local Guard."

Yon looked down his nose at Noa. "I guess I'll have to take your word for it, Kenji," he said. His face remained completely impassive. He looked down at Noa's hand. One of his eyebrows rose. "You're married ... what does your husband think of having a pilot for a wife?"

And this was why Noa could never come home. Yon might have climbed the ranks on merit, he might be able to see the value of people beyond the offspring of the Firsts, but he would still have a blind eye to female talent. Even though, despite his higher rank, Noa had seen more combat, and had more genuine experience than he had or was likely ever to have.

"I don't have a husband," Noa said, not surprised Kenji hadn't bothered to mention that she was widowed. It was the sort of thing that would slip his mind, even though he had teared up at Timothy's memorial.

The Captain's brow furrowed into a scowl. The corners of his lips curled down. His gaze shot to Noa's rings, and then back to her. Maybe if she said she was a widow he'd give her a look of pity instead of a look of disdain that bordered on betrayal. She really didn't want his pity. When his eyes met hers again, Noa gave him a tight smile.

Not returning the smile, he excused himself, and crossed to talk with another two officers of the Guard across the room. The slight smile on Kenji's face as Captain Yon left gave Noa pause.

Later, when they were back at Kenji's place, her brother

surprised her by saying, "I'm sure Captain Yon will offer you a better position in the Guard than you have in the Fleet." While she was straining a splash of potent redfruit juice into two mugs of steaming soy milk, Noa looked up in alarm. "Kenji ... he's not going to offer me a position in the Guard."

"Of course he will," Kenji said. "I recommended you—and after System 6 and the Belt Wars—he'd be a fool not to."

Noa looked down at the juice. "Well, he'd be a fool, alright."

"Think of it, Noa, you could come home every night to Prime."

Noa looked up.

"You could have a place like this instead of the tiny one room you and Timothy had on the ship." Kenji spread his arms, gesturing toward the admittedly expansive two-bedroom apartment. Two bedrooms and a prayer room. Noa's eyes slid to the cross on the wall, and the Three Books below it. Kenji was an atheist, but he always said he respected the peace religion brought Luddecceans.

"I'm not his idea of a Lieutenant Commander," Noa said, throwing the strainer in the sink.

"What do you mean?" Kenji asked.

"Didn't you see the way he looked at me, Kenji?"

Her brother stared at her blankly.

Noa's heart fell. "You didn't see, did you? Is something wrong with your app, Kenji?"

"I must have forgotten to turn it on," he said, meeting her eyes too firmly.

"Why would you have turned it off to begin with?" Noa demanded.

"Because caring what people think takes too much energy," Kenji said. "It distracts me from my work."

"But with the app—"

Kenji's face got flat. "Did it ever occur to you that I was born the way I was for a reason? That maybe my ... my focus

265

… is a gift, not a handicap?"

"You always said your app made you feel connected, not alone … "

"Sometimes people need to be alone," Kenji said.

"Yes, but … "

"I'm less alone here in all the ways that really matter," Kenji said, taking a step toward Noa, head lowering and shoulders rising in a way that would be threatening if Noa didn't know sixty ways to kill a man with her bare hands … Still, she found herself taken aback. She scolded herself. Kenji didn't mean it like that.

Halting, he ran a hand through his hair. "I don't have to depend on the charity of my family anymore for company."

"It's not charity; we love you!" Noa said.

Closing his eyes, Kenji said, "Let me finish."

Noa took a breath.

Opening his eyes, Kenji said, "I get respect here. More than that, I have friends. I go to parties like the one we went to tonight."

Noa hadn't thought the atmosphere there was friendly, the focus was more to see and be seen; but she held her tongue.

"I'm even … " His face darkened and he looked down at the carpet. "Courting … "

Noa's eyes widened and her jaw fell. "Who … what … " Kenji had a girlfriend or two in his past. But none of his relationships seemed to last long. He blamed his app, said he had a lag.

Kenji met her eyes, blinking slightly. "Yon's daughter."

Noa felt her excitement evaporate. The daughter of Yon, she suspected, would court whomever her father told her to. She bit her tongue—this time, literally. In as civil a voice as she could manage she said, "And is it serious?"

Kenji rubbed his neck and looked down at his feet. "I dunno, she's pretty, and very nice … but I'm really too busy right now." He shrugged and met Noa's eyes. "She seems to like me, though."

Noa didn't know how Kenji could verify that without his app; but, considering the other domineering men the girl had probably been exposed to, she might like the distracted genius more. "Of course she likes you."

Shrugging, he smiled. "Well, maybe someday. I know here it's a possibility." He walked over to the window. "I know it's hard to understand, but here I can disengage my app and be treated more as a normal person than I ever could on Earth with my app engaged."

Noa thought to herself, if she were in his shoes, she wouldn't get the same respect. An eccentric man could be useful; an eccentric woman, though, would not be acceptable.

He gazed out the window. "I know you think this planet is backward, and it is in some ways, but it's also wonderful." She walked over to him. Turning to her, he said, "I know you face less prejudice for your appearance in our hometown than anywhere else in the galaxy."

"Except for the Fleet," Noa said.

Kenji looked out at the park land as though he hadn't heard her. In the rays of the setting sun, the lush greens were turning to rich browns and vibrant orange. "You say you'd give your life for the Fleet," he whispered. "I'd give my life for the people here."

***

"No," Noa said, her avatar hunched on the floor of her brother's apartment, clutching her head. James's avatar sat down on his heels, unsure of what to do. In the physical world, he held his breath.

The scene around their avatars melted, and they were lying in the dirt, in mind and in body. "No, he'd give his life for this world," Noa whispered, in the physical world and in his mind.

267

She took a breath that was ragged and too shallow. By now only James's arm was laying on top of her, but he moved it, afraid that even that small weight was hindering her breathing. She clutched her head in her hands, dark fingers scissoring the cable that hard linked them but not pulling it out. Emotions sparked across the link, too quickly for him to sort through them all, but anger was at the forefront. "No, he wouldn't want me to risk it." She snarled softly. "But I can't let them hurt him!"

And James remembered a conversation from when he was James Sinclair, the professor, with an older colleague. The colleague had said the only thing that came close to the love for children was the love for siblings. "They can be as different from you as chalk from cheese, they can annoy the hell out of you, but you still would kill for them. It's just as irrational."

James was an only child and childless, but he grasped hold of that memory, turned it around in his mind, and decided he had to convince Noa that dying for Kenji would be in Kenji's worst interest. "Noa, they won't harm him," he whispered into her mind. "They haven't hurt him yet and they won't hurt him later. You told me he is a genius and that they need him."

Certainty slipped across the link from Noa. "They do need him."

"You might make it across the field," James said, hoping that he was pressing an advantage. "Would Kenji? Is he strong enough to make it … what if they killed him during the escape?"

He heard Noa suck in a breath, and he kept going, giving his imagination free reign. "No, they'd kill us, but they'd be very careful not to hurt him. They would believe he was in league with us, however."

Noa took another long breath that seemed to shake

through her entire body.

"You said he'd die for this world," James said. "But he doesn't have to. You can save your world and save your brother—but for now, that means leaving him where he is."

Noa trembled.

James slowly exhaled, waiting …

Noa took a shallow breath. "I hate this, I hate this choice … "

James took another careful breath. He was grateful his app didn't show emotion. He suspected that, on principle, if she knew just how much he did not want to try and retrieve Kenji, she never would agree not to try and rescue him. As soon as he'd seen the spotlights, the rifles, and the Guard, his vision had gone black and a sense of failure had flooded every cell, nano, and fiber in his being. He'd sorted through his memories, desperately trying to find a way to convince her, and realized she'd only ever backed down from a plan for the greater good. Instead of trying to argue odds of survival, injury, or capture, he'd used that personality trait in his favor. Or her favor. And even then, that hadn't been enough … would appealing to her desire to save Kenji tip the scales?

He looked at Noa. The sharp angles of her shoulders contrasted sharply with the memory of her avatar's smooth curves, and also her breathing—

"James, can you look at the field?" Noa said across the hard link. In the physical world, a breath rasped out of her fragile body.

Across the hard link, Noa projected an image of herself, skirting past the spotlights to the first line of patrols, stealing a weapon, and firing until she ran out of ammo … until she succeeded or they killed her. James froze, not about to let her use what he could see to plan a course across the spot-lighted terrain. Her body shuddered, and in the physical world her voice cracked. "That's what I want … but I … I won't, James." As her physical body tensed, her avatar said coolly, "We need to leave here, but if they've moved the spotlights or if the teams have gotten closer, we may need to choose a different route."

James didn't look out across the field. Noa's avatar's eyes met his, and she let sincerity cross the hard link. Words could lie, but emotions could not. She was telling the truth—the vision of her storming the patrol was just a dream, a wish—James's body relaxed just slightly. He looked out over the field and transmitted what he saw.

"They haven't," Noa's avatar said smoothly. In the real world, she shook. He looked down and saw her face was wet. Her avatar continued without emotion. "We need to go back to the Manuels' before they do move." In the real world, she ripped some small plants out of the ground and her lip curled as tears dropped from her chin.

Taking a deep breath, she tried to push herself up, but in that breath James heard something that made him grip her more tightly.

"What?" her avatar said. In the physical world she hissed.

"I need to listen," James replied. Like he had needed to follow her here, like he had needed to pull the trigger in the forest. He pressed his flesh-and-blood ear to her back.

"What are you doing?" Noa's avatar protested. He didn't want her to be repulsed, but he had to hear her lungs. Instead of explaining with words, he let the concern slip across the hard link. Her whole body went rigid. She took a deep breath—and he heard a distinct crackle. His body went cold.

"What was that?" she said.

"You have some sort of lung infection," James replied. Movement caught his eyes. Raising his head, he saw the Guard team moving across the field. He sent the vision across the link, and then yanked out the cord, and helped Noa to her feet.

Panting, Noa said, "That isn't … what I … meant." But she didn't explain.

CHAPTER FOURTEEN

"Exhale," Hisha said, pressing a plastic mask over Noa's mouth and nose. Sitting on the side of the bed, Noa did as she was bid. The deflation of her lungs burned.

The trip back to the Manuels' home had gone completely without incident. Part of her had wanted to run into a patrol. She'd been filled with rage that had no outlet—rage at what the Guard were doing to Kenji, at the impossible choice she'd had to make, and at herself. She was leaving Kenji, Ashley, and a thousand faces without names behind, not knowing if she was doing the right thing. She'd felt rage at James, too—because she'd been weak and shaky, breathing too hard, and he'd asked if he should carry her as her pace had lagged. It had been humiliating. More humiliating, she had almost said yes.

She glanced past Hisha. James was standing in the door frame. The townhome was old, probably almost as old as the colony, and it was built when materials were scarce. The hallways and doorways were narrower than a starship's. James's head almost brushed the top of the door frame and he made the place look like a dollhouse. He was leaning in the doorway, arms casually crossed, and his face showed no concern; but he'd nagged her like a mother hen to wake Hisha as soon as they'd returned last night. It was Noa who had insisted they wait until morning.

He'd relented, but as soon as he'd heard Hisha stir when the baby woke, he'd gone off to tell her about Noa's condition. Hisha, being doctorly, had immediately insisted on examining her. Noa's eyes went to the crack beneath the blinds. It was barely even light yet.

"Breathe in and exhale again," said Hisha. In the doorway James shifted so his body filled the entire frame, as though he expected her to bolt. Noa had no intention of doing that. She knew when it was time to admit she was sick—most of the time, anyway. She did as she was bid, but glared at him on principle. His eyes narrowed. Over the doctor's shoulder, James stuck out his tongue—just as she had done last night, the third time he'd offered to carry her. Not very professional on her part, though in her defense, she had apparently been oxygen starved at the time. Seeing James stick out his tongue while he maintained an expression of gravitas in the eye and brow region, Noa laughed uncontrollably and so suddenly that it triggered a burning cough. A slight beeping came from the mask. Hisha pulled it away. As Noa's hacking subsided, Hisha said, "You have a cryssallis infection in your lungs."

Noa groaned. Cryssallis was a type of Luddeccean fungus that occasionally set up residence inside human and other mammalian lungs. It was fatal if not treated. The treatment wasn't painful, but it was long and cumbersome. James was suddenly standing next to Hisha, looking down at Noa. He wasn't frowning, but his jaw shifted, and his sudden proximity ... he was concerned. Noa ducked her head, remembering the sudden flash of emotion he'd hit her with over the link, so strong it briefly incapacitated her.

"Bloody bastard of a dung weevil," Noa muttered, because the fungal infection fit that description, and also because she didn't want to think about that emotional rush.

Hisha's delicate features drew into a frown. "It isn't particularly contagious. It usually only occurs when the immune system is weakened. Even Oliver is in no danger from it."

"Would severe malnutrition make me susceptible?" Noa said, looking down at the tattoo on her wrist, mind wandering back to the disgusting gruel that she'd devoured at the camp. She almost shuddered.

"Yes, it would," said Hisha. Noa noticed the doctor looking down at the stumps on her hand. She closed her fingers instinctively.

"I'd like to do a complete physical," Hisha said. Her voice was soft, but the concern in her words rang loud and clear.

James took a step closer. "That sounds like a good idea."

"Sure," said Noa. She knew it was a good idea, too, but instead of admitting it, she glared at James and said, "Happy now?"

James said in that deadpan voice of his, "Yes, Commander, I am overjoyed that you have a potentially terminal lung infection."

"I'll let you undress then," said Hisha quickly. Turning to James, she raised a hand as though to put it on his sleeve but then stopped. "Let's give her some privacy."

James looked over Hisha's shoulder, obviously wanting to say something to Noa. Since the doctor's back was turned, Noa stuck out her tongue at James. He wasn't Fleet, after all; and she didn't have to be professional. He raised an eyebrow, and said, "Very mature," as though he hadn't stuck out his tongue at her just a few minutes before. He was out the door before she could offer a witty comeback.

As she undressed, she heard Manuel getting ready to leave, and Eliza reassuring 6T9 that it would be best if she went to "meet some people" alone. Eliza and Manuel were going to round up the crew. It was dangerous, letting Eliza drive—dangerous to Eliza, passengers, pedestrians, and other drivers—but they were desperate. They had very little time to put together a crew, and Eliza's semi-celebrity status as a first colonist gave her some leeway with the Guard. If

Noa, James, or 6T9 were captured in a random hover stop, the mission would end before it began; and so they were staying put. Noa needed to use the day to come up with a firmer plan. Hisha had a day off and had intended to stay home to watch Oliver.

A few minutes later, Hisha came back into the room. Noa could hear a kid's holo playing before Hisha shut the door, and guessed that was what Oliver was up to. What followed was a physical exam and all the questions Noa would have expected: Did she need to be screened for sexually transmitted diseases? It was a nice way of asking if she'd been raped. She hadn't, and she told Hisha so. Was she having trouble sleeping? Yes. Did she want something for it? Not yet.

After the physical exam and routine questions were completed, Hisha said, "Aside from the lung infection, the malnutrition, and your hand injury, you seem fine."

Noa slipped on her shirt. She was actually relieved. The lung infection had been a shock, although it shouldn't have been; all the signs had been there. After the diagnosis, she'd wondered if her body was harboring other dark diseases.

Hisha touched her lips, eyes on the scar on Noa's abdomen. "Mr. Sinclair … he's not from Luddeccea. His augments are extensive and they look cosmetic, too."

Her accusatory tone gave Noa pause. But then she remembered her own first impressions of James—she'd thought of him as "too perfect." On Luddeccea, even doctors like Hisha frowned on "frivolous cosmetic augmentation." When she had first met James, Noa had thought he—or his family—had gone "too far." But she'd ceased to think of his enhanced features very much at all. It was strange how even perfection became normal and invisible after a while. She blinked down at her fingers on the buttons of her borrowed shirt. It wasn't just that his perfection

275

had become invisible—somehow, over the past few days, she thought of him less and less as Tim's doppelgänger. She wasn't sure if she liked it.

"You're sure you can trust him?" Hisha asked, startling Noa out of her reverie.

"He's saved my life a few times now," said Noa, carefully keeping her voice light.

Hisha flinched. "He seems ... different ... the authorities, they're saying that aliens are infecting augments. If he is somehow contagious ... "

Noa froze. Her skin crawled. Of course, Hisha was worried about Oliver; with parents, every decision would always come back to their children. Nonetheless, she didn't respond at once. A day ago she would have jumped to James's defense immediately, but after last night ... When people felt emotions, electrical activity occurred on the surface of the brain. Nanos could pick up the location of the activity, transfer a similar electronic pulse to nanos in another human via hard link, and they could in turn "feel" a shadow of that emotion. The emotion James had transmitted last night had hit her like a bright lance of light; that was the only way she could describe it. Her brain hadn't been able to recognize the pattern. She'd even had a brief hallucination ... the ground had fallen out beneath her, and James was trying to hold on to her. She thought that the hallucination was a product of her confused brain trying to make sense of what James felt. It had been surprising, intense, and ... alien. Her lip curled in disgust, not at the memory of the strange emotional charge, but at her own reaction to it. That she could even think that way about another human made her ashamed. She met Hisha's gaze. "The same authorities saying augments are being possessed by aliens would rip your son's arm off without anesthesia and let him bleed to death."

276

Hisha's face became pinched. "My son's augments are necessary."

Noa secured the last button. "James was in an accident back on Earth. He fell from high enough to crush bones and pulverize internal organs. On Earth, they don't feel the same way about cosmetic augments as we do—but he would have needed them just to look human."

Hisha bit her lip. "His mannerisms ... I've never seen anyone so ... composed and unemotional."

Smoothing out the sleeves of her shirt, Noa took a breath. "More recently, our friendly Local Guard shot his hover out of the sky. The facial reconstruction augments he received were damaged. He may not appear to feel emotions, but he has them." And no one would ever think him unemotional after feeling that bright charge of pure feeling he'd hit Noa with last night, but she'd never say that aloud.

Hisha didn't precisely look convinced; but instead of questioning Noa further, she said, "I'm going to have to go into the hospital to get you the treatment."

Trying to smooth over the last few awkward moments, Noa gave her a respectful nod. "Thank you."

Opening the door, Hisha gave her a tight smile. "I can't have you passing out when you're piloting the ship. I can tell them that Oliver's death has made me not want to be at home alone." Leading Noa down the stairs, Hisha cleared her throat. "Of course, I need someone to watch Oliver."

Noa felt her nostrils flare as they stepped into the kitchen. Hisha was a civilian, and she didn't understand what they were up against. She tried to keep from snapping at her. "I can't watch him. I have to work out a plan with James for commandeering the Ark. Now that we have the protest marches to factor in, we'll be able to change our strategy."

"But he's too young not to have supervision," Hisha

protested, going over to Oliver. Sitting in the corner of the kitchen in a bouncer contraption and sucking on his knuckles, he barely looked up at Noa. He was gazing intently at a holo.

Noa's eyes fell on James. He was eating a bowl of what looked like oatmeal with a fist-size helping of shredded coconut and a giant square of butter on top. Carl Sagan was at his feet. Noa would need James, preferably not hungry. She didn't distract him with a joke about his culinary choices. Her gaze flicked to 6T9, standing unblinking in hibernation mode, and was hit by inspiration. "6T9, wake up!"

The 'bot's eyelids fluttered and a soft hum came from his chest cavity and his head.

"No," said Hisha, apparently guessing her intentions. "No, no, no … "

Noa turned to her. "You said that you'd do anything so that your child could live."

Hisha took a step back. "But I can't let a se … a 'bot watch my son. Who knows what he might do to him? And he's unclean."

Noa rolled her eyes. "I'm sure he's been bathed since his last escapade."

"I have indeed," said 6T9 brightly.

"And he'd never have sexual relations with a minor," Noa supplied.

6T9's jaw dropped, and he stood up straighter. "Indeed, I would not. That goes specifically against my programming." It was the first time Noa had heard 6T9 sounding so affronted. Come to think of it, had she ever heard him sound affronted?

"Can you make sure the minor doesn't harm himself?" Noa asked.

6T9 smiled. "I am programmed to recognize harm, even self-harm, and to stop it with physical restraint if necessary, and a call to the authorities." A light buzz came from his chest. "Although, with the ethernet down … "

"You could call for James or me," said Noa. "We'll be upstairs."

"Oh, yes! I could call for James or you," said 6T9, eyes widening. He smiled and nodded, as though that was the most ingenious idea he'd ever heard.

"No," said Hisha. "He doesn't know how to take care of a toddler!"

Voice dry, James quipped, "I'm sure he knows lots of games."

Forcing herself to frown instead of laugh, Noa shot a glare in his direction. The cheeky bastard raised an eyebrow.

"Indeed, I do know a lot of games!" 6T9 chirped. He frowned. "Although most I could not play with a minor, as they would violate my programming."

Sighing, Noa said, "You can throw a ball, right, Sixty?"

"Yes."

"Make hover noises?" Noa supplied, remembering watching Kenji when he was a baby.

"Actually, yes!" said 6T9.

Noa nodded. "You'll have to do."

"No, he won't!" Hisha stamped her foot. "He needs instructions on feeding, and potty training, and nap time."

"Then give him instructions," Noa snapped.

"But make them simple," said 6T9. "I'm dense. Literally and figuratively."

Hisha glared up at Noa, and Noa swore the smaller woman trembled with rage.

Leveling her gaze at her, Noa said, "If you have problems with 6T9 watching your son in your kitchen, you better be ready to park yourself on this planet and stay behind. These are ideal conditions compared to what we'll face soon. If you think your son would be better served by staying here, then you say so, now."

Hisha's mouth opened as though she was about to speak. But then she snapped her jaw shut.

Noa let her stance soften and spoke gently. "I'm trying to save everyone's lives, not just your son's."

As Noa expected, the doctor deflated a bit at that. She turned to 6T9 and started to give him instructions for feeding, naps, and nappies. Noa took a deep breath and felt a sting in her lungs. Thank the universe, the rest of her crew would be military and disinclined to confront her over trivialities.

Motioning for James, she headed to the stairs. Grabbing a piece of fruit, he followed. "And that is why I didn't want a child on the ship or anywhere near this mission," she half-muttered, half-panted as she climbed the steps. She paused to catch her breath at the top of the landing.

"Maybe he won't survive the commandeering," James said.

Noa's head snapped in his direction. His tone was so flat, she couldn't tell if he was joking ... if it was a joke, Noa couldn't imagine it being in poorer taste.

"What?" said James, with no eyebrow raise and no expression in his lips, of course. A shiver swept through Noa, and she didn't think it was just because the Manuels kept the air conditioning too damn high.

"What is it, Noa?"

Somewhere, an air vent clicked off. "You don't sound as though you care, either way," she said softly and then mentally castigated herself. It was just his damaged augmentation—of course he cared, even if he couldn't express it.

"I should care?" said James.

Noa wanted to step back, but her back was already to the wall. The situation suddenly felt wrong, backward, and inside out. "Yes," Noa whispered, hairs on the back of her neck rising.

James's head dipped. The air vent clicked again, and she heard air rushing into the other room. "You care," said James. A slight crease appeared between his brows. "More than you would about an adult."

"The death of a child is the death of hope," Noa whispered, her hands fluttering to her abdomen. "It would be terrible for morale."

"Oh," said James. He shifted on his feet. "Have you caught your breath?"

Noa started at the lack of segue, but then she shook it off. They had too much to do, and too little time.

***

James watched Noa's avatar prowl through a three-dimensional map of Prime generated by his app. Her avatar's face was lit from below, her hands were clasped behind her back, and as usual her avatar wore her Fleet grays. James's avatar, this one in more casual Earth attire—a long tunic and loose slacks—walked along beside her. In the physical world, they were sitting across from one another, cross legged on the bed, Noa leaning slightly against the headboard. Occasionally he diverted his attention to the sound of her breathing. As she'd rested, it had become less ragged. He was worried about what lay ahead. He knew the first treatment for the infection would give her improved lung function immediately, but she still would be far from well. He didn't let that concern, or any other emotion, cross the hard link. She kept her feelings to herself as well.

"A disturbance there should divert the Guard," Noa's avatar said, pointing at the entrance to the museum complex.

Her words brought his full focus back to the mental map he'd conjured. Their avatars were in the courtyard of the Tri-Center where the Ark was docked; the mental model of the Ark rose just to her hip. She was pointing at the restricted wing of the complex where Luddeccea's spaceport and Central Authority were located. "With the protests going on, the ranks of the Guard will already be thin—they'll have to divert some forces to protect the rest of the city. The Guard left behind will fall back to protect the Central Authority wing or go to the main gate, if they detect a disturbance. That's when we'll have to move in."

James tilted his head. "What sort of disturbance were you thinking of?"

"I'm sure with Manuel's help we could improvise a bomb," Noa's avatar said, tapping her chin.

In his mind, he ran through his near-contacts with the Guard, remembering in particular that they were solicitous when not threatened. James took a step closer to the gate. "Maybe we should use another sort of distraction, something that won't immediately be perceived as an attack, that generates confusion instead of aggression?"

Noa's avatar snapped her hands behind her back again. "Agreed. Have any ideas?"

Instead of answering, James expanded the scale of the map until the main gate was as high as the walls of the room; it was still only one-quarter of its real size. The gate was an antiquated-looking structure of metal bars embellished with decorative curling ferntree leaves. Looking out from the museum campus, it was possible to see traffic streaming by. Luddeccea's Tri-Center was in the heart of Prime. The First Families had built outward from the Ark's final resting place, a few kilometers from the sea where it had landed. There were Guard posts on either side of the main entrance. Each post shot beams of light into the sky at a thirty-degree angle. A stone fence connected to the gate and continued around the museum complex port and the central headquarters; the fence emitted a circle of similar beams. Altogether the beams of light created a funnel-shaped fence of light in the sky. To cross the beams was to violate a no-fly zone. Only ships specifically authorized by the Port Authority were allowed to take off and land. Hover craft approaching the port, museum, and Central Authority were allowed to do so, only at ground level.

"It's slightly blurry," Noa said, indicating the gate and the hover traffic staying low, carefully avoiding the beams of light.

James nodded. "This is from my memories, before I fell. I was just a child when I visited the Tri-Center."

A brief surge of emotion sparked over the link from Noa—sympathy—and he felt his neurons jump, as though he'd been waiting for exactly that. He wanted to pause everything, to examine that feeling; but there was no time. In his mind, the countdown clock to Manuel's expected arrival ticked along, unstoppable. He focused on the present, and mentally opened the gate. Luddeccea had no history of insurrections, so the gate was seldom closed. Blurry shapes of hovers swept in and turned, either to the left toward the museum complex and Central Authority, or to the right toward the space port. Noa's and James's avatars were standing in a pedestrian area, backs to the museum. There was a stone wall between them and the Ark, and enormous stone bollards between them and the main gate.

James tilted his head, studying the bollards and the traffic speeding through the gate. "What if we caused a hover crash pile up at the gate?" he said. "We could make it look like an accident—"

Emotion sparked across the link again from Noa, causing James's neurons and nanos to spark with so much electricity that he couldn't identify her emotion. And then he did. Happiness. It sparked through his nervous system like a drug.

Her avatar beamed. "We could program hovers to crash. None of our team would even have to approach the gate." Her brows furrowed. "But if the hovers were unmanned, the Guard would know immediately that it was a ruse."

James's nanos and neurons spun. "We need a decoy of some sort." As soon as he said it, he was struck by an idea.

Noa's eyes widened in real life and on her avatar. "Ghost's 'bots!"

It was exactly what he'd been thinking. James's avatar smiled. The body he was in wanted to smile, too, but couldn't. "Yes."

Noa exhaled, and there was a ragged edge to it. Her avatar said, "You know, for someone who called this a crazy plan to begin with, you're being really helpful."

His avatar's smile dropped. "I still think it's a crazy plan. But if we stay here, we're not likely to survive until the Fleet arrives; maybe a year or so at most."

And he couldn't have left her. The mental map faded, and he was staring at Noa in the physical world, the hard link a tether between their minds. If he focused his hearing, there was still a slight rasp to her breathing. A thought occurred to him. "If we hadn't come to Prime, if we hadn't sought out help, your infection might not have been discovered. You would have died in months … or less."

She shook her head. "You don't know that. You would have discovered the infection either way."

"Would we have been able to find a doctor who wouldn't turn you in?" James asked.

"Who knows?" Noa and her avatar shrugged. "Unhappy what-ifs. Not worth thinking about."

But James couldn't help thinking about it. The Noa before him wasn't the vibrant woman from his memories, but she was alive, complex, unique, brave, and still beautiful, even with the sharp angles that had replaced smooth curves.

If he lost her … his vision, his whole mind went dark, as though the possibility was too great for his neurons to contemplate. Failure. His body shuddered.

"James?"

He felt her hand on his shoulder. The world stood still. Noa was close, he could feel her breath on his cheek. His gaze fell to her slightly parted lips. The edge of her teeth, very white, flashed in the dim room. One had a barely discernible chip. A tiny flaw that would have been covered up on Earth.

"You alright?" she said.

He couldn't answer. He didn't know. The moment felt real, and everything beyond the moment felt like a dream. The time before he fell on Earth, that felt like the biggest fantasy of all, but it hadn't been … He tried to focus on the memories of himself as a history professor in Sol System. He had loved his career, he knew that intellectually. He remembered his mind had always been racing with ideas for his next paper or presentation.

He "had" loved his career, past tense. The dream was fading. Noa's hand on his arm by contrast was in brilliant focus.

He put a hand on top of hers. "I'm here," he said. He met Noa's gaze and her dark eyes did not avoid his. He could feel her pulse beneath his fingers. "I'm alive." His gaze dropped again to her lips that were so close. "I'm more alive than ever before. It's a cliché, isn't it?" At least according to the books he'd devoured before. There was some comfort in that; the dream that was the past was helping him cope with the reality of the present. He would have smiled wryly if he could.

Noa gave him a lopsided grin, and something warm sparked through the hard link. "Just because it's a cliché doesn't mean it's not true."

The spark of emotion, that was also real. He wanted more of that—of her. He couldn't leave her, couldn't abandon her, even if it meant death. The same books, that history that he was connected to, told him his attachment bordered on obsession. His hand tightened on top of hers. He wasn't the type to become obsessed with a woman. And, as right as she made him feel, the obsessive nature of his emotions also filled him with apprehension. Something was off. "I don't know if it is the extreme situation, though … I worry it is more—"

From behind him came 6T9's voice, "Oh, you're hard linking! You should have told me. I have some apps with built-in themes. Roman coliseums with gladiator avatars, cowboy ranches, dragon lairs with shapeshifting dragon knights … "

Noa projected what she saw over the hard link—6T9 with Oliver practically draped over his shoulder. Despite 6T9's rather loud declaration, the child didn't stir.

"Go away, 6T9," Noa said.

"Yes, ma'am," said 6T9, and through the link James saw him disappearing down the hall.

Noa's hand was still on his shoulder, and his hand was still on top of hers. He could feel the bones beneath her skin, and the light throb of her pulse. To think of her frailty was too much. To think of everything that felt real being wrong was also too much. He understood now, at some deeper, intrinsic, hard-wired level, why Noa joked in the face of danger and despair. It was to avoid launching one's mind on inconvenient mental trajectories. Seeing her laugh would be infinitely better than worrying.

Cocking an eyebrow, he said, "I think that reviewing the sewer maps would have been much more interesting if our avatars had been dressed as gladiators."

Noa laughed, and let her good humor slip across the hard

link. It fused with the sense of victory he always had when he made her laugh, and that emotion and his own laughter exploded in his mind like fireworks. He let the sensation slip back across the link.

Pulling her hand away, Noa gasped and sat back fast. The cable between them drew tight.

He felt confusion across the hard link, and then nothing. She'd shut him out. "What was that feeling?" she asked.

The question echoed in his mind through her avatar, and in his ears, as she'd spoken the words aloud, too.

"I just … laughed," he said. He wanted to lean close again, but didn't.

Noa stared at him wide eyed. From the front of the house came the sound of a hover landing, and then the click of a latch as the front door opened. James heard Hisha's footsteps in the foyer. "Noa, you need your treatment … now!" the doctor called.

Noa yanked the hard link out. Leaning forward, she whispered, "Don't worry, I don't think anything is wrong," she said. "You just startled me."

And then she was hopping off the bed. At the door, she stopped and leaned on the frame, as though in pain—or weariness—and the awkwardness he felt over the situation was replaced by dread. She could still die. His mind went dark, and he heard a single word echo between his nanos and neurons.

Failure.

He shook his head. Obsessive. He was being obsessive … or maybe it was just stress, and adrenaline. Rising from the bed, he followed her. The reality that he was in didn't give him a choice.

***

Noa held a plastic ventilator mask to her face. Her nostrils were filled with the slightly acrid smell of her treatment, and it left a bitter taste on her tongue. Although the day had been sunny just hours ago, clouds had rolled in; and she could hear a gentle rain on the roof. Through the cracks in the blinds, she watched the afternoon gray turn to the dark blues of a rainy evening. The wet season was coming. In a few weeks the Guard wouldn't have to patrol the sewers—they'd be flooded.

"You're almost done," Hisha said. "You should feel the treatment begin to work immediately, but you won't be better."

Noa nodded. She could already feel the beginnings of relief.

While the inhalation device quietly hummed and delivered the rest of her treatment, she reviewed the plans she'd made. She tried not to think about the emotional surge she'd felt over the hard link. She'd hallucinated again; this time, she had hung suspended in zero G and watched a star go supernova. It had been strange and surreal and … more. Beneath her mask, she licked her lips, flushed and scowled; she had no time for foolishness. She readjusted herself in her chair and tried to relax. Carl Sagan, padding around the room, stood up on his four hind legs and nudged her hand. She ran her fingers between his soft ears—and her thoughts drifted back to that strange emotion and hallucination like a leaf caught in a stream. She told herself that she wouldn't even think the word "alien" and of course did think that … She searched the room with her eyes. James wasn't with her now. Cocking her head, she heard him eating in the kitchen. He had complained that the cold in the house made him want to "eat like a horse." She guessed a guy who played polo would know about horse appetites. Beneath the mask, she smiled. Polo was one of the most expensive sports she could think of, especially on Earth. Even on Luddeccea a horse was an expensive item. Horses ate a lot, and required a lot of pastureland and care. Perhaps that wealth was the key to James's strange, intense emotions; he had some hyper-weird expensive augments. Crazy Earther.

"You're done," said Hisha, walking back into the room, holding Oliver's hand.

"Shixty," the toddler gurgled, looking over his shoulder to the kitchen.

"Hush!" said Hisha.

"Shixty!" said Oliver.

From the kitchen came 6T9's voice. "Does he need a nappy change?"

James's voice floated from the other room. "I think that's his name for you."

"Are you sure? It sounds like he is saying a word Eliza finds too offensive for me to say," the 'bot replied.

Hisha picked up her child, her face crumpling in a way that foretold tears. "Hush, don't say that, Ollie," she murmured.

Noa took off the mask. Through the front door, she heard the sound of another hover outside. "That is Eliza," said 6T9, passing down the hallway between the kitchen and the living room.

Exhaling in relief that Eliza had made it back, Noa tucked the mask away. She joined 6T9 and Hisha a few minutes later in the foyer just as Eliza burst in. The older woman immediately reached for 6T9. He pulled her into an embrace and Eliza leaned against him. Her breathing was labored.

Looking over Eliza's shoulder, Noa saw—much to her disbelief—that the hover didn't have a single nick. But her heart dropped in dismay. "You didn't rendezvous with any of the Fleet members Manuel assigned to you?"

Eliza shook her head, still panting loudly.

"Check her for a cryssallis infection!" said 6T9, turning

to Hisha.

"I'm fine," Eliza said, turning to Noa. "They weren't there! All of them … gone. I went into their homes and to their work places, and then I was stopped."

Noa's eyes widened.

Still trying to catch her breath, Eliza said, "I told the authorities … I have a grandchild … in the Fleet … wanted to visit him."

Hisha snapped a breath tester over Eliza's mouth. It blinked green after a few short seconds and Hisha pulled it away. "She's clean."

"I'm fine!" Eliza snapped, but she was still breathing deeply.

"Sweeping you off your feet!" 6T9 declared, putting a hand behind her back and another behind her knees.

"I'm fine!" Eliza said again, but this time more softly. 6T9 gathered her in his arms with such slow grace and gentleness, it looked like he was performing a dance.

Eliza took a deep breath and then turned to Noa. "I'm so sorry," Eliza said. "Their houses were all vacant." There were tears standing in her eyes.

Noa took Eliza's hand. Her skin felt papery and thin. "I know you did your best, and if it had been anyone else, they would have been arrested."

Behind Noa, James's voice rumbled like a storm. "This isn't good. If she went to their homes and was stopped … "

"Their homes may have been under surveillance," Noa finished, still holding the older woman's hand. "Which could mean they followed Eliza back here." She felt her heart rate pick up in her chest. The acrid taste of the treatment was replaced by adrenaline. She felt her senses sharpen the way they used to just before a piloting mission. It felt good, and she realized just how much the illness had been hurting her. She almost smiled.

290

"I didn't mean to … " Eliza protested.

Noa gently squeezed her hand. "There is nothing you could have done. But we will have to leave."

Eyes wide, lip trembling, Hisha said, "We have to wait for Manuel."

"Yes, we do," Noa agreed.

"Really?" said James, peering between the blinds by the door. He didn't turn when Hisha's head whipped around and she aimed a glare at him.

"We need a crew," Noa responded.

Hisha's shoulders sank. She met Noa's eyes, the death glare she'd shot at James completely gone. Dropping Eliza's hand, Noa put a hand on her shoulder. "But be ready to move out."

Nodding, Hisha tore out of the room and up the stairs, leaving Oliver at Noa's feet.

"Mub out," said Oliver, sucking on his knuckles again. Noa looked down at him. He barely came past her knees. He grinned up at her, chubby cheeks splitting in a lopsided, oblivious grin. The almost-smile on her face melted and her chest constricted. She had to get this adorable lump of uselessness aboard a spaceship while taking fire—and Eliza as well. If 6T9 malfunctioned …

"Blasted heap of a leaking fission reactor," she muttered, and silently prayed that Manuel would bring her some Fleet personnel.

At her feet, Oliver giggled.

***

A few minutes after Eliza's arrival, Noa heard the sound of Manuel's hover. She peeked through the blinds on the second floor and saw he wasn't alone in the craft. Her heart soared. Carl Sagan apparently caught her mood, because he hopped and gave a happy hiss. She reached out to him and he crawled up her arm and curled behind her neck.

She scratched him behind the ears. "You're coming with us, Buddy. The Ark is a tourist attraction now and has a snack shop aboard." Her nose wrinkled. "And that means rats." Carl Sagan bounced and hissed happily as she strode down the hallway to the stairs.

Moments later, downstairs, her heart sank, again.

Noa's eyes swept down the line of men and women in Manuel's foyer as the werfle sniffed at them. Putting her hands behind her back, she tried to hide her dismay. There were six of them, four men and two women; all wore hats or hairstyles that hid their neural interfaces. Noa reckoned that only two of them were Fleet—an old man and a young woman who looked all of sixteen years old. Noa could tell they were Fleet by the way they stood—or in the case of the woman, how she sat in a wheelchair—at attention. Gripping her wrist tighter, Noa went first to the man, Manuel beside her.

"This is Gunnery Sergeant Phil Leung," Manuel said. The engineer's voice was shaky. He knew he'd let her down—or that circumstances had let them down. Since Eliza's targets had disappeared, Noa guessed that these were the only Fleet personnel he'd been able to find. She wished she could take him aside and tell him not to let his nervousness show in front of this motley crew. Normally, she would ethernet such information to her second-in-command—as soon as they were out of space and out of range of amplifiers, she would hook up a local ethernet on the Ark. In front of her, Leung snapped a neat salute and she gave him a tight nod. "Commander," he said, "it's an honor to serve with another veteran of Six."

Scanning her data banks, she pulled up Leung's file and, for the first time, felt hope. Leung had a potbelly that doubled his girth. His East Asian eyes were bright hazel flecked with orange, but bloodshot. His golden skin was marred by a bulbous red nose that spoke of too much drink, and his hair was thin and graying at the temples. He was out of shape, and possibly drank too liberally; but he was a veteran of the Io Company and had served in Sixth during the Asteroid war. She felt like singing Hallelujah. Gunny Leung's platoon had been in the thick of it—cleaning up the pirate compounds after Noa and her pilots had blasted the pirates halfway to kingdom come. She gave him a curt nod instead of singing, but she knew he could see the slight smile on her lips. "Glad to have you aboard."

Gunny's eyes went to Carl Sagan. The werfle gave a happy hiss and leapt onto Gunny before Noa could stop him. Gunny smiled as the creature climbed to its favorite spot, behind his neck. "We goin' someplace where there'll be rats, Commander?" he asked, scratching the werfle behind the ears as it relocated on his broader shoulders. Noa didn't answer that, but her lips turned up. Werfles weren't as common as cats on starships … but they were just as appreciated.

"And this is Ensign June Chavez," said Manuel, moving Noa down the line. Noa looked down at the woman in the wheelchair, sitting at attention. Chavez's legs were cut off mid-thigh. Most people tended to look like blends of all the human races, and as a result, didn't look like any race in particular. Chavez was the type of person who had distinct features of all the races. She had hair that was almost as tightly curled as Noa's, but it was red. Her tan face was dotted with freckles, and she had generous full lips. Her eye shape suggested East Asian heritage, but they were a vivid green.

"Do you have prosthetics, Ensign?" Noa asked as she pulled up Chavez's history. Chavez had lost her legs when she'd been caught in a landslide on System Ten's fourth planet. She'd been helping some colonists evacuate a set-

293

tlement at the time. No combat experience—but notes in her file said she'd served bravely and had volunteered to be among the last to lift out.

"Yes, Sir, in the hover, Sir," said Chavez. "Temporary ones, but they work decently enough after they warm up, if they don't get wet. I was waiting to rejoin the Fleet after surgery for the permanent ones." The words tumbled out of her mouth so quickly it took a few seconds for Noa to catch it all.

"We had to hide them in case we were stopped," Manuel said.

Noa exhaled in relief. "Go put them on," Noa said. "Now."

"Yes, Sir, right away," said Chavez, wheeling herself quickly into the garage.

Noa's eyes went to the other three men, and the one woman. They all looked terribly young. Behind her back, her fingers went to fidget with her rings and found them not there.

"These are rebellion sympathizers from my shop," Manuel said. "They should do as crew." His voice was gruff, and Noa heard him gulp. "This is Bo," he said, indicating with his head to the tallest of the young people. He had typical Euro-Asian African looks—black wavy hair, green eyes, and he appeared to be in good shape, at least.

Giving a salute that looked sincere, but was obviously unpracticed, Bo broke into a lopsided grin. "I was on my way to join the Fleet when the time gate closed. I'm ready to get off this rock." The grin got wider. "Really excited." He bounced on his feet. Noa's hands tightened behind her back and she made a mental note to not give him a firearm. Inside her head, her chronometer was ticking down fast. Noa's eyes went to the other three sympathizers.

The girl looked quickly at the other two boys, and then blurted out, "We're all augments. I have an artificial lung …

294

please don't leave us behind. Augments are disappearing."

"We are all engineers," said another, shifting nervously on his feet.

"Students," said the girl, dropping her eyes. "Engineering students, ma'am ... I mean, Sir."

Behind her back, Noa's nails bit into her wrist. "No one is being left behind."

The chronometer in her head was almost at zero. She turned to Manuel. "What weapons do we have?"

"I couldn't get to the facility we're using as an armory. We've got what Gunny had in his basement."

Noa didn't sigh. The chronometer in her head ticked down to zero. James poked his head in from the garage. Yanking at the hard link he'd used to program the hover, he said, "We're ready."

Hisha appeared on the stairs. She'd tied a complicated-looking sling thing to her front. Oliver was passed out inside of it. Meeting Noa's gaze, she stammered, "He won't cry. I ... I ... sedated him, just as I promised."

Noa nodded at her. "It was the right thing to do." The doctor didn't look mollified.

Noa glanced at the rain-spattered window. It was dark at least. "Time to move out."

A few minutes later, the hover was set upon by Guard ships as soon as it left the Manuels' townhome complex.

Fortunately, they weren't in it.

CHAPTER FIFTEEN

James watched from the roof as the hover sped down residential streets, bright with the shine of lights on rain-slicked pavement. Sirens from the Luddeccean Guard's hovers screamed behind and above it. He let out a breath of relief. They'd put pillow cases stuffed with hot water bottles into the vehicle and sent it on its way, hoping the vaguely body-shaped pockets of warmth would confuse any heat scanners—not that it had been necessary. The rain had picked up. It was pouring in rivulets off the roof, off the hovers he saw parked in the complex, and down his neck—the cool water would throw off heat scanners. He'd also programmed the vehicle to follow the streets instead of taking flight; Noa had suspected it would be shot down if it took to the air. On the streets, still busy with evening traffic, the Guard would hopefully be more restrained, and hopefully they'd get a little extra time to flee before the ruse was discovered.

"It worked." The words from Noa were spoken directly into his mind. They were hard linked. Noa had dispensed with propriety the instant they hit the roof. Noa was crouched beside him behind the wall of the home three doors down from the Manuels' residence, crouching under the leaves of the neighbor's rooftop garden. The rest of the "team" was with them. James's eyes flicked in their direction. He knew they were there, but all that he could see were Chavez's legs. They'd duct-taped plastic bags over her prosthetics—from where James sat, it looked as though someone had left a bag of garbage on the roof. His gaze went to the roof of the Manuels' home. They'd gotten out of the house just a few minutes before the Guards dropped men to the roof from a hover. The Guards on the Manuels' roof were following the hover chase with binoculars, laughing amongst themselves. All that separated them from James and the team were leaves, darkness, and rain.

The link hummed with equal amounts of determination and focused fury from Noa. It was oddly reassuring. James wondered if the Fleet trained its officers to transmit such feelings.

Over the link, Noa spoke to him. "The Guards on the other roof—are they distracted by the chase?"

There was a reason they hadn't moved farther. There were two more Guards on the next roof. James looked over the edge of the wall separating the rooftop garden they were in from the next.

"Yes," he responded over the link and sent her an image of what he saw: two men, rifles slung on their backs, gazing through their binoculars.

Noa transmitted data on their weapons to him. They were sniper rifles. "With built-in transmitters," Noa said. "We can't steal them."

One of the snipers said, "Did you see that MX? Just jumped 100 meters straight vertical." He whistled. "Sweet machine."

"Think they'll ever sell those hovers to civilians? I sure want one," said his companion.

"We got 'em!" said the first sniper, springing a bit.

The second said, "Not yet."

And then there was the crackle of a radio device that looked like it might have been transported straight from the 1990s on one of the men's thighs. "Team S1, report!"

"We're here," said the first sniper. "All's well. Almost in position."

"Unprofessional," Noa whispered into his mind. "Lucky us."

Noa turned to Chavez, Manuel, and Leung and delivered some quick hand gestures. The three officers nodded.

Over the link, Noa said, "James, you and I are going to take them."

She slipped a stunner from a holster on her thigh—a weapon from Gunny Leung's "arsenal." They also each had a pistol and a rifle, but they were too loud. A stunner pressed against a man's side would be nearly silent.

"I'm allowed to use deadly force?" James said, taking out his own stunner, but eyeing the Guards on the Manuels' roof standing outside of the back door.

"Of course," Noa said into his mind, eyes on the two snipers. "Try not to let the sound of his body hitting the ground alert the others."

"Understood," James replied across the link. They didn't just have to worry about the other Guard team hearing. 6T9 was programmed not to hurt humans and to offer assistance in the event of injury. Such programming would override any orders Eliza gave him.

"Now," said Noa, yanking out the hard link between them.

She slipped over the wall between them and the two snipers. Her breathing was steady and even, her movements sure. James followed. Crouching low, they hugged the shadow of the wall that separated the rooftops.

From the hover chase blocks away, an explosion went off, briefly illuminating the rooftop. The snipers whistled and chuckled. As soon as the light subsided, Noa and James rushed forward. James put his right hand around his target's mouth. James was wearing a thin, stunner-resistant glove on that hand. Pressing the stunner to the man's side, he hit the activate button. James heard a soft click as two twin prongs sprang from the stunner's business end. He prepared for the man's body to convulse. Nothing happened. Recovering from his mental shock, the man began to struggle.

James pictured the man flipping him over his shoulder, and the Guard being alerted to their presence in the resulting scuffle. He acted before any of that happened.

***

Noa restrained a grunt as she lowered the sniper's body gently to the roof. In the periphery of her vision, she saw James do the same. She'd known he could do it. Chavez would have been an obvious choice, but her temporary limbs creaked. Leung was out of shape. Manuel was an engineer—he had the training, but not the experience.

From her right, she heard shouts. Every hair on the back of her neck rose, but then she saw it was just the rooftop team at the Manuels' house flooding into the dwelling. She heard the front door burst open from below, and shouts as the home was invaded from both directions.

She signaled the rest of the team to follow James and herself. Chavez launched herself over the wall and the rest followed, with Gunny, Carl Sagan wrapped around his neck like a shawl, taking up the rear.

At James's feet a muffled voice crackled, "Team S1, report."

"The radio," James said.

"Find it!" Noa hissed, rolling over the man James had stunned.

James plucked a device the size of a brick from the man's side pocket and began fumbling with the buttons.

"Mimic his voice!" Noa whispered.

James blinked at her. "Mimic his voice?"

"You mimic me all the time!" Noa said.

"I hadn't thought about it … " said James, staring at the radio.

"Team S1?"

"What do I say?" James said.

"That we're in position!" Noa said as Chavez slid over the wall of the adjoining roof and the rest of the team followed.

"In position," James said. Noa breathed out a sigh of relief. He'd perfectly mimicked the sniper who'd spoken earlier.

An order crackled over the device. "Keep your eye on the cul-de-sac, make sure no one climbs out a window."

Noa rolled her hands, trying to urge James to keep speaking.

James's eyes got wide, but then into the radio he said, "We got 'em."

Noa's brows drew together. That was exactly what the man had said earlier—maybe he could only mimic phrases he'd heard?

She breathed out a sigh of relief when there was just a chuckle from the other end. "Yeah, I think we did."

Checking over her shoulder, she saw that the two remaining Guards on the Manuels' roof weren't looking in their direction. "Keep that," she said, pointing at the brick-like transmitter he was carrying. James nodded.

Gunny Leung stepped over the man James had stunned and looked down. Noa followed his gaze on reflex. For the first time, she noticed the sniper's neck was at an awkward angle and his eyes were wide. His neck was broken … but she remembered James taking out the stunner. Gunny grunted. Noa put her finger to her lips for silence. She looked to James; he was motioning for her to move quickly. She and Gunny loped to the next wall. But the sniper's empty eyes stayed in her mind.

***

The eyes of the dead sniper were still in Noa's mind as she stood guard in an alley just beyond the townhome complex, pistol in hand. James was across from her, looking the other way. Chavez and Manuel had the other side of the narrow thoroughfare. Gunny Leung and the three engineering students were struggling with a sewer grate while Hisha waited with Oliver in his carrier, and 6T9 stood with Eliza in his arms. On either side of them, tall residential buildings rose steeply.

Behind Noa and James, Bo grumbled. "I could be more help if I had a rifle or a pistol."

Gunny Leung answered. "Lift the grate if you want to be any help at all, son." Carl Sagan gave a tiny growl from Gunny's shoulders as though to emphasize the old sergeant's point.

"His venom sacks have been milked, right?" asked Bo.

"Not in a long, long time," said Gunny. Bo seemed to redouble his efforts.

"Eliza," 6T9 whispered, "I am sure one of the gentlemen from the authorities on the rooftop had a broken neck."

Noa's whole body tensed.

6T9 continued, "Shouldn't we call an ambulance for him? One of the dwellings in these buildings should have one of those telephone lines."

"No, no, no," Eliza said back. "They were just sleeping on the job. Nothing to worry about, my beloved."

"If you are certain," said 6T9.

Noa exhaled.

Gunny's eyes flitted to James and narrowed. Noa couldn't decide if he looked suspicious or just appraising.

"I meant to tell you, the stunner didn't work," James whispered. His voice made her jump. He was still facing away, looking out onto the street beyond the alley. "I had to break the man's neck."

He said it so easily … because it was easy for him. She shivered, and it wasn't because of the rain. She remembered him saying, "I have no misgivings about killing, but I wonder if I should."

A history professor, even one that was an avowed adventurist, should not be able to break a man's neck with such ease. There was more to him than met the eye. She bit her lip. Of course there was. He was the "archangel," she'd known that since she'd awakened next to him in his parents' cottage. She'd thought it was a mistake then, just the authorities targeting an off-worlder out of some mistaken intelligence and religious nuttiness. But maybe there was a kernel of truth in their paranoia? A tiny part of her whispered that James was dangerous, that he might be part of some conspiracy. She scowled. Of course, the Luddecceans thought she was dangerous, too—and also part of the Archangel Project.

"Noa?" said James, holding the stunner toward her.

Glancing down at it, she said, "Stow it. Maybe Manuel can fix it."

"Hmm … good idea."

As he slipped it into a pocket, the girl whose name Noa still did not know, said, "I wonder when they'll realize that the hover doesn't have us in it."

At that moment, the radio in James's pocket burst with static. "Suspects were not apprehended. Repeat: suspects were not apprehended."

"The house is empty," another voice said over the radio.

"They were never in the hover," said yet another voice.

Behind Noa, Leung said, "Grate's off. Only room for single file."

"Gunny, Chavez, you first," Noa ordered. She gestured to the students. "You next—help Eliza and Hisha down."

302

As everyone snapped into action, the radio-brick thing hissed, "Team S1, report."

James pulled it out of his pocket and stared at it.

"Say something," Noa said.

"In position," James said in the sniper's voice.

"I can't get a visual on you, S1," said another voice.

"In position," James said again.

Another voice crackled over the radio. "Is everything alright?"

James blinked at the radio.

"Make something up! Stall for time," said Eliza, lifting her head from 6T9's chest. "Quickly!"

Lifting the radio to his lips again, James mimicked the first sniper. "That MX is a sweet machine." He coughed, and repeated the second sniper's words verbatim. "Think they'll ever sell those hovers to civilians? I sure want one."

Noa winced. Catching her eye, James shrugged helplessly, looking not so much dangerous as befuddled. Noa felt her heart growing lighter. James wasn't part of some alien conspiracy. And if he was tied to the "Archangel Project," it was only in whatever oblivious way Noa herself was tied to it.

"It was a boring conversation anyway," Noa said, wondering if he'd catch the reference to that old move-ee he'd shared with her.

Chatter exploded from the radio again. Someone said, "S1, I'm going to send a team to your position."

Noa's heart beat fast. Hisha was handing Oliver to someone below, and her movements seemed to be in slow motion. They were steps from the townhome complex, and any minute their path would be discerned.

Over the radio, someone said, "Team S1 is down. Repeat, S1 is down."

"Should I tell them we're having a reactor leak, too?" James asked, apparently having caught the reference. He raised an eyebrow—it was his 'I am teasing you look.' And, damn it … she needed someone to joke with at times like this, when everything could go down a mine pit at any moment. Grinning, Noa gave him a wink. That earned her an eye roll. She motioned to Manuel. "You go down, we'll follow."

Manuel slid down through the grate and James said to Noa, "After you."

Noa slid through the grate into the darkness and fell into line behind Hisha, Oliver's sleeping cherubic face just visible above the folds of fabric of his carrier. She flipped down some heavy, ancient night vision goggles that had belonged to Gunny's grandfather and only slightly improved her vision.

She frowned. The darkness and the cluster of frightened civilians in a tunnel brought back memories of the evacuation of New Rio. The colony had been infected with a plague that was incurable at the time. Most of the carriers were oblivious. She felt herself shiver, even though it was warm. Being oblivious to his part of the Archangel Project didn't mean James wasn't dangerous.

It didn't mean she wasn't dangerous, either.

***

James poked his head around the intersection. He scanned in both directions. All he saw was the glint of the water running through the tunnel. "Clear," he said.

Noa slipped past him, pistol raised, and then gestured for the people behind him.

"Not clear back behind us," Gunny whispered. "We've got four incoming, 725 meters. Tunnel from the left."

"We're almost there," Noa whispered. "We'll make it."

James focused behind them. He heard the splash of footsteps, but couldn't detect the exact location or the number of men. Gunny must have had more sophisticated augmentation. It made James jealous—and that was ridiculous. He was a history professor; he wasn't supposed to have sophisticated locator apps.

The team walked a few more meters down the new tunnel. It was cooler in the tunnels, now that it had rained; their clothes were drenched. James felt a tightness in his skin, and knew that if he looked he'd find his bare arms to be as pale as bone. He found himself wishing he'd had a chance for a snack. He had the sensation of his vision and focus tunneling, as it did whenever he was hungry. The footsteps trailing the team faded out of his consciousness, and then he was aware only of himself and Noa. She was slinking through the darkness beside him with amazing stealth. Her breathing was no longer raspy, and her movements were fluid; she wouldn't need his arm this time. At that thought, he nearly tripped over his own feet.

Noa's eyes met his in the darkness. He shrugged, trying to convey nothing to worry about. He blinked, and remembered he had a snack on him. He pulled out half of a protein bar and started to munch. His vision cleared and his focus expanded. Beside him, Noa drew her head back, and then looked heavenward. He recognized the gesture from their time in the freight car, and remembered the words that normally went with it. "Eating again?" she would say.

He shrugged again, and put the tiny remainder of the bar back into his pocket.

A slight red glow fell on his shoulder. He spun, pistol raised, and found himself staring at a tiny blinking red light at the side of 6T9's head.

Staring at the muzzle of the pistol, Eliza gasped. 6T9 made no indication that he noticed the weapon. In a mechanical voice the 'bot said, "I am no longer able to assist." He set Eliza gently down and then started to waver. Before James's brain had caught up to what was happening,

Noa, Manuel, Chavez, and the engineering students were grabbing the 'bot by his arms and were easing him to the ground. As they settled him down, 6T9 said, "Thank you."

Hand to her mouth, Eliza leaned over him.

"Low on power," 6T9 said, thankfully quietly.

"Leave him here," one of the engineering students whispered.

"That might be wise," said 6T9.

"No!" cried Eliza, putting her hands on the 'bot's shoulders. "If he stays, I stay, and there goes your mission bankroll."

"6T9, will you be able to walk another 600 meters?" Noa asked.

"Of course he will!" said Eliza, her voice too shrill.

One of the engineering students put a finger to her lips.

"I cannot walk any farther," said 6T9.

"You can, you can," Eliza said in a trembling voice. "Get up!"

"I cannot walk any farther," 6T9 repeated, not moving from where he sat.

"Shixty," said Oliver, drawing James's attention. The toddler was rousing, poking his rumpled head over his mother's shoulder.

As his mother hushed him, Eliza said, "He just needs power. There wasn't an adequate charger at the Manuels' home."

Under Eliza's hands, 6T9 slumped forward like a doll, and the light behind his eyes went out. Eliza gasped.

"Shixty," sniffled Oliver, as Hisha slipped an injection of something into his arm.

Taking advantage of the delay, James pulled out the rest of his protein bar.

"We should leave him," said Gunny, as James popped the last of the protein bar into his mouth.

"No, Noa!" said Eliza. "I'll need him to carry me later. I can't make it on my own."

Licking the sheen of fat from his fingers, James said, "Ghost has 'bot parts. He could probably put one together for you."

Eliza's face fell. "I don't want just any 'bot! I want 6T9." She turned to Noa. "The deal was, you took him and me!" The volume of her voice was rising.

Noa put her hands to her lips in a sign for silence. Somewhere in the distance, James heard a shout. They were so close to Ghost's home and safety. Were Eliza's hysterics going to get them shot down anyway?

Noa sighed. "You're right, I promised you passage."

"I'm not carrying him," said one of the engineering students. The young woman drew back.

Hisha and Manuel were quiet.

Gunny said softly, "It would be better to leave him." He closed his eyes and put a hand to his data port. "They're closing in on us."

Chavez's gaze was darting between all the other members of the team. Eliza started to cry, her sobs echoing through the sewer tunnels.

"Shhhh … " said Noa.

"Do you have more sedative?" Manuel whispered.

"I'll scream!" Eliza hissed.

Noa's eyes went to 6T9 and back to Eliza again. She eyed the team. "I did promise Eliza—we can make this work."

James noticed the 'team' shifting on their feet.

"He's not just any 'bot," Eliza interrupted. "If he was human, you'd bring him."

His eyes slid to Noa. Her jaw was set, her shoulders squared. She wasn't going to leave 6T9. James could see it already.

"We have to leave it!" Hisha said.

James felt his nerves spark beneath his skin at the word 'it.' Noa's stance … that word … before he knew what he was doing, he was sitting on his heels beside the 'bot.

Someone whispered, "What are you—"

Pulling one of 6T9's arms over his head, James swung the heavy 'bot over his shoulder. Standing up, he found all eyes on him. "Move!" he said. He wanted to frown, but he could only manage to shift his jaw. "We don't have time to argue about this!"

Gunny's eyebrows were at his hairline. Manuel's jaw dropped. "Do you know how heavy those things are?" the engineer asked.

Before James could respond, Noa said, "Move out. The longer we're here, the greater the danger we're in."

No one argued this time. The young woman and one of the men went to help Eliza. There were echoes and shouts in the tunnel—but the voices were confused. They weren't sure where the team's voices were coming from in the maze of tunnels, so they were traveling more slowly than James's team. He would have felt more satisfied if …

"I'm hungry again." The words were out of his mouth before he'd thought of them. He couldn't care if he was overheard; his vision was tunneling in again.

***

"Here," Noa whispered, slipping James a protein bar. She'd been feeding them to him, like stoking a furnace, since he'd heaved 6T9 over his shoulder. But he could eat all of it, as far as she was concerned. He'd saved her neck, and her authority, and the sorry excuse she had for a crew, by hauling 6T9 up on his back. She took a deep breath—for once, not because she was exhausted—but to keep her anger from boiling over. She told herself that Gunny would have been right, under ordinary circumstances. 6T9 was a waste of resources. But these weren't ordinary circumstances. Eliza would need the 'bot to care for her aboard the Ark. Noa had heard 6T9 talk knowledgeably about Eliza's ailments. He had some expensive apps to augment his native programming. And she'd seen the way he cradled her gently in his arms and took her hands with the utmost care—that was knowledge that would have been integrated in the circuits of his titanium bones and synth muscles. Even if they were to install his motherboard in one of Ghost's 'bots, not all of 6T9's working knowledge could be transferred with the motherboard.

A light went off in her mind, and she drew to a halt. Craning her neck, she looked up at the place her locator app told her was the entrance to Ghost's lair. It looked no different from any of the ancient cement surrounding it.

"My coordinates right?" she asked James, keeping her voice a low whisper.

"Yes," he said as the others caught up to them.

Noa held up a hand for a halt and silence.

"Leg up?" she whispered.

James slid 6T9 from his shoulder. Before he lifted her, Noa put a hand on his shoulder. Inclining her head to the 'bot, she asked, "You'll be fine hoisting him up too? Should I get some rope?"

James cocked his head. "I believe … yes, I will be fine … save the rope for Eliza." He cleared his throat. "Although another protein bar would be helpful."

Noa gave him her last one. He stowed it in his pocket and wove his fingers together. Noa gave a last look to the 'bot lying like a discarded doll in the middle of the sewer, a trickle of runoff pooling at the small of his back. And then she slipped her foot into his linked hands and said, "On three."

"What?" said Manuel.

Noa was already leaping up to the seemingly cement ceiling. As she expected, she passed through a hologram, into the vertical shaft below Ghost's abode. She caught the rung of the ancient metal ladder and looked down. Her legs were swinging through a shimmering floor of light. She heard hushed cries of surprise. Ghost had disguised the access tunnel to look like the rest of the sewer. She looked up and saw another shimmering veil of light between her and the grate above. The ancient metal door to his abode was gone. There was just the appearance of crumbling cement in front of her nose. Understanding hit her in a flash. Ghost was going through extra trouble to hide his dwelling. He was concealing himself even more than before … and he had been well-concealed before.

She shook her head, reached out, and felt the door. It wasn't locked. "Send Manuel up next," she whispered. After crawling into the tunnel, moments later she reached Ghost's lair. This time there were no holos of the Ark's engine room. It was just his place—the bed, the dirty kitchenette, the clutter of electronic bits and parts—among them a sex 'bot splayed out in a chair, arms and legs missing, eyes open to the heavens. It was dark even though the geothermal unit was still on. It was humid and too warm.

There was no sign of Ghost.

***

Feet in the relative safety of Ghost's abode, James bent into the crawl-way entrance and pulled on 6T9's shoulders.

"Thank you so much for doing this," Eliza said, already in the room, just behind him. "I won't forget it."

"Where is Dan?" he heard Manuel say.

"I don't know," Noa replied. "But he left the holos on to cover the back entrance, so he must be coming back."

James gave one final tug and pulled the 'bot out onto the floor. Hovering behind him, Eliza said, "The geothermal unit has chargers. It will take him a few hours to completely recharge."

James only grunted. He was exhausted, hungry … and cold. Slipping through the tunnel after the 'bot, Chavez said, "A geothermal unit? I can recharge my legs, they're starting to die on me." She began tearing off the plastic bags covering her prosthetics, revealing metal knee joints and plastic. At the juncture of plastic and flesh, there were bands of fresh duct tape. "Hisha put that on so water wouldn't get into the connections."

James saw one of the young men roll his eyes at the sight, and another turned up his nose. James blinked. He didn't find the sight off-putting, but a memory came back to him of eyeing a woman walking in front of him wearing her prosthetics unabashedly. He had said to a friend, "If you can have synth flesh and look perfectly normal—why wouldn't you?" He clearly remembers being repulsed. He looked at Chavez's legs again. The duct tape, the metal, and the plastic—he didn't find her more or less attractive for it. His eyes went to her face. She winked one of her startling blue eyes at him and grinned. "Where did the Commander find you?" Her Luddeccean accent was thick. He noticed a crucifix hanging at her neck. "And are there any more like you?"

One of the engineers coughed behind his hand. Another scowled at James.

It took a moment to realize she was flirting with him. In another life, would he have smiled at her … or would he have recoiled at the sight of her legs? Would he have turned up his nose at her accent? Would he have looked down on her because she was like Noa, too earthy, too brash, and too loud? Something in him went still and cold. Noa didn't flirt. Sometimes she recoiled at his touch.

His vision tunneled to the point where he saw only his hands. Hefting 6T9 up like a potato sack, he carried him to the geothermal unit. Setting him down without bothering to be gentle, he let Eliza plug the 'bot in.

Chavez gingerly picked up a duplex charging wire from a pile of equipment, plugged the single end into an outlet, and the double end into the backs of her prosthetic legs. James's eyes slid to the kitchenette. On the counter was a jar of peanuts. He looked at the geothermal heater—it felt so good to be close to it. It was so warm, but the peanuts looked delicious. He looked at the wires attached to 6T9 and Chavez and sighed. "I wish I could recharge so easily."

Rocking on her artificial limbs, Chavez gave him another grin. She was pretty. Her features might be unusual, but they were open and … he tilted his head … symmetrical. She looked healthy and energetic. He remembered a few of his other self's short encounters. He'd pursued far less attractive women for brief flings. And yet he wasn't drawn to Chavez at all.

Lifting an eyebrow at his own musings, James retrieved the peanuts, but then immediately returned to the geothermal unit and the halo of warmth around it.

With his first mouthful of food, the conversation around him began to come into focus.

Eliza was clucking at the dismembered 'bot.

Hisha had taken Oliver out of his carrier, and was gently rocking him while eyeing the same 'bot. Her nose was wrinkled in disgust. "That is so distasteful."

Farther away, Manuel was saying, "How long should we wait for Dan?"

Noa answered, "If he doesn't return, we're pretty much dead in the water."

"We could shoot our way up to the Northeast Province," said Bo excitedly.

Gunny, Manuel, and Noa all looked up at him, and then back to each other.

Manuel said, "If Dan doesn't get back—"

"I never left!" The buzz of conversation stopped. All eyes went to the door that led to the hallway. Ghost was standing there; he had his hologram projecting necklace on, the glow of it seemingly illuminating perfectly chiseled features.

"You're not Dan," said Manuel.

The necklace dimmed, and there was the slightly pudgy face that James remembered.

"I prefer to go by Ghost," he said, lifting his nose.

Noa rolled her eyes over to James. He mouthed "ebatteru." It was Japanese, but translated roughly into "arrogant" with implications of "attention seeker." He saw her chest heave, and she abruptly coughed. But there was no rasp to it. His jaw only shifted, but internally he smiled.

"Ghost?" said Manuel, his voice dropping an octave.

"Humor him," said Noa.

Ghost's beady eyes darted in her direction, but he didn't respond. Instead his eyes went to the others in the room. His lip curled up. "I suppose these are passengers you used to raise money for my services … but where is your crew?"

There was a short silence. Noa stood a little straighter. "These are the crew."

Ghost's mouth gaped. His eyes fell on the engineering students. "Is this a joke?" he whispered.

Noa took a step toward Ghost. "A deal is a deal, Ghost. They'll do, especially if you can generate one of your stellar holograms to introduce them to the Ark's engine rooms and to review my plans."

Ghost stared at the engineering students. His eyes passed over James, lingered on Chavez, then went to Eliza and 6T9, and stopped at Hisha and Oliver. Staring at the boy, he demanded, "What is that?"

James felt his neurons spark. That … denoted something

313

less than human. James didn't feel the way Noa felt about children, but he felt annoyance sparking like static beneath his skin at Ghost's wording.

Hisha drew the child tighter to herself. "My son."

Ghost shook his head; lip trembling, he looked away. "They'll have to do." And then his eyes went to Noa. "We have to leave soon. There have been crackdowns, more arrests."

Noa said, "We put that together."

"I had to mortar up the other exit," Ghost said, lip still trembling. "There are too many Guards in the alleys. I think your disappearance has made them nervous."

"We are all ready to leave as quickly as possible," Noa replied.

Ghost began to pace. His eyes went up to James's and then down to the peanuts. "You're eating my peanuts?"

He didn't sound angry; he sounded surprised.

"What else would I do with them?" James said.

Ghost's eyes flicked to the peanuts and back to James. "You've got nerve."

James shrugged. "And an appetite."

Ghost ground his jaw. His eyes fell to James's arms. "Interesting tattoos."

"They are amazing," said Chavez. "Where did you get them?"

James was saved having to answer by a sudden hum and click from 6T9. "Oh, look, it is one of the XTC 100 models."

All eyes turned to 6T9, whose focus was on the dismembered female 'bot on the chair.

"Don't let it distress you, dear!" Eliza said.

Ghost snorted.

"Why would it distress me?" 6T9 said, turning his eyes to Eliza.

"Because it's a 'bot like you and it's chopped to bits?" said

Bo.

6T9 tilted his head. "Only the health of humans matters." He smiled at Eliza. "And yours more than all others, my love."

Ghost snorted again. One of the students choked out a strangled, "Blech."

James's eyes went to the empty eyes of the dismembered 'bot on the chair. He found himself rolling his sleeves down to cover the tattoos on his arms.

***

A semi-transparent holographic image of the Tri-Center and the sewers beneath it floated in Ghost's lair. The team gathered around it. Everyone was standing except Eliza and Oliver. Eliza was sitting in a chair. Oliver was on Ghost's bed, sleeping off the remainder of the sedative he'd received. Carl Sagan was curled up in a ball beside him.

The team had long since gotten past the "how is this possible?" questions about the hologram. James had again asked, "You're really not using quantum entanglement to pull data from the Luddeccean mainframe?" He had a snippy response from Ghost about frequencies beyond the scope of Luddeccean devices' ability to detect, that were "beyond your understanding." Now they were reviewing the final details of the plan.

Noa asked, "Can we get a close-up of the Ark?"

The holo of the ship expanded to fill the tiny room. Designed to take off upright and to glide to a water landing, it looked almost like the old space shuttles of the twentieth century, or like a submarine. Its nose was currently pointed to the sky. From this perspective, they were facing the bottom, the rounded surface that would slide into the water, gracefully slipping across waves, or potentially submerging in inclement weather, and then bobbing up to the surface to float to the nearest shore. The other side, just out of view, was flat and would be the top side if it were horizontal. Unlike the space shuttles of old Earth, the Ark didn't have bulky external rockets. Instead it had four small rockets at its base. Silver "timefield generator bands" encircled the full 78.5 meter circumference of its exterior hull and short wings. The bands were only a hand's width wide and were set at intervals of half a meter apart on the Ark's eighty-meter length. The Ark's computer didn't have enough computing power to create a stable bubble in time. Instead, the bands created an unstable bubble that had to be continuously regenerated, similar to antigrav engines. Unlike antigrav engines, the time space "bubble" would encompass the entire ship and allow the Ark to escape gravity when in orbit. Once it reached zero G, the timefield bands would allow the vessel to achieve effective light speed. As the Ark moved into and out of that shifting time space, the vessel would be flung through space as though from a slingshot.

"We'll be moving at a different time from our folks back home, won't we?" said the female engineering student who Noa now knew as Kara. Her tone was mournful.

"Yes," Noa responded. Unlike ships that passed through time gates, the Ark with its timefield generators would experience the time paradoxes of light speed travel theorized by early physicists. Time would move faster aboard the Ark than it would planetside. The difference would fluctuate with the efficiency of the ship's timefield bands, and hopefully wouldn't be more than double, but even at optimal efficiency, if they had to make it all the way to Time Gate 7 … she banished the thought.

She heard a few gulps among the assembled team.

Noa took a step toward the hologram. "Rotate it," Noa said. The portion of the craft that would be top-side during landing appeared. This side was flattened. There were doors set into it, but the view of those was blocked by an elevator shaft. The elevator was not native to the craft; it had been built to take tourists to the various decks of the vessel. The Ark's original grav generators had depended on acceleration. Those had since been replaced so that the vessel could have gravity even while stationary; however, the design of the vessel still hadn't changed. Instead of having decks set longitudinally in the long vessel, they were set horizontally. On board, "down" would be the tail, and "up" would be the nose.

Noa pointed to the first door, twenty meters above the ground. "This is the door that leads to the main engineering deck. We'll get out of the elevator here. It's possible we'll be receiving fire at this point, and it would be best if we took cover."

"The Ark's hull should be more than sufficient to protect us from ordinary laser fire and bullets," Gunny said.

"Agreed," said Noa. Even the more delicate timefield generating bands had been designed to survive for decades in deep space. The forward guns could prevent collision with large asteroids—the hull was designed to withstand the impact of asteroid fragments, should the forward guns be used.

Pointing at the vessel, Noa said, "Gunny, Chavez, James, and I will head to the bridge. Manuel, you'll lead the team including Ghost to the engineering deck."

Ghost snorted and the hairs on the back of Noa's neck prickled. Of course, he expected to be the "leader." Keeping her voice level, she said, "Ghost, show them what they'll be dealing with while you're busy shutting down the defense grid."

No snort followed that command. Instead, he projected the engineering room. Noa resisted the urge to roll her eyes. He was such a genius that he couldn't foresee the need for Manuel to lead the team while his brain was busy with the much bigger task of keeping them from being shot out of the sky.

She followed along as the engineers went over exactly what they'd need to do to get the engines ready for lift-off, and then to gear up for light speed. Then she walked the bridge team through their tasks.

At the very end of the meeting, Gunny said, "You know, I think this just might work."

Noa felt muscles that she hadn't even realized were tight loosen in her back and neck. Gunny's opinion meant more to her than Manuel's, Ghost's, or James's. Gunny was the only one in the room with extensive ground combat experience.

"After we get to light speed, it should be a piece of cake," Noa agreed.

The older man nodded. "The time paradox will make their weapons useless, and we'll be nearly untraceable."

Noa actually smiled. If Gunny believed it, she could believe it. She felt her hopes rise and saw several tentative smiles around the hologram.

Scratching his stubble, Gunny said, "And no one will expect us to try to steal this old hunk of junk."

Chavez made the sign of the cross, and Kara echoed it. Noa's smile dropped. That hadn't been the most encouraging way to put it.

Oliver chose that moment to raise his head and cry, "Spaceshit!"

Gunny choked. "Sort of."

Hisha ran through the holo toward Oliver. "He can't say ship," she said apologetically.

Hopping from the bed, Oliver dashed toward the holographic controls. "Shit! Shit! Shit!"

Sitting up suddenly in her chair, Eliza shouted, "I just remembered. Sometimes when the timefield generators stalled, engineer Rodriguez would hit the transformer box with a hammer!"

Ghost snorted, "Crazy old woman."

James said, "It could be true … every ship has eccentricities. Even I know that."

Jun, one of the engineering students, said, "In our case, all the eccentricities will be aboard."

Bo laughed as all eyes in the room shifted to Jun. Jun shrugged. "You gotta admit, we're all pretty crazy to be planning this." Noa raised an eyebrow at him. Rocking back on his feet, he held up his hands. "Not that it's worse than staying here and waiting to be picked up by the Guard."

"Well, as long as we're clear on that," said Noa, sensing a chance to repair the mood of optimism.

"Hey, get away from that!" Ghost shouted as Oliver, evading his mother, activated one of Ghost's holographic necklaces.

The hologram of the Ark dissipated, and Ghost ripped the necklace from Oliver's hands, prompting the child to wail. Hisha picked him up and began consoling him. Oliver still screamed.

"I think we need more fire power," Gunny said to Noa, somehow ignoring Oliver's screams.

James, evidently hearing the comment over the screaming Oliver, said, "Ghost has some empty bottles here—maybe we could scrounge together the makings of Molotov cocktails, maybe even IEDs."

"How did you come up with that idea?" Ghost said, his tone oddly accusatory.

Noa blinked. It was true that Molotovs were an ancient technology normally only encountered in military history classes, but … "He's a history professor."

Ghost's eyes narrowed at James. "Huh," was all he said. Noa found herself biting her lower lip. Her fingers bit into her palms. Ghost's distrust almost made her trust James more, as illogical as that was, maybe because Ghost's judgment of character was about as reliable as a lizzar's.

"Molotov cocktails sound like a good idea to me," said Gunny, nodding his head at James.

Noa almost sighed with relief at the slight sign of cooperation … and the dropping decibel level of Oliver's cries.

Ghost muttered, "Next we'll be using flint arrows."

"Well, you seem to think we aren't capable of understanding more sophisticated technologies," James snipped back. Noa glared at him and Ghost. She took a deep breath, prepared to scold them both—and felt a sting in her lungs.

On cue, Hisha said, "Commander, you need to take your treatment."

Before Noa could get a word in edgewise, a plastic mask was slapped over her face.

A few minutes later she sat in a corner, plastic mask still on, the acrid smell of treatment in her nose. Her eyes were on James's back as he began assembling Molotov cocktails next to Gunny. The two men were working companionably, which gave her some hope. This might work; this really might work.

Her eyes slid down James's back. He'd stripped down to only a short-sleeved undershirt, and his tattoos were standing out in sharp relief on the pale skin of his well-muscled arms. She shook her head and reminded herself that those shapely muscles were probably bought. She tilted her head—they didn't look oversized, though—some augmented men looked as though they'd stuffed balloons in their biceps.

Chavez sat down next to Noa abruptly. "I think something came loose in my left leg's connectors," the other woman muttered. The ensign began ripping duct tape off her left limb. "How did this get in here?" Chavez wondered aloud. Noa's eyes flitted over briefly, and she saw the ensign holding up a single pebble. The ensign tossed it aside, grabbed another roll of tape, and began re-taping the joint of her artificial limb. Noa looked away.

"Errr … " said Chavez. "Ummmm … Commander … so I didn't realize that you and Professor Sinclair were a thing."

It was at that moment that Noa realized her eyes had roamed back to James's back. Averting her gaze quickly, Noa blinked over her mask at the young woman. She almost pulled the mask off—but there was Hisha again. "Oh, no you don't," Hisha said, putting her hand over the plastic.

The ensign continued, "I never would have flirted with him if I'd known."

Noa took another deep breath of acrid vapors. She'd missed that flirtation and felt a bit annoyed. She told herself it was because they didn't need that sort of drama this early in the game. Her brows drew together … and what made the ensign think that discussing this right now was a good idea? Or discussing it ever? Although it didn't break any rules per se, it was just not done. The young woman had no sense of proprietary and … Noa's shoulders fell. This woman was part of her crew.

Jun said, "Why don't we just walk through the gates of the museum like normal tourists?" He was assembling 'bots to go into the decoy hovers that would crash inside the Tri-Center.

"Because we were in Manuel's hovers and they have a visual ID on us," Bo answered in a voice that said, idiot.

"Mr. Ghost says he doesn't have enough holographic necklaces for all of us, either," said Kara softly. "And we should all probably stick together."

Kuin, one of the engineering students, said, "What is this?"

6T9 replied, "You asked for a woman's arm. It is a woman's arm."

"The skin tone is too dark and it's too large, you stupid 'bot."

"Would you like me to get a smaller one that is more appropriate in complexion?"

"I'll get it myself, you useless hunk of silicone."

"Don't say that to him!" said Eliza.

"Useless hunk of silicone," said the student, and Noa's skin heated in anger. It might not be hurtful to 6T9 to say such things, but it was hurtful to Eliza.

Noa nearly pulled the mask away to correct the boy, but Hisha's hand was suddenly on the mask again. "You can't miss any of this dose, Noa." Her brow was furrowed with concern. Noa scowled, but didn't argue.

"Don't touch that!" Noa's eyes went to where Ghost stood over Oliver. Ghost raised his hand as though he might strike the toddler.

"Don't touch him!" shouted Manuel, grabbing Ghost's arm.

Kara gasped. All the attention in the room went to Ghost and Manuel. The engineer growled. Hisha darted over and picked up the little boy, snatching him away from Ghost's reach. The timer on the treatment dinged. Noa ripped the plastic from her face, but before she could say a word, beside her Chavez said, "He's pretty to look at though, ain't he?" Noa's head whipped in the girl's direction and followed her gaze. She was staring unabashedly at James.

A scream ripped through the small space from the far corner. Noa's head whipped again, this time to see Kara standing with her hand over her mouth. Kara's eyes were riveted on Carl Sagan. Darting past her, the werfle was carrying cybernetic eyeballs in his mouth and with the tiny hands of his midsection.

"Stupid girl," muttered Ghost, before resuming his quarrel with Manuel.

Kara quickly shuffled away, hand still on her mouth.

Noa felt her stomach turn. This was never going to work.

***

James looked from side to side in the intersection in the sewers. His hearing caught the sound of footsteps—it was impossible to tell how far—his tech didn't adjust for the echo. But they sounded too close. The water in the tunnel had increased exponentially, but he could avoid splashing in the stream that ran down the center of the tunnel if he skirted the walls. He turned a corner, listened and verified that the Guard was coming in his direction. He heard someone say, "Jericho team will head down the tunnel beneath Liberty Avenue."

Turning, James rapidly signaled the team some 405 meters away. Gunny's augmented vision caught the signal, and he halted the others. They immediately began crawling into an accessory tunnel located about six and a half feet from the ground.

James approached them slowly, carefully checking side tunnels before he crossed. By the time he reached them, everyone but Gunny and Noa were in the accessory tunnel. James kneeled down by Gunny, and offered a "leg up."

Slipping his boot into James's hands, the older man nodded and murmured a barely audible thanks. James didn't respond, just lifted the man up into the small tunnel. He heard scuffling inside, and a hiss from Carl Sagan. He nodded to Noa, and she put her boot in his hand, and he lifted her in a fluid motion. He followed her up into the tunnel and there was more scuffling as the team moved farther back.

Outside James heard a Guard say, "I heard something!" and he felt Noa stiffen beside him.

There was some light from a grate in the tiny space,

and James saw one of the engineering students touch his forehead, his stomach and his shoulders. It took a moment, but James realized he was making the sign of the cross. For some reason, James felt as though someone had doused the lights within his mind with a cold pail of water. Leaning against the tunnel wall, he tried to make himself small.

The sound of footsteps outside the access tunnel got louder. "I definitely heard something!" a Guard said.

"Check that accessory tunnel!" someone in the main tunnel commanded. In the dim light, he saw Noa raise her pistol, and Gunny and Manuel did the same. James was so close to the opening of the tunnel he was afraid to move, afraid that any motion he made might be seen from below. A flashlight beam jumped along the wall in front of his nose.

"I don't hear anything," someone outside his line of vision said.

Deeper down the tiny accessory tunnel came a sleepy cry from Oliver.

"I heard it!" someone said. "Give me a lift!"

James reached for his pistol. Beside him, silent as a snake, Noa shifted so she was sitting on her heels, pistol raised at the tunnel opening. Before the Guard was lifted, Carl Sagan's body went hurtling past Noa and over James's lap. The werfle hissed and poked its head out into the main tunnel.

Noa's chin dipped. She readjusted her finger on the trigger of the pistol.

In the main tunnel line, someone said, "Oh, look. It's just a werfle."

"Someone's escaped pet by the look of it."

"Probably down here looking for rats."

A hand from one of the Guards shot up so it was in view of James, but the owner's face was not in view. Carl Sagan hissed.

"Easy, Mister," said the owner of the hand, giving Carl Sagan's chin a scratch. "We're not taking you in."

"We're not?"

"Hot cores, no. These guys eat rats. Let him stay down here and clear the rest of 'em out."

The hand retreated, and then the light. James sat motionless. Noa lowered her pistol, but touched a finger to her port, and met James's gaze. James pulled a few lengths of cable and a square port box from his pocket as quietly as he could, and he handed all but one cable to Noa. Plugging one end of the cable into his port, he saw Noa do the same, and then her avatar flickered in his mind's eye. "The 'bot controlled hovers should be ten minutes from the crash site." There was no segue, no, "that was close" or "thank the stars for Carl Sagan." The werfle settled onto James's lap in the physical world, and he idly scratched the creature behind the ears.

Another avatar flickered to life in the shared space between their minds. It was a young man in the camis of the Fleet: loose shirt and trousers speckled drab gray. "Who are you?" James's avatar asked.

Noa's avatar's lips pursed. The new avatar also looked at him curiously.

"It's Gunny," said Noa.

"Old avatar," said the mental projection. "But I didn't think I looked that different."

James studied the new avatar. He had trouble reconciling it with Gunny. The face was younger, clean shaven, and there was no gray hair or beer gut. However, the avatar did carry the same firearms and other assorted weapons as Gunny carried in the real world, and the eyes were the right color, James supposed.

Chavez and Manuel's avatars came online. James had less trouble identifying Manuel—though the avatar was slightly more fit, he looked about the same age. Chavez's avatar was indistinguishable from her person—minus cybernetic limbs. Ghost's avatar appeared, too. It didn't look military issue—it wasn't in his Fleet grays, and it had the same sculpted face as the holographic necklace.

"We're close to the Tri-Center now," Gunny's avatar said. "'proximately a kilometer."

Noa's avatar, bearing the same arms she did in the real world—an extension of the Fleet avatar programming, James decided—holstered her pistol and swung her rifle around. "Remember, we are bound to encounter resistance in the tunnels below the museum. They may fall back to protect the more sensitive areas of Central Authority, but we can't count on that."

"Aye, Commander," said Chavez and Manuel.

Ghost's avatar also bore a weapon—a rifle from his personal armory. Back in his lair, the engineering student, Bo, had asked if he could have one of the rifles, but Ghost had snorted and said, "I'd give it to the girl first."

The engineering students weren't in the shared mental space. They didn't have avatars. They were commonplace things on Earth, but on Luddeccea, apparently, they were considered an extravagance. In the physical world, Bo was petting a Molotov cocktail. The other students were more subdued. Kara sat next to Noa, and James was certain he could hear the girl's heart beating too rapidly.

"You all know your roles," Noa's avatar said. She nodded at James's avatar. "Let's go." And then her avatar reached up and motioned pulling the data cord from its socket. All the avatars copied the motion, and James was suddenly completely alone in his own mind. The break in the connection felt like a cold slap. He yanked the cord out of his own port. Noa motioned for it, and he let her gather up the length of the cable. It kept his hands free as he slipped into the main sewer line. As soon as he was down, he swung his rifle around and focused his hearing. He couldn't see anyone, but he could hear voices approximately 100 meters away. Catching Noa's gaze, he reached up and touched her hand, the signal that the team could follow. As soon as they touched down, he touched one ear and then the other—the sign that they could be overheard. Everyone nodded—except for the drugged Oliver and 6T9. The 'bot was blindfolded. Eliza had given him the exact route they were taking and told him they were playing an exciting new "game," that "only he could play with her." The 'bot was smiling blissfully beneath the blindfold. There was no doubt that there would be resistance—and 6T9 couldn't be allowed to see, lest he seek to render assistance—or report the team.

As the fastest member of the team with the best eyesight and second-best hearing, James took point, Noa and Ghost beside him. Chavez, Manuel, and Gunny were at the end of the line, the rest of the group in between. James's dancing neurons homed in on the distant voices of the Guard beneath the Central Authority. James expected at any moment that the darkness would be split by a UV spotlight, or laser tracer, but none came. Within a few minutes, they were at the first hurdle: a gate that spanned the width and height of the entire tunnel.

Most of the sewer lines were open; gates like this one were traps for garbage and debris that could block the flow of water during the flash rainstorms frequently experienced by Luddeccea Prime. But they were almost directly beneath the Central Authority, and as Gunny had explained it, "'ccasional floods are worth the added security of a gate."

The gate was made of crossed steel beams seven centis in diameter, set at intervals of fifteen centis apart. Set at the center was a locking mechanism—a steel plate as wide as

James's spanned hands. He knew, without knowing how, that he wouldn't be able to open it with brute strength. It was not like the lock on the train … That had been brute strength, hadn't it? Not a rusty lock as he'd first believed, or wanted to believe. He felt a rush of static beneath his skin.

Putting these thoughts aside, James carefully focused on the ceiling by the gate. Something glimmered in the low light—a holocamera—just as Gunny had suspected there would be. Noa lightly tapped James's arm. Turning, he took the cable she had between her fingers. Ghost took the other end. It was too dark for Ghost to see without augmented vision. They plugged the cord into their ports, and there was the familiar rush of electricity and connection as James shared with Ghost what he saw across the link. Ghost's avatar flickered in his mind's eye and said, "I can handle it."

"They will have frequency jammers here," James responded.

Ghost's avatar rolled its eyes and smirked. "I told you, I have something special."

James knew he did have something special—they would never have been able to retrieve data from the mainframe without it; but, still … he felt his skin crawl as though expecting a bullet. He wanted to know how Ghost was connecting to the central computer. Next to him, he heard Noa shifting slightly on her feet. She was so close he could feel the soft kiss of her breath against his cheek. He wanted to take her hand, but didn't.

Ghost abruptly ripped the cord out, and the stream of electrons running between their minds stopped. For a moment James saw stars behind his eyes, and then his gaze slid to Noa. She was biting her lip so fiercely it went pale beneath her teeth. There was no link between them, but he knew what she was thinking. If Ghost got this wrong, the whole show was over. Noa's eyes went back to Hisha, and then to Oliver strapped to her chest. The toddler was sleeping in a drug-induced stupor, drool slipping from his lips to his carrier. Oliver was, perhaps more so than Eliza, the most vulnerable member of their group. James's eyes went back to Noa, and he remembered what she'd said, "The death of a child is the death of hope."

He didn't believe it—not for himself—but he took in her pained expression and realized it wasn't just a cliche for her, a sound bite picked up from a political speech. It was real. He tilted his head. Oliver wasn't even her child, and he knew she'd been annoyed by the prospect of babysitting.

He heard a soft thud above, and looked up. "That's the hover crash happening right above our heads!" someone whispered, before another person hushed them. From the Guards down the tunnel he heard someone say, "Did you hear that?"

He heard an intake of breath from someone on their team, and then a crackle of static from a radio in the distance. His neurons and nanos dancing in anticipation, James focused on the sound. He heard another person say, "There was a four-hover pile-up above. Looks like a bad accident—Yao, Parvati, and Khan, go offer assistance." James's dancing neurons almost relaxed, but then from the gate came a loud clanking, like heavy unused gears grinding into motion.

Ghost spoke sharply in the darkness. "It's all done. Cameras are disabled. Run." James's brows drew together. Ghost wasn't supposed to say that aloud. Hunching over his rifle, the little man ran down the tunnel toward the gate. That wasn't the plan either; James was supposed to go first. Shaking his head, he ran after Ghost and quickly overtook him. He heard the team following, and down the tunnel shouts from the Guard. "What was that?"

James reached the groaning gate. It was slowly opening,

the gears clanking faster and faster. James pushed against the ancient metal to hurry it along. Nothing happened.

Taking a step back, he rushed the metal bars, hitting them with his side with all his might. There was a loud groan, a snap, and the gate sprang open and James crashed through, just as a beam of ultraviolet light flashed in his eyes. "Incoming!" he said, flinging himself to the floor and raising his rifle as water trickled around his body. The rifle sights had built-in light adjustment; even without his augmented vision, he would have seen fine. Noa belly-flopped onto the ground beside him and lifted her own rifle. Ghost dove to the ground and crawled to the farthest edge of the tunnel before lifting his. There was the sound of rifle fire from the Guards, and bullets ricocheting off steel. Oliver screamed, and it pierced James's consciousness just for an instant, but he blocked it out and fired. He fired off one shot, Noa fired off another; and from behind, two more went off simultaneously. He barely had a chance to blink … and it was over. Just like that. He looked back and saw no one else had come through the gate yet. Chavez and Gunny's rifles were poking through the bars.

Manuel cried, "Is Oliver hurt?" and 6T9 said, "Eliza, this game doesn't seem to be safe."

"It is just a game," Eliza said, "It's safe."

"He's fine," said Hisha. "Just scared."

"Move!" said Noa, already on her feet. "We may encounter more resistance!"

And then it was chaos. Ghost was running ahead again, Noa was screaming for him to get back, Oliver was crying, and 6T9 was saying, "I am not allowed to play games like this with children!"

"It's not a sexual game," said Eliza. "Just exciting."

James heard shouting down the tunnel, footsteps, and the hiss of the old-fashioned radios the Luddeccean Guard used. But then the footsteps stopped. James heard one of the Guards say, "Protect flight control and the Central Authority." He felt a jolt of shock hit his system, a cocktail of relief, and bewilderment. He hadn't, he realized, believed that this plan would really work, but Noa had been right. They weren't expecting an attack on the museum, and no one thought about the flight capability of the Ark.

They swung a hard right and entered a narrower dead-end tunnel just as gunfire erupted behind them. James stood back with Gunny. The older man handed him a case of women's makeup powder that belonged to Eliza. "Check to see if they're approaching." He needn't have said it. James remembered the plan. He flipped the mirror open, held it around the corner, and shook his head. "They're not moving."

"Not yet," said Gunny.

"James!" shouted Noa. He turned. She stood in a natural spotlight cascading down from the manhole cover that was at the center of the courtyard that the Ark was housed in. Manuel was climbing down. "It's heavier than I thought." Manuel panted and dropped to the ground. "Have to lift it up and over."

From behind him, he heard the Guard in the tunnel approaching.

He appraised the height from the top of his head to the manhole cover ... two and a quarter meters. He remembered the tree he'd hurdled in the forest without a second thought. He felt as though he could do this ... not knowing how he knew made him uneasy, but the footsteps were getting closer, and Oliver was crying.

"Out of the way," he said, handing the mirror to Gunny.

"Out of his way," Noa cried, motioning people to the side. "You heard him."

Sprinting forward, James leaped into the air. Electricity

331

and pain shot down his shoulder. He heard the scrape of metal on metal, he felt the manhole give, and then collided with the wall of the dead-end, barely grabbing the ladder with one hand. He looked above. The manhole cover was only partially covering the drain.

"The human cannonball," someone said.

"Are you sure you're not Fleet?" asked Manuel.

"Your arm and shoulder!" Noa cried, voice strained.

At that moment, he realized he was cradling both against his side. "Will be fine," he ground out. His neurons weren't dancing anymore. They were red and angry. And his vision took that odd moment to blur and tell him he was hungry. He forced the arm he cradled to move—and it did, slowly, at first, but then with increasing ease. Managing to climb a few rungs, he turned his head sideways and pushed it through the narrow gap between the cover and drain wall. From the sewer he heard Gunny say, "They're almost here. Now!" There was the crash of glass, and he knew they'd set off the Molotov cocktails. From above, he heard an alarm go off and screams. Ignoring the screaming of the nerves in his shoulder and the alarm and cries of tourists, he pushed his head completely through the manhole, effectively using it as a wedge. The heavy metal cover slid to the side and his top half emerged into the warmth of the Prime mid-morning. The sun had come out and it was hot. The only sign of the rain was lingering humidity in the air. He found himself in an empty, paved, circular depression that was slightly taller than him. At the top of it were decorative planters filled with two-meter tall tropical grasses. In the rainy season, they would be deep purples in hue, like the pines in the north, but now they were a faded violet. Above the tops of the decorative plants loomed the Ark. There were stairways at north, south, east, and west, and the rest of the perimeter of the circle was ringed with a bleacher-like seating area. Half-eaten food and food wrappers littered the seats. A woman carrying a baby was rushing away. He lifted his eyes up and saw more tourists at the base of the spaceship dodging through more decorative planters, making a break for the exits. His eyes drifted upward again along the lines of the ancient craft. There was a wide awning surrounding the vessel—it looked like what it was … an exhibit, a curiosity, a relic. His eyes went upward and he felt as though all his neurons and nanos had come to an abrupt halt. There was probably a reason why no one expected the Ark to be used as an escape vessel.

CHAPTER SIXTEEN

Noa hung on the ladder in the wall next to the manhole. "James, what's wrong?" she half-shouted over the sound of screams, rifle fire, breaking glass, and the museum alarm. Her partner in crime … or whatever … stood half-in, half-out of the tunnels. He didn't answer. Perhaps his injuries were worse than she'd feared? "James, can you move? Can you climb out of the way?"

She could feel the heat of the flames from the Molotov cocktails against her back. They'd hold the Guard back for a while, but soon they'd figure out their ruse and their destination.

James quickly shimmied up the ladder, and Noa felt relief uncoil in her belly. She scrambled up as he gave the signal for all-clear above. Gunny must have seen because he shouted, "Everybody up!" Noa popped out into the hot sunshine of the Prime morning. James stood, a rifle sagging in his arms. His neck was craned upward. Noa looked beyond him, out of the artfully-designed picnic area that could serve as a catch-pond during the rainy season, to the hulking shadow that was the Ark.

"I remember it as being bigger," James shouted over the roar of the museum alarm, stretching out the arm he'd just been favoring, and giving his hand a shake.

Noa squinted up at the vessel. "It's large enough for our founding families." She took off toward the steps.

James caught up to her. "It looks older than I remember.

And … mutated."

Noa scowled. Picky off-worlder. True, the ship looked a little beat-up. The sides were scarred with over a decade's worth of asteroid impacts, and the Central Authority hadn't bothered to give it a paint job—paint was chipping off its dirty, rain-streaked hull. Also, the holo Ghost had projected for them was of a ship of the same class, but new. The ship in the holo hadn't spent years in deep space, endured a rough landing, and served as housing for the First Families for over a decade. It was evident from the Ark's not precisely streamlined form that the crew had had to make some special modifications during that time—however, "By Republic law, it has to be space worthy!" she shouted. "It looks old—"

"It looks mangled," James interjected.

Ignoring the comment, Noa continued, "It has all the comforts of modern times—real grav and food." Pausing almost at the top of the steps of the picnic area, she ducked to scan the courtyard through her sights. The base of the Ark was surrounded by a decorative awning that allowed tourists to walk the perimeter of the base without being drenched in the rainy season or scorched in the summer. No one seemed to be hiding in the shadows, and she caught no signs of movement through the decorative planters. The Ark's exhibit was situated between two prongs of the Tri-Center Building. On one side was the museum. Through glass walls she could make out three stories of exhibits. On the other side were walls of stucco and less glass—the wing of the spaceport. She saw no one in either direction; no tourists, no passengers, no members of the Guard. Just to be sure, she tapped James's shoulder. Sparing her vocal cords, she pointed to her eyes, and back to the building, a silent sign for, "See anyone?" Meeting her gaze, he shook his head. She took a deep breath. The tourists and guides had fallen back into the heart of the Tri-Center building. This was working too perfectly, and she felt a stab of dread.

Bringing her focus back to the courtyard, she muttered, "This is too easy," too softly to possibly be heard. But James must have heard her. His head whipped in her direction faster than a gray snake. She couldn't hear him, but she saw the startled, "What?" on his lips.

She gave as much of a shrug as she could with the rifle in her hands. There was no way she could explain it. She glanced back quickly in the direction they'd come. Ghost was cowering in the depression with Hisha and the students. Oliver was stirring on Hisha's shoulder, and 6T9 was standing up, shaking his head, blindfold still in place. Manuel was trying to push him down. The 'bot was frowning, saying something to Eliza that Noa couldn't hear over the alarm. Gunny and Chavez were standing over the manhole, Molotov cocktails in their hands. Gunny met Noa's eyes and Manuel did, too. They both gave curt nods. Leaving Manuel to keep 6T9 in line, and Gunny and Chavez to keep any pursuers from below confused—or at least busy—Noa and James darted quickly to the awning surrounding the Ark.

The contents of shattered souvenir hologlobes dropped by tourists crunched beneath their feet. She heard far-off screams, muffled explosions, and the alarm—she knew it would be ringing in her head for days. She wished she could turn down her hearing and use the ethernet to communicate to James and with her team. She wanted to feel the gentle flow of electrons that would let her know they were well, even without their conscious thoughts. She silently cursed having to rely on her battered eardrums.

Reaching the base of the Ark, Noa and James put their backs to the hull in the same heartbeat. Noa glanced toward the picnic area again. She couldn't see the team—Manuel must have convinced 6T9 to sit. As she thought that, Manuel's head popped over the top of the steps. He met Noa's gaze. Noa gave him the all-clear. Manuel turned and said something Noa couldn't hear to a member of the team. He disappeared for a moment, and then reappeared an instant later.

Carrying his rifle in one hand and seemingly dragging Ghost by the collar, Manuel hurried in toward the Ark. The rest of the team hid in the depression, taking cover in case they had to beat a fast retreat. Noa took a deep breath. She didn't believe there could be a retreat now. This had to work. Just before Manuel and Ghost reached them, she turned to James. He gave her a tiny nod, and raised his weapon. Giving each other a tight nod, they walked around the Ark in opposite directions, like well-oiled parts of the same machine ... even without the ethernet.

Noa circled around the Ark with her rifle up, ready for incoming fire. It never came, which made her gut constrict. Her eyes met James's as he rounded the base from the other side. Noa darted to the cage-like elevator for tourists that ran up and down the side of the Ark while James covered her. Whoever had been operating the elevator when the alarm went off had had the presence of mind to lock it. The doors were closed and wouldn't budge. Cursing, Noa tested the buttons. Nothing happened. For a moment, she thought of asking James to try, but then she thought better of it. Brute force might damage the lift and make it unusable, and then they'd have to climb twenty meters up to the entrance. There might be a better way ... Giving the signal for "wait" to James, she ran around the base, the alarm still blaring in her ears.

Ghost was cowering beneath the awning, back pressed to the hull in the cluster of thrusters at the base.

"Ghost!" Noa shouted. "Need you! Elevator locked."

"What?" Noa saw the word on his lips, but couldn't hear it over the sound of the alarm. Grabbing his arm, she pulled him toward the lift. For an instant, he dug in his heels, and her heart skipped a beat. But then, overcoming his fear, he followed her, letting his rifle hang from his back and covering his ears.

As they rounded the base, the alarm abruptly shut off.

"The elevator," Noa shouted, her ears ringing even with the alarm gone. "It's locked—"

"And undoubtedly shut down," Ghost said with a scowl.

"Can you do anything?" Noa said in a normal voice.

Ghost's eyes darted side to side. "I built the mainframe. The mainframe that controls everything!" His voice was angry, defensive.

"Can you open it?" Noa demanded.

"If it's connected by hardline. These things are quite primitive and … "

"Do it," Noa commanded.

Ghost continued to look around nervously.

"James and I will cover you," said Noa.

"Okay, okay, yes." Ghost shook his head, sank to the ground, and pulled his knees to his chin. "Trying to access now … "

Noa kneeled on one knee, and James did the same. Swinging her rifle around, she peered through the sights, looking for any sign of movement, but saw none. In the direction of the depression, she heard the sound of glass crashing and Gunny shouting, "Another." Oliver was crying, and 6T9 was saying, "Eliza, I believe the child is in need of assistance." But other than that, and the ringing in her ears, it was eerily quiet.

"I don't like this," Noa said.

"You'd rather they be firing at us?" James said.

Noa's fingers twitched on the trigger. "Someone should have confronted us here."

James only grunted.

"Ghost," she said. "Can you open the elevator?"

She only got a mumbled chant in response.

High above them, a ptery called out. Noa felt a bead of sweat prickle on her brow. Peering through her sights, she methodically swept the museum wing, first floor, second floor, and third floor. No one moved inside, and then she dropped her gaze to the junction between the branches of the building. In the double doors there, she saw a shadow move. She heard one of the doors click. "We've got incoming!" she said.

"I only see one figure," James replied.

"Could be a single guy making sure the museum has been evacuated." Noa continued to gaze through her sights. "Could be armed … Be ready."

Over the sound of her own heart, she heard the door click again. Noa was ready for the Guard, or even just museum security. She expected to see a weapon raised. She expected gunfire. Instead, a man awkwardly sidled out the door, holding his hands above his head. The instant she saw his profile, Noa screamed.

***

Noa's shout nearly split James's eardrums. "Don't shoot! Don't shoot!" An instant later, she was springing to her feet, lowering her rifle, and shouting, "Kenji, Kenji, it's me!"

It took a moment for James to recognize the man. He'd seen the adult Kenji in Noa's memories, and at a distance when they'd approached his condo unit. Time must have added wrinkles to Kenji's face and gray hair at his temples, because he looked much older than James remembered. He was broader, too. And he wore head-to-toe Luddeccean Green. James's mind snapped the pieces together. Kenji followed the Luddeccean doctrines on anti-augmentation; he looked his natural age so, although he was younger than Noa, he looked older. And he was working with the Central Authority. He'd come from that wing to the courtyard, but why had he come here, unarmed?

"I knew it was you, Big Sister," Kenji said. "And I know what you're trying to do." He gave a slight smile and nodded. "It's a good idea."

James couldn't see Noa's face from where he still half-kneeled, scanning the two wings of the complex, but he could hear a half-sob in her voice when she said, "We tried to come get you, but we couldn't; now you're here, and we can escape."

"No, Big Sister, no one's going anywhere," said Kenji, his voice soft, his words slow, as though he was talking to a frightened animal. "I'm going to get you help. I tried before … this time it will work. I'll oversee your re-education myself."

At the words "I tried before" and "re-education," James felt a prickle in the back of his neck, and heat race along every inch of his skin. Kenji … Kenji had sent Noa to the camp.

Noa gasped and backed away. "What?"

James was on his feet. "Manuel, cover Ghost!" he roared. He heard the engineer rounding the base of the Ark, but didn't turn to look. He strode toward Noa and Kenji, imaging Kenji's spine snapping in his hands, but then drew to a stop. The side of his lip ached to curl in a snarl. Noa would never forgive him if he hurt her brother.

Kenji grabbed Noa's hand. "I'll get you help. You were always there for me, Big Sister. I'll be there for you. I know you're wrapped up in that Archangel Project, but I'll get you help."

"No, Kenji, no," Noa said, shaking her head and pulling

her hand away.

Kenji's brow furrowed. And then he said, "I intercepted the signals, Noa ... maybe you don't know it ... "

Noa put her hands on his shoulders. "You have to come with us, Kenji."

Putting his hands over hers, Kenji guided her hands gently down. "No one is going anywhere, Noa," Kenji said. "I changed all of the passcodes on the Ark—and Dan's access codes to the mainframe. But it will be okay, you'll see. I'm protecting you." Kenji looked down at her injured hand. "What happened to your fingers?"

A ptery screamed above their heads.

"They cut them off at the re-education camp," Noa said in a strange, flat voice. James found himself taking another step forward. Noa tried to pull away, but Kenji caught her fingers—the ones she had left, James thought darkly.

"No, Noa, you must be mistaken. I told them you were not to be harmed when I turned you in."

James felt like his skin was burning from within. He took another step toward Noa.

Noa pulled away from Kenji, shaking her head.

"Noa, it's okay, it's okay," Kenji said, closing the distance between them.

Noa jerked backward. And James couldn't stop himself. He darted forward, rifle raised. "Stay away from her!"

Kenji turned to him. His eyes went up and down, and his lip curled. "Noa, do you know what this is?" He pointed at James, took a step back, and his voice rose in volume. "He's one of them!"

"No, Kenji, no," Noa said, shaking her head.

"I've seen his picture from the chase footage in the North! He's the one! He's the one!" Kenji was screaming now. "You are consorting with the end of the human race!"

"I've got it!" Ghost shouted.

"No!" cried Kenji, looking over Noa's shoulder in alarm.

And then too many things happened at once. James heard an explosion from the direction of the sewer line. In the periphery of his vision, he saw shadows moving in the windows of both wings of the building.

Spinning in place, Kenji threw up his arms. "No! Wait! Don't shoot my sister!"

Not trusting Kenji's pleas for mercy, James wrapped an arm around Noa and guided her toward the lift. She didn't precisely protest, but she stumbled beneath him, and he heard her half-sob, "No, Kenji, no."

Somewhere, Gunny shouted, "Go, go, go!" and he saw him maneuvering the civilians toward the Ark, 6T9's blindfold still on but falling.

"Eliza!" the 'bot shouted.

"I'm fine, I'm fine," the old woman cried, "keep going!"

Gunfire erupted from the building, and a bottle went rushing over James's head. Others shattered on either side of him and Noa. The remaining Molotov cocktails, he realized. The bottles caught in the decorative planters and the tall, dry tropical grasses erupted in flames and smoke, putting a curtain of fire between the Ark and the Guard in the building.

"Kenji!" Noa cried under James's arm as they reached the now-open elevator.

"Get in," Ghost shouted, to everyone and no one.

And suddenly the sky went orange and dark. "Fire retardant," Noa said as James pushed her into the elevator.

"Hisha!" screamed Manuel. A bullet whizzed by. Manuel stumbled backward and clutched his arm, his rifle sagging from the strap on his shoulder. He was pushed into the elevator by the still-blindfolded 6T9 carrying a wide-eyed Eliza. Tripping backward, Manuel fell to the floor—and James could smell blood in the air.

"Get 'em in there, Chavez!" James heard Gunny roar, and a moment later Chavez shoved the rest of the team in, trapping Manuel, James, and Noa in the back of the elevator with their bodies. The flames, smoke, and fire retardant were so thick that through the wire cage James could only see a few meters. He felt something on top of his foot and blinked down to see Carl Sagan scurry over him and up the metal cage of the lift. Gunfire was going off in an angry staccato from both directions, but he couldn't see the shooters. Gunny stumbled into the elevator, face orange, rubbing his eyes. "I can't see!"

"Where is Hisha? Where is Hisha?" Manuel stammered on the ground. He tried to raise himself, but slipped. Metal creaked above their heads, and the elevator jerked into ascent.

From the ground came the sound of Oliver's wail, rising over the scream of bullets, and the roar of flames.

Eyes tearing, Gunny was hanging out the still-open door. "She was ahead of me! Oh, God, the kid!"

"The child is in distress," said 6T9, setting Eliza down quickly.

"Help him! Help him!" said the old woman.

Noa was already pushing toward the front of the elevator. 6T9 was instantly beside her, blindfold gone. James felt his mind alight in fear and frustration. Couldn't she ever keep her head down?

Oliver's wail rose again above the sound of flames. "Hisha," screamed Manuel from the floor. James looked back to see him crawling, one-armed, toward the front of the elevator between the press of legs.

"Manuel!" Hisha's breathless call just barely rose above the din.

"Stop the elevator! Stop the elevator!" Manuel shouted. The elevator jolted to a stop ... but then began to ascend again, this time a little more slowly.

"I can't stop it!" Ghost panted. "A bullet … something is jammed."

Noa dropped to her knees. The ground was over two meters below. "Hisha!" she shouted, reaching out a hand.

"6T9, help Noa, you're stronger!" Eliza shouted.

The 'bot reached out a hand to Hisha, too. The woman was jogging toward the elevator, clutching Oliver who was screaming louder with each bullet that fired and ricocheted off the hull of the Ark— each one seemingly closer to the pair despite the curtains of smoke and fire retardant ... They couldn't see Hisha. A thought struck James. "They are aiming at the child's screams."

As soon as the words and thought had passed from him, Hisha fell. Noa screamed, and James could see the muscles in her arms strain and knew she was going to jump. Oliver was still wailing on the ground. In his mind, realizations collided in a stinging flurry of electricity. Noa wouldn't leave the child, she'd jump down there, attempt to rescue him, and make herself the target. Before he could second guess himself, or had even formulated a plan, he shoved Noa down and leaped over her and 6T9, landing on the ground next to Hisha. Above him, he heard Noa say, "Chavez, let loose with all you've got!" He heard Noa and Chavez firing above his head. Noa wasn't going to jump down—she was going to try and cover him. It was oddly a relief even as return fire came from all directions. James knelt down on the ground next to the fallen woman. She'd landed on top of Oliver, now only whimpering. Another bullet hit her side right before his eyes and her body jerked. Oliver wailed. "Hisha," James said, getting closer, eyes stinging with the fire retardant that was congealing near the ground in a thick cloud. She didn't move from where she lay, body huddled over Oliver. He touched her shoulder, and felt slick hot blood. He lifted her up and realized there was a bullet wound in the back of her head—and another in the front right above her open eyes. The wailing Oliver was coated in red and gore. The child took a deep breath, and for a moment his cries became soft gasps. James ripped the cloth of the carrier, picked up the child roughly with one arm. His mind went still, blank, and dark. The elevator was too high. He couldn't make it. He knew it like he'd known how to kill a man with a roundhouse kick, or a quick twist of the neck, or that he could leap two and a quarter meters into the air. Oliver wailed again. Bullets screamed by them.

He should run.

Instead, against all logic, he jumped. Some useless part of his brain calculated that he would miss the platform by a good half meter, and even 6T9's extended hand by at least forty centis.

Even as that thought was passing through his mind, 6T9 slid down so he was hanging over the edge by his waist and caught James's hand. And it was like a light had gone off in James's mind; it spread to the world and every fiber of James's being and for an instant, everything was brighter.

And then 6T9 began to slip forward.

***

Noa was fighting tears as she sprayed bullets haphazardly into the wall of red fire retardant. It wasn't all because of smoke or the cocktail of chemicals doused on the flame. She aimed high, telling herself their snipers would be on the roof. It was also where Kenji wouldn't be. The elevator shuddered beneath her, and Noa hazarded a glance down just in time to see 6T9 catch James's arm. Laying flat on the floor of the elevator, 6T9's entire torso was hanging over the edge. And then it was like a slow-motion nightmare. James was dangling, Oliver was screaming, and bullets were still raging. One of the bullets hit 6T9 square in the arm, leaving a black hole. The 'bot didn't flinch, but he was quickly sliding forward. Eliza toppled on top of the 'bot, shouting, "He caught them!" Manuel threw his weight on one of 6T9's legs. Noa braced a foot on 6T9's backside, trying to help, but she didn't dare stop shooting, for fear the return fire would intensify. As she thought that, another bullet whizzed by James so close she saw a piece of his shirt rip and catch in the breeze. His face remained impassive, but his eyes briefly met hers. He could have climbed up 6T9's body if he only let go of Oliver, but he didn't.

For an instant the scene was crystal clear, in the way that only battle could be. The Luddecceans were firing at James and 6T9. The sex 'bot, a symbol of all that was degenerate, and the fallen angel of their twisted fantasies were trying to save a human child.

"Pull them up!" Eliza said.

"Oliver!" screamed Manuel.

"I have no leverage, my darling Eliza," 6T9 shouted.

Still spraying bullets, Noa half-turned her head and snarled at the students, "Pull him up!"

Snapping out of their shock-induced comas, the students dropped to the floor and began pulling the 'bot backward with Manuel and Eliza. Chavez and Noa kept firing into the red cloud. Even Gunny was firing. His eyes were weeping and shut from the sting of fire retardant—but they were all firing blindly anyway.

The elevator jerked so quickly she nearly lost her footing. Just as she ran out of ammo, she heard scraping behind her, felt cool air against her back, and Ghost shouted, "It's open!"

"Eliza! Help guide Manuel and Gunny!" Noa shouted, dropping her useless weapon and falling to her knees to help the students pull the 'bot, James, and Oliver into the elevator as Chavez continued to spray bullets.

"Hurry, come!" Ghost shouted. Kara took Oliver from James, and James slithered on his stomach up into the elevator cab. Chavez grunted. "I'm out of ammo—"

"Then go!" screamed Noa. "All of you!"

Everything was a confusing blur of moving legs, intensifying gunfire, and another sound—a low roar. Engines. The Ark's engines were starting. Noa gaped. Kenji had been wrong—about the mainframe, the elevator ... and everything.

"Keep down!" Noa shouted into James's ear as he began to stumble upright. Nodding, he kept to his hands and knees. Joining him, she turned to the door of the ship. The door was an archway of light. She saw bullets impacting into the wall just beyond the entrance. She scuttled forward, James was beside her ... but then he slipped and crashed to his belly.

"James!" she shouted, grabbing him beneath the arm, preparing to drag him. But he got up a moment later, and they scurried into the Ark. "Down!" Noa said as soon as they were inside. Flinging herself over James's shoulders, she pushed. His body gave way beneath hers and they flopped together on the floor with James cushioning Noa's fall. "They're in!" Chavez shouted. She stood by the door, intermittently swinging around the door frame to fire a small pistol ... a pistol that wouldn't even be powerful enough to break the glass of the museum windows from where she was standing. Before Noa could shout at her to get out of the line of fire, the door slid closed. There was a sound like raindrops on a tin roof ... it was the sound of bullets hitting the hull.

She took a deep breath that came out shakier than it should have, even after taking fire. Her thumb found the stumps of her fingers. Kenji's betrayal was so fresh that it made her feel physically heavy. The fingers of her left hand curled—and she felt the absence of her ring and pinkie finger. Her breath quickened, as though she were starting to hyperventilate, and she felt like she might be sick. Noa forced herself to calm, bit her lip, and told her stomach to untwist from its knot. She could not break down. Not now. Sliding off James's back, she rubbed her hand over his shoulder, not letting him go—to anchor herself, maybe, or to comfort both him and herself. He was warm, solid, and real beside her, his tattoos dark on his arms, but fading. He had been a perfect stranger, not Fleet or Luddeccean. She'd met him in the snows of the North, and he'd had no reason to save her, but did anyway, whereas her own flesh and blood had sent her to a prison camp—and would have again, claiming it was to save her. Her eyes briefly caught sight of Carl Sagan, standing upright on his four back legs, waving in the air, his nose twitching. James moved, and she turned toward him. His cheek was pressed to the floor, his shockingly blue eyes were on her. He wasn't a stranger any more. They were bound as tightly as anyone she'd served with in the Fleet. Her mind instinctively reached for James's, and she let loose a flurry of emotions—relief and gratitude, and shame for Kenji—but James wasn't hard linked to her, and the emotions never crossed the empty air between them. There was no time to say all she felt. "Come on," she said, heaving herself up. "It's not over—" And then her eyes caught sight of crimson on the floor, smudged by her body.

"James?" she said.

He sat up, gingerly touching his side. His fingers came away bloody.

***

James stared at the crimson stain on his fingers. His shirt was wet, as was his knee.

"James!" Noa said again, alarm ringing in her voice.

"They have a sickbay," he heard Chavez say. "Commander, I can take him there—"

"I'm fine," James said. And he knew he was, without even touching the wound in his side. He'd felt a brief shock when it had hit him—a sensation of danger, and warning—but strangely no pain.

Noa put a hand on his shoulder. "James, you collapsed outside—"

"I slipped on the blood on the elevator floor," he said, climbing to his feet. "But the wound is minor." The wound in his side didn't hurt at all. He was more annoyed by the relative chill of the Ark interior.

Tugging his arm, Noa said, "No, Chavez is taking you to medical—"

James could feel the thrum of the Ark's engines beneath his feet, and heard the sound of bullets outside on the hull. Pulling her hand from his arm, James met her eyes. "I'm fine—courtesy of my augmentations." He didn't know that, but it was as good a hypothesis as any. "We don't have time to argue—and you're shorthanded as it is."

At his words the thrum beneath his feet increased in intensity. Manuel's voice cracked from a round circular grate in the wall. "Commander, I'm in sickbay, but on my way to engineering, Ghost is in command there—"

Ghost's voice cracked over Manuel's. "I'm working on the ground defenses. As soon as I get in, your darling brother is going to go to work getting me out."

"Can he really shut off the ground defenses?" Chavez said. "Without ethernet access?"

James's eyebrows rose. "He got us this far." But how … it still nagged at James. He didn't think 'scrambled transmissions,' as Ghost had said, was explanation enough.

Noa touched a red button beneath the grate, as they'd all

learned to do in Ghost's lair. "Understood. On our way to the bridge."

As she released the button, Chavez stared at the speaker. "This ship is so primitive. Maybe we can set up a local ethernet—"

"We have to survive the next twenty minutes, ensign," Noa snapped.

James realized he was still staring at the speaker, mulling over Ghost's mysterious access to the mainframe, and whether they might have only scant minutes to live. Even if Ghost could shut down the ground defenses, they still had an armada to face. Noa was already walking over to a sliding door of the airlock they were now in. A moment ago, he'd heard the worry in her voice—heard her heart race at impossible speeds when she'd thought him injured. She pressed a button, the door slid open, and she stepped through. Apparently she'd recovered from the shock of thinking him near death. James followed her past the airlock, and Chavez followed him.

Moments later, Noa summoned the lift that ran through the center of the ship from engineering to the bridge. As they waited, James looked around and located the hatches in the floor and ceiling that could be lifted for ladder access in case the lift did not come. As he did, he couldn't help but notice the walls of the corridor. They were gray, but not austere. There were faded drawings painted on the walls— stick figures of men, women, and children; plants in pots; hearts and crude stars. All the drawings ended at about the level of his waist. He remembered his last visit to the Ark as a child—the tour guide had said that the Ark had been a family ship. During the voyage a few children had been born. They'd been allowed to paint on the walls ... and yet, people of the same philosophy that would allow such humanity had just shot at him for being ... for being ...

He gripped his side where the blood was rapidly drying, a testament to his frailty, his humanity. They believed he would be the end to the human race. His gaze shifted to Noa. Her chin was high, her shoulders squared, her dark skin in sharp relief with the pale gray walls. He wasn't sure what he would have done if she'd gone with Kenji ... his vision dimmed. It would have all been over then ... everything ...

His vision went completely black. The thoughts in his mind stilled to all but one. Everything, what?

Metal screeched below them, and the engine grew louder. Chavez jumped, and Noa looked down sharply.

"Is that normal?" Chavez said.

The lift opened, and Noa stepped into the small cylindrical space. The ceiling was shaped like an oblong pill. Noa's eyes slid to James's.

"Sure," she said, raising an eyebrow as though daring him to contradict her. In Japanese she muttered, "I have to keep morale high."

James remembered standing below the elevator, contemplating not jumping—all would have been lost if he'd given in to the sense of inevitable failure. Raising an eyebrow of his own, James said, "Perfectly normal sound."

"Are you sure?" Chavez asked, metal limbs creaking as she shifted on her feet.

"I'm a historian," James said. "I have studied these ancient ships."

It was the most blatant lie he'd told in his life—or at least since he'd awakened in the snow—it felt oddly liberating. Noa's eyebrows rose and he thought he saw the hint of a smile on her face. There was a ding and the lift door opened. Noa gave him a tiny nod, and they stepped into a space scarcely larger than a coffin. James stood to one side, Chavez to the other, and Noa stood sandwiched between them facing the front. The door shut, but the lift did not move. "Bridge," Noa said, looking upward.

Nothing happened. Chavez drew against the wall. Eyes flitting side to side, she held the pistol in her hand so tightly her hand shook. James saw what looked like a small gray door on the wall just as wide as his hand, and about as tall. He opened it, revealing some buttons. James pressed the one that was the highest. The elevator started to move. Touching his chest, James said to Chavez, "See, historic spacecraft, my specialty."

Chavez's shoulders loosened and she grinned.

"Well done," said Noa, the edge of a smile definitely on her lips.

Looking up at the ceiling, James said in Japanese, "I hope we're going to the bridge."

Noa coughed just as the lift jerked to a stop. The doors did not open. Instead, the ceiling slid away, and the walls dropped.

CHAPTER SEVENTEEN

They were standing in a beam of light, in a circle of stairs much like the one that led out of the rain catch, but not so high. The bright sun outside made it lighter on the out-side than in, and Noa had a perfect view of the city. In the distance, she saw smoke rising. For the first time since the skirmish outside the Ark, she thought of the protests Man-uel had promised. Her hands turned to fists at her side. The uprising, the 'civil disobedience' that was distracting the bulk of the Guard forces, had turned violent. She had no doubt that the protesters would lose … and also, that they were probably responsible for the relative ease with which Noa and her people had made their way onto this ship. "Make this work," Noa told herself. "For all of them out there." She must have said the words aloud, because Chavez turned to her sharply.

"It will work," said James, and then he added in Japanese, "and if it doesn't, it is better than the alternative."

Noa thought of Ashley and the scars where her prosthet-ics had been pulled off, of little Oliver somewhere down the decks, and the man standing beside her whose mind would be picked apart. She felt herself turn to liquid steel. She shifted her gaze back to the bridge. At the top of the short stairs were six chairs tilted backward. Two for the pilot and co-pilot, two for passengers on either side of those, and two for the gunners manning the cannons.

Eliza poked her head around the seat next to the pilot

chair. "Hurry! The engines are almost ready to go."

Gunny poked his head out from the chair for one of the cannons. "Guns are still charging." His face was completely red from fire retardant, except for where it had been washed away with tears. His eyes were still bloodshot.

"To the other cannon, Ensign," Noa commanded, striding up to the captain's chair. She didn't bother asking Gunny if he could see well enough to fire—he was the only one on the ship that had any experience firing a cannon. Granted, that had been with ground cannons that were far more maneuverable, and he'd never had to allow for changes in gravity or firing at near light speeds … She pushed those thoughts to the side as she snapped herself into her chair. James snapped himself in beside her in the co-pilot chair. Manuel and Ghost both had experience that would have made them better co-pilots—but they were needed in engineering. As soon as he was secured in his seat, James started swiping at buttons. Screens in the instrument panel in front of Noa sprang to life with grainy images from outside of the Ark.

"It doesn't have a data port link," Chavez said, as though she didn't quite believe the holos she'd practiced at Ghost's place had been real.

"The red button fires," said Eliza. "You can practice maneuvering the guns if you press the little blue button next to the screen."

"Screen?" said Chavez. "Oh, right, no neural interface … the screen is so tiny."

There were steering bars directly in front of Noa. Ignoring both of those, Noa focused on the buttons and dials laid out on the dash. She pressed a button that the admiral had never needed to demonstrate for her. As soon as she did, the sound of hissing pipes and Manuel's shouts of, "Make sure that coolant pipe isn't leaking," filled the bridge.

"Engineering, are we ready to go?" Noa asked, as though they had a choice.

"Hold on, Commander," Manuel said. And then she heard him call out, "Timefield generator array?" and someone else respond, "All units online and operational."

Manuel continued down his checklist. "CO_2 filtration system?"

Another voice responded, "I … uh … think … yes, the light is green."

Gunny whispered what sounded like a prayer under his breath; Noa bowed her head and silently echoed it.

"Manuel …" Noa said.

"We're ready as we'll ever be, Commander," the engineer responded.

"Ghost?" Noa asked.

"Still working," Ghost grunted back.

"We have to go now," said James. "They have … I think those are ground cannons?"

Noa looked at the screen he was pointing at. "They wouldn't fire on a national monument, would they?" Noa asked, staring at the blurry image and at the same time diverting the engine power to the antigravs and main thrusters.

A whine sounded from below.

"That doesn't sound right," said Chavez.

Not answering, Noa gritted her teeth. She wasn't precisely sure if the Ark had ever been tested since it had been refitted at the Republic's order. "No time like the present," she muttered to herself, and then louder said, "Belt in, everyone!"

Manuel's voice filled the bridge. "All in."

Kara's voice cracked over the speaker. "Oliver and I are belted in in sick bay."

"Let's go, then," said Noa. Grabbing hold of the steering

bars and one hand on the throttle, she said a prayer, the same one she'd used in the Asteroid War in System Six.

Interrupting her concentration, 6T9 said, "Shouldn't we be alerting the authorities to the dangerous rebels taking control of the museum?" Noa's heart caught in her chest. Of course, 6T9 didn't think that the Guard had fired on them. If he had thought he was with the real rebels, he probably would have turned himself in.

"Dangerous rebels?" said Gunny.

"They shot at a child!" said 6T9.

"So that's how he's rationalizing it," Gunny said, as though to himself.

"How can you rationalize shooting at a child?" 6T9 cried.

"Shut down," said Eliza.

"Yes, ma'am," said the 'bot, and slumped forward in his seat.

Noa pulled back on the throttle. There was a shearing noise. Nothing happened. She swore she heard the entire ship collectively taking a breath.

And then an earsplitting roar filled the bridge, and before Noa could even glance down, her back was slamming into the seat and they were hurtling toward the clouds.

***

The force of the Ark's acceleration pushed James's body into his seat. His eyes watered, and his skin felt tight, his hands reflexively grabbed the arm rest. The pressure on his lungs was too intense to breathe. He wondered if something had gone wrong. Sixty seconds into the sky, the G forces suddenly lessened. The dome of the sky above their heads was still unblemished, perfect—but he knew the armada was up there, waiting.

"Fire cannons, now!" Noa said.

The ship rocked in rapid succession four times as plasma fire ripped out of the vessel. As the beams sped away, they fanned out.

"That should clear our path," Gunny said. "Plasma will play havoc with the external sensors of anything that isn't outright destroyed ... We're in the clear."

From the intercom there were cheers, and James wanted to smile, too. The ships in their immediate trajectory would be incapacitated, unable to fire or move, and they'd be in the way of any other vessels that might fire on the Ark. The Ark would fly right through the "donut hole" left by the cannons, and jump to light speed.

"Now all we have to do is blast out of the atmosphere and hit light speed," someone said.

Unfortunately, the timefield bands couldn't counteract substantial gravitational forces and shoot them through space at the speed of light.

"We're ready for it!" Manuel shouted. There was another cheer.

James craned his head to look at Noa. He wanted to congratulate her. To tell her she'd been right and he had never been so happy to be wrong.

But he found her frowning. "Do you hear that?" she said.

James opened his mouth, about to say no, when from below he heard a loud shearing noise.

"Oh, dear," said Eliza.

"What happened?" said Gunny.

Ignoring him, Noa said, "Manuel, that was the timefield generator array, get it back online!"

James's hands tightened on the armrest. Without the timefield bands, they'd never make it out of the atmosphere.

"I'm trying, I'm trying!" Manuel said.

"Going to do a gravitational turn, hold on," Noa said. "Performing calculations."

"A what?" said Eliza.

Noa just growled, so James answered for her. "We may be able to get out of orbit if she uses Luddeccea's spin as a slingshot … if she gets the angle right." But they'd miss the donut hole created by the cannons.

"Oh, I remember, the ship has an onboard computer that can—"

"I have a computer onboard my shoulders," Noa said. And of course she did. She was a pilot in the Fleet of the Galactic Republic; such apps would be standard. James saw the instant Noa's own navigational app finished the calculation. Her head snapped back, her eyes widened, and then she depressed the steering bars. The Ark leveled off at a more horizontal angle, and the chairs they were on all pivoted so that everyone in the bridge was right side up.

"I'm not a damn bat!" Ghost's voice cracked from the radio. Apparently, not all the seats on the Ark could remain orientated to Luddeccea's gravitational pull.

"We're not going to have a clear path," Gunny said, his voice hushed. "And the cannon needs to recharge … "

"I could divert some power from the timefield generators," Manuel's voice cracked over the line.

"No," said Noa. "If we don't hit light speed, this is all over!" Her chin was dipped low, her nostrils were flared, and James could see the muscles and tendons in her arms.

Ghost's voice cracked over the radio. "The armada is using older, non-ethernet dependent communications. I can't take the ships down that way … but I can try to scramble their detection and ranging instruments on the surface. It could create confusion."

"You do that!" Noa ordered. She gave her head a tiny shake and muttered, "The heavy cruisers won't be able to turn around that quickly."

"We should be able to take a few hits from a small fighter," Gunny said.

Noa nodded. James could see the steering bars in her hands vibrating to the same rhythm beneath his feet. He looked out at their trajectory. As the atmosphere became thinner, the ambient noise within the bridge dropped a few decibels—they were leaving the friction of oxygen, nitrogen, and carbon-dioxide molecules behind. After the roar of takeoff, he felt as though the cabin had grown hushed. The sky was rapidly changing from crystalline blue to the velvet black of space. He'd never experienced a takeoff that was as beautiful, and he wondered if it was because he suspected it might be his last.

"What do you see in the scopes, co-pilot?" Noa said.

James looked down at the screen showing the view directly above Prime, behind and above them. Six giant cruisers were clustered around Time Gate 8. He tilted his head. Of course they would be grouped around the station. It was controlled by aliens … or demons, or djinn. In the estimation of the Luddeccean authorities, anyway. His head ticked to the side.

Time Gate 8 had its own defenses. It was evenly matched with the cruisers and their small squadrons. His head ticked again. Four of the cruisers were dark … the station was dark, too. Time Gate 8's ring should have been lit from within. So aliens didn't need light? Had they been routed? Motion on the screen caught his eye. "Eight small fighters heading this way." They looked like delicately gliding snowflakes at this distance.

Noa's eyes dipped to the screen and then up to the window. "Five seconds until they're in range," she ground out.

James could do nothing but watch helplessly as the snowflakes approached. His grip tightened on the armrests.

"Four seconds," Noa said, although she needn't have, the countdown was playing out in his mind now in giant numbers.

"Three seconds," Noa said. Her voice was steady and calm, as though the situation was under control. His voice would be that way too … it always was that way … even times like now, when he wanted to shout, to scream, to frown, or to cry. The armrest snapped beneath his fingers.

"Two seconds," said Noa. On the screen, the snowflakes lit up.

"And—"

Noa's voice was cut off by the sound of explosions topside and rear of the ship.

"We're hit!" Manuel cried. Though he need not have.

"Damage report?" Noa said.

The ship's path changed, and it veered up sharply. James stared at the rapidly changing screens in front of them. His chair spun around, righting him so that the planet was below again. The ship was performing a huge arc. In a few minutes, the loop would be complete and they'd be plunging headfirst into Luddeccea's atmosphere.

"Engine One is damaged," Manuel's voice cracked. "And the thruster at one o'clock."

"I copy! Cutting Engine Three and thruster!" Noa said.

The Ark's flight stabilized, but with just Engine Two on the starboard side and Engine Four on the port side, they could only move left or right.

James looked up through the dome of glass. He didn't need to look at the dashboard to see the enemy. The Ark was heading straight toward the armada and the dark time gate.

***

Noa felt sweat prickling on her brow. The fighters that had fired on them split up to avoid the Ark hurtling in their direction, but others were dropping out of one of the heavy cruisers, just ahead and above them.

"Manuel! How is it coming?" she said, trying to keep her

voice level.

"We can fix it! It was just a short."

"How long?" Noa asked.

He didn't answer, but over the intercom she heard him yell, "Duct tape! I need more duct tape for this circuit!"

"The fighters are regrouping," James said.

Noa's eyes slid up. The fighters were beginning to glow at stern and starboard. She took a deep breath and hit the starboard hard, veering the huge ship left. Plasma fire ripped past them. Some of the screens in front of them went dark.

The small fighters flew off in every direction.

"The large ships … " James whispered. "The patterns of those lights ..."

Noa's eyes went to the large fighter-ships. Their cannons were arming, which was why the small fighters were getting out of the way. Noa's hands were damp, and she clutched the steering bar tighter to keep her palms from slipping. "Manuel!" she said. "I need timefield generators and I need light speed, now."

His voice cracked over the intercom. "Working on it!"

She saw the light of the cannons on the big ships of the armada grow brighter as the fighters flew off, almost leisurely. Of course, the Guard wasn't in any hurry. The Ark was dead in the water. Noa thought of giving power to Engine Three, and plunging the Ark into Prime; she could take out the Central Authority in one brilliant flash. Thousands would die. Order on the planet would break down; the people in the camps would be able to free themselves.

Her fingers twitched on the throttle. She swallowed. No, the people in the camps wouldn't go free. They'd die faster as the small shipments of food would never arrive. They were in no condition to fight off their guards. They were in the middle of nowhere, they wouldn't get aid …

"The time gate!" Eliza whispered.

"It's lighting up," James said.

Noa looked up and her jaw dropped. Time Gate 8 was lighting up at very specific intervals. "Those are the station's cannons!" she said.

The cannons on the huge fighter-carriers appeared to dim—in reality, Noa knew they'd just spun around to face off against the gate's defenses. Fighters dropped out of the large ships' hulls like rain and swirled in a swarm toward Time Gate 8.

"What …?" said Gunny.

Noa's mouth gaped as she watched bolts of plasma shoot from the gate's cannons, directly at the large carriers. Smaller bolts knocked into the small fighters. One of the large freighters managed a direct shot to one of the gate's cannons. Noa braced herself for the explosion … but instead, as the plasma fire hit, it appeared to disperse around the cannon in a glowing sphere that reminded Noa of nothing so much as a soap bubble. Then the glow appeared to be drawn into the cannon … and suddenly it was fired back out, directly at the carrier that had shot the initial blast.

"Some sort of energy transfer?" James said.

Noa had seen it before—but only in a demo holo. "That is only theoretical."

"Not anymore," James whispered.

But Noa couldn't respond; bits of shattered carrier and fighter were spinning in their direction. Gritting her teeth, she tried to steer the Ark around the debris as best she could.

"Who's onboard the station?" Gunny asked, "and are they on our side?"

"Trying to open a channel," James said. In the periphery of her vision, Noa saw his pale hands flying across his dash. She kept swerving left and right—but debris was everywhere.

A sight hurtling before her made her eyes widen. "Manuel! I've got a big ol' chunk of freighter coming this way! I need that engine!"

"I'm trying to give it to you!" Manuel cried.

"We need something! Anything! Thrusters won't be enough!" Noa said as the huge chunk veered toward them. She readjusted the Ark's course as much as she could, but they needed just a few degrees more … her internal apps were buzzing, warning her they were on course to lose a wing—and a large hunk of the hull with it.

"We're going to get pulverized," James said, voice as usual without inflection, and in that instant she hated him for it.

"There's always hope," she muttered. "Manuel!"

The ship suddenly veered away from the debris.

"What was that?" Manuel's voice cracked over the intercom.

Ghost's voice buzzed, breathlessly. "I discharged all the material from the toilets on the bottom of the ship."

Beside her, James said, "Well, isn't that the shi—"

His voice and her laugh—that wasn't a real laugh, but relief and adrenaline caught in a gust of breath—were both cut off as a chunk of debris tore against the bottom of the wing. The vibration echoed through the ship, making the hair on the back of Noa's neck stand on end. It was so loud, it hurt. Gunny screamed, and so did Chavez—maybe she did, too. The noise died down. Her gauges told her the wing was still there, and there was no hole in the hull; Ghost's ploy had been just enough. Tears streaming down her cheeks from the pain in her ears, she tried to say something, anything to James—a triumphant, "See, hope?" but as the scream of shearing metal quieted, she realized that the bridge was filled with another sound, a buzzing hum from the dash in front of James.

"Is it on our side?" Gunny shouted again as a carrier exploded in front of them, and Noa gaped. Carriers and fighters were scattering. The Ark was on a path to fly directly into the ring of Time Gate 8.

"Not yet determined," James might have said. It was hard to hear over the stream of unintelligible buzz coming from his dash.

A light flashed from one of Time Gate 8's cannons. Noa didn't need her furiously calculating apps to know that they were about to be hit. The beam of plasma fire streaked through space in an instant that felt long but was too short for her to respond.

She blinked as the ship shook. For a moment she was in shock. They were still in one piece. She had expected to be free falling through space.

"That was a light blast," Gunny said.

"A warning shot of some kind?" Noa asked.

The chatter from James's dash grew louder. Noa turned to James just in time to see his dash light up with electricity that danced up his hands. He slumped in his seat, and the cabin was silent except for Noa's shout and the continued sound of static.

***

He fell.

He heard Noa call out his name. "James."

James. A jumble of syllables that meant nothing, and everything. Him. His universe tied up in a word. His name, who he had been.

The hero never died in stories. But this wasn't a story.

His feet moved beneath him, and it took a moment to realize he wasn't dead. He was walking through darkness, and he knew where he was. He was in the unmanned portions of Time Gate 8, the parts of the station that had "grown" almost organically since its construction above Luddeccea.

And he knew where he was going—a shuttle that would take him to the surface of the planet. Somewhere he heard an explosion. And a signal struck his mind. There were no words, but he understood: he would face resistance. He continued to walk undeterred, and as the scene played out in hyper detail, it occurred to him that he was dreaming.

Maybe he was dead. To sleep, perchance to dream, wasn't that what Shakespeare had said? He'd never actually read Shakespeare, he knew it from twentieth-century movies. The movies he had been obsessed about, but now only cared about because they gave him frame of reference. No, that was not all. They tied him tighter to Noa every time they watched one together. Thinking about her, he saw the first image of her, in her Fleet grays, the wide smile on her face, her eyes averted. Because he couldn't do anything else, he continued to walk, getting closer to the sound of explosions, but the image of her hovered before him like a will-o'-the-wisp. He reached the end of the unmanned portion of the station and a door opened before him with a whoosh of air that, according to his senses, was too laden with CO_2 to be breathable by humans. He stepped into a secondary hallway, off the main boardwalk that continued around the whole ring. There was a dead human male at his feet in Luddeccean Green. The human had a pistol in one hand, and another was stretched out in front of him. James looked up the wall in the direction of the stray hand. There was an access panel with wires yanked out. Had the dead man been trying to open the door James had just stepped through? He looked back at the doorway—the door frame was pockmarked with bullet holes and darkened by flame. He looked around the space. There were more dead humans spread out on the floor. Most wore Luddeccean Green, but there was a woman and a child collapsed in a corner. Part of his mind screamed, "Go to them, Noa would want you to go to them," but his dream self walked on unburdened by the scene. He had a shuttle to catch. He walked to another airlock and it opened before him into the main promenade, where the sound of explosions was very loud.

Something alighted on his forearm, light as a bird. But he couldn't look to see what it was. The weight tightened, but not painfully. He heard Noa's voice. "Hang in there, James. I'll get you to sickbay as soon as I can." Her voice was a whisper, but it rang in his mind louder than the other voices, the same cacophony that he hadn't understood before, but now oddly he did understand.

"The Archangel Project will continue." It was the buzz from his dash, but now it was comprehensible.

Beyond his closed eyelids, he heard Gunny say softly, "Cannons are charged."

"Hold your fire!" said Noa.

The buzzing conversation in the strange language went on. Was it language? There were no words ... but he understood it. "The Archangel Project will continue." The phrase was repeated, nine times in different voices. Were they voices? Or just different frequencies of signals? Another voice said, "They attacked us."

One of the first voices said, "We cannot lose this opportunity."

"Data is still being collected," said another voice.

"Time Gate 8," Noa said. "Do you require evacuation?"

"The Heretic," said one of the nine.

"Cannot provide assistance," said the same one that had said, "they attacked us."

A blur of buzzing opinions followed.

"More data is required."

"Continue the Archangel Project."

"Gate 8, do you require assistance?" Noa's voice hitched

slightly. James could hear the tension in it, the note of fear, but he knew she would not waver in her offer.

Ghost's voice cracked over the intercom. "The ground defenses are back online. Commander, we have to get out of here!" James's eyes were still closed, but he could hear the man's lip trembling, imagine the sweat beading on his brow.

"Forget ground forces, I'm worried about who … whatever … is in Time Gate 8, Commander," Gunny whispered. "I think the Green Coats were right, something's aboard that thing … something dangerous."

Noa did not reply.

"Engines are operational!" Manuel declared. "We can go."

"Time Gate 8, do you copy?" Noa asked again. The pressure on James's forearm increased. No … not pressure singular, but pressures plural, three tiny pressures from Noa's left hand. The recognition sent an electric pulse through his body at the same time his mind was churning.

The ground defenses were arming … but she wouldn't leap to light speed until she was certain there was no one aboard Time Gate 8 who needed assistance. But no one was there. He knew that, just as he had known he could lift 6T9, he had known how high he could leap, and he had known that the wound in his side was not dangerous. At least, no one human was aboard. He struggled to open his eyes, to pull himself out of his fog, and warn her. At the same time, his mind screamed to the voices he'd heard in his head, "Answer her!"

And then he heard the reply, "The Archangel speaks."

"The Heretic still supports us," said another.

"Answer," one voice said. Eight more repeated the phrase.

James's eyes bolted open and his head jerked backward with such force, his vision faltered. When it returned, he found Noa's eyes on him, her arm stretched across the space between them. Her lips were parted, and James answered her unspoken question. "I'm fine," he lied. He swore he felt something snap in the back of his mind.

Giving a tiny nod, Noa slipped her hand back to the steering bars. Her eyes went heavenward toward the massive form of Time Gate 8's ring. The Ark was minutes away from coasting through the ring. The voices over the intercom were once again an indiscernible blur. Had he been hallucinating? Dreaming?

Noa began to speak again. "Time Gate 8—"

The voices coming through James's dash coalesced and merged and this time spoke in Basic. "We hear you." The words sounded like they were spoken by a choir.

Noa began to speak again. "Can we assist—"

"You cannot assist," the strange choir continued.

"We have room for—"

"We are not your kind," the choir said. James heard a collective intake of breath on the bridge. Noa's hands, up until this point tightly gripping the steering bar, went briefly slack.

The choir continued, "The ground forces prepare to attack."

Noa squared her shoulders. "With your defenses, we still might have time—"

"Assist us by continuing," the choir sang. "Go!"

"Commander, their cannons are targeting."

Noa's order cut through the bridge, "Light speed, now."

Nothing happened.

"I thought it was fixed," Manuel said. "I thought it was—"

"Hit it with a hammer!" Eliza screamed.

"They've fired, Commander!" shouted Ghost.

James felt a chill rush over him, but then Noa pulled back hard on the steering bars. His head flew back into the headrest, and he felt as though his body was being crushed against the seat. He blinked, the pressure lessened, and the stars blurred into a single glowing mass. They were at light speed, they'd left normal light behind, and only the ancient glow of the Big Bang remained to light the way.

The bridge was absolutely silent, except for the chirps of the timeband indicators, and then there was a crackle of static. For a moment, every muscle in James's body tensed, expecting another alien transmission, but instead Manuel's voice crackled over the intercom. "Wow! Hitting the transformer box with a hammer actually worked."

A collective breath escaped the crew in the bridge. "We're safe," Eliza whispered. "6T9, wake up! We're safe!"

"We're not safe," Gunny whispered. "Not with whatever that thing was out there."

James kept his eyes studiously ahead. His hands tightened on the arm rests … whatever was out there … was it already in here, somehow, in him?

***

Noa sat on the steps of the bridge, a cup of coffee beside her. It was oddly good coffee. The galley of the Ark had been converted into a cafe for tourists, and only the best Luddeccean bean was served up there. She idly rolled the paper cup in her hand. It was emblazoned with the emblem of the Ark—a dove with a green sprig in its mouth.

Manuel was sitting on the steps opposite her. His face looked waxen, his eyes vacant and far away. Gunny was in between them, James was directly to her left, and Ghost was between him and Manuel. Above and behind Noa, Chavez was in the helm seat, one of the students beside her. Eliza was off minding Oliver—or more, minding 6T9 as he minded Oliver. The other students were in engineering.

"It looks like they were right," Manuel said. "Time Gate 8, it is controlled by … something."

Noa rubbed her eyes. How could the Luddecceans have been right? None of the intel she'd had access to as part of the Fleet had pointed to alien sentience. "It could be some sort of terrorist organization," she said. But she didn't believe it.

Manuel's voice was a low rumble. "They are converting incoming fire into energy blasts! Terrorist organizations are seldom better-equipped technologically than established societies."

"Seldom, but sometimes," said Noa. Manuel's eyes narrowed, but then he shook his head and looked away, as though it was too trivial to worry about. Noa swallowed. She'd been in Manuel's shoes before ... everything but survival for his son, and then himself, would feel trivial to the engineer for a very long time.

Gunny sat up straighter, catching Noa's attention. In a hushed voice he said, "If augments are controlled by whatever is on the station, and it spreads over the ethernet as the Authority says, are we assisting it to spread to other systems by returning to Earth? Should we be continuing?" His eyes were wide, and he looked more frightened by that possibility than he had in the line of fire. It made Noa's heart ache.

"Yes!" Ghost cried. "We should continue." He waved his hands. "We can't stay out here! We'll die." Noa eyed the man sharply. He looked visibly shaken—his lower lip was trembling, and there was still a sheen of sweat on his brow. Her mouth twisted. Not that it took much to shake Ghost. The man was a coward ... but he had saved them by blowing the contents of the toilets out into space. It had given them just enough boost to avoid being pulverized by debris. Still, something nagged at her ...

"Even if whoever was on the gate wasn't human ... " she paused. She had trouble saying that aloud. It was so ... unbelievable ... none of the intel they'd collected in other systems pointed to the presence of extraterrestrial life. And she certainly didn't believe the talk of demons or djinn. Her brow furrowed. Or fallen angels heralding the end of the human race, for that matter. Taking a deep breath, she continued, "That wouldn't mean that their interests and ours don't align." She sat up straighter. "And even if the Luddeccean Authority is right about there being an alien intelligence aboard Gate 8, that does not mean that they are right about that intelligence possessing human augments." She waved a hand back toward Chavez. "The ensign seems completely in control of her legs—"

"Yes, Sir!" Chavez said.

Noa waved a hand at Manuel. "Your son hasn't tried to strangle you with his augmented hand."

The engineer hissed and drew back. "Of course not. He's a baby!"

Noa's eyes went to James. He was looking at a spot in the floor. She almost said, "And James seems in full control of his augments," but found those words wouldn't come. James wasn't in control of his augments. She let out a bitter laugh instead. "James, the most augmented individual aboard saved an innocent child from the Guard. If augments are demons and devils, give me demons and devils." Shaking her head, she said, "And James had many opportunities to kill me in my sleep—"

"No!" James said, lifting his head sharply, eyes wide with alarm.

Noa started. The outburst was out of place, too emphatic. All heads in the room turned in James's direction. He went quiet and dropped his gaze.

Noa stood, purposely drawing all eyes back to her. "I've been to the camps where they warehouse the missing augments." She rubbed the stumps of her fingers almost instinctively, and saw all eyes drop to her scars. "What I saw there ... the inhumanity I saw from my fellow humans, the inhumanity that is still going on ..." Her jaw got tight. "We continue to Earth, we let the Republic know about the slaughter. At this point, I trust whoever is aboard Gate 8 more than I do Luddecceans."

"We have to go on," said Manuel, empty eyes focused on a nondescript point on the floor.

Gunny looked nervous, but he nodded.

Ghost sighed. "Thank God."

Gunny cleared his throat. "Any idea what 'Archangel' and 'Heretic' might mean?"

The hairs on the back of Noa's neck rose.

"What?" said James, head snapping up again.

Noa's muscles tensed. He was tied to the Archangel Project—just like she was. Her eyes went to Gunny. He was shifting nervously in his seat. If he knew Noa and James were involved in the project, would he trust them more or less?

"It came over the comm device," Gunny said to James. "'Archangel' and 'Heretic' were the only discernible words in all that buzz ... until whatever it was started speaking Basic."

James stared at him blankly.

"When you were unconscious," Noa said.

James looked away too quickly.

Ghost's eyes narrowed at James, and then at Noa. A tiny smile came to his lips. Noa didn't like that smile. She made a decision. Taking a long breath, loud enough to be heard and draw even Manuel's attention, she said, "When I was first captured by the Guard, they interrogated me." She rubbed the stumps of her fingers again, looking for her rings. She saw Gunny and Manuel's eyes widen, saw Ghost's Adam's apple bob, and realized they were inferring that her fingers were cut off as part of her interrogation. She bit her lower lip. The torture in the interrogation room had

372

been only mental—she'd thought that she'd implicated her brother, that he'd be undergoing the same scrutiny she was. But he hadn't. He'd turned her in.

She closed her eyes. Oh, Kenji. Her stomach dropped. He'd been so misled.

Remembering where she was, she opened her eyes. Manuel and Gunny were looking at her with bright eyes. Gunny gave her a tiny nod.

She took a steadying breath. "As a Commander in the Fleet, I am privy to a lot of classified information … things they never asked me about." She looked down at the floor. Her voice, when she spoke, was softer than she meant it to be. "During the interrogation, they kept asking me about the Archangel Project. They swore I was a part of it." She met their eyes again. "I've never heard of the Archangel Project." Gritting her teeth, she said, "I thought maybe they'd just been trying to break me."

"But they didn't," said Gunny. His voice was thick. Noa met the older man's gaze. She might outrank him, but she respected him, and she got the feeling deep in her gut that he respected her … more than that, he'd be loyal despite his own misgivings.

Her eyes slid to Manuel. He was looking at the ground, nodding to himself. He'd be loyal because of his son. She didn't look at James. She didn't need to. He wouldn't let her down, she knew that like she knew how to walk, to talk, and to breathe.

"Well, glad that's settled," said Ghost, wiping his hands on his thighs. "Are we dismissed?"

Noa's eyes went to the little man. She needed him, even if he was a coward; he was brilliant and useful. "That was very clever, Ghost, ejecting the contents of the toilets."

Ghost shrugged, but she could see a hint of a smile on his face.

"You'd make a hell of an engineer," said Manuel, his voice oddly monotone. He was saying it by rote, Noa realized. Playing the role of the encouraging leader and offering praise on autopilot.

Ghost's smile dropped. "Too boring," he said dismissively.

Manuel scowled and Noa contained the urge to roll her eyes.

And then it hit her, something that had been bothering her since they crawled into the Ark's airlock. "And it's a good thing you were able to stop the elevator," she said.

"What?" said Ghost.

"When it got jammed … " said Noa. Her jaw tightened. He'd claimed he hadn't been able to stop for Hisha … but he'd stopped at the first deck with a door, instead of the one at the top, where the elevator would have stopped on its own.

"Ah, well, got lucky," said Ghost.

Noa met his eyes. He might not be lying. He had his direct brain-to-mainframe connection, or whatever—he could have found the problem. She blinked. But that isn't what he said, he said they "got lucky." When did Ghost not claim responsibility for any sort of genius? She surveyed the slight smile on his face, the way he looked at her too directly. Her jaw got tight. If the Ark had a computer error, they needed Ghost. There weren't any other options. Purposefully relaxing her frame, Noa said, "Of course." Her voice must not have been as neutral as she had attempted, because a light went on in Manuel's eyes. He looked up at Noa, and back to Ghost. She could see the question playing out there.

Noa forced herself to smile at Ghost, and hoped it didn't look too fake. "Dismissed," said Noa.

Manuel and Ghost headed toward the lift platform at the center of the floor. Manuel cast a dark glance at Ghost.

Ghost lifted his nose.

She bit her tongue. It was going to be a long trip. "Forget about aliens—humans are more dangerous at the moment," she thought as the lift descended.

"Noa?"

She jumped and found James very close. "Did I say that aloud?"

He raised an eyebrow, but didn't answer with words. He didn't need to—she could read him by now. It was oddly comforting to know, even if yes, she did say that aloud.

* * *

James sat at the edge of the bed in the room that was his quarters. It had just enough space for a double bed that could fold into a couch, and a chair that was next to a portion of wall that could lift up and become a desk. There was a tiny porthole that showed the blur of stars, a sink in the wall with a mirror. There was a small lavatory with a toilet. An ancient notice on the wall on some sort of plasticized paper reminded him that food was strictly forbidden outside of the galley, lest they had accidentally picked up rats.

There was also a screen above the area that was a desk. James had been informed that it worked a lot like his father's laptop, and the Ark had movies on file, mostly religious in orientation, all of them ancient. He should be curious about what entertainment the ancient ship had to offer, or, barring that, too tired to be curious. But he wasn't. The hallucination—or the dream—that he had had while unconscious played over and over in his mind. It didn't feel like a hallucination or a dream; it felt like a memory—a memory that was bright and clear, like anytime after he'd awakened in the snow.

He swung himself back onto the bed. It had to be a dream. He wouldn't have walked calmly and unafraid over dead bodies. He might be callous—but he wasn't without fear. It had been a dream. He had not understood what the voices were saying before he fell into unconsciousness, or after he woke up. He'd latched onto the words 'Archangel' and 'Heretic' and imagined he understood, that must have been what happened. Curling on his side, he closed his eyes and tried to sleep, or to sink into the half-waking state that passed for sleep lately. Like every other time, his mind started to replay the events of the day with astounding clarity. His eyes bolted open. He did not dream.

CHAPTER EIGHTEEN

Visions of Ashley waving her crutch danced before Noa's eyes. She woke up with a start. Her bed smelled stale. She closed her eyes, and let her mind focus on the hum of the engines. For a moment she had a sensation of stepping into sleep as though it was a deep dark pool—but then in the darkness the face of the woman in the corpse wagon took form, and the form stretched forward, reached toward Noa with waxy arms, her mouth opened, and ...

Noa awoke, shaking, curled in on herself, and clutching a pillow. She looked across the bed. It was too large for one person aboard a spaceship—but the Ark was a colony ship—during the first voyage, even the Captain had a wife.

She took a deep breath, squeezed her hands into fists, and felt the absence of the last two fingers on her left hand. She felt tears prickle the corners of her eyes. She thought of Kenji, and Ashley, and the dead woman in the wagon and desperately wanted drugs to help her sleep. There was probably something in the sickbay ... she shook her head. The crew would know. A crew this small, they were all going to know everything about everyone really soon. Having their commanding officer hooked on sleeping pills would not inspire confidence.

She wished James were here. Chavez had actually asked if she'd be billeting with him. Her hand clenched on the covers. She missed him ... she hadn't slept without him since the camp. He'd become associated with safety in her mind.

Rubbing her eyes, she sighed, thinking of some of the erotic dreams he'd inspired. Waking up to him after those had been awkward, but erotic dreams were better than nightmares.

Maybe he wasn't asleep. She reached out with her mind … and before she could reprimand herself, she touched the ethernet. She blinked. Not just the local ethernet—Ghost had promised to establish one. With her mind she saw little lights for each member of the crew and felt a wave of happiness. They were connected, if only to each other. She tried to access the ship's functions—and found she still could not—baby steps, she reminded herself. Her mind flitted back to her crew, and to James. The light for his consciousness was white … he was awake. She reached out to it, and felt his reply in her mind. "I am here."

"I think I'd like a snack," she replied across the shared channel. "Meet you in the galley." James was always up for a snack. She flung on the clothes she'd laid out on the chair beside her bed, and was out the door less than two minutes later.

She nearly bumped into 6T9. He was pacing the hallway, Oliver on his shoulder, a long power cable with an extension attached to his back. The other end was inserted into the wall. 'Bots were so energy intensive. 6T9 gave her a smile. She nodded, though it was unnecessary, he was only a 'bot and wouldn't have cared. She turned to the lift, but before she'd even taken a step, James emerged from the sliding door. She blinked.

Over the ethernet, he said, "I was on my way to see you when you called."

"Couldn't sleep?" Noa said aloud, and stifled a yawn behind her hand.

"No," he said, approaching her slowly, almost cautiously. His eyes went to 6T9. There was a line between his brows.

"Me either," she said. "Kept thinking of everyone we left behind." 6T9 wasn't human. Speaking so plainly wouldn't make him think less or more of her … or make him think at all.

James's gaze returned to her. He tilted his head, and lifted his hand toward her, but then dropped it. "We will reach the secret time gate. The Fleet will return to Luddeccea and end the genocide; we could not do that ourselves."

It was the wrong thing to say. Noa's heart sunk. By the time she brought the Fleet, Ashley could very well be dead. Kenji … well, she had no idea. The Fleet would save others, possibly millions, but not the people she knew, and not the ones she'd seen die already.

Pacing back toward them, 6T9 leaned close to Noa, putting Oliver's drowsing drooling little noggin right next to her shoulder. The 'bot whispered, "Whoever saves one life saves the world entire," and gave a bright smile.

Noa's breath caught at the words, and at the smell of Oliver's sweaty little head. He smelled like toddler and hope. The words were heavy, but lightened her heart. He was right, and she was letting herself sink into a vortex of despair she'd never known before—not even during the Asteroid Wars of System Six. For all of them, she needed to pull herself out. She put a hand to her mouth, her vision got blurry, and she almost cried from relief. She'd just been delivered grace by a sex 'bot—who would have thought?

"That is profound," James murmured.

Lifting his chin, 6T9 nodded. "I have a proverbs and idioms app. Just like a pig in a poke."

Noa's lips parted. That made no sense.

One of James's eyebrows shot up. "Are the idioms set to cycle randomly?"

"Yes, how did you know? Guess it takes one to know one!" said 6T9, walking away and gently shushing Oliver.

Noa laughed, and rubbed her temples.

"Not so profound, after all." James sighed, looking after him.

Noa shook her head. "The words are still profound, even if the messenger is a sex 'bot." She looked up at James. He was watching the 'bot walk away. The crease was still between his brows. She wasn't hungry, but she said, "Want to get that snack?" She didn't want him to leave.

"Actually, I needed to speak to you," James said, his voice low and hushed. Leaning closer, he whispered, "Privately."

Her eyes slid closed as his warm breath tickled her ear. She felt herself flush, but then her brain caught up with his words and the reality of the situation. He had already been on his way to her quarters when she'd contacted him, and it wasn't a romantic visit, despite the hour. His caution, the concern in his eyes, said otherwise. She shouldn't be disappointed. She was too old for such sentimentality.

"Right," she said, "this way."

She commanded the door to open, and it didn't. With a huff, she found the open button and gave it a shove. The door slid away, and James followed her into the tiny space.

When he spoke, it was over the ethernet. "Can we have a truly private conversation, even here?"

Noa looked above their heads. Could they be private over Ghost's ethernet? She suspected not. Her eyes went around the room. 6T9 was just outside the door; he might not listen on purpose, but she had no idea what his auditory abilities were. He might hear, and if anyone asked him to repeat what he'd heard, he'd doubtlessly tell them. And even if he didn't … She looked to the intercom on the wall. The whole place was linked by the ancient communications system. You were supposed to touch a button to transmit, but still … Without a word, James lifted a hand. For the first time, she noticed he was carrying a roll of hard link.

Noa laughed. It was a brilliant idea. The direct connection would circumvent eavesdroppers of the electronic and physical variety—and even if someone burst into the room, they'd think they were just up to some kinky sex.

James tilted his head, and one eyebrow shot up. Noa motioned with her hand for an end of the cable. Plugging it into her port, she said across the well-used line, "If 6T9 saw this in your hand … " She rolled her eyes, and said across the link, "He'd think we're hard linking in all sorts of ways."

As she said it, she felt a slight stir of disappointment in her chest. She didn't let that slip through. She was lonely; and these past weeks … today … she hurt. It struck her that she desperately wanted contact, an embrace—her eyes fell to James's slightly parted lips—or more. Why was she thinking this right now? She'd been alone with him before, even had more privacy. But they'd been on the run, not even as safe as they were here, and she'd been dying. Now she was like a spring that had been tightly coiled for weeks, and she was bursting free. But it still was not the time. She snapped her eyes back to his. He wasn't saying anything; he was completely motionless. She wasn't sure how a human could stand so still. It was obvious, though, that he hadn't been amused by the joke.

"I'm sorry," she said, crossing her arms, suddenly uncomfortable. "That was off color, I—"

"I am not offended," James said. "The opposite."

Noa felt her breath catch. James dropped his gaze to the floor. Across the hard link he said, "But there is something I must tell you—it could be important for all of us. It's something I remembered, from the time before I landed on Luddeccea … " He took a long breath. His head ticked to the side a few times. "It … it … came to me when I was unconscious."

The stutter, the head tic. Noa put her hand on his arm

without thinking. His eyes slid to it and then slid up to her face. Blue eyes on hers, his lips did not move as he whispered across the link, "I think it will be easier if I showed you."

She nodded. And then the world went black.

***

James showed her everything: the walk through Gate 8, the darkness behind his eyes when he had listened to the transmission—and he translated the transmission for her, too. Noa's avatar had stood quietly the whole time, arms crossed as they were in real life, as close to him as they were in real life.

When it was all over, they stood in the mental space between their minds. Noa looked up at him and said nothing for a long while. "It could have been a hallucination," Noa's avatar said.

"It wasn't," said James.

"A dream."

"I don't dream—I recycle memories, that's all—and that's what this was," James's avatar responded.

In the mindscape and the real world, Noa narrowed her eyes up at him. "So, this ... " she waved a hand and turned the scene to the interior of Gate 8. "Is your way of telling me you might be an alien?"

In the real world James's head ticked. "I ... I ... " His avatar ran a hand through his hair, and then chuckled mirthlessly. "I wish I could say that for certain." He met the eyes of Noa's avatar. In the darkness of the mindscape, they were nearly black. Her avatar still had the scar on her cheek, but her hand was whole. Her brow furrowed, and her mouth opened. Before she could speak, he said, "Noa, I know I'm wrapped up in the Archangel Project somehow ... "

"And I am, too," Noa said.

He shook his head. "No, not like me. We both know the

evidence points to me being the Archangel—"

"And I'm probably the Heretic."

James's avatar blinked.

She held up her wrist, and then scrunched her eyes at the sweep of dark brown perfect skin. "In real life, it has the tattoo … " James looked down at her avatar's wrist, and remembered the tattoo from the physical world in perfect detail. Running his hand down her avatar's wrist, he left the tattoo behind. H0000616.

"The 'H' stands for 'Heretic.'" Her lips stretched into a thin, bitter smile. "They never told me why." The smile crumpled. She hissed, and he felt frustration, anger, and despair seep across the link.

"Noa … " James stammered. "Something is wrong with me. The time before I woke up in the snow, it feels like a dream, less clear, hazy, as though I was a completely different person." He closed his eyes. "Before I got to Gate 8 … I was a different person. I couldn't have killed anyone." He looked down to the ground. "I couldn't have walked past a dead mother and child and not felt something, not tried to help."

"You don't know you didn't feel anything!" Noa snapped. "It was the dream, the memory, something was wrong with your recall."

"I can't even smile, but I have all these abilities that I don't even remember I have. Noa, something is wrong with me. I'm broken."

"We're both broken!" Noa said, throwing up her left hand. On her avatar it was whole … and two platinum bands were on her ring finger. Noa's eyes widened as though she'd just noticed them. Her avatar pulled her hand close and suddenly they were surrounded by wraiths. A woman on a crutch holding out her hand, a corpse's face frozen open in a scream, a guard beating a woman bent over a sewing machine. Long lines of women trudging between barracks, and Kenji throwing up his arms before a wall of fire. Noa's memories, James realized—or her fears.

A hazy recollection came to him, of the man he'd been before, with another woman—her father had just died, her face streaked by tears. James's other self hadn't felt anything particular for that woman, but he'd felt for her loss. He had gathered her into his arms and pulled her close.

With his avatar and his real self he reached out and pulled both Noas to him. It felt awkward, like his arms didn't belong to that man in the memory who'd comforted the woman so easily. Maybe his arms didn't belong to that man. But as soon as he touched her, Noa practically melted against him, as though she belonged there. It was so right, it was overwhelming; he found he could say nothing. Noa was quiet too, but the wraiths receded.

He felt her take a deep breath. She didn't pull away, and he didn't let her go. Two bands on the ring finger of her left hand. She might be married. He felt as though she wasn't for some reason … but he found he didn't care either way. He dropped his cheek on the top of her head and pulled her tighter.

"See, both broken," she said.

He rocked her, his hand trailing along her back. He could feel the tiny ridges of her spine. "There are too many coincidences, Noa." The words came out of his avatar in a sigh. "We both know the same dead language, I found you in the snow using a frequency that should be secure. I knew your name, your age, your rank."

She pulled back and looked up at him sharply. "And?"

He shook his head. "That's too much, you have to find that odd."

She pulled farther away, and his stomach fell. Looking away, Noa crossed her arms and shook her head. Her jaw hardened. "No."

"Don't tell me you don't believe that there is an alien force at work," James said, stepping toward her. She didn't look at him. He persisted. "You saw what happened at Gate 8, not just in my memories, but in reality."

"No," she said again. The set of her jaw became even more stubborn. She glanced quickly at him but then away. "I still think you're a hyper-augment, wrapped up in this madness for no other reason than I am. But it doesn't matter."

"Noa, you can't be in denial anymore."

Still not looking at him, she shook her head. "Doesn't matter."

James rolled his eyes. "The Luddeccean forces were shot down with technology you admit humans don't have yet. You can't ignore that."

"I'm not ignoring it!" Noa snapped across the link. Her avatar turned to him, arms crossed. Lip curling, she said, "I'm saying. It. Doesn't. Matter."

James's avatar's jaw dropped. In real life, his jaw remained shut as though snarled in wire.

"I'm saying I don't care."

James blinked, in real life and in avatar form.

"You saved me," Noa said. "You saved Oliver. You're helping me save my whole damned planet. I don't care who you are … or … or … " she waved a hand. "Or what! If you're an alien, well, you've treated me better than my own people."

James eyes widened; he realized he hadn't taken a breath in several long minutes.

"I don't care." She waved her hand again and shook her head. "What you are!"

His head ticked to the side in real life. A feeling hit him with such force he couldn't even name it. Relief, gratitude, victory, and a seething desire for more, all wrapped up in a

385

neuron and nano screaming explosion. It took him by surprise, and ripped through his mind with such intensity and speed it overwhelmed the applications that kept emotions from slipping across the link.

Noa gasped and rolled back on her feet.

In the dark mental mindscape, a huge metal door suddenly appeared, so large it would have stretched up to the bridge if it had been real. Before James could ask for an explanation, the door swung open with a clang, and Noa's and his avatars were bathed in white light.

James gasped in wonder. Noa dropped her eyes, and then looked at him and shrugged. "That's me … sometimes when you send emotions over the hard link I hallucinate. This one slipped."

She wasn't doing anything to hide it. He supposed a several-story door with white light pouring through was hard to disguise.

He looked back to her, suddenly embarrassed. "I didn't mean to send you that." It had been rude. And too much.

Her eyes stayed locked on his. "It's really alright."

He still felt ill at ease. Raising an eyebrow, he tried to make a joke of it. "Another odd coincidence?"

She didn't say anything, but he thought he saw the corners of her lips curl up just slightly. A feeling slipped across the link, and it tugged him toward her before he'd even deciphered it. When they were standing so close there was no distance between them, his mind caught up with what his body already knew. She wanted him, too. He felt the familiar tug of longing swirled with something else. He felt like if this were it, if the ship were to disintegrate, if they never reached the Kannakah Cloud, he'd accomplished something, something enormous, and this moment meant as much as life itself. The door in Noa's hallucination disappeared and there was only her and him and blinding white light. He lifted a hand to touch her cheek—in real life and to her avatar. Her eyes closed. Her lips parted slightly. And if he was an alien, he had some very human desires. His forehead fell onto hers. If he was alien … "I'd never hurt you, Noa. You must know that."

Her hand caught his. "I know." She let her assurance slip across the link and it filled him with relief. He sent the feeling back and the floor beneath them vanished in the mindscape.

For a moment they stood, the shared desire flaring across the hard link between them, and the white light of Noa's hallucination turning to orange. Her more fragile body pressed against his, and electrons streamed between them. The hallucination, everything—it felt right. They were two nuclei about to fuse in the heart of a star, and he had never felt more human.

CHAPTER NINETEEN

Kenji stood, head bowed, finger on his lips, listening to the static that was the transmission from Time Gate 8. In the midst of the static the words, "archangel" and "heretic" rang like bells. The rest was incomprehensible. "New code," he said when the recording stopped. "It will take a while to decipher it, but with the clues provided by context and—"

"Why did they say 'archangel' and 'heretic?'" shouted Counselor Zar. He sat at the left of a long dark table in the bunker conference room at Central Authority.

Kenji lifted his head, and had a moment of claustrophobia. The ceiling was low, the room was cave-like, despite the Luddecean Green paint on the concrete-block walls. At the other end of the table, behind the premier, was the emblem of the dove. It smelled like dust, and the dryness of the air prickled his nostrils, pumped as it was through filters for disease and chemical agents that seemed to extract every bit of moisture from it. The room was packed with twenty military advisors, counselors, and the premier. All his friends, all his allies in this war for the soul of humanity.

… but it was too much. Too many people, too many faces, he couldn't keep track of all the shifts of bodies, flickering frowns, and narrowing eyes around him. He looked back down at the long conference table. Its highly polished black surface reflected only himself. "That is impossible to say definitively at this time."

Zar spoke. "They've cracked our code for their … their

… thing … " Kenji dared glance up at Zar; his face was unusually red. Kenji squinted. Was he angry? Embarrassed? Frightened? "And they're throwing it back in our faces."

"We don't know that," Kenji protested, staring back down at the table. Hadn't they heard what he'd just said?

"Maybe they have a sense of humor," said Counselor Karpel.

"Why would you think that?" Kenji raised his head to the Counselor, genuinely curious. It seemed far-fetched that the intelligence would bother with something so trivial as a joke.

Ignoring Kenji, drumming his fingers on the table, Karpel said, "We should have never given it such an obvious code name."

And that Kenji agreed with wholeheartedly. But it had been important to some people that the code reflect the apocalyptic nature of their enemy.

The hall erupted in a buzz of conversation before Karpel replied. Kenji tried to focus, but all the different words, and the inflections they were spoken with … they were dizzying. He put his hands to his ears in frustration.

"Quiet!" said a voice from the end of the table. Kenji looked up to see the Premier Leetier standing there. Leetier was slightly shorter than Kenji, and broader, his hair straighter—he was older, but had less gray hair. He possessed an ability that Kenji found nearly magical—the ability to silence a room. And sure enough … the room was now quiet, except for the distant hum of an air vent, and farther off, a drip. "Mr. Sato, we have something else I'd like you to analyze."

"Yes …" Kenji stammered. "Please." No arguments, no emotions, just analysis. He nodded, glad and relieved. There were footsteps and several sheets of glossy paper, each long as one arm laid before him on the table. Kenji lifted the still damp pho-toe-graphs. A buzz rose in the room, but with something before him to concentrate on, he could ignore it.

The pho-toes were an ancient technology, but what Kenji had to work with. They might have been able to form a three-dimensional representation of the battle with images captured from the satellites that had once ringed Luddeccea, but the Guard had destroyed the satellites. He scowled. Gate 8 and all the major time gates needed to be shut down, but the satellites weren't part of the intelligence. Their destruction had been a waste. He shivered, and suddenly felt heavy.

He shook his head and tried to dampen the coil of dread loosening deep within him, and to ignore the chill that was spreading to his limbs. He focused on the pho-toes; they showed two-dimensional images of the Ark mid-battle. There was one taken just before the torpedo had grazed the hull. He stared at it, estimating the damage the ship had received, and then closed his eyes and whispered a prayer, "Thank you, great Jehovah." Kenji didn't really believe in God, at least not the way most Luddecceans believed in Him; but he found praying focused him, kept him centered.

He lifted his head, and found all eyes at the great conference table on him. "They've sustained damage to a time-field band midway down the hull," he said. "They won't be going very far."

A breath of relief escaped his chest and he looked back down at the pho-toe. They could still save Noa. He put a hand through his hair. He had tried to warn her … He felt his stomach churn, like he needed to vomit.

"We may not be able to save your sister, Kenji." The words came from the opposite end of the conference table. Kenji's head jerked up. The premier was the only other person in the room who was standing.

Kenji's jaw sagged. "But ... she's a victim. You saw him, he looked like her dead husband. Of course she would be drawn to him." His hands began to shake. He'd never given much credence to the Luddeccean view of women being creatures too ruled by their emotions for the hard tasks of leadership and governance, but seeing Noa fall so easily into the clutches of one of them, so easily enthralled ...

"The lives of millions of Luddecceans are at stake," the Premier said. "The virus they carry on the Ark could spread to the other colonies in the system."

Rolling back on his feet, Kenji swallowed hard.

"Forget about them," said a gruffer voice. Kenji turned to the Admiral of the Luddeccean Guard. Sitting next to the premier, he was leaning forward in his seat, eyes on Kenji. Was he angry? Suspicious? Kenji couldn't tell.

"We've seen the power of Gate 8, and we know the devil isn't above using it."

Kenji tilted his head. Did the admiral believe the station was possessed by the devil? It was hard for him to tell who in the Premier's council were devout, who were opportunists, and who were people like himself—people who didn't believe the letter of the prophecies, but believed in the spirit. The spirit was what mattered, wasn't it?

"As long as it's up there," the Admiral continued, "none of us are safe on Luddeccea. We are all hostage to its whims."

The table erupted in debate. Kenji heard someone say, "Hunt down the Ark, destroy the pet monstrosity aboard, and show that devil in the sky we aren't above using our force."

At those words, the pho-toe slipped from Kenji's fingers. He nearly fell over, but caught himself on the table. His breathing came so fast and so hard that the debate in the room faded into a distant hum. He'd almost thought he'd lost Noa just a few hours ago, and now they were talking about destroying the Ark and his sister. He had to save her from the monster she was with and the Guard. His fingers curled, and his body trembled. He had to save her … she would have saved him.

"Hostage!" He barked out the word with such force his body straightened.

The room went silent.

"Kenji?" said the Premier.

Kenji put his hands at his side and tried to meet the Premier's eye. He hated eye contact. It was a struggle with some animal part of his mind that wanted to look anywhere else. His eyes watered with the effort and he blinked.

Someone started to talk, but the Premier held up a hand again and once more the room went silent.

Fingers jerking uncontrollably at his sides, Kenji tried to keep his voice level. "The intelligence, it values its … avatar … "

"Archangel," someone hissed.

"Devil," someone else whispered.

"Djinn," said someone else.

Licking his lips, Kenji said, "We can use it as leverage. To prevent Gate 8 from destroying our planet."

"We can take it apart," said someone else.

Kenji released a breath. "And we could save Noa."

Someone inhaled sharply. Kenji swallowed. He heard someone whisper, "He couldn't stop her before."

Someone else whispered, "He was right about the plot to steal the Ark … "

Kenji bowed his head. His fingers twisted with his heavy robe.

"Of course we will try to spare her." Premier Leetier's voice cut through the whispers. Kenji's eyes drifted closed, and he couldn't bring himself to meet the man's eyes again. But he nodded and whispered, "Thank you."

The Premier's voice rose in volume. "Kenji Sato's unique mind is of essential use to us. He is proof that together, humans can prevail against any demons of spirit or technology. If his sister is valuable to him, she is valuable to us."

Kenji opened his eyes. Blinking, he tried to meet the Premier's gaze, but still couldn't manage it. His gaze settled on the man's lips instead. They were curled up sharply on one side ... a smile was friendship ... a smile meant honesty, as did meeting someone's eyes, which the Premier was trying to do, though Kenji was failing miserably to do the same.

"Thank you ... Sir ... thank you!" Kenji stuttered.

"Don't worry, Mr. Sato," the Premier said. "We'll apprehend that devil and take care of your sister."

The admiral added his voice. "Yes, we'll take care of them both."

Unaccountably, Kenji shivered.

AUTHOR'S NOTE

Thank you for reading *Archangel Down*. Because I self-publish, I depend on my readers to help me get the word out. If you enjoyed this story, please let people know on Facebook, Twitter, in your blogs, and when you talk books with your friends and family.

Made in the USA
Middletown, DE
03 March 2018